To Colin
from Jane + Murray

November 1979

A1018

# Adventure Stories for Boys

*The four hurried down the promenade.*

# Adventure Stories for Boys

*Illustrated by*

PAUL SHARP

HAMLYN

LONDON •NEW YORK• SYDNEY •TORONTO

First published 1967
Seventh impression 1978
Published by The Hamlyn Publishing Group Limited
London · New York · Sydney · Toronto
Astronaut House, Feltham, Middlesex, England

ISBN 0 601 07070 4

Printed in Great Britain by
Butler & Tanner Ltd, Frome and London

# CONTENTS

# ACKNOWLEDGMENTS

The publishers wish to express their thanks to authors and publishers for permission to include the following stories:

THE CRIME WAVE from THE ADVENTURES OF BILL HOLMES (Oxford University Press) © Fielden Hughes, 1950
THE SPEED KINGS © Robert Bateman, 1963
ADVENTURE INCORPORATED © James Kenner, 1963
SPELL OF MAGIC © Harry Harrison, 1963
THE SHIP THAT VANISHED © Odhams Press Ltd, 1963
HIGH QUEST © Odhams Press Ltd, 1963
HOODOO ON THE RANGERS © Odhams Press Ltd, 1964
A MAN'S JOB © Odhams Press Ltd, 1964

All first published in Eagle and Boys' World

# The Crime Wave

by
FIELDEN HUGHES

'Come in!' said the Headmaster in response to a sharp little tap on his study door.

The door opened, and in came Mr Snooks, the English master, who was also Bill Holmes' form master.

'You wanted to see me?' inquired Mr Snooks.

The Headmaster, wearing an anxious look on his red, clean-shaven face, waved his hand towards a chair. 'Yes,' he said. 'Sit down.'

No sooner had Mr Snooks accepted the invitation to be seated than the Headmaster rose from his own chair, pulled his pipe out of his pocket, and began to stride about the room. A look of polite irritation appeared on the English master's face. He did not care for the Head's habit of prowling to and fro when he was worried and deep in thought. It was too much like watching a tennis match without the fun of the tennis. If he wanted a walk, why not take one and invite Mr Snooks to accompany him; not root his visitor to a chair. However, he concealed his annoyance and patiently directed his attention and his remarks at various points in the room, wherever the Head happened to be at that moment.

'There's a wave of petty thefts going on in the school,' said the Head, stopping for a moment to glance out of the window at nothing in particular.

'Dear me,' said Mr Snooks to the Head's broad back. 'How irritating.'

Some people might suppose that this remark was a trifle

weak, considering the seriousness of the matter; but the fact is that nothing is more irritating to schoolmasters than this very thing, and the Head found Mr Snooks' comment both just and satisfying. He turned from the window and set course for the bookcase on the opposite side of the study. Mr Snooks followed with his eyes until, for comfort, he had to turn his head a little also.

'It is. It is,' said the Head testily, looking severely at his books behind their glass doors. 'It's exceedingly vexatious. I hate this kind of thing *so* much. It's difficult to locate. It breeds suspicion, and it tends to increase unless it's stopped very quickly.'

'Exactly,' said Mr Snooks, as viciously as if he had spent years among convicts, 'what kind of things have been stolen?'

By the time the question was out the Head was at the other side of his desk, opening a drawer to find his tobacco pouch. Mr Snooks felt as if he were writing his words in the air, like an aeroplane advertising something with a smoke-trail. The Head found his pouch and, to Mr Snooks' great relief, sat down to fill his pipe.

'Money,' he said. 'Small possessions. The usual things that boys have. I sent for you because, with two exceptions, the complaints of losses come from boys in your form.'

'Nothing has been mentioned to me,' said Mr Snooks.

'No,' replied the Head, 'because, as you may recall, when we last had trouble of this kind I ordered that all cases of loss should be reported direct to me, and not otherwise referred to. You will agree that the less said, the better the chance of detecting the thief — if there is a thief.'

'If there is a thief? I gathered that you thought there was.'

'Yes. I'm sure of it. Sometimes — you know what boys are — there's a run of losses due to absolute carelessness with personal property.'

Mr Snooks nodded. He certainly knew what boys were, and looked as if he did not like them any the better for it.

'But in this case —?' he said.

'Too many. And much too similar. Besides, all boys aren't equally careless.'

Again Mr Snooks looked knowing — this time as if he could not have disagreed more.

'How many complaints have you had?' he asked.

'Eight in three days — six from your form.'

'So you think the thief — if any — is in my form?'

The Head spread his arms and shrugged his shoulders.

'It's at least possible,' he said, 'isn't it?'

'Oh, yes,' agreed Mr Snooks, passing before his mental eye the faces of his form, and finding how difficult it is to believe that anyone you work with every day could be a thief. 'Well, what would you like me to do?'

The Head picked up a note on his desk. 'Here,' he said, 'are the names of boys who have reported losses, and a list of the articles they say have been taken.'

Mr Snooks took the paper and ran his eyes quickly down the list. The eyes stopped at the fifth name, and a look of rather scornful disbelief came into them. He tapped the paper with his finger.

'Carfax,' he said disdainfully. 'Carfax. There's an ass for you.'

'What about Carfax?' said the Head shortly.

'He told you he'd lost his stamp album?'

'That is so,' said the Head. 'That is exactly what Carfax told me. You sound a little doubtful, but I assure you that he said so. Is there anything wrong with the statement?'

'Everything,' said Mr Snooks with deepening scorn, 'considering that the album is at this very moment lying in my desk, where I put it after confiscating it. He was persistently looking at the book in my lesson the day before yesterday.'

'Good heavens!' cried the Head. 'You don't mean to say, Snooks, that he has the audacity to try and report you for theft?'

Mr Snooks snorted, and almost said 'Nonsense!' However, with an effort, he refrained.

'No, no,' he said, with a rather forced smile. 'Of course not. But if you knew Carfax as I know him you'd realise that he has wholly and entirely forgotten where it is. He merely knows the album isn't in his possession.'

'Oh,' said the Head deeply. He pressed the bell on his desk and his secretary appeared.

'I want to see Carfax,' he said. 'Mr Snooks' form.'

Mr Snooks sat back and began to nurse one thin knee in his two hands. This was more in his line.

In a few moments the door was opened by the secretary, and a tall boy with a mass of curly hair and a rather vacant though amiable expression came in.

He seemed to make a mechanised entry, as if the secretary had propelled him forward with one hand while she opened and then shut the door with the other. The boy glanced at the two masters with a look of apprehensive interest.

'Carfax!' said the Head.

Carfax swallowed so hard that his head came forward before he replied.

'Yes, sir?' he said, and then shot Mr Snooks a swift smile that made him look like a friendly hare.

Mr Snooks did not return the compliment.

'You reported that someone had stolen your stamp album,' said the Head conversationally.

'Yes, sir. That's right, sir,' said Carfax, brightening as he gathered the subject of the interview. There was much relief in knowing what it was and thinking what it might have been.

10

'Has it turned up, sir?' asked Carfax, smiling hopefully.

'When was it last in your possession?' asked the Head.

Carfax, in spite of Mr Snooks' rather acid view of him, was a nice, friendly boy, and it came into his mind that it was awfully decent of the Head to take all this trouble about his album, because the Old Man must be terribly busy with other matters, even if of less importance. Therefore he smiled.

It was quite a mistake. Mr Snooks looked at the Head as much as to say: 'You see? This is the genuine Carfax. An ass, if ever there was one.' The Head rapped smartly on his desk.

'Don't stand there grinning, boy,' he said. 'This is a serious matter. Answer my question.'

The smile vanished like a light. 'Oh, well,' thought Carfax, 'the Old Scout's a bit on edge. Better be careful.' Now he wrinkled his brow in thought, and made a supreme effort to look like one making a supreme effort.

'Well, sir,' he said, 'I *know* I had it on Sunday night because I was mounting my new pictorials — the ones with Kilimanjaro on them — they're worth twenty pence, sir, without the album.'

'Will — you — tell — us — when — you — last — had — the — album — in — your — hands,' demanded the Head.

'Yes, sir,' said Carfax hurriedly. 'Sunday night, sir.'

'Then it can't have been stolen at school,' said the Head with deadly logic.

'Oh, yes, sir. That's right. No, I'm wrong — I brought it to school on Monday.'

'How do you know?'

'Because I showed it to Williams...'

Carfax's voice tailed away. The bell had rung — a dreadful bell. It all came back to him. He went very red, and shot a look at Mr Snooks and then returned his gaze to the Head.

'Well?' said the Head. 'You showed it to Williams, and then?'

11

'I've —' Carfax cleared his throat. There was an obstruction in it. All was clear from the silence. It was one of those moments when speech is unnecessary, because everyone knows what everyone else is thinking. But the Head wanted to hear a few more words from Carfax. 'You were going to say?' he remarked.

'I've remembered where the album is.' murmured Carfax, with great shame, and as much of a melting smile as he could manage.

'Good. Good,' said the Head. He turned towards Mr Snooks. 'We can leave you to deal with the theft of Carfax's album, Mr Snooks, I think.'

'Safely,' replied Mr Snooks.

The silence fell again. But Carfax broke it.

'Shall I go now, sir?' he said.

The Head nodded and Carfax left the room hurriedly. He would have liked to have vanished in a puff of smoke but, what with the laws of nature and the demands of politeness, he went with all the speed he might, consistent with these two terrible handicaps. The Head knew, for his part, that Mr Snooks wanted to say something that respect for Heads did not permit, so he said it for him.

'Well. Are there any more simple cases on that list?'

'I'm afraid I can't clear up the others like that,' replied Mr Snooks, smiling a little.

'A pity,' said the Head. 'I think you enjoyed that one.'

Mr Snooks did not reply, except with a little smile.

'Very well, then. Take the list with you, and make some cautious inquiries. We must try and lay hands on the culprit.'

Mr Snooks rose and nodded. Then he went out of the room, for he had a few words to say to Carfax.

There will never be any telling what success the Head and Mr Snooks might have had in their efforts to detect the thief, for the incident of Mr Snooks' fountain pen, occurring within an hour of his talk with the Head, gave the whole affair a new importance. When the other boys in the form were dismissed at four o'clock, two members remained in the form room. One was Carfax, to whom Mr Snooks was giving a long lecture on his careless, forgetful ways; the other was Bill Holmes, sitting at his desk rewriting an essay on the character of Long John Silver. On the original copy Mr Snooks had written in red ink: 'If I could read this it might be good. I doubt it, but it's worth trying. Re-write at 4 p.m.'

Bill had been moved from his old position at the back of the classroom to a desk right under Mr Snooks' nose. The reason was that he would be less able to indulge in what the form master sometimes called 'less worthy pursuits', sometimes 'nefarious activities', according to his mood.

'Very well, then,' said Mr Snooks to Carfax, 'I shall look for some improvement.'

'Yes, sir,' said Carfax, estimating that another two minutes would about see the end of the lecture.

Mr Snooks looked disapprovingly at Carfax's attire.

'Another point,' he said, 'while we are having this heart-to-heart talk, Carfax.'

'Oh, yes, sir,' said Carfax, picturing a clock in his mind.

'You have good clothes. Why don't you take care of them? Your appearance is an absolute disgrace. Pull yourself together. Make an effort to be tidy. The outside not only expresses, but even affects, the inside.'

'Yes, sir.'

'You say yes, but do you agree? Words are cheap. Let me see actions. All right. You may go now.'

'Yes, sir,' said Carfax joyfully. 'Good afternoon, sir.' He was away to the door like a bird this time, when Mr Snooks called to him·

'Carfax.'

'Yes, sir?' said Carfax, as he skidded to a halt.

'Come back here.'

Carfax returned and looked inquiringly at the form master.

'Walk out of the room. This is not a race track.'

'No, sir.'

When Carfax had gone, Mr Snooks walked out of the room and left Bill to break the dead silence with the scratching of his unwilling pen. He knew where Mr Snooks had gone — to wash and brush-up before setting off home for tea. He raced on so as to finish with Long John Silver and Mr Snooks by the time the master returned.

Bill was writing his last word as his master came through the door, rolling down his cuffs and then smoothing his hair. Bill sat still and watched him lock his cupboard and hang the key on the nail in the side. Then he went to his desk and Bill saw him looking for something on his inkstand. Mr Snooks looked in vain. Whatever it was had gone. He went over to the door and closed it. Then he came over and stood by Bill's desk. Bill held the finished essay towards him.

'Never mind that,' said Mr Snooks in a strange voice. 'When I went out just now I left my fountain pen on my desk. It's not there now. Do you know anything about it?'

'No, sir,' said Bill. 'I haven't seen it.'

'Yet you were the only person in the room,' said Mr Snooks, looking with hard eyes at Bill.

'There was Carfax, sir,' said Bill.

'Nonsense, boy. You don't suggest that Carfax would take it under my very eyes?'

'I don't know anything about it, sir,' said Bill, staring at Mr Snooks' face, which had gone quite pale.

'Stand up,' said Mr Snooks.

Bill obeyed, his essay in his hand. Mr Snooks compressed his lips, stared back at Bill for a second, and then whisked up

14

the lid of the desk with an expression of contempt on his face.

'Look there,' he said, pointing an accusing finger at the interior of the desk. Bill looked, and there, lying on top of his books and papers, was Mr Snooks' fountain pen. The master picked it up, and put it into his waistcoat pocket, where he usually kept it when it was not in use. The action looked accusing, and as he did it he spoke one word to Bill.

'Well?'

'I don't know how it got there,' said Bill.

'No?' said Mr Snooks. 'Well, I do. And there are various other little matters that you could clear up if you wanted to.'

Bill stared in amazement at Mr Snooks.

'What other matters, sir?' he asked.

Mr Snooks produced the slip of paper the Head had given him and read it to Bill.

'Of course,' he said sarcastically, 'you will be quite unaware — quite unaware — that the following thefts have taken place. You don't know that a ten pence piece was stolen from Greville; a pocket-knife from Haine; a purse containing twelve pence from Colevil; a propelling pencil from Hardsby; and a book about football from Jennings, for instance?'

'First I've heard of it, sir,' said Bill.

'Why lie about it?' said Mr Snooks fiercely. 'Of course you know all about it.'

Bill drew a deep breath.

'You don't think I took those things, sir, do you?' he said.

'Don't try to fool me, boy,' said Mr Snooks. 'You tried to steal my pen — did in fact steal it — and I think it's very likely you stole all the other things as well. However, it's not for me to deal with — you must come with me to the Headmaster.'

But when they reached his study, they found that the Head had gone.

'Very well,' said Mr Snooks, as if Bill had stolen the Head

and spirited him away on purpose to foil the ends of judgement. 'Get out now. But first thing in the morning you shall be dealt with.'

Bill left the building and began his walk home. For some time he couldn't think, for the shock of all that had happened.

Half-formed thoughts passed across his mind. The pen in his desk — it was as if there was magic at work against him. It would be hard for them to prove anything against him about the other thefts, but how was he to prove that he did not put the pen in his desk. It was hardly credible, even now, that the pen had really been there, and that the whole scene with Mr Snooks had really taken place.

'You're very quiet, Bill,' said his mother as he sat gloomily at tea.

'Am I?' he said mechanically.

'Yes. You haven't said a word since you sat down. What's the matter? Don't you feel well?'

'I'm all right, Mum.'

'Something gone wrong at school, I suppose?' she said, looking closely at him.

'I wish you wouldn't keep on,' said Bill. 'Really, there's nothing wrong. I'd tell you if there was.'

Mothers have to make decisions. Mrs Holmes made one now.

'You're overtired,' she said. 'Why not have a hot bath after tea and go to bed very early. Get a good long night's rest.'

That wouldn't do at all. Bill had other plans that didn't fit in with that in any way. He shook his head.

'I'm really quite all right,' he said, putting a false cheerfulness into his voice. 'I'm just thinking something out, and

I've nearly got it,' he said, trying to sound convincing.

Secretly, Bill wished he were as near a solution as he had told his mother. But a solution there would have to be, before nine the following morning, or things were likely to rise to a pretty fine temperature. When he had finished tea he picked up his cap.

'Where now?' said his mother.

'Just a stroll round.'

'It'll do you good.'

'Thank goodness for that,' thought Bill, for though he loved his mother, there were moments when he wanted a little peace from her — and this was one of them.

He walked straight to the rectory, leaned against a tree outside the garden wall and, putting his fingers to his mouth, sent out the long doleful whistle that was his signal to Tony. His friend's window went up, and a hand waved, then the window went down again and in a minute or two Tony joined him. 'You look depressed,' said Tony.

'Let's walk,' said Bill. 'I've got a lot on my mind.'

'Yes,' said Tony, 'I can see that. What is it? A case of more than usual difficulty?'

'Listen,' said Bill, as they walked along, 'and don't say a word till I've finished.'

Tony listened with growing seriousness as the tale of Mr Snooks' missing pen was unfolded.

'Well, Bill,' he said, 'I must say it looks pretty black for you.'

'Thanks,' said Bill gloomily. 'In a minute you'll be asking me if I'm sure I didn't take it after all.'

'Good heavens, no — but you must admit — I mean, you can hardly expect your Headmaster to take as good a view as I do.'

Tony fell silent and was evidently deep in thought. Bill did not disturb his reverie, having enough to think about. Suddenly, Tony seized Bill's arm and they halted under a street lamp, face to face.

'Now,' said Tony, spreading one hand out and ticking off the points on his fingers, 'let's get this clear. Someone planted that pen on you. Why?'

'How should I know?' demanded Bill.

'Have you an enemy in the form?' asked Tony with a searching glance.

'No.'

'Then I'll tell you what it is. The thief who took the other things scented a row from afar, and planted the pen on you so that you'd get the blame. Yes, that's it.' Tony was delighted at his progress with the case. 'Now then,' he went on swiftly, 'all you have to do...' His voice tailed off.

'Well?' said Bill. 'All I have to do — is — what?'

'Er — I'm afraid I'm a bit off it there. I was just going to say that all you have to do is to discover who took the other items — but that's rather the point, isn't it?'

'It is rather,' said Bill grimly.

'You don't mind my asking you questions?' asked Tony, looking closely at Bill.

'Ask what you like,' said Bill, 'but let's keep walking.'

'Certainly,' said Tony. 'Now do you think it's possible this Carfax took the pen?'

'No.'

'Is he likely to have taken the other things?'

'I've no idea.'

'Could it have been an adult, and not a boy at all?'

Bill shook his head.

'You have to suspect everyone in cases like this, and proceed by elimination,' said Tony, using the many lessons he had learnt from Bill in the past. 'Do any adults have access to the rooms?' he asked his friend hopefully.

This time Bill made no response of any kind.

'Bill!' said Tony sharply. 'What was my last question?'

Bill shook his head. 'I don't know,' he said.

Again Tony halted the party. He shook his head sorrowfully.

'I quite realise that I'm not in the same street as you are as a detective,' he said, 'but I'm trying to help, and I should have thought I was entitled at least to politeness.'

'I'm sorry, Tony,' said Bill, smiling a little. 'My mind wandered, I'm afraid.'

'That's all right,' said Tony immediately. 'I should feel the same way if I were in your place. But I'll tell you one thing.'

'What's that?' said Bill.

'The great detective is slipping, and for one reason only.'

'And that is?'

'Because you're the case yourself. If it had been anyone else, you'd have been half-way to a solution by now.'

'Perhaps,' said Bill.

Tony suddenly took notice of the direction in which they were walking.

'Here,' he said, 'where are we going?'

'The scene of the crime,' said Bill, more cheerfully. 'If you're going to solve this case and get me out of this hole, you'll want to see the place for yourself, won't you?'

'Yes,' said Tony, peering down the road towards Bill's school, which was not more than five minutes' walk from where they were. 'But we won't get in at this time of night, will we?'

'There's sure to be someone about,' said Bill. 'Anyway, we'll get in, even if we have to climb over the railings.'

'That'll help, if we get caught, I must say,' said Tony.

'It can't make things much worse,' replied Bill.

They reached the school, and found the main gate still

*A booming voice hailed them as they crossed the yard.*

open. They crossed the yard boldly, and had nearly come to the Boys' entrance when a booming voice hailed them.

'Hoy!' it cried. And the cry did not sound friendly. The two stood still and the figure of Charles Wintney, the school keeper, hurried towards them. He was a tall, heavily-built man. He wore a boiler-suit and limped a little, for he had an artificial leg. He was known to the boys as Hoppy Wintney, but Bill greeted him very politely.

'Good evening, Mr Wintney,' he said.

Hoppy did not return the greeting. He looked with wide blue eyes — rather fishy, Tony thought — at his visitors, and the look was full of suspicion born of years of dealing with boys.

'An' what might you be arter?' he demanded.

'I'm sorry to trouble you,' replied Bill. 'But I've left something in my desk — something important.'

'Well,' said Hoppy, 'yer can sleep sound, because whatever it is will be as safe as the Bank of England. I'm just going to lock up. But I'll tell yer what I'm not a-going to do. I'm not a-going to climb them stairs again tonight, not if you've left yer heart in yer desk, I'm not.'

'Oh, please, Mr Wintney. I've never troubled you for anything before, and it's terribly important. Please,' said Bill with all the persuasion he could manage.

A cunning look came into Hoppy's eyes.

'And wot is it,' he said, 'that a young lad might have left that's so important?'

Tony took charge. First he jingled his money in his pocket. Then he took out ten pence.

'It's his homework book, Mr Wintney. I'm sure you'll oblige us.'

Hoppy turned his suspicious gaze on Tony.

'And who might you be, then?' he demanded. 'You don't

come here, do yer? Nothing whatever to do with the place?'

'No,' admitted Tony. 'I'm just a family friend.'

'Oh,' said Hoppy. 'A family friend.'

Silently, Tony passed the coin over to Hoppy, who palmed it without a word, and slipped it swiftly into the pocket of his boiler-suit.

'Well, sir,' he said, 'it's against the rules, but seeing as the documents are all that important I'll go so far as to let you in. But I'm coming with yer, mind. And I'm staying with yer.'

Nothing, not even good silver, could melt away the deep suspicion of Hoppy, but soon they were in the form room, strange and silent in the evening light. Bill went to his desk, opened the lid slowly, and Tony stared over his shoulder, while Hoppy leaned on the broom he still carried with him. He soon saw the position.

'They're not there, are they?' he said. 'I didn't think they were. More than likely you left 'em at some shop. Still, you've had your look. Come on, now. I've got to lock up quick. If anyone came and found you here there'd be trouble all round.'

As they went down the stairs Hoppy seemed to be in quite a good humour.

'Yer'll have to get a new one if yer don't find yer old homework book,' he said. 'Well, it'll teach yer to be more careful.'

As they emerged into yard he turned to Tony. 'All boys is careless, yer know,' he said. 'Your young pal's the second I've had here tonight. There was a lad here half an hour before you came, wanting to get in for something he'd left behind at four o'clock.'

Bill felt as if he had had an electric shock. He tried to sound casual as he spoke to Hoppy.

'Who was that, Mr Wintney?' he asked.

'Chap in your form, now I come to think of it,'

replied Hoppy. 'Tall, cheerful feller with a lot of hair.'

'Carfax?'

'Yes. I asked him his name, and he said it was Carfax.'

Tony laughed, as one man might laugh to another at the follies of boys. It sounded a bit hollow, but Hoppy seemed to notice nothing amiss with it.

'What was *he* after?' asked Tony. Bill held his breath for the reply.

'Foreign stamps,' he said. 'Worth a bomb, he told me.'

'Did you let him get them?' asked Bill.

'No fear. His stamps is safe where they are till the morning. Now off you go and look fer yer homework book elsewhere.'

'Well?' said Bill, when they were clear of the school.

'Well?' said Tony, looking at Bill.

'We've got to see Carfax,' said Bill.

'What — *now?*'

Bill looked very seriously at Tony.

'I've got till nine o'clock tomorrow morning,' he said.

'Sounds as though you're going to be executed,' said Tony.

'Well, almost,' said Bill. 'Come on.'

'Where's this Carfax live?'

'Quite near, as it happens.'

'It's pretty clear, isn't it?' said Tony as they hurried along.

'What is?'

'That this chap Carfax took the pen and slipped it into your desk. Then, when he thought the coast would be clear, he went back to get it. But our crusty friend foiled him, so Carfax thinks it's still there. He'll get a shock in the morning.'

'Somebody's going to get a shock in the morning,' said Bill. 'I wish I was as sure as you are who it's going to be.'

'You must expose him. No doubt about that, Holmes. It's you or Carfax.'

'You think I should?' said Bill.

'Why, of course,' replied Tony warmly. 'You've either got to show Carfax up, or you'll get punished for something you didn't do.'

'How do you think Carfax actually got the pen into my desk?' asked Bill.

'That's an easy one,' said Tony. 'At the front of each of those desks there's a slot big enough to stick an atlas in —'

'Just what the slot is for,' said Bill.

'Well, that's the way the fountain pen got into your desk,' said Tony.

'You're probably right,' said Bill. 'Well, this is where Carfax lives.'

They were outside a large, red-brick house in a long road of similar houses. Bill was about to go up the two stone steps and ring the bell when Tony seized his arm.

'Wait a minute,' he said.

'What for?'

'Let's have a plan,' said Tony firmly. 'What are you going to say to this fellow?'

Bill shook his head. 'I haven't any idea.' he said.

Tony glanced at his watch.

'You've only got this evening to solve the mystery,' he remarked. 'You'd better get an idea pretty quickly.'

'I couldn't agree more,' said Bill. 'But as time's short hadn't we better ring the bell for a start?'

'Wait,' said Tony again. 'Leave this to me. I've got the hang of this case. Already I've got over one fence tonight.'

'You were pretty good with Hoppy,' said Bill. 'He took quite a fancy to you. All right. I'll leave it to you.'

Tony mounted the steps and put his hand to the bell. Then he withdrew it.

'What's this fellow's Christian name?' he said.

'Harry,' said Bill.

Tony pressed the bell and waited. In a moment a stout lady opened the door.

'Good evening,' she said, and smiled at Tony.

'Good evening,' he said, smiling politely. 'Is Harry Carfax in?'

'No?' she said. 'He's not. Who is it wants him?'

Tony glanced round towards Bill; but Bill had vanished as completely as if he had been spirited away.

'Why, I —' Tony paused, and glanced again to make sure Bill had disappeared. 'Why, I had a message for him; nothing important.'

'What is your name?' asked Mrs Carfax — for it was Carfax's mother. She wore a smile as if she were dealing with a harmless lunatic. Tony saw it and liked it little enough.

'Oh, he wouldn't know me,' he said. 'The message is from a friend.'

'Indeed,' said Mrs Carfax, smiling more broadly. 'And what is the friend's name?'

'Er — Holmes,' said Tony. 'He's in the same form at school.'

'Well, if you'll give me the message, I'll pass it on when Harry comes in.'

'Oh, I won't trouble you with it,' said Tony, in an agony of impatience to be off after Bill, wherever he might have gone. 'It's nothing — nothing at all.'

'No trouble,' said Mrs Carfax pleasantly. 'Do tell me and I'll see he gets the message.'

'It'll keep till they meet in the morning,' said Tony desperately. He bowed quickly. 'Good night,' he said, and fled.

'Good night,' said Mrs Carfax, and closed the door.

Tony glanced both ways, and there, at the corner of the road, he saw Bill talking to another boy. Rather annoyed, he swiftly made his way towards them.

'Look here, Bill,' he said reproachfully, 'it was too bad of you to clear off like that. This fellow was out, as it happens. But he might have been in, and I should have looked a pretty fool without you there.'

'I'm sorry I went off, Tony,' said Bill, 'but I knew he wouldn't be in.'

'You knew he wouldn't be in?' said Tony. 'How did you know that?'

'Because just as you had rung the bell, I saw him coming along the road. Allow me to introduce you — Harry, this is my friend Tony Harries. Tony, this is Harry Carfax.'

'Well, I'm —' Tony stared at the tall boy with the friendly face and the mop of hair. 'How d'ye do?' he said.

Harry Carfax ducked his head, gave Tony a friendly grin, and said, 'Hello.'

'What about a walk, Harry?' said Bill.

'Yes,' said Harry agreeably. 'Good idea.'

The three moved off along the road, Bill and Harry on the best of terms, Tony silent and amazed. When was Bill going to get down to business and charge this affable rogue with his wickedness? He looked at his watch. The minutes were rushing by, and nothing was really done or established yet.

For a while, Bill and Harry talked of school matters: swimming, football, sports, in which it appeared that Harry took little real interest, but Tony could not fail to observe that the boy was so cheerful and friendly a chap that he was prepared to take a kindly interest in almost anything that pleased his companions. When the conversation turned to personalities in the school, especially masters, Harry Carfax revealed a sense of humour that made what he said very entertaining indeed. But though he saw all that, Tony was not in a mood to be entertained. Here, by all the signs, was the ruthless thief who was endangering Bill's good name and running him into grave risk. If all this talk was part of the hunt, when was the kill going to take place? They hadn't much time left.

Tony glanced at his watch and gave Bill a nudge with his elbow.

'Here,' cried Bill disconcertingly. 'That hurt, Tony. What was that for?'

'Time's getting on,' said Tony darkly. 'We've a lot to do.'

'That's all right, Tony,' said Bill. 'You're not in a great hurry, are you?'

'*I'm* not,' replied Tony meaningly. 'No- *I'm* not in any hurry at all.'

'Harry,' said Bill, turning to Carfax, 'what was Snooks jawing you about at four today?'

Carfax gave his amiable grin, as if he greatly enjoyed the memory.

'You'll laugh when I tell you,' he answered, and forthwith told the whole story of the album, the report to the Head, and Mr Snooks' lecture.

Then, to Tony's satisfaction, Bill fired his first shot. 'We heard you'd been round to the school tonight. Did you go to pinch your album back again?'

Carfax was not in the slightest degree put out by this question. He did not even inquire how Bill knew he had been back to school.

'Of course not,' said Carfax. 'I couldn't anyway. Snooks takes his desk key home with him on that bunch — you know?'

Bill did know. Everyone in Mr Snook's form knew that bunch, for the master had an endearing habit of tapping a particularly thick head with it.

'Besides,' went on Carfax, 'I'm in the black as it is. I don't want any more trouble just yet. No. I went back to get my new packet of Argentine stamps that I left in my Bible.'

'In your *Bible?*' said Tony.

'Yes,' said Carfax. 'I put them in there for safety this morning, shoved the lot in my desk and forgot the stamps because of Snooks jawing at me. They're worth a bomb, those Argentines. But Hoppy wouldn't let me go up and get them.'

'I know,' said Bill, grinning. 'Hoppy told us.'

'You've been there tonight, too?' asked Carfax.

Tony was puzzled. He listened to every word Carfax said on the theory that he was listening to a thief and a rascal. Yet the impression he got was that he had never met a kindlier, more transparent boy in his life; a quiet, humorous philosopher of a boy, who got excited about nothing, and suspicious about nothing. Either he was what he seemed to be, or else he was the most accomplished rogue and superb actor in the world.

'Yes,' said Bill. 'I wanted to get into the form room, too.'

'Well,' said Carfax. 'No wonder Hoppy was peevish. You must have been the third tonight!'

For the second time that night, Bill felt as if he had received an electric shock.

'The third?' said Bill cautiously. 'Who was the other one, then?'

'I don't think he actually spoke to Hoppy. He may have done. But I saw him as I was going away.'

'*Who was it?*' said Bill, trying to keep exasperation out of his voice at the kindly Carfax's reply.

'H'm — that's funny,' said Carfax. 'I never can remember that chap's name — wait a minute — I'll get it — always annoys me if I can't remember a thing like that.'

'Is he in our form?' asked Bill. Tony walked along with his hands clenched in agony.

'Yes. It's on the tip of my tongue. Talk about something else. It's sure to come back to me just when I don't want it. Probably I shall remember when I'm just dropping off to sleep.'

Bill could keep his temper no longer. Suddenly the astonish-

28

ed Harry found himself pinned in an iron grip. Bill glared at him, and words came out from between closed teeth.

'Never mind his name,' hissed Bill. 'Tell us what he looks like, you silly ass.'

'Here,' said Harry, staring. 'What's up?'

'WHAT'S THIS CHAP LOOK LIKE?' demanded Bill.

'It's that chap with a glass eye, or anyhow, he looks as if he has a glass eye,' said Harry.

'Fratton,' said Bill, releasing Harry.

'That's the name. Fratton. Know him as well as I know you. But what's the excitement about?'

'You didn't speak to him?'

'What — when I saw him in the yard tonight?'

'Yes.'

'No. I couldn't. I doubt if he saw me. I only just caught sight of him.'

'You're sure he was going into the school?'

'Where else would he be going?'

'I don't know. You saw him, not me. How do you know he was going into school?'

'Because he was trying to dodge Hoppy and get in the Boys' entrance.'

'Did he fix it?'

He may have done. I don't know. I cleared off. I didn't want Hoppy reporting me in the morning.'

Bill said nothing and they walked along in silence for a while. Then Carfax's curiosity began to stir. Anyone else's curiosity would have been aroused long before. However, even he could not fail to see that the interest of Bill and Tony in the matter of Fratton was a little intense.

'What is all this about?' he asked. 'Why are you so interested in Fratton?'

'Well, it's about this pinching that's been going on in

the form. You must have heard all about it, surely?'

'You don't think Fratton did it, do you?'

'Well, it's possible.'

'I don't think it is,' said Carfax, wrinkling his brow.

'Why not?'

'Why should he pinch anything? He's got more money than anyone in the form. His father owns those restaurants by the football ground.'

'But why should he go back to the school?'

'Well,' said Carfax, grinning, 'you did that, too. And so did I.'

'So what?' said Bill. 'How do you know I didn't do it? And how do I know you didn't?'

'Well,' said Carfax simply. 'I just didn't. And I don't think you did, either.'

'Why not?' asked Bill shortly.

'I just know it. You're too decent a chap to do it.'

Bill smiled and thumped Carfax on the back.

'You're a good fellow yourself,' he said. He turned to Tony. 'What's the time?' he asked.

Tony looked and told him.

'Gosh!' said Carfax, when he heard what time it was. 'I must go! I've just remembered. I promised I'd stay in tonight and let my parents go to the cinema while I look after my young sister. There'll be a row if I make them late. Cheerio.'

Bill and Tony grinned at Carfax's hasty departure.

'The man who forgot his own funeral!' said Bill. 'Well, you're in charge of this case. Do you think he's our man?'

'Frankly, Bill,' said Tony, 'I don't. I did at first, but not now.'

'Why not?'

'I've a hunch that it's someone else. Carfax just isn't the type at all.'

'Much too nice a chap? Yes, I'm inclined to agree with you.'

'Well — yes. I suppose that's it.'

It was Bill's turn to shake his head.

'No good at all, Tony,' he said. 'You believed everything he said — why he went to school, what he went for, his denial of intention to steal his album back again — everything. And what's worse, you've fallen for it because he's such a nice chap. No, no. That'll never do.'

'Well, you don't think he's the thief any more than I do.'

'Well, I'm sure he didn't take the pen. I was there all the time. I saw him leave. He couldn't have done it.'

'Then why have we been wasting our precious time on him?' demanded Tony. 'If you knew all the time that he didn't take the pen?'

'Two reasons, both so good that either of them would have been enough. The first, that we don't *know* that the chap who took the pen also took the other things. Snooks jumped to that conclusion. Besides, if it could all be pinned on me, that clears it up nicely, doesn't it?'

'And the other reason?'

'That Carfax was the only clue we had. You must agree he helped us quite a bit.'

They reached the rectory gate and stopped outside.

'I'm afraid I've not been much help,' said Tony. 'All we know is that Carfax couldn't have taken the pen, and that a chap called Fratton went back to the school after hours.'

'That's the lot,' said Bill. 'And it's not much help. What's the time now, Tony?'

Tony looked at his watch.

'You've got precisely twelve hours in which to solve the mystery,' he said.

'Thanks,' said Bill briefly.

'Let me know what happens, Bill,' said Tony, reluctant to

appear callous by departing, yet unable to suggest anything helpful.

'I'll let you know,' said Bill lugubriously. 'Good night.'

'Good night,' said Tony, and with a kind of dumb sympathy stood watching the departing figure of Bill until he was out of sight. Then he turned and went straight to his own room to go over every item of the case in the hope of being able to offer Bill the correct solution.

When he reached home, Bill had his supper and went to his room, saying he was tired and would go to bed straight away. When he had gone, Mrs Holmes looked at her husband.

'There's something wrong with that boy,' she said.

'Oh?' said Mr Holmes, from the depths of his comfortable chair. 'What is it?'

'I don't know. I wish I did.'

'Have you asked him?'

'Yes. But he says there's nothing wrong.'

'Well, then, perhaps there isn't.'

'I know there is. He's in some trouble. I hope it's not serious.'

'Well, my dear,' said Mr Holmes, folding his paper back to see it more comfortably, 'if it is, we shall hear of it. If not, you're worrying for nothing.'

Mrs Holmes was understood to say that men were all the same, which was, of course, true in one way and remarkably untrue in another. Bill, if he had heard his mother's remark, would almost certainly have told her that there were at least two sorts of men — the crooks and the honest ones. But he was upstairs, deeply occupied with thoughts of his own. He lay in bed, his arms under his head, staring at the ceiling, his mind examining the whole matter of the missing pen, and all he knew about it. An hour or so after he had retired, he saw his door begin to open quietly, whereupon he instantly feign-

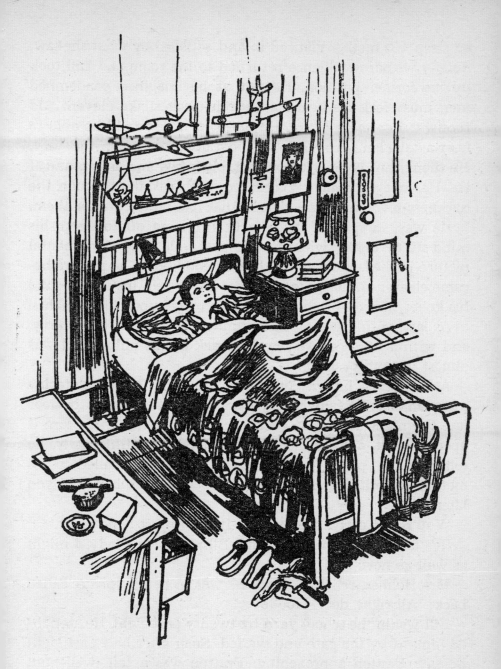

*Bill lay in bed, trying to solve the mystery.*

ed sleep. His mother glanced in and, satisfied by what she saw, quietly withdrew. Silence returned to the room and Bill took up his former position. He felt as he imagined condemned men must feel. He heard a church clock strike eleven, and thought: *Ten more hours.* He doubted if he would be able to keep awake long enough to get hold of a loose end in the story. He thought of Mr Snooks comfortably in bed and asleep, and of the Headmaster similarly situated, both rushing through the darkness towards a nine o'clock that had no terrors for them.

He was, in spite of his efforts, dropping off to sleep, his mind stil revolving, when he was shot wide awake by a mental picture pushed up out of his drowsy condition. The picture became clearer and brighter. Bill sat up in bed, his arms round his knees, his eyes bright, his attention rigid upon his thoughts.

At last, with a feeling like a hunter in sight of his quarry, and with a satisfied 'Ah', he lay back on his pillow and was almost instantly asleep.

At breakfast he was bright and cheery. By his plate lay a note in Tony's handwriting, evidently pushed under the door late the night before, or even early that morning. He tore it open, read it, and grinned widely. Then, whistling gaily, he took his cap, put it jauntily on his head, and called to his mother, who had gone upstairs: 'Goodbye, Mother. See you later.'

'You're off early, aren't you? It's only just gone eight.'

'It's a lovely morning,' replied Bill, 'and I'm ready. I might as well go now.'

Mrs Holmes, relieved to see he was in better spirits, called back: 'All right, dear. Goodbye.'

Bill was in the school yard by twenty past eight. He stationed himself by the gate and waited. Soon after half past eight he saw Fratton approaching. Fratton was a tall, well-built boy, with dark, short-cropped hair, and brown eyes, one of which was artificial. As soon as Bill saw Fratton he went to meet him, walking slowly and casually, his hands in his pockets. They met a little distance from the school gate.

'I want to see you, Fratton,' said Bill, stopping in front of him.

Fratton stopped and looked at Bill.

'What about?' he said.

'Snooks' pen,' said Bill.

Fratton's face betrayed no emotion.

'Snooks' pen?' he said. 'I don't know what you're talking about.'

He was going to walk on, but Bill, taking his hands out of his pockets, stood in his way.

'Oh, yes, you do,' he said. 'You took it off his desk yesterday afternoon and dropped it into my desk through the slot.'

'It's not there now,' said Fratton, looking very cunning. 'Ten to one you stole it yourself and want to push the blame on to someone else.'

'So you did get in last night,' said Bill. 'Well, I could have saved you the trouble. Snooks found it there and has it safely in his pocket.'

'And knows where to look for the thief, it seems.'

'Not yet, he doesn't,' said Bill. 'But he's going to.'

'You're going to tell him I took it? Well, get on with it. You'll find it pretty hard to prove.'

'I'm not going to tell him,' said Bill. '*You're* going to do that.'

'Oh, yeah?' said Fratton.

'And at the same time,' said Bill, 'you'll tell him that it was you who took Greville's money; Colevil's purse; Hardsby's pencil; and Haine's knife.'

'You clever Dick,' said Fratton. 'What makes you think I took that stuff and if I did, what makes you think I'm going to tell Snooks? You must think I'm completely mad, Holmes!'

'I'll tell you what,' said Bill, suddenly going red with anger. 'Snooks keeps moving you about the room. I don't care where he moves you, but it happens that those are the chaps he's moved you next to. And you're going to tell him, because if you don't, I'll give you such a hiding he won't be able to recognise you when you go into school.'

'I see,' said Fratton. 'Snooks found you out, and this is your idea of getting out of it. Well, you're not getting out of it at my expense. Now get out of the way.'

Bill seized Fratton without hesitation. On their side of the road there was a narrow passage between the houses. Under the impact of Bill's attack, Fratton staggered into this passage and in a moment the battle was raging. Bill was the lighter of the two, but Fratton reeled under the whirlwind of his onslaught. The walls were blank each side and no one saw or came.

The sound of the whistle in the school yard came to their ears. Fratton leaned against the wall, feeling his face and groaning.

'Now then,' panted Bill. 'Maybe you'll think again and do what you've got to do.'

So saying, he ran to the yard and fell in with his form.. In the form room, Mr Snooks looked gravely at him.

'I've seen the Headmaster,' he said. 'You will go to him now.'

'May I wash first, sir?' asked Bill.

'No!' said Mr Snooks angrily. 'You may not. Go at once.'

The Headmaster was standing in front of his fireplace when Bill entered. It was a bad sign. It meant that he was ready for action.

Bill stood before him. The Headmaster stared at him, stern eyes resting on his rather battle-grimed face. But he said nothing about that. Instead he began one of those conversations where only formal replies are expected from the other party.

'You know why I've sent for you?'

'Yes, sir,' said Bill.

'There is no doubt at all that you tried to steal Mr Snooks' pen,' said the Head. 'So we need not even discuss that. But there is reason to think that you have been guilty of other thefts. Pleased with your success in smaller things, you were encouraged to try something more dangerous. Is that not so?'

'No, sir,' said Bill.

'I am giving you an opportunity, before you are punished as you deserve, to confess all that you have done, and so remove suspicion from other boys — a suspicion that your wicked actions have brought on your innocent class-mates.'

'I didn't take the pen or anything else,' said Bill, 'so I haven't anything to confess, sir.'

The Headmaster looked even grimmer than before.

'Very well,' he said. 'I've given you your chance. I can do no more.'

Bill watched him as he went to his cupboard and took out a cane. He was just thinking what he would have to do to Fratton to square their account, when there was a scuffle at the door, and without any knock Mr Snooks entered with Fratton.

'Excuse me, sir,' said Mr Snooks urgently.

The Headmaster stared coldly at the intruders.

'What is it, Mr Snooks?' he said irritably.

'This lad Fratton has just confessed to me that he took my pen and the other things you told me about.'

It was a study in expressions. Mr Snooks stood with his hand resting firmly on Fratton's shoulder, his eyebrows raised and his mouth slightly open in his eagerness to prevent the injustice of an innocent boy being punished. Bill's face wore a look of triumph and relief, and he let out a slow breath at the narrowness of his escape. Fratton glowered sullenly at the Headmaster, his lip split from the recent battle, and his nose swelling almost under their very eyes. The Head stood with the cane in his hand, his eyes, recently so stormy, now bulging slightly at the sudden change in the situation. There was what seemed a long silence, then the Head spoke.

'Good heavens,' he said. 'What have you done to your face, boy?'

'I was in a fight, sir,' said Fratton sulkily.

'M'm,' said the Head, silently assessing the dishevelled boy in front of him.

'Let me be quite clear — you wish to confess that you took the pen, and certain other articles?'

'I don't wish to, sir,' said Fratton, truthfully enough.

'Don't hedge, boy,' said the Head loudly. 'Did you steal them, or didn't you?'

'Yes, sir,' said Fratton. 'I did.'

'Then there's no more to be said,' remarked the Head, as if there were quite a lot more to be *done*. 'Except for me to tell you, Holmes, that I am sorry you were wrongly blamed. I will see you later. Meanwhile, I will personally deal with Fratton.'

Mr Snooks and Bill withdrew from the study. In the corridor, the form master turned to Bill.

'For goodness' sake,' he said, 'go and wash your face. I can't think how you got it into that state.'

'No, sir. Yes, sir,' said Bill happily, and hurried off to the cloakroom.

At midday, when Bill came out of school, an anxious Tony was waiting for him outside.

'Well, Bill?' he said urgently. 'What happened?'

Bill, all smiles, took Tony's arm and began to march him along the road.

'They found the thief,' he said, unable to stop grinning.

'They did?' said Tony, blowing out a long breath. 'Well, that's a relief. Did you get my note?'

Bill silently took out the note he had received at breakfast and handed it to Tony.

'I delivered that at two this morning,' said Tony, with an air of having contributed to the final victory.

'Look at it,' said Bill. 'You may need it again.'

'I know what's in it,' said Tony, pulling it out and glancing at it nevertheless. Then he started and turned very red.

Bill chuckled.

The note read:

'Dear Jane — I'll meet you at six on Friday. Better not walk up this way in case you're seen. If you're late out, I'll wait till you turn up. Yours, Tony.'

Tony looked uncomfortable.

'That's done it,' he said.

'Who's Jane?' asked Bill, grinning.

'She's a very nice girl. I met her a few weeks ago,' explained Tony.

'Where's the note you meant for me?' asked Bill.

'In the post,' said Tony with a groan.

'What's in it?'

'Proof that Carfax is the thief. Was I right?'

'That's absolutely brilliant, Tony,' said Bill admiringly. 'Now Jane knows who did it!'

'Oh, do shut up,' said Tony. 'I feel bad enough about it as it is, Bill.'

'How did you arrive at that conclusion?' asked Bill.

'When I thought over our talk with Carfax,' said Tony, 'it became quite clear to me. He was lying about Fratton.'

'Lying about Fratton?' asked Bill in some surprise.

'Yes. Fratton never went near the school at all last night.

'Is that a fact?' said Bill, amused at his friend's intensity.

'Certainly. If old Hoppy had seen Fratton, he'd have told us. And it Fratton had been there the porter would have seen him. Dash it, I gave him ten pence. And he did tell us about Carfax. No, no. The more I thought about it, the clearer it became that Carfax told that lie to put us off the scent. It shows you how easy it is to be deceived by a pleasant manner. I was absolutely taken in — I don't mind telling you. Pity I made a mess of it by putting the letters in the wrong envelopes. Still, they got him, you say?'

'Oh, yes. Fratton owned up to all the crimes this morning,' said Bill.

'Good. Good,' said Tony. Then he started. 'Carfax, you mean.'

'No, Fratton.'

'Fratton?' said Tony, gaping foolishly at Bill.

Bill laughed at Tony's expression.

'Yes — Fratton. He went and owned up to everything in the Headmaster's study.'

'What on earth made him do that?' said Tony.

'I did,' replied Bill grimly, pointing to his face.

'I see,' said Tony. Then he grinned. 'I must admit you've got a very fine black eye coming up there. You'll have to do something about that. But, tell me, Bill — what made you think it was Fratton?'

'I did what you did last night — went to my room and thought for hours. I wasn't getting anywhere until I suddenly remembered two things, neither of which you could possibly have known. The first was that Fratton, who doesn't get on too well with Snooks, has been moved round the classroom quite a bit. And every boy he's sat next to has lost something.'

'That's all right. But my case was the pen. What about the pen?'

'Snooks marks the absences with it at the beginning of the afternoon, and leaves it on the desk till the end of the day. I've often seen it there. Well, it couldn't have been taken under his nose, and it couldn't have been put in my desk while I was there.'

'True enough, said 'Tony. 'But I don't see why it should have been Fratton any more than anyone else.'

'No? Well, I suddenly remembered that I went out of the room for two or three minutes because I'd left my English essay book in the gym after P.T.'

'Proves nothing,' said Tony.

'Only that someone had the chance while I was out. At the time, Snooks had a few boys round his desk while he was marking essays.'

'With the pen?'

'No. He uses an ordinary pen and red ink for that job. I remembered he was called out of the room for a minute. The boys at the desk started messing about and no one would have noticed Fratton taking the pen. When Snooks came in, I asked to go to the gym for my book, and that's when Fratton could have put the pen through the slot in my desk. I sit in a front desk and it would have been quite simple for him to put his hand behind him and drop it in while he kept his eye on Snooks.'

'But why didn't he put it in his pocket?'

'Obviously he wanted to plant it on someone else, in case Snooks realised his pen was missing during the afternoon. I can only guess that putting it in my desk was the easiest way, and that Fratton meant to pick the pen up later. That's why he went back to the school.'

'Couldn't Carfax have done all this?'

'Fratton was one of the group at Snooks' desk — Carfax wasn't.'

'Well,' said Tony, looking at the ground. 'I still think it

might have been Carfax, although he seems a pleasant fellow.'

Bill grinned. 'But it was Fratton who owned up, and you can't argue round that!'

'And you charged him with all the thefts on that evidence?' asked Tony.

'I certainly did,' said Bill cheerfully. 'It was quite a gamble, but it came off!'

When Bill arrived home, his mother stared at him in dismay.

'Good gracious me, Bill!' she cried. 'How did you get that terrible black eye?'

'Well, it's quite a long story, Mum,' laughed Bill. 'After dinner, I'll tell you all about it...'

# A Man's Job

by
L. J. White

'We work all day —
For very little pay —
That's what puts us in a rage — ta ra ra —
We go down white —
And up we come at night —
Like a lot of little blackbirds in a cage --'

The raucous voice died away to a chorus of shouts of 'Put a sock in it' from all sides of the bath-house.

Jack Byers paused in the act of undressing. The narrow aisle between the rows of cubicles was crowded with men. Night shift workers scurried in from the showers and hurried to dress. Day shift men stowed their clean clothes in the narrow lockers, then ran naked across to where their pit clothes were hanging, aired and dried.

Fat men, thin men, tall men, short men; old-timers who dawdled, boys who raced with each other; all jostled good-humouredly together, gossiping.

At this early-morning hour, at the changing of shifts, pandemonium reigned in the bath-house. Some live spirits persisted in singing under the showers, others larked about or exchanged jokes as they washed each other's backs.

It was Jack's first day at the mine, and he was bewildered. His pal Bob Wingate touched his arm.

'It's all right, Jack,' he assured the boy. 'You'll soon get used to it. Everybody's in a hurry, either to get to work or to get home. We've plenty of time, really.'

43

Jack resumed his undressing, watching the other men to see how they tucked their clothes away so that they remained uncreased. Then he wrapped his towel about his bare body and followed Bob through a narrow passage that led to the dirty clothes cubicles.

He was lacing up his heavy pit boots when the same raucous voice struck up again, the words echoing back from the vaulted roof above.

When the harsh voice died away into a whisper, Jack looked at Bob, who burst out laughing.

'That's Nobby Niblett coming off the night shift,' he explained. 'He always sings that one if he knows there are new starters about. "Blackbirds in a cage", indeed...'

The two boys made their way to the pit, pausing only to get lamps from the cabin near the pithead. Bob was a veteran of some months, and was proud to be able to initiate the new boy into his job. Also to ward off the chaps who itched to play good-natured tricks on an unsuspecting new recruit.

As they waited their turn to descend, Jack was suddenly confronted by a frowsy individual who thrust stubby fingers into his pockets. Jack recoiled in alarm, but Bob quickly enlightened him.

'He's only searching you, Jack.'

'Searching me? What for?'

'Oh, of course, you don't know. He's searching for cigarettes and matches.'

'But I don't smoke — you know that.'

'He searches everybody.'

'Why?'

The searcher had moved on, however, and Bob was saved the explanation then. The cage had arrived at the surface, and they followed the throng of men crowding into it. It was soon packed with men and boys, and descended with a thud and rattle of chains. It sounded and felt quite insecure.

Jack held his breath at the swiftness of the descent and swallowed hastily. Bob had prepared him for the peculiar sensations he would experience, and he strove successfully to overcome his feeling of nausea and alarm.

Before he realised it the cage had dropped with a soft thud on to the shaft bottom, and they all streamed out. Jack immediately compared what he saw with a tunnel on the London Underground. His pal read his thoughts at once.

'It's like the Underground, Jack, isn't it?' he remarked. 'It *is* really an underground railway system that brings the coal from workings a mile away to the bottom of the shaft. Come on, we'll go and find the train.'

'Train?' echoed Jack.

'That's what I said. We'll ride in the train for a part of the way. Come on, or we'll miss it.'

The two boys followed a file of men to the station where the underground train waited. Jack stared curiously at the black curved walls and the arched roof, supported by curved steel girders. The spacious gallery was well lit by electric lamps suspended from the roof. They picked their way carefully between long lines of tubs filled with coal waiting to be wound up the shaft. The new boy voiced his surprise.

'I never expected it to be like this!' he exclaimed.

Bob Wingate laughed.

'This is the best part of it,' he remarked. 'Wait till we get into the workings.'

They had reached the train now, and joined the men climbing into the empty pit tubs. The train of tubs would be drawn later through one of the tunnels, hauled by a steel rope driven by an unseen engine.

The train was soon filled, the guard's whistle blew, and they moved off. The boys squatted in the bottom of a tub,

*They joined the men climbing into the empty pit tubs.*

striving to make themselves as comfortable as possible in the springless vehicle. The other men took it all as a matter of course, but Jack thought it was the most uncomfortable journey he had ever made. The train gathered speed, jolting and jarring over the uneven track, the noise making conversation a matter of shouted phrases. Jack noticed, in the light shed by the men's bobbing headlamps, that the tunnel was getting lower and narrower as they progressed.

At last the train stopped, and everyone climbed out. Jack at least was not sorry, and he was astounded to see that some of the boys had fallen asleep and had to be roused.

'When you've worked in here as long as they have, you'll be the same, Jack,' Bob said. 'When you've been out dancing half the night like some of them, and work on the early-morning shift, you'll sleep on your nose.'

Jack pondered this in silence. He was finding out already that work in a coal mine was not as easy as some people made it out to be nowadays. Still, it was his first day.

His pal was calling.

'Come on, Jack. We've a long way to go yet.'

A long way to go! Jack's idea of descending a shaft and starting straight away to cut coal was a long way off the mark. What lay before him? His misgivings mounted as he followed his friend into a dark and narrow tunnel.

After walking for what seemed hours, the boys arrived at the deputy's station. The deputy was the man responsible for their safety, and would give them their instructions.

A big man, he was clad only in shorts and singlet, for the air at this distance from the shaft was already warm. He was giving each man a few words of warning or instruction. He motioned to Bob Wingate.

'You youngsters can go and work with Old Moore until you get your pit-sense '

They followed the deputy, Jack ducking his head to avoid the timbers, and pondering over what he had just heard.

What was 'pit-sense'? Who was Old Moore? What sort of a job was this he had let himself in for?

The deputy paused for a moment and Jack whispered.

'What's pit-sense, Bob?'

It was Jack Byers' first day in the mine. His pal, Bob Wingate, was a veteran of six months. Bob knew the answers — or thought he did!

'It's a sixth sense all miners get when they've worked in the pit long enough,' he explained. 'They can tell when there's danger without being told.'

'Who's Old Moore?' Jack asked again.

The deputy chuckled.

'You're thinking of Old Moore's Almanac, *I'll* bet. His name is really Jacob Moore, but everybody calls him Old Moore, because he's always telling people what's going to happen in the future. He's right sometimes, too!'

In a few minutes they arrived at the place where the old man was working.

'Jacob!' the deputy called. 'Look after these youngsters!' He turned to Jack. 'This is a small area of the seam that is not worth working by machinery. Elderly miners finish their time out here, training the new recruits. Old Moore isn't sixty-five yet, but he looks like Methuselah already. I bet he'll see eighty, at least.'

The old man gave the boys a quizzical glance. He was quite bald under his safety helmet, his chin covered with a grey stubble. Short and squat, his arms bulged with muscle. He was something of a character, Jack decided.

Old Moore turned to the deputy.

'Eighty? he grunted. '*I'll* never see eighty. One of these days I'll be buried alive if you keep sending that wild pony in here!'

The deputy laughed, and slapped the old man on the back. 'That's how he always talks,' he remarked to the boys. 'But he's all right, really. He'll look after you until I come back.'

The deputy left them, and Old Moore looked the boys over appraisingly, then sniffed.

'They send all the newcomers in'to me to start with,' he grumbled. 'Then off they go to work on the machines. I don't hold with the newfangled ways. Machines make men lazy.'

He turned to the coal face. The boys stripped to their singlets and joined him there. He showed Jack how to hew coal and shovel it into a tub, then set props to the roof where required. It was all a novelty to Jack, and the fact that Bob was with him was an added interest. Bob kept talking about what the machines could do.

Eventually the tub was filled, and the old man began grumbling about the horse that would come to haul it away.

'What do we do now, Jacob?' asked Bob.

'Sit down and rest,' the old man retorted. 'I reckon we've finished work for today. The driver of that horse is as afraid of it as I am. He'll be hiding out of the way. We won't see either of them today.'

Old Moore's prediction was right about the driver and their work being finished, but not about the horse. They were still sitting in a group, the old man rambling on, when they heard a commotion back along the gallery. What happened next was so confusing to Jack in this strange environment that he was never able to remember in detail all that happened.

He was aware of the old man, with an agility surprising for someone of his years, leaping over both Bob and himself as they squatted against the coal face. Jack peered up to see the bloodshot, staring eyes of a huge animal behind the coal tub. Its bulk almost filled the gallery, its flailing hooves threatening to dislodge the timbers that supported the roof.

The boys sprang to their feet in alarm, wondering what to do. The old man was tugging away at the animal's bridle, cursing and swearing at the top of his voice as the horse plunged and kicked. Something must have frightened it so that it was fast becoming frantic, and Old Moore's shouting and bawling wasn't helping.

Suddenly, disaster struck. The horse made a wild attempt to turn around so as to get back out of the gallery.

In doing so, it dislodged the timbers around it. A stream of debris came from above, the roof groaned and cracked, and eventually collapsed with a thunderous crash.

The two boys crouched against the coal seam, terror-stricken, expecting that they would be buried at any moment. Clouds of dust whirled around them.

At last all movement ceased, the dust settled, and the boys were able to see the extent of their predicament. A huge mound of debris stood where Old Moore had struggled with the horse, but of man or animal there was now no trace.

Then the full realisation of their plight struck Jack, and tears welled up into his dust-filled eyes. They were entombed!

A huge mound of rubble blocked their way to freedom, and beneath it, they thought, lay the body of the elderly miner with whom they had so recently been working.

Jack's thoughts were gloomy. Would they die of hunger or lack of fresh air? Would they be rescued in time?

Bob shivered and jumped to his feet.

'Jack!' he exclaimed, 'we must do something.'

The other boy clambered slowly to his feet.

'I'm trembling, Bob,' he quavered. 'Is there anything the matter with me?'

His pal clapped him on the shoulder. It was his place, with six months' seniority, to take the lead.

'That's the shock, Jack,' he explained. 'You're as right as rain, same as I am. We're not giving up already, are we?'

Jack gazed at the heap of stones and rubbish that confronted them and groaned.

'I ought to have listened to my father,' he grumbled. 'He wanted me to go and work with him, on the railway...'

Bob interrupted. 'Would you like to be cleaning engines all day and getting covered with oil and grease — and making tea? This is a man's job, down here.'

Jack refused to be comforted.

'We'll be dead men if we're left here long,' he objected, then burst out laughing as he stared at Bob.

'That's more like it,' his pal remarked. 'But what's the joke?'

'I was thinking of that song we heard this morning — "Like a lot of little blackbirds." Your face is as black as the coal.'

Bob stared at Jack in his turn, then he, too, laughed.

'Yours is the same. It's the dust from the fall.' He became matter-of-fact. 'Well, Jack,' he went on, 'we'd better do something.' He looked around their narrow prison. 'I don't think any more will fall, but we'll put up some more props, to make sure.'

The two boys got to work at once. Bob knew what to do from what he had been taught, and Jack did as he was told, working with a will. They gathered some props that were at hand and, after several trials and misfits, at last made all as secure as they could.

Suddenly Jack straightened.

'Did you hear a sound?' he queried.

'I thought I heard a shout,' Bob whispered.

'D'you think Old Moore can still be alive under that pile of rocks?' Jack asked.

'Not under that lot,' Bob replied. 'But he may have managed to escape to the other side. That's what I was hoping — and then he'd soon get help and get us out...' He broke off, and put his hand up. 'Listen!' he commanded.

The boys gazed at each other. A faint echo of a cry came from one side of the fall.

Bob was the practical one. He immediately began to scrape away the rubbish from one side of the heap, where broken timbers were jammed together. He called to Jack.

'It's Old Moore, Jack. It's a miracle. He must be under this heap of timbers that are forming a pocket. He's alive, all right. Clear those stones from behind me. We'll soon get him out.'

They worked quickly, the old man's shouts getting louder every moment. At last Bob stopped and leaned towards the hole he had made.

'Jacob!' he yelled. The answer came at once, louder than expected.

'What's the matter with you boys?' he grumbled. 'I've been calling for ages. Don't you want to see Old Moore again?'

After much scratching and scraping, heaving and pushing, they at last got the old man over to their side of the pile of debris.

There he stood, rather like a shaggy black bear, breathing in gulps, gazing around the confined space.

'Well,' he got out at last, 'this is better than crouching down beside that pit tub, swallowing dust.' He looked at the newly-erected props. 'Who put these up?' he demanded.

'We did,' replied Bob.

'Oh! You did, did you? Not so bad for a pair of youngsters.' The old man suddenly sat down. 'I'm hungry,' he grumbled. 'Wonder how long we've got to stop here?'

And that was a question that neither of the boys could answer. They would just have to wait and hope rescue would come.

52

*At last they managed to pull Old Moore out of the debris.*

'What time is it?' Old Moore grunted, some time later. 'One of you boys got a watch?'

Jack and Bob stared at the old man from where they sat with their backs resting against the coal face. He chuckled. 'I'm forgetting myself — always doing it. Most of our clothes are the other side of that danged pile of muck.'

He turned from the boys and stared at the heap of debris that marked the three sides of their prison. Old Moore was certain that they would be rescued eventually, but the wait seemed interminable.

The boys struggled to their feet. They were clad only in the singlets and trousers in which they had been working when the accident happened.

Jack shivered.

'I'm getting cold, Bob,' he quavered.

'So am I,' agreed Bob. 'But that's a good sign, isn't it, Jacob? It means that the air is fresh, and we won't be choked by gases.'

Old Moore turned round and surveyed the two boys.

'That's quite right, young Bob,' he pronounced. 'When I was a young man, my old Dad used to say the best cure for feeling cold was to work to keep warm. Come on, let's do some exercises.'

'Not enough room,' Bob objected.

'Room be blowed!' retorted the old man. 'I'll show you.'

He did! The contortions he went through as he threw his legs and arms about made the boys laugh their heads off. In the end he collapsed, puffing and blowing.

'Cor,' he wheezed. 'I'm too old for that — anyway, I'm warm enough now. Come on — get going, you two. Legs first, up and down. One, two, one, two. Now your arms. In and out, up and down.'

Away they went, until at last they, too, were out of breath.

'I'm warm enough now,' gasped Jack. 'Are you, Bob?'

Bob was listening intently, his ear against the pile of rock. 'Hush, Jack. I can hear something.'

Jack bent and shook Old Moore's shoulder where he lay resting.

'D'you think they're coming to rescue us at last, Jacob?' he pleaded.

The old man rose to his knees and listened, too. Suddenly a prop cracked with a loud snap and some stones rolled down from the top of the pile.

Jack jumped back hurriedly and stumbled over Old Moore. Bob crouched back as far as he could.

The old man admonished them.

'Now, now, young Jack. I know it's your first day in the pit but you must keep calmer than that. And *you* ought to know better, young Bob...'

Another crack sounded as he finished speaking, and a cloud of dust rolled down from the heap of debris.

'They're shifting it from the other side,' explained Old Moore matter-of-factly. 'The deputy's brought a gang of men to shift the fall. He's a good 'un, is Webber, though we mustn't tell him that.'

Another stone rolled down, and Jack began to whimper.

'Old Moore doesn't seem to be worried at all,' he whispered to Bob. 'D'you think we'll ever see daylight again, Bob?'

The old man turned abruptly and shook the young boy's shoulder.

'No more of that, young Jack,' he warned. 'Of course we're getting out. Now, boys, we've got to get busy. When they move the other side it may collapse on us. Hand me some props, Bob.'

Fortunately, there were props available, and the old man pushed and heaved as he manoeuvred them into place. Sounds from the other side got louder, while the roof creaked and groaned continually. The boys did their best to assist, but most of the exertion was borne by Old Moore.

Soon he was wheezing and gasping as he worked. The climax came as a miniature avalanche of rocks slid into their chamber.

At the same moment the old man collapsed in a heap.

A beam of light played through the cloud of dust on to the little group, and a voice called out. It was the deputy.

'Are you all right in there?'

'It's Jacob,' shouted Bob. 'He's ill, I think. None of us is injured.'

'Stand back, I'm coming over.'

Sliding down the heap of rock, the deputy swiftly bent over the old man, and felt his chest.

'He's winded, I reckon,' he said as he straightened up. 'We can't do anything in here, though. Up you go, boys. There's plenty of help now.'

The two boys were pushed and pulled through the narrow hole, then Old Moore was hauled carefully out and placed on a stretcher.

'Will he die, Bob?' asked Jack fearfully, as he eyed Old Moore.

One eye opened and a voice croaked.

'Die? Not me! Didn't I tell you I'm going to see my hundredth birthday? Just having a ride out, I am.'

And ride out on the stretcher he did, too, until they reached the shaft. A first aid man examined him, then remarked:

'You're as crafty as ever, Old Moore. You're quite all right. You can walk now.'

Before the old man could reply, they were in the cage and being whisked up to the surface.

'There you are, Jack,' shouted Bob over the rattle of the chains. 'There's the daylight you wondered if you'd ever see again. You've finished your first shift. What do you think of it?'

Jack was gulping the fresh air and blinking in the sunshine. 'Well!' He deliberated a while, then prodded his pal playfully. 'I think I'll try it again tomorrow. It's certainly a *man's* job!'

# Hoodoo on the Rangers

## by
## W. McNeilly

Jackson Haig was conscious of only one sound — the whirr of his 16-millimetre film camera — that and the picture he could see through the view-finder. Jackson had the one ability every film cameraman must have — concentration.

Right then he needed it. For Jackson was hanging upside down from the roof of a blazing building, held only by the ankles. Beneath him was the wreckage of a plane. It had crashed, slid along the ground through a score of back gardens, and smashed into the rear of the very house that Jackson was using as his perch.

'Going to be long?' complained a voice from above. 'It's not that I mind. But the roof's starting to burn through...'

Big Bill Gormley was Jackson's sound engineer. His hands were gripping Jackson's ankles. His teeth held the flex of a microphone which was picking up the crackle of the flames.

'Right!' Jackson coughed through the smoke. 'That's it. Up!'

His arm went protectively round the camera as his partner heaved him to the roof.

'I'm not sure about the light,' he complained. 'But I think I got some nice shots.'

Bill wound up his microphone flex and hoisted his portable tape recorder on to his back.

'We'd better get down,' he said mildly in a soft, slow, northern accent. 'The roof is liable to collapse any time.'

They scrambled together down through the skylight and

into the attic of the house and stopped to gain their breath.

'Come on,' called a third voice from below. 'We haven't all day to play around. We can catch the six o'clock news with this little lot and I want an interview to round it off.'

Futuric Films were at work. Jackson, Bill and Brendan O'Hara *were* Futuric Films. They had pooled their money and started a little independent company which filmed news and features for the television companies.

The plane crash had been a routine job... so far. But before they left the house it was to become something very different.

Firemen were running through the house, unwinding hose behind them, as Jackson and Big Bill joined Brendan at the foot of the stairs. The firemen were too intent on their work to bother about the intruders. They were used to seeing cameramen and reporters wherever there was a fire.

'There's someone in this room through here,' Brendan said quickly as the others joined him. 'I'll try to get him to talk.'

The team always tried to work an interview into every film. It meant a higher rate of payment for one thing. And it made for better stories.

The man in the drawing room looked dazed. He was quite young and he seemed to be having difficulty in focusing his eyes. Brendan jabbed the microphone under his nose as Jackson focused the camera.

'Maybe you'd like to tell us what happened?' Brendan suggested.

'Uh?' said the man.

Jackson frowned a little. The man's face was familiar. Where had he seen him before? A vague acquaintance? A public personality? A face in the newspapers or on the TV screen?

Brendan kept trying.

'How do you feel about having a plane crash in your back

garden? Was it a shock? What were your first reactions?'

The man looked blankly at the interviewer. He was swaying a little on his feet.

'Better drop it, Brendan,' Jackson advised. 'That man isn't well. The shock of the crash has probably...'

'Vultures!' barked a voice from behind. 'That's all you are. A pack of hungry vultures preying on the helpless. Out, now! Out of it, the lot of you, before I charge you.'

Inspector Clark had nothing particular against camera-men, sound-men or interviewers. Sometimes he watched TV himself. But somehow, when his path crossed that of Futuric Films, sparks always flew. Sometimes he stopped the team getting film. And there had been times when they had shown film which made him look a little less than dignified. When a runaway bullock had careered down a main street the team had been on hand to let the nation see Inspector Clark vanishing into a horse trough — head-first.

'Breaking and entering, I wouldn't be surprised,' he said briskly as he strode over to the man in the room. 'Being on enclosed premises. Obstructing an officer... Send the doctor in as you go out.'

The worst of the fire had died as the trio made for their battered-looking station-wagon. But though it looked battered, it had a highly-tuned three and a half litre racing engine below its bonnet. It could touch the 140 m.p.h. mark on the open road. Bill Gormley tended its engine with loving care.

'A couple of quick interviews with the neighbours,' Brendan insisted. 'That's all we need to round it off...'

'Not for today's news, we don't,' Jackson answered as he got behind the wheel. 'We're cutting it fine now.'

An ambulance pulled in as they swung away. In the mirror Jackson saw the man from the house being led out to the ambulance. A doctor ran towards the man and lifted an eyelid

*The worst of the fire was over when the trio left the scene.*

with his thumb, then a crowd of onlookers surged round.

'Concussed,' Brendan remarked. 'That's the test. They look at the pupils.'

'It's also the test for drugs,' Jackson pointed out. 'If the pupils are contracted...'

The station-wagon screamed to a halt, and as Jackson looked back the ambulance was already moving off.

'Thank you,' Brendan muttered crossly. 'I always did like bashing my head on the windscreen...'

'I've remembered... just remembered who that man was. I knew I'd seen the face before... It was Charlie Offsal...'

'The Glendale Rangers' new centre-forward!' Brendan gulped.' You could be right. Oh, what a time to remember...'

'That's another knock for the Rangers,' Brendan remarked as the car sped towards the city and the nearest TV studio. 'Without Offsal they just won't have a chance in their match tomorrow. You know, you'd really think there was something in this story of a hoodoo on the Rangers.'

Glendale Rangers were a First Division team, one of the most famous and glamorous in England. For years they had dominated football. Then, late last season, disaster after disaster had struck.

'They've won only three matches this season,' Bill said as he opened up Jackson's camera and took out the film which had been shot. He slipped it into a can, ready to hand to the film-processing laboratory as soon as they reached the studio. 'And they've lost the last seven running.'

Jackson drove swiftly but without taking a ghost of a chance through the growing traffic.

'There could be a film in this,' he said suddenly. 'In the story of the Rangers... or rather of the hoodoo. What do you say?'

'You mean follow them up for a week or two?' Brendan

echoed. 'We could do that, get interviews, films of their matches... It could build up into something quite big...'

Just how big it was to build, none of the Futuric trio could have guessed at that time. They could not know that they were embarking on a story that would bring them into the shadow of peril, disgrace and death.

The next day, the sports pages of the papers were full of the new disaster to the Rangers. Could the ill-fated team hope to win the match that day without their centre-forward? The general opinion of the sports writers was that they could not.

And that seemed to be the opinion of the crowd waiting for the gates to open as the Futuric Film Company drove up.

'I'll do some quick interviews,' Brendan said. 'See what the crowd have to say.'

Tall, shining blocks of new office buildings towered over the football ground, for Glendale was a town which was growing swiftly.

Jackson set up his camera and tripod. Bill swiftly rigged the sound-recorder and Brendan went to work along the waiting queue.

'Are you a regular supporter?' Brendan asked one sour-looking man.

'Supporter! We don't get nothing to support, mate. I'll tell you why I come here. I like a good cry. That's why.'

Most of the supporters spoke in the same vein.

'Pathetic!' was one comment.

'I only come to see just how bad they can get,' was another.

Brendan turned to face the camera and gave a few quick comments of his own. Then the gates opened and the crowd surged in.

For most matches the Futuric team would have gone to the Press box. The view of the field was best from there. But Jackson, Bill and Brendan had already agreed that it was not so much the story of the match they were after as the story of the hoodoo.

'We'll try the Chairman of the Board first,' Jackson said. 'Jason Arkwright. He's a big property man. I think he owns most of the block of flats and offices around here.'

Arkwright was a tall, red-faced man with a mop of black hair and cold, pale blue eyes.

'What do you mean, hoodoo?' he snarled, when Brendan tried to interview him. 'There's no hoodoo here. Rangers are just having a bad run, that's all. It's people like you spreading this hoodoo story who have caused it. Once we win a few games you'll hear how the tune changes. And we'll win, all right...'

He turned back into the board-room and slammed the door.

'Charming!' Brendan murmured.

The film team moved out to the embankment. Jackson set up the camera at the very top, where he could cover the whole field. Bill Gormley rigged a long lead to the sound-recorder so that Brendan could move among the crowd.

By now the teams were trotting out on to the pitch. The Rangers were playing Grinton United and for the first few minutes it did indeed seem as if the days of the hoodoo were over. Rangers were constantly on the attack, and Martin, the reserve centre-forward, seemed to be linking up perfectly with the rest of the team. The United goal was under constant siege and a Ranger's goal seemed inevitable.

Then a hard-pressed defender got his foot to the ball and kicked it wildly upfield. The Rangers' backs were all up in attack and when a United winger burst through there was no one to stop him but the goalkeeper, Victor Wills. Wills made a despairing effort to cut off the shot but the attacker had all the time in the world to shoot past him.

The sudden turn of fortune seemed to take all the heart

out of the Rangers. Their attack lost its sting and they fell back on the defensive more and more.

United slammed another goal past Wills before the Rangers began to recover. But later, Martin robbed a defender of the ball, side-stepped cleverly and shot low into the net.

As the crowd roared its startled applause, Jackson swung his camera to the director's box. With his zoom lens he was able to bring Jason Arkwright into close-up.

'That's funny,' Jackson muttered. 'Arkwright should be cheering. But he's scowling!'

Almost as if Arkwright had heard Jackson's comment, he began to smile and applaud.

It was half-time now and Brendan hurried through the crowd, gathering their comments on the match — and especially on that last sizzling goal.

'Maybe it's a pity we didn't lose Offsal before. Martin's playing a blinder. Why was he only reserve?' was the general view.

And that made the shock even more surprising when the Rangers trotted out on the field again for the second half. As they lined up it could be seen that Martin was now out on the left wing.

'He'll never get a pass there. He'll never get another shot,' the fans shouted angrily.

The forecasts were proved only too dismally true. Martin saw little more of the ball — and the other Rangers seemed unable to do anything with it when they had it. They were sluggish and unsure of themselves and they had no answer to the two more goals that United slammed in.

The crowd was in a real ferment by the end of the match. And more than one voice was eager to record its views into Brendan's microphone.

'I blame the manager,' one man said. 'He should never

have switched Martin over. I just can't understand it!'

Before Brendan could record more, a little knot of big, hardfaced men forced their way through the crowd.

'It's you and the likes of you that caused it,' snarled the leader. 'Putting out these hoodoo stories, making the lads feel they've got the blink on them.'

'Shouldn't be allowed,' another man agreed. 'They should be shown they're not wanted here. They should get a good lesson, they should.'

'And we're just the boys to give them it,' agreed the leading tough.

Without warning he lashed out at Brendan with a vicious right.

'Bash 'em up,' he yelled. 'Smash their cameras. We'll give them hoodoos.'

The toughs surged forward on the camera team. Jackson saw the glint of metal knuckle-dusters on one fist. A bottle was being waved. An angry growl filled the air as the thugs moved menacingly towards them.

Jackson Haig thought quickly. For this was not the first time he and his young partners had been threatened with violence when out on a job.

'Plan three!' he shouted and snatched up his camera and tripod.

Big Bill Gormley grabbed up the portable tape-recorder and swung behind Jackson. Brendan O'Hara swung behind Jackson on the other side as the mob closed in.

The trailing lead of Brendan's microphone made a first class trip wire and brought down three of the attacking thugs. And they were the lucky ones.

For now Jackson swung up the feet of the tripod so that three stout, sharp-pointed lances were thrust towards the gang.

With his two partners at his shoulder, Jackson pressed forward behind the long, deadly, three-pronged lance. The thugs who had been so keen to push forward now bellowed for those behind to get out of the way. There were screams of pain and fear as the tips of the tripod feet jabbed and pricked.

Those tips were sharp. But they were short. They could do little more than prick through the clothing of the thugs. But that was enough. The gang wavered and broke.

'Smash their camera,' yelled a voice in the crowd.

But a thug in the front of the battle line shouted back:

'If you want to do any smashing, mate, come and do it yourself. I'm getting out of here.'

Futuric were through. At gathering speed they headed for the exit and their waiting station-wagon. The powerful engine beneath the battered bonnet howled into life.

'That's that, then,' beamed Bill Gormley as Jackson drove the car away from the football ground. 'A bit of a punch-up that, eh? But I suppose that's the end of it.'

'I wonder,' Jackson answered. 'I just wonder.'

And he said little more until they were back at their headquarters in South Kensington. The film had to be processed and this was Bill Gormley's work. While he was in the darkroom, Brendan and Jackson played back the tape-recording. A later process would be to marry up the sound with the pictures. But first they wanted to know just what sounds they had recorded.

'Isn't it a funny thing,' mused Brendan. 'There was hardly one in the whole crowd of supporters who was really supporting the team. They didn't believe they had a ghost of a chance...'

Jackson waved him to silence.

'Listen to that again... run it through once more — the very last bit...'

Again the shouts of the angry thugs rang through the office.

'Why were they so keen to smash the cameras?' he demanded. 'That's not normal. They were deliberately set on to us by someone. There must be something on that film that someone doesn't want to see broadcast... Bill, is that film nearly ready?'

A little later, the puzzled trio were watching the film run through on the 'Editor', a device which projected it on to a small screen. There was also a splicer on the editor so that sections could be cut out of the film and joined up in different order if that was necessary.

'There's that interview with Jason Arkwright. He was furious when we mentioned the hoodoo... but turn the film on a bit to the point where Martin scored,' said Jackson.

'Now look. I got a big close-up of him then... Wouldn't you think a director who had just seen his team score would be pleased?'

'But he smiles a little later on,' Bill pointed out.

'It could be that he saw Jackson's camera turned on him,' Brendan said thoughtfully.

'What I can't understand, is why Martin was transferred to the wing,' pondered Jackson. 'It could have been an act of deliberate sabotage. Maybe it isn't a hoodoo that's wrecking the Rangers. Maybe it's a traitor.'

'Let's get over to wherever Martin lives and ask him just why he was transferred at half-time. Let's find out what happened in the Rangers' dressing-room.'

Futuric had lots of contacts among the newspapers and a few calls to Fleet Street soon produced Martin's address. Again the battered-looking station-wagon went snaking through the traffic towards Glendale.

Martin had lodgings in an exclusive private hotel on the outskirts of the town. But now the hotel did not look nearly so exclusive. Outside, a hungry-eyed crowd surged backwards and forwards, pressing against a ring of policemen.

From an upstairs window a wisp of smoke streamed.

'I've got a feeling we're too late,' Jackson said grimly.

As he jerked the car to a halt, a familiar figure strode up.

'The "vultures" again,' snarled Inspector Clark. 'But you're too late this time.'

'What do you mean?' Brendan demanded.

'A bomb was planted in the bedroom of Martin, the Rangers' reserve, but Martin wasn't there when it went off.'

'Where is he?' Jackson asked.

'If I knew I wouldn't tell you,' growled the Inspector. 'But I don't know ... Martin has vanished.'

'I suppose it's no good asking you any more questions?' Jackson Haig grinned.

'You suppose right,' snapped the Inspector. 'Now buzz off with your cameras, you vultures. You make me sick.'

'Sticks and stones...' quipped Jackson. 'Come on, boys, let's get to work. Brendan, you grab some interviews while I see if there's enough light here to film.'

Futuric Films were at work again. Jackson swiftly set up his 16-millimetre cine camera on its tripod and glanced at the light-meter dangling around his neck.

'It won't be beautiful but it all carries the story on,' he said.

Big Bill Gormley set up the sound-recording equipment and Brendan O'Hara moved through the crowd, doing snap interviews with everyone willing to talk.

Jackson filmed the hotel first, concentrating on the window of Martin's room from which the smoke of the bomb explosion still drifted. Then he turned to the eager crowd, gawping at the scene of the crime. What made people come to stare, he wondered. It was a perfectly ordinary private hotel — except of course that a bomb had just gone off in a bedroom.

A shot of the police followed. Then Jackson zoomed in for

a close-up of Inspector Clark leaving the hotel. Brendan returned then and whispered excitedly in Jackson's ear.

'Hey, Inspector!' called the cameraman. 'Any clues?'

The policeman gave him a tight-lipped glare. He would have stalked past but for Jackson's next words.

'Don't forget the window-cleaner!'

The Inspector jerked to a halt. Jackson explained.

'Brendan's been talking to someone in the crowd who saw a window-cleaner at work a little while before the bomb went off. Window-cleaners don't usually work at night.'

Plainly the Inspector had not heard of this.

'Thanks,' he said sourly. 'Well... in return I'll tell you something. There was a typed, anonymous note in his room, telling him to get out of town — and stay out... You needn't bother thanking me. It'll be in the papers in the morning.'

Back at their South Kensington headquarters the Futuric team considered the matter.

'One thing's for sure. This is a lot more than just a hoodoo story. Someone's definitely out to wreck the Rangers. They're in the open now.'

The other two nodded their heads in agreement with Jackson.

'Which means that it's going to be still harder to get a decent story,' Jackson went on. 'They'll be besieged with reporters. The ground will have a real security guard on it. We won't be able to get inside at all with our equipment. What do we do?'

Bill Gormley thought hard.

'Couldn't we hire a plane and fly overhead,' he suggested.

'A lot we'd see that way,' sniffed Brendan. 'Even if they didn't bring out anti-aircraft guns to shoot us down. And the way things are going, that could happen.'

'Apart from the cost of a plane,' Jackson added dryly.

Bill went to the dark-room to process the film they had shot that evening. He wasn't in for long — about half a second.

'Hey!' he gulped. 'Brendan — Jackson — quickly!'

His face was pale.

Jackson was on his feet in an instant, darting for the dark-room door.

'Something wrong?' he demanded. 'The film?'

But it wasn't the film which had given Bill Gormley such a shock.

In the dark-room, sprawled on the floor, lay the body of a man. He was quite dead.

Inspector Clark was his usual acid self.

'I wouldn't be a bit surprised if I couldn't book you for manslaughter. That bit of uninsulated wire probably constitutes a man-trap in the legal sense.'

'I... I've been going to fix it for a while,' Bill muttered.

Jackson broke in. 'That man had no right in there. He was burgling the place, after our equipment, no doubt. He put his hand on a live wire and conked out. We didn't invite him to burgle the place. You can't hold us responsible.'

The Inspector gave a nasty smile.

'You don't know much about the law. Even burglars have their rights.'

But at last he went — after the body had been removed from the dark-room, and innumerable statements taken down. Again the Futuric team were left alone.

'Was he after our gear — just some chance sneak-thief?' mused Jackson. 'Or was it the film he wanted?'

'Things are warming up,' Brendan answered. 'Whoever's behind it — they seem to believe that we know something... and that we've got film to prove it.'

'If only we could get a bit closer to them,' Jackson sighed.

71

'They're on the alert now and to bring a camera within a mile of the ground is going to be dangerous. How do we get closer?'

'What about the ground staff?' suggested Bill Gormley. 'They must want the thing cleared up as much as anyone.'

'Not as much as the players,' Jackson answered. 'Now if we...'

He broke off, staring at Brendan.

'Of course,' he breathed. 'Yes. Of course. That's it. That's the very answer.'

Brendan shuffled uncomfortably.

'I don't know what's in your mind, Jacko. But from the way you're looking at me I don't like it.'

'Why shouldn't you like it?' Jackson answered. 'Think of the honour. Think of the autographs. Think of the fans filling the streets round your house, cheering you like mad.'

'What are you getting at?'

'Glendale Rangers' new centre-forward... Brendan O'Hara! You are going to join the Rangers, Brendan!'

... The bare-headed lad who walked up to the entrance of the Glendale Rangers' ground looked, and was, nervous and ill at ease. His rather soiled raincoat and badly cut suit sat uneasily on him.

It was quite a while since Brendan O'Hara had worn a suit costing less than thirty pounds.

From a window overlooking the ground a cine camera peered down. Jackson Haig was behind the view-finder. The third member of Futuric Films was crouched beside a small radio receiver which was linked to a tape-recorder.

'He's coming through now,' said Bill Gormley. 'Good reception, too.'

Brendan's voice seemed to fill the room.

'Me name's Brendan O'Hara,' he said in an exaggerated Irish accent. 'Oi'm after havin' a letter here in me pocket from Mr Burton, the manager, of the Glendale Rangers.'

There was a moment's silence and the rustling of some paper. The sound came from a microphone in Brendan's lapel which was linked to a miniature transmitter in his pocket. The transmitter's range was short. But it was enough to reach the waiting receiver. Another voice came over the air, that of the gatekeeper.

'This is an invitation to sign professional papers for the Rangers. You were a schoolboy international, I see... But it's dated a year ago. Why have you been so long in replying?'

'Oi'd say that was me own business,' Brendan answered tartly. 'But since yer interested I'll tell ye. I'm only just after getting the letter. Oi was over in Oirland, don't ye know, and me mail didn't catch up...'

The gatekeeper seemed satisfied. The whirr of Jackson's camera stopped as Brendan vanished within the ground.

'So far so good,' he said. 'I wonder if they'll sign him on.'

'He was pretty good,' Bill answered. 'I think he'd have been playing professional football before this if he hadn't been so keen to keep his amateur status. I think they'll jump at him.'

Bill was right. From what came over the radio, Mr Burton remembered Brendan's promise as a youngster. He was given a quick work-out on the field and then taken to the board-room. Now came the harsh voice of Jason Arkwright, Chairman of the Board.

'Well, O'Hara. Mr Burton and Mr Legge, the trainer, tell me you gave a pretty good display. We're going to sign you on. And what's more — we're putting you straight into the team for tomorrow's match.'

Brendan's gasp almost wrecked the microphone.

'Faith, that... that's marvellous, sorr,' he answered. 'Oi had no hope at all ye'd think so highly of me.'

Jackson grinned mirthlessly.

'They're putting him in the team because they can't get anyone else,' he commented. 'They've been trying to sign on players all week. But no one's going to Rangers as long as they have the hoodoo hanging over them.'

'I just hope we haven't put Brendan's neck on the chopping block,' Bill commented gloomily.

'He'll pull it in in time,' Jackson said. 'Don't worry. You know him.'

Yet he could not help worrying himself. Brendan was a fast-talking, quick-acting interviewer for the team. But now they seemed to be dealing with a completely ruthless enemy of the Rangers, someone who wanted to crush the team out of existence. How would Brendan match up to that challenge?

Bill suddenly shouted in alarm.

'The transmitter has gone dead!'

But it had only gone dead because there are no lapels on a track suit. Brendan was out on the pitch again as they soon saw. He had no way of wearing the radio.

From their window, Jackson and Bill were able to watch a good bit of the training-session that followed. The team started with some interval running and followed this by some heading practice, standing in a ring and heading the ball from one to another. Then followed a favourite of the trainer, running along a zig-zag line of old motor tyres, a good exercise for helping a quick side-step.

'Brendan's puffing a bit,' Jackson chuckled. 'We can't have been working him hard enough.'

But the next item on the training programme made Jackson frown. Brendan was given the ball and, plainly, told to try to dribble it through the rest of the team. Naturally he failed, as tackle after tackle was hurled at him.

Jackson winced as he saw Brendan brought down time after time.

'That's daft,' said Bill. 'They could crock him ... or maybe that's what they're after. Do you reckon he's been twigged?'

'Legge has a reputation as a tough trainer,' Jackson answered. 'But a good one. I don't know any other way you could really teach people to dodge a tackle. Well, I suppose we'll have to wait now for Brendan to report. I doubt if he'll risk using the set again while he's inside the ground.'

Jackson was right. The receiver showed no more signs of life and it was more than an hour before they saw Brendan's slim, athletic figure come striding from the ground. He headed down the road towards the café where they had agreed to meet.

But he had only gone a few paces when a lank figure suddenly slouched out of a doorway to confront him.

'Is he going to be attacked?' Bill gasped.

'Not physically,' Jackson grinned. 'It's only Jim Hardy from the *Echo*.'

It was even hotter than they realised. For when Jackson and Bill found their friend in the café he had the miniature transmitter on the table before him. It was disguised to look like an ordinary transistor set and indeed an ordinary receiver was part of its circuit.

Brendan's face looked strained.

'It's the news,' he said. 'They've found Martin, the missing reserve centre-forward ...'

'Has he told them anything?' Jackson asked eagerly.

'He's not likely to,' was Brendan's sombre answer. 'He's dead.'

The hoodoo had struck again!

'How was he killed?' demanded Jackson.

'A car accident,' answered Brendan. 'That's what the news bulletin said. He ran off the road ... the Southampton road.'

'Trying to get out of the country,' Jackson mused. 'I suppose he hoped to get aboard a liner, skip the country ...'

'But why?' Bill demanded. 'Why should he want to leave the country?'

'Why should anyone want to put a bomb in his bedroom — but they did!' Jackson countered. 'Because he knew too much about the hoodoo — or someone thought he did.'

The trio fell silent round the grimy café table.

'Whoever was responsible for Martin going out on the wing is behind the mystery,' Jackson said. 'And he was determined Martin wouldn't tell what happened in the dressing-room at half-time. That means Burton, the manager, or Legge, the trainer...'

'Or Hewitt, the centre-half. He's the captain,' Brendan put in. 'He could have ordered the change in tactics. That gives us three suspects... at least. But which one is it?'

'That's for you to find out,' Jackson said. 'That's why you signed on for the Rangers.'

Bill Gormley coughed unhappily.

'Perhaps we should pack it in,' he suggested. 'If they've got to the stage of knocking blokes off... Well, we might have a job finding an interviewer as good as Brendan.'

'Thanks for the comfort,' Brendan grinned. 'And the compliment. But I didn't join Glendale Rangers to pack it in the next day. Now — where do we go from here?'

'You make yourself scarce,' Jackson answered. 'Bill and I are going down to have a look at the crashed car. We'll need a few shots of it to keep the story complete... And watch it, Brendan. Bill's right. We don't want to have to look for a new interviewer.'

... 'The vultures are late this time,' said Inspector Clark grimly, as Jackson set up his camera tripod on the roadside and began to film the police at work on the wreck of Martin's car. 'I thought you had an unerring nose for blood.'

The daylight was fading fast and Jackson did not answer

at first as he took a light-meter reading, swiftly focused the camera and set its motor whirring. He took half-a-dozen shots from different angles, close ups of the police, wide-angle shots of the whole car, and assorted shots of the spectators who had, as ever, appeared on the scene. When the whole story of the hoodoo was edited this scene might be wanted. On the other hand, it might be thrown away. That was something you could never know in the film business.

As he finished, Inspector Clark approached him. Bill Gormley could not hear what was being said as he packed away the equipment. But as soon as the Futuric unit's battered-looking old station-wagon was streaking away, Jackson began to laugh.

'Old sour-puss Clark,' he chuckled. 'He knows Brendan's in the Rangers' team. He wants us to keep him posted. Imagine — asking for help from us "vultures"!'

Bill and Jackson did not return to London. Instead, they made for Seaport, near Southampton, for the next day Rangers were playing Seaport Mariners. Futuric would be there to see if the hoodoo struck again.

The evening paper was full of Martin's death. The headlines screamed: 'RANGERS' HOODOO STRIKES AGAIN'. But the report added nothing to what Jackson and Bill already knew.

After a meal, Jackson and Bill went out for a walk. They headed for the Mariners' ground to get some idea of what filming conditions would be like the next day. It was a smaller ground than most of those in the First Division — overshadowed by the bleak shapes of factory buildings and warehouses. Fog had crept down on the port and the mournful groaning of ships' sirens filled the air.

'There's a light on in the office. We'll see if we can fix something up,' Jackson commented.

As they headed for the pavilion door at the rear of the

ground, a figure stirred in the shadows ahead. It hurried on ahead of them, as if unwilling to be seen. Jackson tensed and then broke into a trot. As he did so, the man ahead began to run.

'After him, Bill!'

The pursuers were running hard when two men stepped out from a doorway into the path of the escaping man. Jackson saw the struggle begin. Then he and Bill were piling into the attackers. They had no idea who the fugitive could be — but two against one was far from fair play.

Jackson slammed a short left hook into the solar plexus of the burly man who was grabbing at the fugitive's arms. Bill thumped an uppercut at the other man. The fugitive was free for a moment.

One of the men on the ground grabbed at his legs and he lashed out wildly, tore himself free and raced on down the dark road.

'Hey!' gasped Jackson, staring after him. 'It... it's...'

Before he could get the words out, something slammed down on the back of his head.

But into the dark wells of unconsciousness he carried the memory of the face he had seen. It was the face of Martin — *the face of the man who had been killed on the Southampton road.*

'Well, well, well,' a familiar voice broke gradually through Jackson's consciousness. 'Our little vultures are in trouble this time.'

When Jackson Haig came round it was to find himself slumped in a chair under lights that sent shafts of pain blazing into his head. He tried to raise a hand to his skull, which felt as if little men with big hammers were doing some road-mending inside. His hands would not move. When he looked down he saw the reason. He was handcuffed.

Blue uniforms loomed all about him and the sour face of Inspector Clark was looking down at him.

'Hey!' Jackson said. 'I was coshed.'

'You were,' agreed the Inspector. 'Or at any rate trunch-eoned. Attacking officers in the course of their duty... I expect you'll get ten years.'

'Where's Bill?' Jackson swung round and saw the sound engineer of Futuric Films sitting sheepishly on another chair. He, too, was handcuffed.

'You mean... those were coppers going for Martin?' Jackson gulped. 'I... we thought they were thugs, more of the hoodoo merchant's men.'

The Inspector said nothing but continued to gaze down at him with his sour smile.

'How did you know Martin was going to be there?' he barked suddenly. 'How did you know he wasn't dead?'

'But... we didn't,' Jackson protested. His brain had begun to work at top speed at last. 'We were only checking what the ground was like for tomorrow... How did *you* know he wasn't dead?'

'The body was short of a finger on the left hand. Martin was all complete. So he must have arranged the accident to cover for himself. You see where that leaves us, don't you?'

'Where?' Jackson asked carefully.

'We've been doing quite a lot of checking. Martin was around for nearly every disaster that's hit the Rangers recently. He himself was responsible for them losing their last match — for it was his own request that he should go on the wing after half-time. The captain told us that... Martin is the man behind the hoodoo.'

'I don't believe it.' Jackson said stubbornly next morning. 'I don't believe Martin's the hoodoo man. Why should he be?'

'It's possible the Inspector's quite right,' said Bill Gormley cautiously. 'It adds up.'

They were back in their hotel, released after a lot of argument. They had the feeling that their arrest had been the Inspector's idea of a merry practical joke. Although there was nothing merry about their aching heads!

'The bomb,' said Bill. 'Martin could have planted that himself.'

'No. I can't accept it,' Jackson sighed. 'There's more to it than that... I wonder if Brendan's on to anything?'

Brendan O'Hara was travelling down to Seaport with the rest of the team. Jackson and Bill had little hope of hearing from him before the match with Seaport Mariners.

As the time for the match drew near, there was still no report from Brendan.

'We'd better get to the ground,' Jackson decided. 'I expect the manager is keeping the whole team under his eye.'

The whole of Seaport seemed to have turned up for the match. How much this was due to their love of the game, and how much to the publicity of the hoodoo, it was hard to tell.

Jackson and Bill rigged up their equipment in the Press box. Then Bill had to act as interviewer in Brendan's absence. Jackson himself tended the sound equipment.

There was no cheering for the Rangers as they trotted out on to the pitch, only a curious hush as if the crowd expected them to drop through the ground. The Mariners, though, got a rousing welcome.

It was the Mariners who kicked off. They pressed strongly from the start, with some neat, quick inter-passing that soon had the ball down at the Rangers' goal. Plainly, they were full of confidence.

They were in for some shocks.

The Mariner inside-left sent a sizzing shot rocketing for the corner of the net. Victor Wills, Rangers' goalkeeper, was up to gather it as if he had springs in his boots. In the same movement he hurled the ball out high and clear to Rangers' centre-half, Hewitt, the captain. Hewitt trapped the ball, swung round and passed directly upfield to Brendan who had not gone back into defence.

Brendan was away like a shot, beating the Mariners' right-back. He had only the keeper to beat and he pretended to shoot hard for the right. As the keeper went that way, Brendan gently lobbed the ball to the left. In the first minute Rangers were a goal up.

Five minutes later, Hewitt himself grabbed the ball from a loose scrimmage in mid-field, swung it out to the right-winger who cut inside and then crossed a beautiful, head-high pass which Brendan had only to nod forward to notch his second goal of the match.

There were few Rangers supporters at Seaport. But what there were kept up a continual howl of encouragement. It was so long since they had had anything to cheer about.

And Rangers responded with two more goals before half-time. One came from the outside-left, a long, beautiful shot that came curling in over the heads of the defenders. The other came from Brendan's boot, a simple goal that was almost handed to him on a plate when the Mariners' keeper fumbled a save.

Jackson glanced over to the directors' box. The Rangers' board was all there. In their midst, Jason Arkwright, the chairman, was applauding furiously as the half-time whistle blew.

A local band played during the interval. Jackson wrote up his 'dopesheet' while it played. This was a notebook in which each separate shot he had filmed was recorded.

'That's funny,' he remarked. 'I don't remember ever getting a dopesheet finished at half-time before...'

'I don't remember as long an interval before,' Bill answered. 'They've been off the field for a full fifteen minutes...'

Abruptly the loudspeakers of the address system crackled into life.

'Ladies and gentlemen,' said a flustered announcer. 'We regret that the remainder of the match cannot now take place. We must ask you to leave the ground quietly and...'

Whatever else he said was drowned in the howl of protest which came from the terraces and stands.

Jackson looked at Bill in alarm.

'What's happened in the dressing-room? What's gone wrong?'

Jackson was already making his way out of the Press box. Something was wrong down below in the dressing-rooms. Something was terribly wrong!

The dressing-room looked like the scene of a massacre. Groaning bodies twisted and writhed on the floor and on the benches.

Jackson Haig halted at the door for an instant in sheer shocked horror. Then, as if by instinct, he whipped up his camera. The motor purred as the lenses took in the scene.

But not for long. A shout rang out.

'What d'you think you're doing? Throw him out!'

It was the harsh voice of Jason Arkwright which barked the order. The chairman of Glendale Rangers seemed beside himself with fury as he charged at the young cameraman.

'Get him!' shouted a hoarse voice from Jackson's side.

From the corner of his eye Jackson saw a punch swinging at his head. He ducked, and as he did so, swung the camera by its handstrap. A 16-millimetre film camera is a solid, chunky bit of metal. When it hit the attacker in the stomach it put all ideas of a fight out of his mind. He doubled up, gasping for breath.

But Arkwright was on top of Jackson now, his red face dark with anger and his fists pounding at the cameraman.

Jackson was beaten to his knees, helpless under the blows.

Arkwright lashed out with his foot, a vicious kick which would have felled Jackson if it had landed.

The cameraman wriggled frantically aside, and as the chairman's foot hissed past his jaw he struck again with the camera, an upward blow which hit Arkwright behind the knee of the leg taking his weight.

The burly chairman came down with a crash. But Jackson did not wait to see him hit the floor. Turning, he darted from the dressing-room and raced for the Press box.

'What's happening down there?' demanded Bill Gormley.

Swiftly Jackson told him.

'It looks as if they've all been poisoned, somehow... But let's get out of here.'

'Poisoned!' Bill gasped. 'But what about Brendan?'

'Brendan's all right,' Jackson answered. 'I saw him. He was the only one of the team still on his feet. Come on, for Pete's sake. There's going to be the most unholy row...'

The row had begun already. The crowd did not like to be told that the second half of the match with Seaport Mariners was cancelled. They were showing their dislike in violent ways.

It looked as if they were determined to wreck the ground. Sticks, stones and bottles flew. So did fists.

Jackson took a few quick shots of the rapidly-growing riot as he and Bill forced their way out.

Thankfully they piled into the seats of their waiting station-wagon and headed for their hotel.

'What d'you make of it, then?' asked Bill as Jackson sent the car roaring through the streets.

'I don't know about the poisoning,' Jackson answered. 'But I'll tell you something else. Jason Arkwright went for me down in that dressing-room — and so did a tough who seemed

to be under his orders. Arkwright doesn't want us shoving
our noses in. Arkwright could have been behind the man who
tried to break into the dark-room ... *Arkwright* could be the
man behind the hoodoo.'


'Well, well, well,' said Detective-Inspector Clark. 'So the
vultures return to their roost.'

He was sitting on Jackson's bed smoking a cigarette.

'I hope you've got a warrant,' Jackson said grimly.

'What a thing to say!' the policeman pretended to be shocked. 'And I thought we were going to be such friends. But
perhaps I should really be speaking to your little Irish play-
mate, Brendan. Did he enjoy the match?'

Jackson said nothing. He eyed the detective angrily.

'I've been speaking to Mr Arkwright,' the Inspector went
on. 'He thinks it's very strange that only one member of his
team should not have been affected by the half-time orange
drinks — to which, the doctors tell me, someone added a gen-
erous dose of croton oil. A nasty thing to do. It doubles you
up for quite a while. If anyone knew the stuff was in the
drink it would be quite natural for him not to take any.'

'Hey!' Bill blurted out. 'You're ... you're not suggesting
Brendan put that muck in the drinks?'

'He could have done,' the Inspector said. 'He's a newcomer
to the team ... and one very interested in getting a good hoodoo story.'

Jackson could stay silent no longer.

'You're off your rocker. Brendan wouldn't do a thing like
that. Anyway — there's one perfectly good reason for him not
to take the drink. He can't. He's allergic to most fruit. He
comes out in great big lumps all over if he so much

as bites an orange. You couldn't possibly blame him.'

'I know,' the Inspector smiled sourly. 'That's why he isn't in the nick right now... And, in a way, that's why I'm here. I want your help,' he said. 'This hoodoo's got to end — and you're the only ones who can end it!'

'You want *us* to help *you!*' Jackson Haig's voice held a sharp edge of disbelief as he gazed at Clark. 'You're joking, of course. You call us vultures. You push us around. You even arrest us... Now you ask us to help you.'

'I was never more serious in my life,' the Inspector assured him. 'This is developing into a thoroughly nasty case. People are getting hurt. Soon they may be getting killed... if you don't help. And you *can* help. Futuric Films have something the police don't have. You've got someone in the Rangers' team. I want you to pass on to me everything that Brendan O'Hara tells you about the hoodoo on the Rangers.'

He walked to the door.

'Think it over,' he said. 'I'd like to believe we were on the same side.'

As soon as the door closed Jackson started to pack.

'What do we do about the Inspector's offer?' Bill asked as he, too, began to collect his clothes and gear.

'We wait till we hear what Brendan has to say,' Jackson answered. 'And we won't be seeing him till we get back to London.'

Jackson was thoughtful as the old station-wagon howled its way from Seaport back to the company's Kensington headquarters.

Was Jason Arkwright behind the troubles that befell his own football team? It seemed absurd. Yet a pattern was beginning to emerge that made it a possibility.

Where did Martin, the player who had seemed to be dead and had then reappeared, fit into the pattern? There was as much evidence against him as against Arkwright.

How did Brendan stand now? Jackson and Bill knew that he had nothing to do with the hoodoo. But the fact that he should be the only person not affected by the half-time drinks at Seaport must make it seem to outsiders that he had doped the orange juice.

And Inspector Clark? What were they to do about his offer ... or demand? By now they had a lot of valuable film. If they worked too closely with the police that film could become evidence in a lengthy law case. It would be infuriating to have it tied up just when the television companies would be at their keenest to buy it.

Back in London, Bill went at once to the dark-room to process the film shot at Seaport. While he worked the phone rang. It was Brendan.

'I'm public enemy number one here,' he complained. 'They all think I put that stuff in the drinks. Nobody's spoken to me since we got back to Glendale.'

Jackson nodded to himself. It was what he had expected.

'We'll be over there tomorrow,' he said. 'You get back to your digs. We'll want the radio working again.'

The office Jackson had rented was in a building overlooking Glendale Rangers' ground. It was a tall, new building called Arkwright House. It belonged to the Rangers' Chairman, as did much of the property in the area of Glendale.

The camera was set up on its tripod on a table in the centre of the room. With the powerful telephoto lens mounted, Jackson could cover almost all the ground and also the administration buildings behind the stand.

'Don't forget — keep well back, Bill,' Jackson warned. 'As long as we're away from the window we can see out but no one can see us.'

Bill had set up the sound equipment. Now the receiver of

a radio transmitter began to buzz with life. The signal was coming from a tiny set disguised as a pocket radio which Brendan O'Hara was carrying.

'Good morning, gentlemen all,' Brendan murmured. 'This is your friendly station Snoop Two coming on the air with all the latest news of villainy in high places. I'm just going into the ground now...'

There was silence for a little and then the voices of the trainer and manager could be heard.

'What are you doing here, O'Hara?' snapped Burton, the manager.

'Sure oi've come to train,' declared Brendan in his over-exaggerated Irish accent.

'With the rest of the team in hospital? You might as well go home.'

'Wait a minute. He can help the ground staff,' chipped in Legge, the trainer. 'They're painting the north stand. Off you go, son... And you needn't take that transistor with you. You'll work better without a lot of rubbishy noise.'

'Ah, now, Mr Legge, sure what's the harm in a bit of music...? What's the word of the other lads, anyway? Are they bad?'

'They'll be all right,' said Burton brusquely. 'And don't forget — you're still under suspicion.'

In the office Jackson heard the radio being put down and Brendan's feet moving out of the dressing-room. It might be quite a good thing that the Futuric interviewer had been forced to leave it behind. There was silence for a little while, then Burton spoke.

'What do you think of that lad?' Jackson heard him asking.

'He'll make a good centre before I've done with him,' said the trainer.

'No, no. I mean... do you think he was the one who fixed

the drinks at Seaport? After all, he didn't have any of it.'

Jackson didn't hear the answer to this. The men were moving away. But he realised that Brendan would have to be careful, as he was still under suspicion.

'Maybe we should switch off?' Bill suggested.

Jackson shook his head and listened more intently.

His ear had picked up a stealthy slithering sound from the receiver. The sound came closer to the hidden microphone. Now he could hear heavy breathing. There was a creaking sound.

'Sounds as if someone tiptoed in and opened a cupboard door,' Jackson whispered intently.

'I wonder what's going on down there!'

Footsteps were approaching along the corridor, heavy, confident steps.

From the sound alone Jackson guessed that Jason Arkwright was approaching. That he was right was proved just a few moments later.

'Burton!' called the chairman.

'Legge!'

There was no other sound for a moment. Then there came again the stealthy creaking of the cupboard door. There was one soft footstep.

Arkwright must have been standing just beside the transmitter. His gasp was as loud as if he had been in the room with the cameramen.

'Martin! What are you ... ?'

There was a grunt, a scuffle of feet and the thudding sound of a heavy blow.

Then there was a great crash followed by a sinister uncanny silence.

'They've knocked the set over. Come on — we've got to find out what happened.'

'I know what it sounded like,' Bill grunted. 'Murder ...'

There was a lift in the tall building, but there are times when lifts are too slow.

Jackson went down the stairs, leaping two at a time. Bill was hard on his heels. Under Jackson's arm was his camera — and in his mind was the memory of the brief struggle they had heard on the radio... a struggle that had seemed to end in death.

But death for whom? For Jason Arkwright, or Martin, the missing centre-forward? As he raced across the road to the ground entrance, Jackson was trying to disentangle the sounds in his memory. Who had hit whom?

A laundry van came bustling out of the ground as Jackson and his sound engineer raced through the entrance. They had to dodge the van — and then the gatekeeper.

'Hey!' the man shouted. 'You can't go in there...'

But by the time he had finished shouting Jackson and Bill were already in and racing for the entrance of the pavillion itself.

The club's manager and trainer were coming down the corridor as Jackson and Bill charged in. They tried to stop the pair — and regretted it as they picked themselves up from the floor.

Jackson led the way into the dressing-room — and halted in amazement.

It was empty.

'Is... is it the wrong room?' faltered Bill.

'This was the place all right and — hey... look at that stain on the table.'

There was no mistaking the dark stain on the corner of the wooden table. Though it had been rubbed roughly — it was blood. Jackson pointed to a cupboard in one corner. It hung slightly open.

'It's my guess Martin sneaked in here, hid in the cupboard and waited for Arkwright.'

'Then that makes him the man behind the hoodoo on the Rangers,' Bill gasped.

'If he's the one who won the fight,' Jackson answered grimly. 'And if he did... what did he do with the body? He hasn't had time to get it out of the building or...'

As he spoke, one question was settled. Feet came thundering down the corridor. Arkwright's voice boomed through the building. Leading the manager and trainer, the chairman of the Rangers burst into the dressing-room.

'I don't know what you think you're doing here,' he snarled, his face even redder than usual. 'But I can tell you where you're going. Straight out...'

'Is that where Martin went?' Jackson put in as the trio advanced.

'Martin? He's not here!' Arkwright thundered.

'But he was. And he was talking to you,' Bill put in. 'We know.'

The manager and trainer were looking oddly at their chairman. For a moment he looked as if he would burst.

'You're being absurd!' he spat. 'I should call the police and have you arrested. But... well. If you think Martin's here... Find him.'

Jackson's heart sank. Jason Arkwright would never have given permission for a search if Martin had been in the building. Yet he made the search, aided by Bill.

From the windows as they searched, they could see Brendan O'Hara, third member of the Futuric Film Company, working with the Rangers' ground staff on painting work at the other side of the ground.

'Satisfied?' demanded Arkwright grimly as the search ended without a trace of the missing Martin.

'I'd just like to check with those people outside,' Jackson answered. 'They may have seen Martin...'

'They didn't. He wasn't here.' The chairman snorted. 'But go on. Ask them.'

It was hard to walk over to Brendan without giving any sign of recognition but Jackson managed to do it. Then Jackson's last hope faded.

'No, I wasn't after seeing anyone at all,' declared Brendan truthfully.

'There hasn't been a soul come in or out except for yourself and the laundry van...'

And that was all he got the chance to say. For before he had finished Jackson was away, sprinting across the pitch and out of the gate without even returning to the pavilion. Bill saw him go and raced after him.

'The laundry van,' Jackson panted as he raced towards their station-wagon. 'Martin could have been lugged out in a laundry hamper and no one would be any the wiser.'

'Then Arkwright's the man behind it all?' Bill gasped.

'It looks almost certain now,' Jackson agreed as the powerful engine howled its way down the street. 'Do you remember which laundry it was?'

Bill luckily had noted the name on the van as they entered the ground. The station-wagon went streaking through the streets of Glendale towards the laundry on the outskirts. But disappointment awaited the pair there.

'The van from the Rangers?' an under-manager answered Jackson. 'Oh, it's on a round out into the country. It won't be back until this afternoon...'

Again the station-wagon streaked away. Jackson's face was grim.

'I don't like it, Bill,' he said. 'Jason Arkwright would know that Martin's body would be discovered as soon as the laundry van got back to headquarters. So he must have known the van wasn't going straight back...'

'You ... you mean ... he's maybe made plans to intercept it?' Bill murmured. 'You could be right, Jacko ... He's had time enough.'

They were out in the country by now, racing down winding roads with high hedges on either side.

Then, as they swept round a sharp bend, Jackson jammed on the brakes with a howl of screeching tyres.

The chase was over. Ahead of them, close to the hedge, stood the van they had sought.

It was blazing fiercely.

Jackson Haig brought the station-wagon to a screeching halt beside the blazing van. As he did so, Bill was throwing himself out and racing for the flaming vehicle.

As he ran he was jerking off his jacket and wrapping his arms and hands in the thick cloth. Clumsily he wrestled with the van's rear door. The smell of scorching cloth was heavy in the smoky air.

The heat-warped door jerked open at last. Bill plunged into the scorching interior. Smouldering laundry hampers were piled high.

With desperate speed Bill pulled them down and hurled them to the road. Was Martin inside one of them? And if so, could he still be alive? If he had lain unconscious and not dead, the heat and smoke would surely have finished him off by now.

It was only when he had emptied the blazing van and thrown himself out into the fresh air with heaving lungs that Bill realised that none of the big hampers had been heavy enough to contain a human body — dead or alive.

Bill was still coughing, doubled up, when he realised something else. He had done the whole job on his own.

Where was Jackson? The answer came a moment later.

'Stagger over to the right a bit, old boy. The light's better there — and if you'd care to throw yourself to the ground . . .'

Film camera to his eye, Jackson had coolly filmed the whole scene.

'Some pal,' Bill spluttered. 'Why didn't you help?'

'And miss a juicy bit of film like that? That's not the style of Futuric Films,' Jackson reproved his pal. 'Besides, I could see you were all right — and there wasn't room for both of us in the van. I'd only have been in your way ... Martin wasn't inside?'

Bill kicked at the smouldering hampers.

'There's no weight to any of them. We could have been wrong. Maybe that wasn't how he left the pavilion.'

Jackson shook his head silently and moved on round the van.

'Didn't you wonder where the driver went?' he asked. 'There are fresh car tracks here. I reckon that Jason Arkwright sent someone to chase up the van while it was still in Glendale. One of his men would steal it and then run it out into the country, followed by the other man in the car ... Pick up the van driver, fire the van ... and they're clear away.'

'But what about Martin?' Bill demanded. 'What have they done with him?'

That was a question for which they had no answer. They were still puzzling over it as the station-wagon streaked back towards the city.

Traffic was heavy as they made for South Kensington.

'I think we should go to the police,' Jackson decided as he halted at the traffic lights. 'We've got something for them now.'

A fire engine came clanging out of a side street and almost automatically Jackson put on speed to follow it.

'If it's a decent blaze we might as well cover it,' he pointed out. 'This hoodoo story has kept us from earning our living these last few days.'

As if joined by an invisible tow-line, the station-wagon fell in behind the fire engine, racing along increasingly familiar streets. Smoke was towering skywards from a block of buildings ahead.

'Hey!' Bill began. 'That looks very like...'

Jackson's mouth tightened to a thin, hard line.

Smoke and flames were gushing from the top of the old building... the top floor that was headquarters to Futuric Films.

'Arkwright!' Jackson gritted. 'A pound to a penny he's fired the place to destroy our film.'

As he jerked on the brake he was already swinging open the door and running. A policeman tried to halt him at the door.

'You can't go... Ugh...'

The policeman was still picking himself up when Bill raced by hard on Jackson's heels.

There was no smoke on the ground floor or the second, but by the time Bill and Jackson had reached the third floor, smoke was belching down the stairway.

'Keep you head well down,' Jackson panted. 'The cold air should be purer...'

A blast of heat met them on the landing outside their own door. Within, the fire was crackling and hissing, and through the open door they could see the angry glow of the flames.

'It's no good, Jacko,' Bill panted. 'We haven't a hope...'

'My turn this time,' Jackson grunted as he plunged inside.

Jackson had taken a huge breath before he ventured into the flat. That breath carried him across the main room to the door of the dark-room. Inside it were all the films of the Rangers the team had taken since they starked on the hoodoo story. This was no accidental blaze.

The dark-room was belying its name. Work benches were ablaze and even the lino on the floor was flaring. The bubbling material clung to Jackson's feet as he dashed across to the cupboard where the developed film was stared. It was a strong, well-made steel cupboard — and it was locked.

Jackson fumbled for the keys in his pocket — and remembered too late that Bill had them.

'Have to go back ... get keys,' Jackson thought as he turned.

The smoky air was blasting a fiery pathway into his lungs. Nose and eyes were smarting in an agony as the cameraman stumbled through the flames towards the door.

But he did not reach it. For, as he staggered, something caught his foot. He fell.

Rising, he saw what it was that had tripped him.

Sprawled on the floor lay a man, dead or unconcious.

And the man was the missing Martin.

Coughing, eyes streaming, he stooped to hoist the figure on the floor to its feet. But though he was able to lift the shoulders a little, he task was beyond his fading strength.

Martin seemed doomed.

Then suddenly the burden lightened. The body seemed to lift itself.

Jackson felt his shoulder gripped by strong arms. He was no longer alone in the flames.

'Come on, sir ... this way ...'

With firemen and policemen all round him, Jackson Haig was eased towards the door.

'The films,' he croaked. 'Get ... get the films.'

Then he did something he had never done before. Overcome by fumes, he fainted.


Inspector Clark's office was usually a very tidy place. There were files, cabinets, drawers — all neat, all in their place. But it was far from tidy as Jackson Haig and Bill Gormley entered.

A lot of the untidiness came from a cine-projector which stood on the desk with its flex coiling out to a light socket. A screen had been set up on a tripod and cans of film were stacked on the desk — Futuric's film!

'Feeling better?' Clark's voice was less brusque than usual.

'Well — I'm right off kippers now,' Jackson conceded.'I know how they feel... And thanks for getting me out, by the way.'

'Well — we did want those films,' the Inspector grinned dryly.

'And Martin?' Jackson asked. 'How's he? Is he...?'

'Alive,' the policeman answered grimly. 'But only just. He's had a nasty knock on the head. He's got concussion, and goodness knows when he'll come round. Now, to work.'

He signalled to a uniformed constable and the cine-projector whirred into life. A picture began to flicker on the screen.

'Your films seem to be the key to the whole business,' the Inspector explained. 'That earlier attempt to steal them — and then the fire. And of course the planting of Martin in your office.'

'A real homely touch that,' Bill Gormley said.' They thought we'd carry the can for knocking him off.'

On the screen the film moved on... shots of the Glendale Rangers' matches, pictures of the crowd, pictures off the ground.

'Wait!' Jackson called suddenly. 'Hold that scene...'

It was a shot of the Rangers' ground, a crowd scene.

'Those men. They're the thugs who tried to beat us up,' Jackson said. 'And see who's talking to them... it's Jason Arkwright!'

He looked expectantly at the Inspector. Clark did not seem to be greatly impressed.

'So the Chairman of the Board of Glendale Rangers has some undesirable acquaintances,' he murmured. 'We can hardly charge him with that. We need concrete evidence.'

'But there's another shot,' Jackson insisted. 'It shows him beaming just after a goal has been scored against the Rangers. Surely that means something. He's the man behind the hoodoo.'

The Inspector sighed as the constable changed the reel.

'I don't want to dishearten you,' he said. 'But that isn't evidence. Let's suppose, just for the moment, that Arkwright is our man. Suppose he's rigging this whole business for his own ends... Just what are those ends? And how do we prove it? In other words, why does he want to ruin his own team — which I, too, believe he's doing.'

There was no answer to that — not then and not during the rest of the impromptu film show. The last reel of film whirred through the projector and the machine was switched off.

'We've missed something,' the Inspector said. 'We must have — but what...? Well, thank you, gentlemen....'

He rose, as if to conclude the meeting.

'And our films?' Jackson asked pointedly.

'They'll be returned,' said the Inspector. 'But just at the moment... they're evidence. Thank you again...'

Outside Scotland Yard, Jackson and Bill made slowly for their car.

'What now?' Bill demanded. 'Where do we go from here?'

'We find ourselves a new office,' Jackson answered. 'We buy ourselves some new equipment... and we feel very thankful that all our gear was insured.'

The newspaper headlines were as big as they could possibly be: WILL THE RANGERS' HOODOO STRIKE AGAIN? SELL-OUT AT GLENDALE PARK.

'That's a thought,' Jackson grinned. 'You don't suppose we've maybe got this thing the wrong way round. Maybe this hoodoo business is a giant publicity stunt. There's one thing

— the Rangers have been packing in the crowds since it started. I'll bet the club's made more money these past few weeks than ever it did.'

'You could be right!' breathed Bill Gormley. 'Anyway, I see they've got their team fit for this afternoon.'

As expected, Glendale Rangers' ground was packed for the match with Dipdale United, the League leaders. But though there was plenty of cheering for the visiting team as they trotted out on the field, only an eerie silence greeted the Rangers.

'You'd think they were waiting for the ground to open up and swallow them,' Jackson breathed. 'Come on — let's give them a heartener. Come on the Rangers!'

His shout broke the silence, and a moment later it was taken up by the rest of the vast crowd. Down on the pitch, Brendan O'Hara glanced up towards the Press box and grinned briefly.

Then the match was on.

There was no trace, after the first few minutes, of any uneasiness amongst the Rangers' players.

Rangers were the first to strike. United had raided up from mid-field and then lost the ball. It was flicked out to the Ranger's left-wing and centred an instant later. Brendan was there to take the pass and slam it into the net without giving the United keeper a ghost of a chance.

'I think he'll stick to football instead of coming back to us,' murmured Bill.

Jackson did not answer. He was not shooting film this time, but using the powerful lens of the camera as a telescope. By a system of prisms, he could see through it while it was still fixed to the camera.

'I don't see any sign of Jason Arkwright,' he commented. 'Surely he's not missing the match ... not the Chairman of the Board.'

98

Back and forth across the crowd the lens scanned, looking for Jason Arkwright, looking for any of the men who had been connected with the hoodoo, seeking anything that might link up with the case. Once Jackson had a glimpse of Inspector Clark, but that was all.

Abruptly he steadied the camera and pointed. 'Hey! Look at that...'

Suddenly his face was grey and lined.

Bill spun round. 'What is it, Jacko? What can you see?'

Jackson did not answer his friend's frantic question. He could only stare — fascinated horror gripping him.

Bill tried to follow the line of Jackson's horrified gaze, but he could see nothing amiss.

Down on the lush green turf, Glendale were storming back into attack — Brendan O'Hara confidently making his way down the middle of the field. By sheer speed he beat United's centre-half and then flicked out a bullet-like pass to his left-wing.

The winger met the pass and rocketed it back into the goalmouth.

Brendan was streaking up to meet it.

'Shoot!' howled the almost deliriously happy Rangers' supporters.

And someone shot all right.

But it was not Brendan — it was someone else with a gun!

For the young centre's arms threw up suddenly and he pitched forward on his face without trying to get a foot to the ball, and the referee's whistle shrilled as trainers and team-mates converged on the slight, unconscious figure on the ground. Only now did Bill know what had horrified his friend.

A hush of horror settled on the ground of Glendale Rangers, a hush that was broken by only one sound... the whirring of a cine camera. Jackson Haig was filming everything.

'For Pete's sake, Jackson! That's Brendan down there!' cried Bill. 'You can't film on in that cold-blooded way.'

Jackson Haig's finger stayed on the shutter release of the camera, picking up every angle of the scene being played out before him. Though Brendan O'Hara was his friend — and partner in Futuric Films — at this moment he was only the centre-piece in a film that had to be shot.

Then the camera stopped its whirring and dropped from his hands.

'Let's go,' Jackson said crisply, grabbing up his equipment.

But it was not for the ground that he made, or the dressing-rooms where Brendan was now being carried.

'Out the back way!' Jackson ordered as he raced down the steps from the Press box.

'But... but what about Brendan?' Bill protested.

'If there was one thing we could do to help him, I'd be with him,' Jackson answered. 'We're not doctors. What we can do is get the man who shot him.'

They ran from the ground. Jackson swung left and made for one of the tall blocks of office buildings that overlooked the ground of Glendale Rangers.

'Shot?' Bill echoed as he thundered along at the camera-man's side. 'Brendan was shot?'

'Why else do you think he went down like that? And I filmed the man who fired the shot.'

The elevator swept them up to the tenth floor.

'Jason Arkwright?' Bill breathed as they halted at a huge and polished door with a tiny gold plate bearing the name of the Chairman of Glendale Rangers.

'Arkwright,' Jackson agreed. 'And the proof's in my camera now.'

He swung the door open and the pair burst into the vast,

plush office beyond. It was empty save for a broad desk and a filing cabinet.

But there was another door beyond the desk and the two film men padded over to it, silent on the thick-piled carpet. Very cautiously, Jackson began to turn the door handle. Within there was a murmur of voices. Jackson gently opened the door a crack.

'I think you've flipped your lid this time, boss,' a man was saying. 'You can't really hope to get away with shooting him publicly like that.'

'Get away with it?' snarled the harsh voice of Jason Arkwright. 'Of course I'll get away with it. There's nothing at all to tie me in with the shooting. The police can't possibly know where the shot came from.'

Gently Jackson pushed open the door.

'Don't count on that,' he said.

For a long moment Jason Arkwright stood perfectly still, the colour coming and going in his cheeks.

'You must be mad to come bursting in here,' he said. 'I'll have you thrown out.'

'I wouldn't try it,' Jackson answered. 'We both heard what you said to your chum there.'

'What you heard isn't proof,' Arkwright blustered.

'What I have in my camera is,' Jackson snapped. 'A film of you shooting Brendan O'Hara.'

'Tcha!' the Rangers' chairman sniffed. 'That could have been filmed at any time. Why would I have shot the man?'

'For the same reason that you ran this whole hoodoo campaign — for money,' Jackson retorted. 'I've got the proof of that in my camera, too. Through my telephoto lens I could see the plans of this area which you had on the wall.

'Plans which show no sign at all of the Rangers' stadium. Plans which show another huge office block on the site of the ground. That's why you wanted to wreck the team — so you could build on their ground. I'll bet that'll be worth a cool half million to you.'

Jason Arkwright's face darkened.

'You know it all, don't you,' he blustered. 'But there's one thing you've forgotten.'

From behind the desk he whipped up a rifle with telescopic sights and a silencer.

'Now ... I think we'll dispose of the proof first of all,' said Arkwright. 'Hand over that camera. That film isn't going to be developed ... *ever.*'

The rifle's muzzle was like a little dark eye staring at Jackson Haig.

'Hand over the equipment, Haig!' repeated Jason Arkwright. 'I'm going to destroy that film.'

Jackson did not move. Nor did Bill Gormley behind him.

'Hand it over!' Arkwright snarled a third time. 'Or ...'

'Worried about your carpet, are you?' Jackson taunted. 'Don't try to kid us. You'll shoot anyway. You have to. You can't leave us alive. We know too much.'

As he spoke, hope was rising in his heart. Outside, the sun had begun to shine. It was a bright clear day.

Jackson swung his whole body very gently. The camera swung with him. The lenses caught the sun's rays — and reflected them. A bright blob of light danced along the wall ... and on to Arkwright's face.

The dazzling reflection hit the chairman full in the eyes. Momentarily he was blinded.

And as he gasped his surprise, Jackson did as he had been asked. He gave Arkwright the camera.

He gave it to him right in the face. The heavy camera hit Arkwright on the temple and he went down in an untidy, crumpled heap.

*Arkwright whipped up a rifle with telescopic sights and a silencer.*

Jackson dived straight across the desk a split-second after the camera, and Bill Gormley raced after him. As they pounded on Arkwright, the fourth figure in the room, the thug who had been under Arkwright's orders, dived for the door.

'Let him go!' Jackson panted, as Bill seemed about to start in pursuit. 'This is the only man we really need.'

Arkwright came round slowly, blinking up with mounting hate at his captors.

'Keep an eye on him, Bill,' Jackson said.

He moved to the window. Even in the short time since the two film men had left the Rangers' ground, most of the crowd had been dispersed. The fallen figure of Brendan O'Hara had been removed from the centre of the pitch, and now a small knot of policemen stood where Brendan had been shot. Jackson recognised Inspector Clark. The Inspector was making measurements. He kept looking towards the office block where Jackson stood.

'Getting the angle from where the shot came,' the cameraman decided. 'Well, we'll be able to save him that bit of trouble.'

He turned to Arkwright.

'On your feet,' he ordered. 'You're going back to the ground — for the last time, I wouldn't wonder.'

Bill and Jackson flanked Jason Arkwright as they entered the stadium again.

Inspector Clark came hurrying towards them.

'Well, we've got him for you,' Jackson greeted him. 'We ...'

Before he could say more, Arkwright took his last chance of freedom. With Jackson and Bill both looking towards the policeman, he took one quick step backward and then broke into a desperate sprint.

He dived for the door leading into the pavilion and slammed it shut. The lock clicked home.

'What on earth...' the Inspector started to demand.

'The other door,' Jackson rapped. 'From the field. But keep this one guarded, Inspector. By the way — Arkwright's your man, of course.'

He was shouting over his shoulder as he ran towards the pitch with Bill pounding along at his heels.

Down the tunnel from the pitch Jackson raced, and into the corridor leading to the changing-rooms.

From ahead there came the crack of a pistol shot, and a bullet hissed over Jackson's head.

'Stop where you are,' Jason Arkwright roared. 'I'm not going to be taken.'

Jackson halted, and Bill with him.

Jackson very deliberately put his finger on the release button of the camera. He could not focus it properly, but at least he should have some sort of a picture of this dramatic finale.

'You can't hope to get away with this, Arkwright,' he shouted. 'The police are on the ground. The exits are blocked. You'll have to give in sooner or later.'

'I'll never give in,' rasped the chairman.

He was standing at the end of the corridor, beyond the open door of the last dressing-room.

'Maybe you think you've beaten me. But Jason Arkwright never admits defeat...'

Jackson kept the camera running. What could he do now? How could he distract the man's attention long enough to get past the menace of the gun?

But it was not Jackson who did the distracting.

From the dressing-room there was a sudden thump.

A football flashed out through the open door, hit the opposite wall and rebounded right into Arkwright's face. It was the sort of shot that would have beaten a First Division goalkeeper without a chance.

For the second time in half an hour, Jason Arkwright crumpled up.

As he did, a figure streaked out in the wake of the football. It was a figure in shorts and blood-stained shirt with a bandage round his head.

'Brendan!' Jackson gasped. 'You're not dead!'

'Not too much,' gasped the third member of the Futuric team. 'Not unless it's the grand, solid ghost I am. I was just creased on the head.'

He spoke from the door, where he was grappling with Arkwright. The pistol had been flung aside as Arkwright fell, and Jackson snatched it up.

As he did, policemen seemed to pour into the corridor from every direction.

'So you got him,' breathed Inspector Clark. 'Good work.'

Brendan turned swiftly to Bill.

'Come on now — give me a microphone.'

With the instrument in his hand, he turned to the Inspector.

'Now then... what about an interview?' he wheedled.

The Inspector's face went red for the moment. Then suddenly he grinned.

'All right, then. This time I think you've worked for it. Ask your questions and I'll do my best.'

The camera whirred on as Brendan interviewed the Inspector on the case of the 'Hoodoo on the Rangers'.

But behind the camera, Jackson was already wondering what new story awaited Futuric Films.

# High Quest

### by
### DONNE AVENELL

John Killick was having breakfast at his home in Cambridge, that morning in late October, when the headline in the newspaper caught his eye.

It read: *Climbers foiled in Alps.* The story underneath told of a party of German mountaineers who had given up their attempt on the unclimbed north face of the Henker, in the Alps, and had returned to Chamonix.

A rock fall had struck the party on an exposed ledge at three thousand feet. Two of the Germans were severely injured. The north face of the Henker had been notorious in Alpine history ever since two Englishmen, Blythe and Killick, had died on it in 1892.

That was all the story contained, but John Killick had turned the page and read the first three paragraphs of a report on the M.C.C.'s current match at Adelaide before he realised he was still thinking about the north face of the Henker.

The Killick who had died on the Henker had been John Killick's grandfather. He knew that, and it was about all that he did know. It was just an odd piece of family history, like knowing that your grandfather scored a century at Lord's.

It was odd, John Killick thought, that he knew so little about his grandfather's death on the mountain. He was keen on climbing himself — not that he had done much of it, except in North Wales. But the story might be quite fascinating if one looked into it.

John Killick put his spoon down, pushed his chair back and

went across to the bookshelves. There was a book of his grand-father's there, he remembered. He had saved it from his father's library, when the old house was sold up, after his father's death.

He found the book pushed away at the back of the shelf. It was entitled: *Ramblers in the High Alps, by Henry Killick.* A stain of damp was on the cover, and the spine had been nibbled by one of the dogs his mother used to keep.

Of course there would be nothing here, Killick thought with a wry grin, about his grandfather's death on the Henker. The book had been published two years before that, in 1890. But there was a frontispiece photograph of the author.

The face was handsome, severe, rather wooden, as all those Victorian faces are in old sepia photographs. A moustache hid his lips, but the eyes were young and alive.

The eyes were so alive that John Killick took the book back to the table and pushed his unfinished egg aside and sat looking at the photograph while he poured another cup of coffee and lit his pipe. The eyes seemed to follow his whenever he moved his head.

He was still looking at his grandfather's eyes, or looking into them, rather, when the thought that he himself might go out to Chamonix came into John Killick's mind.

He snapped the book shut. Those eyes made him uneasy. He turned around in his chair and looked out of the window. Really, the idea of going out to Chamonix was not a bad one.

He had a month's sick leave left, anyway. And the doctor had told him he needed a change of scenery. The mountains would certainly be a change from the dismal autumn back gardens of Inkerman Street, Cambridge.

He could do a spot of rock climbing and, if the weather was bad, he could spend a few hours in the local museum, if there was one, and dig out the facts about the accident on the

108

Henker which had killed his grandfather. It might be fun.

John Killick got up, half-opened the cover of the book, and shut it again with a wry grin. He went out to the landing for his raincoat. He ought to sound the chief about the trip before he did anything else.

He walked round to the laboratory in Cavendish Road through the drizzle and the damp leaves. It was rotten weather. A good, honest snow storm in the high mountains would be a tonic after this.

The chief agreed. At least, he raised his head from the drawing board in his office and said: 'I envy you,' although John Killick knew that when the chief had a new formula under his fingers it could snow sky-blue elephants and he would never notice.

'Chamonix, eh?' the chief said, fiddling with his stylo and trying to keep his eyes off the drawing board. 'Climbing, eh?'

'I might do a bit,' Killick said. 'The easy stuff, of course, nothing strenuous. And then there's a bit of family history I might dig into while I'm there. My grandfather was killed climbing the Henker.'

'Oh, bad luck,' the chief said. He was looking down at his drawing board hungrily. Killick grinned and turned to go, and the chief said: 'Don't follow your grandfather's example, my dear chap, will you?' as he closed the door.

Killick was still grinning when he came out of the laboratory and turned towards the High Street. He had worked with the chief for three years on this new theory of his, researching into molecular structure, and he was fond of the old man.

In fact, it was his fondness for the chief, as well as his own interest in the research project, which had made John Killick overwork and led to his breakdown at the end of the summer. The breakdown was nothing serious, the doctor had said, but

Killick ought to take a month or two's rest, get away for a change, perhaps.

The lab work had been done anyway, and the chief could get on without him for a while. John Killick felt pleasantly irresponsible as he stopped at the window of the travel agency in the High Street and looked at the sun-tans and bikinis on the posters.

He had meant only to make a few inquiries about Chamonix when he went inside, but the young man behind the counter got so busy with the timetables and weather reports and slee-per reservations that, by the time he came out, the trip was fixed.

He would spend three weeks in Chamonix, the young man said. He would leave Cambridge in four day's time, spend the night in London, cross the Channel on the boat from New-haven, get the night express from Paris through St Gervais, and be in Chamonix by noon the next day. No trouble at all, the young man assured him, enthusiastically.

Between the young man and his grandfather's eyes, John Killick thought with amusement, as he strolled along after-wards, he had been practically shanghaied into this Chamonix trip.

But remembering his grandfather, and with time on his hands, he went that afternoon to the public library. He might as well find out what there was to know about that accident on the Henker in 1892.

There was not much. The incident got a brief mention in a couple of guidebooks and a page to itself in a 1912 survey of Alpine exploration, but even the survey admitted that no definite evidence had ever come to light to account for the death of the two men.

Apparently, Blythe and Killick had set off early in Novem-ber, 1892, from Chamonix with a couple of French guides. They had been watched with telescopes from the hotel (the book did not say which hotel) as they climbed the lower slopes of the Henker through the first and second day.

They were at three thousand feet at dawn on the third day when the clouds came down over the mountain. After that, the only evidence came from the two guides.

The two Englishmen, according to the guides, insisted on continuing the climb. They struggled on for another day through cloud and snow flurries and the frequent rock falls for which the Henker was notorious.

On the fourth day, the two guides had refused to go any farther. They had gained only three hundred feet in twenty-four hours and the weather conditions were getting increasingly worse. They were being paid to climb, not to die, they said.

There had been an argument then, between the two Englishmen. Killick ended the argument by starting to climb upwards again, and Blythe — 'with a face like thunder', as the survey put it — had climbed after him.

The two Englishmen had stopped to rope themselves together, the guides said, before continuing to climb into the mist above. But they were unroped when they fell to their deaths twenty-four hours later.

The guides had paused to rest on a rock ledge during their descent that fifth day on the Henker. They had heard a cry from above. The first body plunged past them thirty yards away, with a length of rope whipping free from it. The second body fell past fifteen seconds later ('not kicking or struggling, but easily, like a diver').

Neither of the two bodies had ever been recovered.

The guides could not say which of the two Englishmen had fallen first. The two men were dressed alike, and there was too much mist on the ice face. They could not say why the two Englishmen were unroped. They could not suggest a reason for the accident.

The survey added that there had been rumours in Chamonix at that time, about a bitter rivalry between the two men, 'but this seems to be at variance with the facts'.

The facts were that Blythe and Killick had been climbing separately in the Alps when they had met by chance in Chamonix in October, 1892. They then decided to team up together for the attempt.

Killick, the survey said, was a gentleman of independent means and a noted Alpinist. Blythe was a former steeplejack who had become a successful builder in south-east London and 'seized the opportunity offered by his affluence to put his early training to a more sporting use.' The pompous phrase amused John Killick. He was smiling when he returned the books to the librarian's desk and went out into the wet dusk. But he had not been smiling when he read the account of the accident on the north face of the Henker.

In fact, the story had made him curiously uneasy. Curiously because, after all, the whole thing had taken place a long time ago. Exactly what had happened between the gentleman and the ex-steeplejack on that mountainside in 1892 could hardly concern anyone living today.

The story was like a badly finished photograph — that was probably what had disturbed him. There were a whole lot of foggy shadows in it, and then you suddenly saw Killick climbing away on his own to settle the argument, and Blythe following him 'with a face like thunder'.

And then there was a second body falling, 'not kicking or struggling, but easily, like a diver'. There was something very disturbing about these brief glimpses. You saw real men, striving and suffering and dying.

But anyway, John Killick thought, as he let himself into his room later, there was no need to wonder now about what really happened on the Henker that day, because if he was ever going to find out he would do it in Chamonix.

The uneasiness had quite worn off by the following evening when a friend of his called Cheever rang him up and came around for a drink.

Cheever was a journalist. Apart from other things, he collected material for one of the gossip columns in the national dailies. And a chap who worked in the Cavendish Road lab had told him about Killick's forthcoming trip to Chamonix.

John Killick told him all about it, then laughed. 'But, good heavens,' he said, 'it can't be of any interest to your readers.'

'Oh, I don't know.' Cheever glanced at the notes he had taken. 'Young scientist takes trip into the past. Probe into death mystery on mountain,' he read out. 'I think it's got something. Mind if I look at that book you told me about?'

Killick gave him his grandfather's book. Cheever flipped through it briefly and found the photograph at the front. He looked up from the photograph to Killick.

'Take away the moustache,' he said, 'and he'd look just like you.'

'No, please!' Killick took the book, smiling. He looked at the photograph again, and it was true. It was something about the eyes. 'Well, I suppose he was about my age, thirty odd, when he died,' he said.

Cheever left after another drink, but he paused at the door and said: 'By the way, Killick, you know what Henker means, I suppose?'

'No?'

'It's the German for "Executioner",' Cheever said.

The fact lodged in John Killick's mind, but it made no real impression on him at the time. It was like the eyes in the photograph of his grandfather and the queer facts in the account of the accident in the survey. They were disturbing when you thought about them, but you had no real need to think about them.

The Chamonix trip, after all, was just a rest cure. He was going to do a spot of rock climbing and get some good mountain air, and the business about his grandfather was just a standby, like the detective novel you packed for a seaside holiday, to be taken out only if it rained.

Even Cheever's paragraph about him in the gossip column of the national daily, which Killick's landlady showed him next morning with great pride and delight, did not alter his mood about the trip. It amused him, with its loaded air of mystery, that was all.

The actual journey to Chamonix three days later (Cheever had called it a 'quest') was prosaic enough to bury any feeling of mystery layers deep in railway tickets, tubes of toothpaste, passports and travellers' cheques.

The youth at the travel agency had planned the whole thing, and John Killick simply carried it out. He spent the night in London. He crossed the Channel on the day boat from Newhaven. He got the night express from Paris, arriving at Chamonix by noon the next day.

It rained most of the way, and at Chamonix a clammy white mist hid the mountains. He had spent a restless night in the wagon-lit and he dozed in the cab which took him to the hotel. All he really thought about with any interest was a bed which stayed in one place.

He had chosen the hotel himself, without knowing anything about it, but because it was called *L'Aigle Irrité* — the Angry Eagle. It was just an ordinary hotel to him.

But it was in the hotel that evening, after he had slept for a few hours and had a bath and dressed for dinner, that he got his first shock.

He was sipping an aperitif in the bar off the main lounge

114

when a big, fair man in an ill-fitting suit came in and went to the bar. He glanced sideways at Killick while he waited for his drink.

Their eyes met. Killick had never seen the fair man before, he was sure of that, and yet he had a queer feeling that he recognised the man.

The man must have recognised him, too, and in the same queer way, because he came slowly across the bar and stood by Killick's chair, looking down at him quizzically.

'Mr Killick?' he said.

'That's my name.'

'I thought it was.' The big man smiled suddenly. 'My name's Blythe.'

John Killick smiled, but the smile felt as stiff as a mask on his face. Behind it, he was trying to cope with the shock.

'Blythe?'

'That's right. Albert Blythe was my grandfather.' He looked at Killick doubtfully. 'You're the chap they talked about in that newspaper column?'

Killick relaxed. 'Yes, I'm the chap,' he said, on a deep breath. 'And Henry Killick was *my* grandfather. You saw that story in the paper, did you? That's what brought you here?'

Blythe said: 'Excuse me,' and turned away to the bar and got the drink the barman was pushing at him. He glanced at Killick, and Killick said: 'No, I'm all right, thanks,' and lifted his own glass.

His face fitted the smile now. There was nothing strange about this meeting after all. He and Blythe were just a couple of men who had been drawn by the same interest to the same foreign hotel. Still, he felt absurdly relieved, as though he had not only been shocked at meeting this man here, but scared.

Blythe took a good, solid pull at his hock and wiped his lips.

He said: 'Yes, well I saw that photograph of you in the paper, and I had a few weeks leave due to me and nowhere in particular to spend it, so I thought I'd come to Chamonix.'

'You're in the army?' Killick said.

'B.A.O.R. Third Royal West Kents. I'm a sergeant.' Blythe looked down at his glass. 'Look, don't think I'm trying to barge in on you. I wouldn't have spoken to you just now, only I somehow felt you were this John Killick chap and it seemed daft not to say something to you.'

'No, I'm glad you did,' Killick said. 'The odd thing is that I recognised you, too. I don't know how. I never saw a photograph of your grandfather.'

'Nor me of yours,' Blythe grinned. 'Maybe the old jossers borrowed our eyes for a minute or two. Sort of recognised each other through us.'

Killick frowned. 'Well they weren't so old, were they? When they died, I mean. They were about our age.'

'I suppose they were,' Blythe said. He glanced at Killick briefly. 'You know a lot about them? About what happened up there on the mountain?'

'Me? Good heavens, no! Do you?'

'I know they got half-way up and then quarrelled or something, but nobody was with them when they had the accident. I don't know much.'

'But you'd like to know more?' Killick said.

'If there's more to know. Yes. Wouldn't you? Isn't that why you came out here, according to that columnist chap?'

Killick got up, looking at Blythe's empty glass. His voice was a bit more casual than it usually was. 'Have another drink?'

From the bar, and turning to face Blythe, he said: 'I'm not as interested as all that. I came out to Chamonix to do a spot of rock climbing, to get a tan. I thought if the weather was bad I could fill in time digging up the facts about that old accident.'

'Well, that's the way I look at it, too,' Blythe said. He took the glass Killick held out to him and said: 'Cheers,' and wiped his lips again. 'I mean, it's all ancient history, anyway. It's not as if it matters to anyone what happened to our grandfathers up on that mountain in the year dot.'

'Of course it doesn't.'

'But, like you say, if the weather's rotten and we've got nothing better to do, we could dig around a bit among the facts.'

'All right, then,' Killick said. 'Let's leave it like that, shall we?'

They left it like that. They had dinner together and sat in the half-empty lounge afterwards drinking coffee and smoking. They talked.

Blythe had joined the army, apparently, in time for the Korean war. He had come back with a bullet scar and a couple of stripes on his arm and a liking for the harsh simplicities of barrack life. He had signed on as a regular.

Killick told him about his own background — public school, university, laboratory. It was a very different background to the soldier's, as different as Henry Killick's had been from Albert Blythe's back in 1892, but the two men got on well together.

It was only when Killick went up to his bedroom afterwards that he began to have doubts about Blythe, and that might have had something to do with the book and his grandfather's eyes.

It was queer about the book. Killick had packed his sleeping things in an overnight bag back in Cambridge. When he pulled out his pyjamas now, in his hotel room at Chamonix, the book with the stained cover fell out with them.

He hadn't remembered packing the book; in fact, he could have sworn he had left it behind. Yet there it was now, lying open on the floor at the frontispiece photograph, and Henry Killick's eyes staring into his as he knelt to pick it up.

Henry Killick must have got on well enough with Albert Blythe when they first met, here in Chamonix so many years ago, Killick thought as he stood holding the book and looking uneasily into his grandfather's eyes. But that hadn't stopped them quarrelling when they were half-way up the north face of the Henker. And that quarrel had led to murder.

What did he really know about the big, fair man he had met tonight, anyway? Blythe had been pretty quick to come to Chamonix when he read that newspaper story. Did he know more about the old accident than he had admitted? Was he afraid that Killick would find out something?

Killick closed the book with a snap. He grinned at himself wryly. This was ridiculous, of course. He was behaving more like a detective than a scientist on holiday.

All the same, he slept badly that night. He slept, but it was a disturbed sleep full of uneasy dreams that haunted him when he woke. Those eyes got into his dreams, too, his grandfather's eyes, and he had a feeling they were watching him carefully.

And then in the morning, when he went downstairs for a stroll on the terrace before breakfast to get the cobwebs out of his mind, the old story of death on the mountain came up again to haunt him.

It was a bright morning, and the snow peaks of the Mont Blanc massif loomed white against the brilliant sky. He was looking at them with a sudden lifting of his spirits when the manager of the hotel came up beside him.

Was Monsieur Killick wondering which mountain was the Henker? Well, no, Killick said. He hadn't even realised you could see the Henker from this hotel. *Mais certainement, m'sieur*, there it was, across the valley, the one with the sheer rock face — the ugly mountain.

Killick looked at the Henker interestedly. It was ugly enough, he had to admit, even in this bright, innocent sunlight, a great towering wall of rock that looked as black and smooth and evil as it had in his bad dreams.

And didn't *m'sieur* know, the manager went on at his elbow, that it was from this terrace, through the telescope over there, that the people watched the *m'sieur's grandpère* and the Englishman Blythe climbing the north face of the Henker?

Killick said, wonderingly: 'Good heavens, no! I didn't know that.'

'No, Monsieur Killick? But I thought it was for this reason that you chose to stay at my hotel?' The manager smiled, shrugging his shoulders. 'Besides, of course, the fact that it was here, at *L'Aigle Irrité*, that *m'sieur's grandpère* stayed that time in 1892, and here that he met Monsieur Blythe.'

'Someone taking my name in vain?' Blythe called out cheerfully, coming across the terrace at that moment.

Killick was too shaken to answer. It was stupid, of course, but the fact that without knowing it he had come to stay at the very hotel where the tragedy on the Henker had started over seventy years before seemed to him, after the haunted night he had just spent, not only queer but sinister.

He tried to explain that to Blythe over breakfast, after he had told the big man what the manager had said.

'Yes, but it was coincidence, you coming to the same hotel that your grandfather stayed at,' Blythe said.

'Was it?' Killick said. 'I feel as though someone else is pulling the strings and I'm just dancing to them. As though someone else wanted me to come to Chamonix and stay at this particular hotel.'

'Someone else?' Blythe looked at Killick. 'Your grandfather? A man who's been dead for more than eighty years?'

'All right, it's stupid. I picked the Angry Eagle because the name caught my fancy. Maybe Henry Killick came here for the same reason. But I say...' He looked at Blythe suddenly. 'You booked in here, too. What made you choose this hotel?'

Blythe grinned easily. 'That's simple,' he said. 'You were staying here. I wanted to meet you, so I just trudged around the town yesterday till I found the hotel you'd booked in at, then I booked in after you. I was sure to meet you, that way.'

John Killick had to laugh. It did him good to look at the big soldier, his clear, honest grin, the healthy square of toast and marmalade disappearing into his mouth. It made his own fancies seem morbid and unreal.

Blythe said, pushing his plate away: 'Well? Are you investigating anything today? Or do we wait till the weather turns rotten, like we agreed?'

'We wait,' Killick said, smiling. 'We make the most of this sunshine.'

The sun shone for three days, and they made the most of it. They spent a lot of time together, and neither of them mentioned the old tragedy on the north face of the Henker, and Killick even managed to forget it for sunny hours at a time.

They spent the first day wandering around Chamonix. They went up to twelve thousand feet in the cable railway on the *Aiguille du Midi* on the second day, just a couple of gaping tourists with peeling noses. On the third day they clambered about in hired boots on the lower slopes of the *Aiguille Rouge*.

Those were the good days. The fourth day was a bad one. It was sunless for one thing, with a sky like a sagging grey blanket hiding the peaks. For another thing, Blythe and Killick had words.

120

Blythe had done a bit of rock climbing here and there, in Korea and Austria and so on, but as far as Killick could judge he was no expert. When he wanted to tackle a two hundred foot slab on the *Aiguille Buet* without pitons, Killick told him so.

Blythe looked suddenly furious and stubborn. He muttered something about know-alls who had been to university, which Killick pretended not to hear, and the two of them scrambled about miserably for the next few hours without speaking to each other. It was a most unsuccessful, irritating day.

It ended with Killick trudging back to the hotel on his own an hour before sunset. There had been no quarrel, nothing as dignified as a quarrel. It was just that the big man's stubborn resentment had got on Killick's nerves.

He was stiff and tired as well, too tired to pay much attention to the man who came up to him as he was crossing the terrace of the hotel.

The man said: 'Monsieur Killick? My name is Paccard.'

He was thick-set, middle-aged with a leathery face and a lot of wrinkles around his eyes — a local guide probably. Killick said: 'Yes?' without stopping.

'Paccard, *m'sieur*.' The man followed Killick across the terrace watching him. 'You know?'

'Why should I know?' Killick said shortly.

'*Pardon, m'sieur*. I thought you would be interested...'

'I'm interested in a bath,' Killick said, pushing past the man, 'and a change of clothes. So if you'll excuse me...'

He forgot about the man while he ran his bath and went back to his room along the corridor for soap and a towel. But when he picked up the towel from the bedside table, that devil of a book was lying underneath it and it was open at the photograph of Henry Killick. And those eyes seemed to be warning him.

Killick went across to the window and looked uneasily across the valley to the ragged mist that was hiding the north face of the Henker. Afterwards, that was the last thing he remembered seeing before the strange twenty minutes that followed, the twenty minutes that made a hole in his memory.

He was turning away from the window when he saw the man who had stopped him, Paccard, talking to Blythe on the terrace.

They were just two men talking, that was all, but the sight had a weird effect on Killick — over which he had no control.

He sidled back into the room and began to drag on his clothes again. He kept going to the window, watching the two men on the terrace, moving softly as though they might hear him. His eyes were as hard and bright as the eyes in the sepia photograph.

He was fully dressed when the man called Paccard gestured in the direction of the town and nodded at Blythe, and the two of them walked down the terrace steps into the street.

Killick saw them go. He stood in the window, noting the direction they took with those hard, bright eyes. He was smiling, but none of his friends in Cambridge would have recognised that smile. He was smoothing his upper lip with the side of his forefinger, too, like a man who wears a moustache.

When he got down to the street, Blythe and the man called Paccard were a couple of hundred yards ahead. They were walking along quite openly in the dusk under the lamps. Killick sidled along after them.

They stopped at a small clapboard building on the northern edge of the town. It was dark and shuttered. Paccard was fumbling at the door, trying various keys by the metallic sound of it, and Blythe was laughing in that deep, clear voice of his.

Killick waited in the shadows until they had gone inside. He waited another three minutes. There was a light glowing inside the frosted windows of the building then, and no one about in the dark street.

The faded board nailed to the wall beside the door read: *Musée Chamonix Ouvrir Décembre à Avril. Entrée gratuit.* Killick looked at the board as he sidled through the open door, smiling at it with that smile none of his friends would have recognised.

He stood just inside the door. There was one light burning inside the museum, enough to scoop the walls out of the shadows, and show where the other two men were standing.

Blythe and Paccard were leaning over a showcase on the far side of the room where the lamp burned. A gold-leafed sign on it said *Killick and Blythe. Henker. 1892.* The glass lid of the showcase was open, Paccard was talking, and Blythe had an old, long-shafted ice-axe in his hand. They had their backs to the door.

Blythe turned round after a little while and put the ice-axe down on the lid of the showcase behind him. The movement brought him facing the door, and he saw Killick.

There must have been something very strange in Killick's face, because Blythe saw it across the length of the room, and even though Killick was standing in shadow.

Blythe said: 'Killick! It's you! It is you, isn't it? Killick, what the heck's wrong?'

Killick walked towards him then. Blythe stood watching him, waiting for him to say something. But Killick said nothing; he just walked stiff-legged across the room.

He stopped a couple of yards from Blythe. He was standing by the closed showcase on which Blythe had laid the ice-axe. He put his right hand down and his fingers felt for the handle of the ice-axe and gripped it.

Killick spoke then, but it was a voice Blythe had never heard before. It said: 'Curse you, Blythe! Curse you!'

The voice was murderous. It was not John Killick's voice, but it came from his throat. But it was John Killick's hand that whipped up the ice-axe and aimed the murderous blow at Blythe's head...

Blythe lunged forward as the ice-axe swung at him. His fingers locked on Killick's wrist.

Death was eighteen inches from his skull, sharp along the cutting edge of the axe. But he was a soldier; he had faced death before. Now he held it at arm's length.

He said: 'Don't be a fool, Killick,' harshly but calmly.

Killick never heard him. There was froth on his lips. The wild eyes were not Killick's eyes, and the vicious strength in the hand which gripped the axe was not Killick's strength.

Locked with Killick, and holding off the downward thrust of the ice-axe at his head, Blythe sensed that it was not Killick who was trying to kill him, but something which was using Killick's body.

Then the man called Paccard moved forward and said stolidly: '*Pardon, m'sieur,*' and gripped Killick around the body and arms from behind.

Blythe freed his other arm and grabbed the ice-axe below the blade. He wrenched it out of Killick's hand.

In that moment, whatever had taken possession of Killick's body released it.

He sagged in Paccard's arms. He shivered like a man waking in a strange room, peering around him at the museum and the big man standing white-faced in front of him with the ice-axe in his hands.

He said, in the pleasant voice Blythe knew: 'What the devil...? Blythe — what's going on?'

Blythe grinned at him carefully. 'If you really want to know,' he said, 'you were trying to brain me with this axe.'

'I — I was?'

There was no mistaking the bewilderment in Killick's voice. Even Paccard recognised it, and helped him across to a wooden bench against the wall.

'I was looking at the Henker,' Killick said, 'out of my window at the hotel, after I'd gone to my room for a towel. That's the last thing I remember. My oath, I must have had a brainstorm or something...'

He looked so miserable that Blythe said kindly: 'Oh, it's not as bad as that. You told me you came to Chamonix because you'd been overworking and needed a rest. You got pretty tired on those rock slopes today, and maybe I got under your skin. Maybe everything boiled up on you suddenly...'

Killick looked up at the big man steadily. He said: 'You're a good chap, Blythe. I mean that. I don't know what happened, what got into me, but I want you to know that I trust you.'

'That's O.K. Killick.'

Blythe was smiling. He put a big hand on Killick's shoulder.

Killick said: 'Thanks, Blythe, anyway,' and looked worriedly at Paccard.

The Frenchman shrugged, spreading his thick hands. 'I would have brought the *m'sieur* here, to the museum,' he said, 'with Monsieur Blythe. But you would not listen to me when I stopped you on the terrace at the hotel. I thought you were not interested.'

'Yes, you stopped me,' Killick said, remembering. 'And I brushed you off, and I'm sorry. But I still don't know who you are...'

'One of the guides who went up the north face of the Henker with Killick and Blythe in 1892,' Blythe said, 'was called Paccard.' He nodded at the Frenchman. 'This chap is his grandson.'

Killick said: 'My oath...'

'I thought you would have known my name, *m'sieur*,' Paccard said. 'The owner of the hotel told me you were staying there and might be interested in talking to me and to my father. So then, when you were not interested, I spoke to Monsieur Blythe and told him who I was.'

Blythe grinned rather guiltily at Killick.

'I'm sorry, Killick,' he said. 'When he asked me if I'd like to see this museum, I thought I'd come round here with him just to — well, to spite you. I was feeling a bit sore with you, see...'

Killick said: 'That's all right, Blythe. I understand.' He rubbed a hand across his face, frowning. 'The funny thing is, I seem to remember seeing you on the terrace together, Paccard and you, just now. I wonder if...'

He got up from the bench suddenly, straightening his shoulders. He said, as lightly as he could: 'Well, it doesn't matter now. I wouldn't be likely to brain you with an ice-axe just because you stole a march on me, not if I was in my right mind. Let's look at the exhibits, shall we?'

He walked across to the open showcase. He looked at the things in there — Henry Killick's leather-bound diary, a silver brandy flask, an 1870 map of the Chamonix valley with routes marked on it in faded violet ink.

It was no good. His old casual, lighthearted interest in these things was gone. These relics of an old tragedy scared him.

He had felt moments of uneasiness right from the beginning, looking at Henry Killick's photograph in his room at Inkerman Road, reading up the meagre facts about the tragedy on the north face of the Henker in the Cambridge library. The uneasiness had deepened when he got to Chamonix. It had become fear now.

Something very strange had happened to him tonight. All right, he was over-strained and tired. But that did not explain the hole in his memory, nor the fact that he must have

126

deliberately followed Blythe and Paccard to this place, nor the ache in the fingers of the hand which had gripped the ice-axe.

Blythe was still holding the axe. Killick said carefully: 'It that thing one of the exhibits, too?'

Blythe held out the axe. There was a label tied to the handle of it. Killick reached forward and turned the label over in his hand. It said: *Ice-axe owned by Henry Killick, 1892.*

Killick shuddered. He said: 'Let's get out of here,' wiping the hand which had touched the label on his windjacket.

He waited for Blythe and Paccard in the icy darkness outside the museum. They were putting the exhibits back in the show-case, turning off the lights. Paccard was telling Blythe about his father.

Paccard's father was in his eighties now. He had been made Curator of the Chamonix museum twenty years earlier when he got too old for climbing. The museum was normally closed until December, but old Paccard had heard that Killick and Blythe were staying in Chamonix and had suggested to his son that they might like to see the relics of their grandfathers.

Old Paccard had been a boy of fourteen in 1892 when Henry Killick and Albert Blythe had been killed on the Henker. He had heard the whole story from his father, one of the Englishmen's two guides on that fatal climb. He knew as much as any living man, Paccard told Blythe as he padlocked the door of the museum, about the tragedy.

'I am thinking, *messieurs,* that you would perhaps care to talk to my father,' Paccard said, as the three of them walked away together. 'He would be glad to tell you what he knows. He is an old man, but his memory is good. You could visit my house tonight, if you wished.'

Killick said in a low voice and not looking round: 'No.'

'Ah, come on, Killick,' Blythe said, good-naturedly. 'He

sounds an interesting old bloke, apart from this Henker business.' He peered sideways at Killick. 'Look, you're not still worrying about what happened in the museum just now, are you?'

'Of course not,' Killick said grimly. 'I only tried to cut you down with an ice-axe.'

'But, heck, I told you, you were overtired, I'd riled you, you must have got worked up...'

'All right,' Killick said, 'all right, if you want to go on digging up the past after what's happened, we'll go on. But I'm warning you. There's something queer about this whole business. I'm not just imagining things. Whatever it was that happened between our grandfathers up on the north face of the Henker years ago, isn't finished yet...'

They were standing still by that time in the dark, windy street, facing each other. Paccard waited for them. Blythe lifted his jaw stubbornly.

'If you're right, Killick,' he said, 'if there is something queer going on, then I say let's get to the bottom of it.'

Killick's face was pale, very serious; he just nodded. He turned to Paccard and said quietly: 'We'll come tonight.'

Killick and Blythe had dinner together in the hotel an hour later. At eight, when Paccard called for them, the first light snow of the winter had begun to fall. They walked through it to the long clapboarded house on the southern outskirts of the town where the Paccards lived.

Old Paccard must have been a big, powerful man in his time, but that time was long past. He sat in a high-backed chair with his twisted, arthritic hands bunched on a stick and his fierce, old eyes the only thing alive in the stretched skin and bone of his face.

Killick and Blythe sat across the fireside from him in the long room which looked out through uncurtained windows

128

to the snow-flecked darkness and the black gloom of the mountains across the valley.

The old man talked a lot, but added little to the story which Killick had already dug out of the guidebook in Cambridge. All he did was to throw light on the facts.

The rope used by Killick and Blythe on the fatal climb, for instance, was the Alpine Club rope, made of manilla hemp with a righthand lay by Beale of Shaftesbury Avenue. A fine, strong rope, old Paccard insisted, and not one that would snap under the weight of one man, however sudden the strain was when he fell, and yet his father had seen that rope whipping free from the first body as it fell past him.

'But the rope might have frayed on a rock edge,' Blythe suggested.

'*C' est possible,*' the old man said, shrugging his ruined shoulders. But he had never seen such a thing happen in all his sixty years on the mountains. Rock edges are not knives, he said, to cut a good new rope in two.

'What you're saying, then,' Blythe put in, 'is that it was a knife which cut that rope?'

'*Mais non*, I do not say that,' the old man answered. 'The rope was never found. I do not know that it was cut. No one knows. But my father told me, in confidence, you understand, but this was a long time ago, that Monsieur Killick and Monsieur Blythe both wore knives. And if they were roped together, and one man fell and was being held by the other, and if that other man cut the rope with his knife...'

The fire shifted in the silence. At least, there was a faint, uneasy sound in the bare room, and the fire was the only thing which could have made it, though John Killick glanced sharply towards the dark uncurtained· window.

'And there was bad feeling between Monsieur Killick and Monsieur Blythe,' old Paccard said. 'You will remember that.'

'We remember it,' Blythe said shortly. 'They quarrelled, didn't they?'

The old guide's eyes flickered curiously from Killick to Blythe. 'You would not say it was a quarrel,' he said, watching them, 'but they were two so different men, your grandfathers. I saw them myself many times in Chamonix, one of them so thin and proud, so much the gentleman, as you English say, and the other so sturdy and strong, a man of the people and so proud of that. C'est vrai, they were alike only in that, those two, they were both so proud — and that was their downfall.'

Killick shifted uneasily in his chair. Old Paccard glanced at him for a moment and then looked away to the window. 'Two men can be proud down here in the valley, messieurs, and it doesn't matter,' he said. 'There is no challenge to the pride down here. But on a mountain, ah, that is different. Is one man stronger than the other? Is one man less afraid of death than the other? These are the questions a mountain asks.

'I think Monsieur Killick and Monsieur Blythe were asked those questions on the north face of the Henker, that time. I think one of them could not bear the answers he got. I think one of them used his knife on the rope because he learned that the other one was stronger, less afraid than he.'

There was silence again in the room, a longer silence. Killick broke it.

'Well, what's so terrible about the Henker, anyway?' he said.

Old Paccard was still gazing at the dark window, gazing into the past, perhaps. It was his son who answered Killick.

The Henker, he told them, was a little over eleven thousand feet high. The lower three thousand seven hundred feet was loose rock and scree, easy climbing to the Henker Nord hut on the ice-field below the north face. The north face itself was

130

another seven thousand-odd feet of sheer rock, ribbed and seamed by ice flaws.

'As a climb, *messieurs*, it is not so difficult,' the younger Paccard said. 'It is, perhaps, of the fourth grade. Such climbers as yourselves could, with a little extra effort, reach the summit, if you had two things on your side.'

He paused. His face was sombre. 'Those two things, *messieurs*, are good weather and good luck. And they are two things which do not exist on the face of this mountain that they call the Executioner. It is a cruel mountain and has claimed many victims.'

He started to talk about the knife-edged wind which scoured the Henker on two days out of three, the blinding snow storms, the mist, and above all, the constant falls of rock which had killed so many men.

'You should see the Henker for yourselves, *messieurs*,' he said. 'I could take you up to the ice-field at three thousand feet. That is a safe, easy climb, and we could spend a night in the Henker Nord hut and come down in the morning.'

He had just said that when the faint, uneasy sound, as though the fire had shifted, broke the silence in the room again. This time, Killick looked quickly at old Paccard.

The old man was still gazing at the uncurtained window. He smiled suddenly. He said in a perfectly normal, rather amused voice: 'You should bring in your friend, *messieurs*, who is outside.'

Killick and Blythe wheeled towards the window. They both saw the face pressed to the dark glass, the thin, white face and the eyes, the bright eyes.

But is was Killick who recognised the face. For those eyes were the same haunting eyes which had stared into his from an old photograph in a book with a stained cover. They were the eyes of Henry Killick...

Killick got to the door first. Blythe and the younger Paccard moved as well, but without hurrying. To them the face they had seen at the window was only the face of a man. To Killick, it was the face of a ghost.

He knew that when he tugged open the door and looked along the wall of the house he would see nothing. It was a shock all the same.

The snow had stopped. It was a clear, black night, with a sheen of moonlight on the glass of the window near which a man should have been standing, if there had been a man. But there was no man — no one anywhere near the chalet.

Blythe said, leaning chummily against Killick's shoulder in the doorway, peering sideways into the empty darkness: 'He must have scarpered, whoever he was.'

'No, Blythe.'

'No? Come off it, Killick. We both of us saw that face peering in. The Paccards saw it, too. You're not saying there was nobody there, are you?'

'Look at the snow,' Killick said flatly.

There was an inch of snow on the ground outside the house. It had covered the footprints Blythe and Killick had left when they walked into the house with the younger Paccard an hour before. It was an untouched white sheet over the path and the strip of earth along the front of the house.

There were no footprints under the window.

Blythe said uncertainly for the first time: 'But that's crazy. We saw that face. Heck — I'm not the type that sees ghosts!'

Killick looked at the big soldier and grinned, but it was a ragged grin. 'I know, Blythe,' he said. 'That's what worries me. The mood I'm in, I'd see ghosts anywhere. I'm tired and run-down, and I tried to brain you with an ice-axe just a couple of hours ago.'

'No look...' Blythe began.

'You look,' Killick said. 'I told you at the museum earlier, there's something queer about this whole business. The more we dig down into the past, the queerer it gets. Do you still want to go on?'

Blythe looked past Killick's shoulder at the empty wall and the sheen of glass in the window. He moved his big, cropped head a little and looked out beyond the house and the sprinkle of lights which was Chamonix, out to the black loom of the mountains across the valley.

'I want to go on,' he said, finally, in a tough, hard voice.

Killick turned back through the door without answering him. The younger Paccard was standing there, watching the two Englishmen with those stolid eyes of his that had seen many high and lonely places and would never be surprised.

'You said you could take us up to the Henker Nord hut?' Killick asked him.

'*Oui, m'sieur.* I did.'

'We want to go, then — as soon as possible. Tomorrow, if that's all right.'

Blythe came back into the room, leaning against the door and watching Killick as Paccard said: 'If the weather holds, *m'sieur*, I will take you tomorrow. I will bring the equipment to the hotel at eight — crampons, axes, pitons, rope. We shall not need these things. perhaps — it is an easy climb to the hut. But with the Henker, one must be prepared for anything.'

Killick nodded, not looking at Blythe. He turned to Paccard's father to say goodnight. The old man put up an arthritic claw of a hand, searching Killick's face with those fierce eyes of his.

'There was no one outside, at the window, *m'sieur?*' he said.

'No.'

'*Alors.* So that is why you decide to climb the Henker tomorrow. But sometimes on a mountain, *messieurs*, there is another man on the rope whom one feels but does not see.

133

A man who is not there. This has happened to me and to others, and it is not a good thing to happen. Be very careful, *messieurs*, on the Henker.'

Neither Killick nor Blythe mentioned the old guide's words on the way back to the hotel afterwards in the cold, black darkness, but they thought about them. The thought chained their tongues.

Only when they got back to the hotel, and were having a last drink in Killick's room, did Blythe bring up the subject they had to talk about.

Killick was over by the wash basin, putting water in Blythe's glass, when the big man said: 'You recognised that face at the window, didn't you, Killick?'

His voice was odd. Killick turned around and looked at him. Blythe was standing by the bedside table and he had a book in his hand, the book from Cambridge with the stained cover. It was open at the frontispiece photograph of Henry Killick.

'Yes,' Killick said. 'I recognised it.'

'You didn't say anything about it.'

'I could have been mistaken. I've had that photograph on my mind ever since I got out here. Any face I saw would look like that.'

'No,' Blythe said. 'You weren't mistaken. I saw the face, too. It was the face in the photograph — Henry Killick's face.'

Killick brought the glasses across to the middle of the room. He put them down carefully before he looked at Blythe.

'All right,' he said quietly. 'I'll tell you what I think. I think Henry Killick's been pushing me into this thing ever since I looked at the photograph in that book in my room at Cambridge. He's been dead over seventy years, I know that, but I think he wants me to find out what happened on the north face of the Henker that day when he died.'

Blythe just watched Killick seriously. 'So old Paccard was right,' he said. 'It was that face at the window which made you decide to climb the Henker tomorrow?'

'Yes, Blythe. Earlier this evening, you said that if there was something queer about this business we ought to get to the bottom of it. I didn't agree with you then. I do now.'

Blythe shifted the book to his left hand and picked up the glass and drank from it. He was that kind of slow-thinking man. He didn't smile.

'Well,' he said, 'maybe old Albert Blythe's ghost is haunting me as well, maybe it was him who got me out to Chamonix, but I feel the way you do about it, Killick. Let's find out what did happen to our grandfathers that day on the Henker.'

They drank to it. Whatever happened, Killick thought in that friendly moment, nothing could go very wrong if he and the big soldier stuck together like this.

He felt that so strongly, and bringing his fears out into the open had steadied him so much, that when Blythe glanced at the photograph in the book again as he was leaving and said: 'You know, the old josser looks like you, too, Killick, the way you looked in the museum tonight,' Killick just smiled.

He took the book from Blythe and tore the photograph out of it. He was still smiling. He tore the photograph in half without looking at it and shredded it in his fingers and threw the scraps of glossy paper into the fireplace.

'Let's forget tonight,' he said. 'Let's start afresh tomorrow, shall we? Let's just buckle down to the climbing tomorrow, and find out what we can about the past, and leave it at that.'

They started afresh in the morning. The weather helped. It was clear and sunny with a sharp wind cuffing the snow off the high peaks in powdered sunlight. Even the north face of the Henker, when they looked up at it from the base of the

*They climbed the first 1500 feet of the lower slope easily.*

mountain three thousand seven hundred feet below, looked smooth and inoffensive.

The climbed the first fifteen hundred feet of the lower slopes easily. The younger Paccard led. He had brought a second guide with him, a lean, dark Chamonix man called Lempeyer, who looked very hard at Killick and Blythe when Paccard introduced them, but said nothing.

Before noon, when the loose scree ended and the steeper slope began, they rested and drank coffee from the flasks. That was when Paccard told them that the guide he had brought to make up the party, Lempeyer, was a grand nephew of the second guide who had climbed the Henker that day in 1892 with Henry Killick and Albert Blythe.

Even this odd discovery, that the four of them were all descendants of the four men who had made that fatal climb seventy years before, cast no shadow on the bright day.

Blythe just stood up and stretched his big chest in the sunlight and said, grinning at Killick: 'History repeats itself.'

And Killick grinned back at him and said: 'Yes, quite a family reunion.'

Afterwards, Killick remembered incredulously those light-hearted words they had used. It seemed weird that they had felt no chill of premonition when Paccard told them about the fourth guide. But their innocent amusement was a fact.

There was just no place for shadows, for ghosts, in the clear hard sunlight on the lower slopes of the Henker that day.

When they had finished their cigarettes, they tackled the last two thousand-odd feet to the ice-field below the north face. Paccard insisted on roping them together, but there was no real need for the rope. The climb was only moderately stiff, and both Killick and Blythe got impatient when Paccard belayed them on some of the traverses.

They reached the ice-field an hour before dusk, physically tired but cheerful, cheerful enough to stand looking up without a qualm at the sheer north face of the mountain rising upwards to the sky above them.

They were standing at the outer edge of the ice-field, with the Henker Nord hut away to their right and the north face three or four hundred yards ahead across the ridges of the ice-field, when Blythe told them he was going forward to get a closer look at the north face. Killick felt the only pang of uneasiness he had felt all day.

There was no reason for the uneasiness, no reason at least that Killick could have know about. But when Blythe started forward, he said sharply: 'No, Blythe. Don't go that way.'

Blythe stopped. Paccard glanced curiously at Killick and said: 'The *m'sieur* is right. That way is bad. There is a crevasse which crosses the ice-field below the north face. There are snow bridges across it, but this crevasse narrows and widens each year a little. It moves.'

Blythe accepted the warning. He wrinkled his forehead at Killick when he came back to them, but he turned the frown into a grin when Killick grinned apologetically at him, and all he said was: 'You're not holding out on me, Killick, are you? You haven't been here before?'

The uneasiness passed. It did nothing to darken Killick's cheerful mood. Even when they got to the hut and the sun went down with a shifting wind and a flurry of snow from the east, the cheerfulness remained.

The Henker Nord hut was just a mountain hut, bare, timber-walled, smelling of bacon fat and leather soap. Henry Killick and Albert Blythe must have spent a night in it on their fatal climb in 1892, Killick supposed, but he did not know how much the hut had been altered since those days.

Paccard would have known, but Killick did not ask him.

The guides were lighting a fire in the wide hearth; the flickering warmth was pleasant on Killick's tired legs, and he was unwilling to break the relaxed mood that was on all of them.

They sat smoking by the fire after they had eaten. They talked about mountains and climbing. They were just two young Englishmen with their guides, pleasantly weary after a day's rock scrambling, with the firelight on their faces and the wind thumping outside at the walls of the hut.

Killick went to sleep like that, tired and happy and relaxed. He fell asleep at once, a warm, deep sleep without dreams.

When he woke up it was still dark. The fire had died down, but the glow of it made a shifting pattern on the walls of the hut. There was a man moving between the fire and Killick's bunk, a big man, shrugging quietly into his clothes, moving softly.

And this big man, Killick knew, lying quite placidly in his bunk and accepting the fact without any surprise or alarm, was the man who had climbed the Henker in 1892 with Henry Killick. It was Albert Blythe.

Killick only saw the man's face briefly when he half-turned to the firelight. In any case it was not a matter of recognising the man. He knew it was Albert Blythe in the way you know a man you are climbing with, without seeing his face, but just because you are sharing a mountain hut with him and you know he will be there when you wake up.

The man stood still for a moment between the firelight and Killick, bulky, big-shouldered. He turned the shadow of his face towards Killick. He might have been listening. After a while he moved away to the door without making any noise. He opened the door and the wind yelled and his body showed black for a moment against the grey light in the doorway. Then the door closed behind him.

Killick watched all this drowsily. There was no sudden

moment when he knew that something was wrong. He just began to feel vaguely uneasy, lying there in the dark hut with the firelight shifting on the walls, thinking about Albert Blythe and knowing that there was something he had forgotten.

It was only when he moved his legs off the bunk and his stockinged feet touched the bare floor that he remembered. Albert Blythe had been dead for over seventy years.

He got up harshly, panicking. He stumbled across to Blythe's bunk on the wall farthest from the fire. The bunk was empty.

It must have been Blythe he had seen going out of the hut, not Blythe's grandfather. But Killick's mind was still foggy with sleep and shock. Why had he been so sure it was Albert Blythe, when he had never seen a photograph of the man who had died on the Henker with his own grandfather?

He was tugging on his clothes while he tried to think it out, not caring if he woke the two guides, knowing with a sick courage that he must follow the man who had gone out of the hut, Blythe or his dead grandfather, whichever it had been.

The light was grey outside the hut. There was a streak of white sky beyond the ice-field, with a hard edge where the black face of the Henker shut it off. The small, grey figure of the man showed against the sky.

The figure was moving. It was near the middle of the ice-field and moving towards the great north wall of the Henker. Killick started to run.

The figure stopped when Killick was fifty yards away. There was a black gash in the ice beyond it. The figure stood facing the gash, looking into it. Killick realised, as he saw that this was the crevasse Paccard had warned them about the day before.

The figure only turned when Killick was ten yards away and shouting wildly. Even then, horribly, Killick was not sure that it was Blythe. It had Blythe's face all right, but the expression on the face was ugly with rage.

It was not Blythe's voice, either — the thick, heavy voice which began to rave and curse at Killick.

It only became Blythe's voice, and the malignant face only became Blythe's face, when Killick took a harsh, desperate step towards him and Blythe turned too wildly and lost his balance on the edge of the crevasse and fell, crying out for help...

Blythe clutched at the air, his struggling body disappearing quickly into the yawning crevasse, but the agonised voice went on screaming for long, terrible seconds afterwards.

Even when it cut off, the echo of it hung in the grey air and was repeated by the great black wall of the Henker north face which shut off the sky thirty yards away across the ice-field.

The silence when the echo died was horrible. Killick could not break it by calling out. He just stood on the black lip of the crevasse, every muscle locked and rigid with shock, looking down into the darkness which had swallowed Blythe.

Only his hectic thoughts moved. He had felt uneasy about the crevasse yesterday. Why? He hadn't even known it existed when they reached the edge of the ice-field and Blythe started towards the north face and he shouted at him to stop.

It was afterwards that Paccard had told them about the crevasse. And even then it was not any physical danger that Killick had been afraid of. He knew that now, staring down into the narrow darkness at his feet. There was something else about that crevasse, something uncanny.

The shout which broke the silence came from behind him. Killick turned stiffly. Paccard was running across the ice-field towards him from the direction of the hut and the other man, Lempeyer, was with him.

Killick was telling the two guides about the accident, trying to explain it, when Blythe's voice called to them out of the crevasse.

141

He must have been twenty feet down, not more. The voice was faint, strangled by the narrow walls of ice, but quite steady. 'Killick! Killick, are you there? Get me out of this! Killick, hurry!'

Killick knelt at the edge of the crevasse. He shouted down: 'We're here, Blythe. Hang on. We'll get you out.'

Paccard sent the other guide back for ropes and axes. He took charge. There was a ledge in the wall of the crevasse, Blythe shouted up to them while they waited. He had fallen on to it and cracked his head and stayed there by a miracle. It was a ledge cutting back into the ice wall, broad and safe enough.

The strange thing was that, though Blythe was alive and safe, Killick still felt this queer uneasiness about the crevasse. It was the uneasiness which made him insist, when Lempeyer brought the ropes, that they should lower him down to Blythe first.

It was broad daylight by the time they had belayed the rope. The sun had cleared the shoulder of the mountain. The wall of ice was blue, transparent as a pane of glass in front of Killick's face as they lowered him into the crevasse.

Blythe was waiting for him on the ledge. It was seven feet across, about as long as a coffin, projecting out over the gulf of darkness below and shafting back deeply in the ice wall of the crevasse. The cold was intense.

Blythe grabbed Killick's body as his feet brushed the ledge. When the rope slackened and Killick was standing safely beside him, he just shifted his hands to Killick's shoulders. They stayed like that for a minute, hugging each other, grinning into each other's faces.

Killick said, still breathless: 'You had me worried, Blythe.'

'Heck, I was worried myself.' Blythe dropped his arms then, not smiling any more. 'I remember falling,' he said, 'I mean, starting to fall. But before that, I don't remember anything. What was I doing up there?'

'Cursing at me,' Killick said. 'I'd followed you from the hut. I never saw you like that before. You looked murderous. You flung away from me and lost your balance. You were too near the edge.'

Blythe looked at Killick, frowning. 'Maybe it's the shock,' he said. 'I don't remember any of that. I don't even remember going out of the hut. It's as if I was completely unconscious.'

'I watched you pulling on your clothes,' Killick said. 'You didn't make any noise. Actually, I thought you were — well, it doesn't matter who I thought you were. It was dark in the hut, anyway...'

'Who, Killick?'

'I thought you were Albert Blythe,' Killick said, simply.

Blythe rubbed a big hand across his face. His eyes looked haggard when he took it away. 'Dead men,' he said. 'Dead men taking us over. Dead men moving us around like puppets. First you with that ice-axe. Now me. Heck, Killick! What do they want with us, those two dead men?'

Killick shook his head without answering. He uncoiled the second rope from his shoulder. Paccard was shouting to them from the edge of the crevasse, and Killick wanted to get out of that cold, narrow place before Blythe asked the question he was afraid of.

Blythe asked it, anyway, before Killick had finished knotting the rope around his body. He looked upwards to the thin slit of sky above the crevasse, downwards to where the ice walls slid through blue and purple and black to utter darkness.

'Why here?' he said. 'Why bring me here? What's a dead man like Albert Blythe got to do with this crevasse?'

Killick was looking past Blythe's shoulder when the big man said that. The sun was higher now, and the light was probing deeper into the shaft of ice at the back of the ledge. And deep in the shaft, in the solid ice itself, Killick saw the answer to Blythe's question and his own queer uneasiness.

There was a rope buried in the ice.

It was lying uncoiled, loose as though it had just been dropped there, frozen into the transparent floor of the shaft two inches below the surface.

A few inches from the rope there was a glove frozen into the ice, a woollen glove. Killick could see the glove to the wrist from where he was standing. The shaft narrowed to a point there and, whatever was beyond the glove, or attached to the wrist of it or to the end of the rope, was hidden.

Blythe had his back to the shaft in the ice wall, but something must have showed in Killick's face because the big man suddenly wheeled around and saw the rope and the glove in the thick-packed ice.

He said: 'My oath, Killick!' in a hard, tight voice.

He got down on his knees on the floor of the ledge and crawled into the narrowing shaft. Killick just stood and watched him. There was nothing queer about those things; they were just a rope and a glove, he told himself — but he knew he was lying.

Blythe got up, brushing his knees, his eyes alight. Killick put a hand on his arm to check him, but Blythe shook the hand off impatiently and went out on to the ledge.

'Paccard!' he called. 'Hey, Paccard! We want you down here. Hurry. We've found something.'

He turned to look at Killick. He grinned. He was the same old Blythe still, only excited.

'Heck! You came out to Chamonix to find out about that accident, didn't you, Killick?' he said. 'Well, that's evidence, buried in the ice there.'

'But it's only a rope, an old glove...'

'It's the rope,' Blythe said. 'The rope Killick and Blythe used seventy years ago on the Henker north face. The rope those guides saw whipping out from the body that fell past them on the mountain that day. Look, we know it's the rope, we know that's what dragged me out here in my sleep. We know now, don't we, what the connection was between old Albert Blythe and this crevasse?'

Killick clenched his hands against his sides. They were shaking. The uneasiness he had felt on the ice-field yesterday was as sharp as that now. 'Yes,' he said. 'We know.'

Paccard was coming down from above now, and he swung on to the ledge beside the two Englishmen. He just nodded when Blythe showed him the rope and the glove in the ice floor at the back of the shaft.

He said, kneeling inside the shaft with his face close to the ice: 'The rope is manilla hemp with a righthand lay. That does not prove it was the rope the *Messieurs* used on the north face that day.'

'But it *could* be the rope?' Blythe said.

'*Mais certainement.* The ice would preserve it. And there are rock overhangs high up on the north face of the Henker. Something falling from such a height would hit the ice-field perhaps thirty yards from the base of the north face. One would expect to find it about here.'

'Or in the crevasse?'

'*C'est possible.* The crevasse is always moving as I told you. Perhaps it was only a shallow gully eighty years ago. Anything which fell into the gully would be hidden from the search parties they sent out from Chamonix after the accident, and then the ice would form over it and the gully would widen and deepen and in time the thing would be buried twenty feet down, frozen solid in the ice, preserved until the crevasse shifted again to reveal it.'

Blythe took a deep, harsh breath. He glanced at Killick, but Killick was not looking at him. He turned back to Paccard.

'And you can see the end of the rope?' he said.

'*Oui, m'sieur.*'

'Well?'

'The rope has been cut, *m'sieur.*'

Killick heard the words, but he did not look at Blythe. He was staring at the glove buried in the ice close to the rope. He just could not drag his eyes away from that glove.

Blythe said harshly: 'Cut? By a rock, do you mean?'

'*Non, m'sieur.* A rock would have frayed the hemp. Or, if it had snapped suddenly, there would be a ragged appearance. This rope has been cut with a knife.'

Killick heard the quick intake of Blythe's breath, but the glove fascinated him. It was buried deep in the ice, and yet it was not flattened. The fingers bulged.

Blythe said: 'So your father's guess was right, Paccard. One of those two men, Henry Killick or Albert Blythe, fell and was being held on the rope by the other. And the other man cut the rope with his knife...'

'If this was the rope, *m'sieur,*' Paccard said, 'then, yes, I would say that happened.'

'Right,' Blythe said.

The energy in his voice made Killick look up sharply. Paccard looked up, too. He was getting to his feet when Blythe stooped down and grabbed the ice-axe out of the sling on the guide's shoulder.

Killick said: 'No, Blythe! For pity's sake, no!'

'Out of my way,' Blythe said.

He moved too quickly for Killick or Paccard to stop him. He brushed Paccard out of the way and crouched in the narrow shaft and swung the ice-axe. There was no room for a swing, but he got a lot of force into the short-armed stab with the pick.

The metal cut an inch down into the ice floor where the rope was embedded, and the glove. The broken chips of ice stung Killick's face as he leant over Blythe's hunched shoulder and tried to drag him back.

'Don't be a fool,' Killick was shouting, and there was horror in his voice.

Blythe just swore, flexing his shoulders to shake off Killick's grasp. 'There's probably a body hidden in there!' he said fiercely. 'But whose is it — Henry Killick's or Albert Blythe's? If we find that out, we find out which one used his knife on that rope. And that's what we came here to find out, isn't it?'

He had swung the axe again while he said that. The pick bit into the ice an inch from the glove.

Killick swayed back sharply as the pick bit home. He thought it was nausea which had weakened his legs, but Paccard was stumbling, too. The whole ice ledge was moving under the impact of Blythe's axe, not shaking, but tilting slowly with a harsh, sullen groaning sound.

Paccard shouted: 'Vite, m'sieur! Quick! The crevasse moves!'

He lunged forward to grab at Blythe, but the big man reeled back past him.

The roof and floor of the shaft in which he had been crouching were moving slowly towards each other, moving with a horrible, slow deliberation, closing like the lid of a coffin on the glove and the rope.

The three men swayed on the ledge. It was narrowing fast as the shaft in the ice wall behind them closed. The bottomless, cold dark of the crevasse yawned at their feet, but the ropes saved them.

Lempeyer, twenty feet above them on the edge of the ice-field, must have realised what was happening. He had the ropes belayed up there, and he began to haul on them one by one. Killick was the last to go up.

He hung for a long time against the sheer wall of the crevasse where the ledge had been. There was no ledge now, no shaft, just this black wall of ice as smooth as the wall of a tomb.

The two men who had died on the north face of the Henker so many years ago were embedded in that tomb. Solid tons of ice had locked up their bodies again, and the secret of their death. And John Killick, shuddering on the end of his rope in the darkness of the crevasse, was glad of it.

It took him ten minutes to get the feeling back into his numbed limbs after Paccard and Lempeyer had hauled him out of the crevasse. He sat huddled in the bright sunlight, letting the warmth soak slowly into his chilled body.

But he had not escaped from the shadow of the past. He knew that when he saw Blythe's face.

Blythe had been standing all that time with his back to Killick and the two guides. He had been looking up at the great north wall of the Henker towering above them. He turned slowly when Killick spoke to him.

'We're going back,' Killick said. 'We're going back to Chamonix now, aren't we, Blythe?'

'No, Killick.' Blythe's face was hard. There was nothing friendly in it now. 'No, Killick, we're not going back. We're going on up the north face of the Henker.'

'Blythe, you're mad...'

'We're going to climb the north face of the Henker,' Blythe said. 'You, and me, and Paccard and Lempeyer here. The four of us, just like it was in 1892. We're going to find out what happened to our grandfathers up there.'

Killick said, sharply now: 'But Blythe — we *know* what happened to them.'

'We know that either your grandfather or mine was a murderer,' Blythe said. 'We're going to find out *which one murdered the other ...*'

In that moment, looking into Blythe's flint-hard eyes on the edge of the crevasse under the north face of the Henker, John Killick knew that he could not turn back.

A dead man had drawn him out here from the quiet back streets in Cambridge to the high Alps. Another dead man had 'taken over' Blythe's big, stubborn body. Henry Killick and Albert Blythe had been petrified in the glass darkness below the ice-field for eighty years, but they were working out their hatred for each other through their two living descendants.

Even now, knowing it was a dead man's voice in Blythe's mouth, Killick felt a sudden loathing for the big soldier. It was the same loathing which had infected him that night in Chamonix when he had attacked Blythe with the ice-axe in the museum. He had to iron it out of his voice now, answering Blythe.

He said: 'Look, does it matter that one of our grandfathers murdered the other?'

'It mattered enough to bring you out to Chamonix in the first place,' Blythe said.

'But I didn't know about the cut rope then, or about the murder.'

'And now you do, you think it's safer to leave the thing alone, eh?'

There was a sneer in Blythe's voice, in his face, too. Killick said thickly, losing control: 'What do you mean by that?'

'It's pretty obvious, isn't it?' Blythe said. 'You've been pulling back ever since you went for me with the ice-axe that night. That scared you, didn't it? You realised then that if Henry Killick had taken over your body and made you try to kill me, that proved he was the murderer.'

'It didn't prove anything,' Killick said. 'You're crazy! It could still have been your grandfather who murdered mine. You've got no proof...'

'That's why we're going to climb the north face of the Henker,' Blythe said. 'To get the proof.'

'All right,' returned Killick flatly. 'We'll climb the north face. Whenever you like.'

The two guides, Paccard and Lempeyer, had been coiling the ropes that had saved three lives in the crevasse minutes before. But they must have been listening, because Paccard looked up at the other man now and said briefly: '*Alors?*'

Lempeyer straightened. He smiled bleakly. 'Seven times I have tried to climb the Henker north face,' he said, 'and seven times it has beaten me. But there has to be a time when the weather holds good up there, when there is no wind and the rocks do not fall. This may be the time. I am ready to go.'

'*Ainsi soit-il*,' Paccard said, 'so be it. We will spend one more night in the Nord hut, and start at dawn tomorrow.'

They were, all four of them, looking upwards by that time at the towering wall of rock which stretched above them. Perhaps they were all thinking of the men who died up there, the many men since Henry Killick and Albert Blythe, pinned to the rock wall like flies or snatched from it by the howling winds and the battering rock falls.

Blythe, at any rate, did not protest at Paccard's decision. He just turned away without looking at Killick and trudged off across the ice-field towards the hut.

Killick kept out of Blythe's way all that day. He liked the big soldier, he still liked him, but he was afraid of the dead man who kept looking out of Blythe's eyes and the murderous rage which infected his own body whenever that happened.

Most of the day he spent outside the hut in the strong, clear sunlight, looking across the valley to Chamonix and the hotel far below. The sunlight reassured him.

Way back in 1892, according to the guidebook Killick had read in the Cambridge library, cloud had shut down on Henry

Killick and Albert Blythe at three thousand feet and hidden their party from the watchers at the hotel. This time, he and Blythe were seven hundred feet higher and the sun was still shining in a clear sky; so at least the events of that tragic climb of 1892 were not being repeated now.

Killick mentioned that to the second guide, Lempeyer, after dark that night, when the two of them had come to the door of the hut to sniff the weather. It was still windless and clear, with stars like chips of ice in the black sky.

Killick wanted more reassurance from the guide, but it was that night, the last before they started the climb on the north face of the Henker, that the nightmare really began.

Because Lempeyer said calmly: 'The guide book is wrong, m'sieur.'

'What do you mean?'

'It speaks in round figures m'sieur. But Monsieur Killick and Monsieur Blythe were not at three thousand feet when the cloud shut down. They were here, at three thousand seven hundred feet, when the cloud hid them from the watchers in the valley.'

Killick said shakily: 'You seem to know a lot about it.'

'Oui, m'sieur.' Lempeyer watched him with those bleak eyes. 'My grand-uncle, who climbed with that party, he kept a diary. The facts are written there. Many times I have read them.'

Killick said quickly: 'Yes, but events aren't repeating themselves, anyway, because it was at dawn on the third day that the cloud came down on my grandfather's party, and we...'

'We have lost a day, m'sieur,' Lempeyer said, into the silence left by Killick's suddenly- strangled voice. 'Tomorrow, when we start to climb the north face of the Henker, it will be the dawn of the third day as it was for that other party.'

Killick did not sleep that night. He lay huddled under blankets by the gusty fire, watching the flare of the coals and listening for a change in the note of the midnight wind, living the nightmare which had already begun.

The sky was still clear an hour before dawn in the morning when Paccard brewed some coffee and they got into their clothes. It was still clear when they filed across the ice-field in the grey half-light and stood under the black wall of the Henker north face and roped together.

Paccard led, Blythe followed him, and Killick was third on the rope, belayed at the first stage, fifty feet above the ice-field, when the cloud came down. The wind blew cold on his face, damp and cold as death.

Killick felt a moment of panic, but it passed. The cloud had come down like this on his grandfather, Henry Killick, as he had climbed upwards to murder or be murdered on the high mountain above. The past was repeating itself, as Killick had known it would.

This was a nightmare he would not wake from until, somewhere on the grim heights of the Henker north face, he found out the truth of that murderous tragedy which had killed his grandfather and Blythe's.

He climbed steadily all through that third day on the mountain. Paccard and Blythe were above him, Lempeyer below, and the rope linked them together, but Killick climbed in a world of his own. It was the black, closed world of an awful nightmare.

It was a hard climb, that third day, with the wind stiffening from the east and the cloud mass swirling around the four men on the rope, chilling their hands, bruising their bodies. Three falls of debris swept down the rock face near them during the day.

Killick hardly noticed the discomfort and danger. The past obsessed him. He felt he was putting his hands on the same holds as his grandfather had used so many years before, wedging his toes into the same cracks, as he swung his body upwards over space.

When they reached the ledge at five thousand five hundred feet with the light failing, and Paccard called a halt, Killick waited until Lempeyer pulled himself up beside him.

Lempeyer must have seen the question in Killick's eyes, because he said, without being asked: '*Oui, m'sieur.* This ledge is called The Slack. That other party, your grandfather's spent their third night on the Henker on this ledge also.'

It was a narrow ledge, so narrow that the four men stayed on the rope while they ate and drank from the vacuum flasks. They wrapped themselves against the wind and huddled, half-standing, with their feet inches from the sheer drop, to wear the night away.

That was a hard night, and the day which followed it was worse. They were stiff and frozen from the long, dark hours, and the wind got stronger at dawn, clawing at their stiff bodies as they squirmed around on the ledge to follow Paccard's lead.

The rock was rotten, too, and the pitons would not hold. They spent most of the morning traversing almost horizontally while Paccard searched for firm rock, gaining a few painful feet in four hours.

Paccard's face was grim when they halted to eat at noon, roped against the rock face. But Killick knew already what was coming. He did not need to see the hopelessness in the guide's face.

By now, Killick was half-living in the past. There were times that afternoon when he was no longer sure whether the big man moving on the rope above him was Blythe or Blythe's grandfather.

The past had merged with the present. Four men were toiling on the north face of the Henker with the wind snatch-

*The four men huddled together on the narrow ledge.*

ing at their bodies and the rock-falls sweeping past them like thunder. They were toiling upwards towards a murder, one which had already happened or one which was going to happen.

Killick had only one brief moment of complete sanity that day, and it came when the four of them reached the ledge at five thousand two hundred feet, an hour before dusk.

In that moment, Killick looked at Lempeyer's face and the guide smiled back at him. The bleak smile told Killick that this was the same ledge on which, seventy years before, the two guides had refused to go any higher with Henry Killick and Albert Blythe.

Killick knew then, with a chill which went deeper into his bones than the bite of the wind, that there was no escape. He and Blythe were trapped in the past as firmly now as the bodies of their grandfathers were trapped in the black ice of the crevasse.

The murderous tragedy which had taken place on the north face of the Henker in 1892 must be played out again to its bitter end.

In a moment, Paccard would tell them that he and Lempeyer would climb no higher. And Blythe would protest. And Killick would sneer at him.

And when Blythe blustered, Killick would turn to the wall of the rock and end the argument by starting to climb upwards again. And Blythe, 'with a face like thunder,' would follow.

It had all been in that guidebook Killick had read in the library at Cambridge. He remembered it now. It was the last thing he did remember clearly, because at that moment Paccard turned on the ledge and put one hand roughly on Blythe's shoulder and the other on Killick's.

'*Alors, messieurs,*' Paccard said, 'we have climbed only three hundred feet in twenty-four hours. Our food is running low.

Lempeyer and I, we are being paid to climb, not to die. We climb no higher.'

Blythe said furiously, shaking off Paccard's hand: 'You're scared, are you?' The look in his eyes, hot and impatient, was the look of Albert Blythe, and his coarse voice was the dead man's too. Everything was happening exactly as it had in 1892.

Killick's smile and his voice belonged to the other dead man. The smile was cold and contemptuous, and the voice was a lazy sneer. 'No one is scared, Blythe,' he said. 'We're mountaineers, not steeplejacks. If you don't dare to go on without the guides, say so.'

Blythe turned on Killick. 'Who doesn't dare?' he blustered. 'I can climb without a guide as well as any soft-faced gentleman. And climb higher, too.'

Killick shrugged. He just turned away from Blythe and found a hold above his head in the smooth black rock and started to climb upwards again.

Blythe watched him for a moment, standing on the narrow ledge with the two guides at five thousand two hundred feet on the north face of the Henker. *Then he climbed after Killick, with a face like thunder* ...

Killick was fifteen feet above the ledge, a climbing shadow in the mist with Blythe harshly following him upwards, when Paccard moved. The guide's face was white to the lips.

'Come back, *messieurs!*' he shouted. 'Come back! This is the Henker north face! You are unroped! You are mad!'

He even groped for a hold on the rock face with a hand too unsteady to get a grip, before the other guide dragged him around on the narrow ledge.

Lempeyer's eyes were hard and bright. He said: 'Let them go, Jean.'

'But they are mad...'

'No. They are possessed, perhaps. You see how the thin

one climbs? On the lower slope he was clumsy, just a rock climber. Now he climbs like a man who has spent a lifetime in the high places, like a mountaineer. He climbs like this grandfather of his who died on the Henker in 1892.'

'*C'est vrai*.' Paccard stared upwards. 'It is true. But I do not understand. Why must they relive this tragedy of the past?'

'Those two are not the two simple young men who came to Chamonix a week ago,' said Lempeyer. 'They have become two other men, whose names are Henry and Albert, two dead men...'

'We are all mad, then,' Paccard said, sagging on the ledge, a shudder in his voice, 'mad to have climbed on this devil of a mountain which kills men and lets the men come back to haunt the living. Paul, those two are doomed. We should have stopped them before it was too late — we who know the Henker, the Executioner...'

Lempeyer did not answer at once. He was looking upwards with those bright, hard eyes. Killick was almost hidden now in the mist which writhed across the black wall of rock. Blythe was still climbing after him, crudely, with a harsh anger in his big body.

'Now there is nothing we can do,' Lempeyer said softly. 'This is the way it has to be, those two climbing towards the moment of truth, one of them killing the other, perhaps, as it happened before, both of them dying. For it is not a mountain they are trying to conquer, those two. It is the past. And men must live with the past to conquer it.'

He was still staring upwards, but now there was nothing to see but the writhing mist and the black wall of rock. Killick and Blythe had disappeared.

High in the blanket of mist the two men were climbing as Henry Killick and Albert Blythe had climbed seventy years before, groping for the same holds, wedging their toes in the same cracks, hauling themselves against the drag of the wind with the same rasp of breath in their throats. Even their voices were the voices of dead men. When the light faded altogether an hour after they had left the guides, and Killick halted with his heel to the rock face and an inch of his boot overhanging seven thousand feet of space on a ledge like the blade of a knife, Blythe said as he swung up beside him: 'You've had enough, have you, Killick?'

His voice was coarse, with a South London edge to the sneer in it. And Killick's voice, when he answered him, was the lazy, contemptuous voice of the amateur, the perfect gentleman.

'Yes, Blythe, I've had enough. I don't climb in the dark. I'm no steeplejack working on overtime.'

Blythe said, between his teeth: 'Look, you fancy gentleman, I don't have to stand here and take your insults.'

'You don't have to, Blythe.' Killick was uncoiling the rope from his shoulder. 'You can find another foothold on this smooth devil of a mountain. But if you stay with me, and we go on together at dawn, I suggest you swallow that clumsy pride of yours and we rope ourselves together.'

Blythe twisted his head to look at Killick. His eyes were suspicious of an insult, but he said: 'If you think so...'

'I don't think, Blythe, I know.' Killick held out the rope contemptuously. 'We shall freeze tonight. If we freeze and we're not belayed, we shall fall. It happened to Lord Churston when I was with him at Zermatt in '84. He was benighted at nine thousand feet on the Matterhorn. They never found the body. I had told him only three days before....'

'All right,' Blythe said, 'you told Lord Churston and you've told me. Give me that rope.'

They roped themselves together. They were already roped together by Killick's arrogance, Blythe's angry resentment, the hatred between them, but, as darkness fell, they tied the manilla with the righthand lay around their waists and crouched close together on the knife of a ledge at five thousand six hundred feet up the Honker.

At dawn, when they began to climb again, they were still roped together and there was still deadly hatred between them.

The hatred must have warmed them, injected hot energy into their cramped muscles. The wind was savage, wrenching at their bodies as they clung to the sheer rock by fingernails and the friction of boots, but they climbed fast. Once or twice they checked, as the rock falls scoured past them down the mountainside like a giant fist cupped to squash a fly, but always they climbed on.

Neither Killick nor Blythe was aware of what had happened to them. Two dead men were driving them upwards in the same bitter rivalry which had led, seventy years before, to murder.

Only twice in that last day, Killick realised the awful truth.

At nearly eight thousand five hundred feet they found a rock chimney. It was narrow enough to let them climb it with a wedging technique — backs against one wall and boots against the other — and wide enough to let them move abreast of each other. They were shielded from the wind and they moved fast.

They were fifty feet from the top when sheer instinct made Killick look up. The sound had not reached him yet, the vicious sound of the rock needle splitting away from the face of the chimney and ricocheting downwards between the narrow walls.

Killick shouted, lashed a hand sideways at Blythe, thrust

him viciously out of the path of the plunging rock. The rock sliced between them one second later.

Killick braced himself against the wall, shaken and sick, eyes closed. It was when Blythe spoke, in the shocked silence after the rock had passed, that he realised the awful truth of what was happening to them.

Blythe said: 'You won't get rid of me as easily as that, Killick,' and his voice was murderous.

'Blythe, you saw that rock come down...'

'I saw you lash out at me,' Blythe snarled. 'By heck, I'd have fallen if I hadn't been ready for something like that. You wanted me to fall, didn't you? You couldn't stomach seeing me climb alongside you, could you? Me, an ex-steeplejack and you a gentleman you and your Lord Churston in '84...'

'Shut up, Blythe,' Killick said. 'Shut up! You don't know what you're saying...'

'I know, all right,' Blythe said, and his voice was cunning, and the cunning was in his face when Killick turned his head frantically to look at him.

The face Killick saw, close to his in the narrow chimney, was the coarse and bitter face of Albert Blythe. And those terrible eyes were looking at him, John Killick, and seeing the man who had climbed the Henker with Albert Blythe and died with him in 1892.

Killick said, desperately: 'Blythe, listen. You've got to listen. You don't know what's happening to us. We've got to stop this before it's too late...'

'Oh, I'll stop it.' Blythe said, in the same voice, with the same coarse, bitter laugh. 'I'll stop it, don't worry. I've downed better men than you, Henry Killick, and I'll get to the top of the Henker before you for all you're a gentleman and I'm just a man who's made his pile. That's what's getting under your skin, isn't it? The thought that I'll beat you? You'd rather kill me...'

'Blythe, for pity's sake...'

It was John Killick's last, agonised appeal. That hot, sour rage, the rage a dead man had felt in the same place on the same mountain over seventy years ago, was creeping along his veins. He tried to reach Blythe first.

But Blythe was already out of his reach. It was Blythe's dead grandfather who grinned malevolently out of the big man's eyes at Killick now.

'Ah, you'd like me to stop now, wouldn't you, Henry Killick? But I know your tricks. And I'm climbing on. I'm going to beat you to the top of the Henker, see?'

The rage boiled over into Killick's brain. He answered Blythe then in the cold, contemptuous voice of Henry Killick.

He said: 'Very well, Blythe. Climb on. We shall see.'

He was already wedging himself upwards in the narrow chimney of rock. Blythe followed him. They moved with the harsh urgency of two men climbing against each other, two men possessed.

They were still roped together. The rope was slack now, but when they cleared the chimney and traversed out on to the rock face again in the battering wind, choosing their own routes, the tug of the rope at their bodies brought them back into the bitter company of each other.

They were tied together by their hatred, anyway, but it was the rope which fanned their hatred into murder.

Slowly, through that grim fifth day on the north face of the Henker, Killick had climbed ahead. Not far ahead, for the rope still anchored him to the big, clumsy body of Blythe, but far enough ahead to let him glance downwards at the man climbing below him, to let him tug at the rope with a harsh, arrogant contempt when he reached for another hold.

Far enough ahead, too, for Blythe always to see that slim, contemptuous body above him.

They climbed all day like that, Killick above and Blythe clambering stubbornly up in his wake. They did not halt at noon. Neither would be the first to admit that the wind was killing, the rock falls more frequent and murderously sudden, the horror of that empty space under the groping boot more paralysing.

An hour before the light failed on their fifth day on the Henker north face, and twenty-four hours after they had left the guides, Killick heaved himself with a last spasm of cramped muscles on to a narrow ledge at nearly ten thousand feet.

He was played out, and he knew it. Exhaustion fanned the hatred he felt for the man stubbornly climbing up towards him from below. He was clumsy, the big man, but he was stronger than Killick. It was monstrous that sheer, brute strength might carry Blythe to the top of the Henker before Killick, who had twice his skill.

Blythe had held him back today, anyway, Killick thought with a stab of jealous anger. He had used the rope that tied them together to put a drag on Killick's skill. It was the rope which had drained his strength.

When Blythe swung himself on to the ledge fifty seconds later, Killick was fumbling at the rope around his waist.

Blythe lunged at Killick. There was nothing in his attack but blind distrust, just as there was nothing in Killick's action but blind jealousy, but the ledge was only two feet wide.

Killick went over backwards, hands clutching at air, muscles clenched in the rigor of shock, a thin, high sound shredding out of his throat that was the scream of a dead man who was dying again.

The rope held. It arrested Killick's body thirty feet below

the ledge. He swung there on his back, helpless, over seven thousand feet of empty space to the ice-field below.

It was only when he looked up, in the sweating agony of fear, that Killick realised the awful truth for the second time that day.

He was John Killick again now. It was the young Cambridge scientist hanging on the end of that rope above the abyss. The shock of the fall had driven the ghost of his grandfather out of his mind and body.

But the man looking down at him from the ledge above, the man with the other end of the rope around his waist and his body braced back on the narrow ledge, the man who stood between John Killick and death, was still the vengeful ghost of Albert Blythe.

And Albert Blythe was grinning. He was grinning at the taut rope which ran from his own big body to Killick's. He was reaching for the knife at his waist; he was dragging it out unhurriedly. He was holding the knife with that terrible grin on his face.

And in the eyes of Albert Blythe there was hatred ...

John Killick knew then how his grandfather had died that day in 1892.

Henry Killick had hung on a rope where John Killick was hanging now. He had felt the same agony of fear. He had looked up to the ledge above, to the man who was braced there with the other end of the rope around his body, and had seen the knife in the man's hand and the murder in his eyes.

John Killick looked up now, in agony, and saw the man on the ledge, the knife in his hand, the murder in the eyes. And though the man was different, the murder was the same, because the jealous ghost of Albert Blythe still possessed the big, friendly body of the army sergeant.

Killick knew that, horribly, when he shouted from a bone dry throat: 'Blythe, help me! Help me!' And Blythe only grinned down at him from the ledge and made a crude sawing motion with the knife two inches from the rope and laughed exultantly.

Blythe was in no hurry to finish the game. He held the knife close to the rope. He shouted, in the coarse sneer of a voice that was his dead grandfather's: 'You never wanted my help before, Henry Killick, you fine gentleman, you. Too good for my help, you were. Why should you have it now?'

'No, Blythe — no...' was all Killick could say now, and the words were a dry whisper torn to shreds by the wind.

Henry Killick had suffered like this, hanging in space with his life in the clumsy hands of a man who hated him. But Henry Killick must have hoped, and for his grandson there was no hope. He knew what was going to happen.

Blythe shouted: 'Well, Killick? You had enough to say before. Well?'

'Please, Blythe...'

'That's better. *Please.* I like to hear you say that, Mister high-and-mighty Killick. Who's going to get to the top of the Henker first now, Mister Killick?'

'Blythe, for pity's sake...'

'Pity, eh? That's a fine thing for a gentleman to have, Mister Killick. But me, I'm no gentleman. A steeplejack, that's what I am. That's what you called me, wasn't it? Well, so now I'm a steeplejack with a knife in his hand — a knife in his hand...'

The knife was an inch from the rope. Over seventy years before, John Killick knew now, it had jerked that last inch viciously and cut the rope and Henry Killick had plunged seven thousand feet from the north face of the Henker to his death on the ice-field below.

And now John Killick himself was doomed. Ever since he had set foot on the Henker five days before, the past had repeated itself mercilessly. Blythe would cut the rope and Killick would fall, and a few seconds later Blythe would plunge after him as the cut rope whipped back, perhaps, and scythed his legs from under him.

But just because he was doomed, because he was hanging helplessly on that rope over the abyss and Blythe was flexing his wrist for the last slash at the rope, John Killick did then the only thing which could have snatched the big man and himself from the grip of the past.

He shouted. He found strength in his lungs and shouted. And the words he used, the harsh, broken words, 'You clot!' and 'Snap out of it, Blythe!' and 'Get the chip off your shoulder!' were twentieth-century words that meant something to Blythe, but nothing to the long-dead man who had taken possession of his mind and body.

The words confused Blythe. He shook his head, frowning, the knife still raised in his hand but the hand no longer clenching it viciously for the last slash of the rope. Blythe was struggling to register those words, to free himself from the dead man, the murderer.

The dead man was losing his grip on Blythe. Perhaps Henry Killick's voice had been scornful, so many years before as he hung on the rope in that last moment, perhaps it had been abject with fear, or silent. But it had not been the hard clear voice that his grandson used now, and went on using desperately as the seconds ebbed.

Blythe shuddered suddenly. He was staring at the knife. He clenched the hilt of the knife in a rigid fist and raised the fist high. Killick shut his eyes in that second, and dragged them open again to see the fist slashing down, but not towards the rope.

Blythe flung the knife with a terrible disgust, far out into the abyss.

Then he shouted, in a voice deep out of his own big chest: 'Hang on, Killick. It's O.K. now. I'll have you up.'

He had shaken off the murderous ghost of Albert Blythe. It was the big, friendly army sergeant who had shouted down to Killick, hanging below the ledge, and Killick had already freed himself from the past. The two of them were struggling for their lives, but those lives were their own again.

Blythe braced himself forward on the ledge and began to haul up the rope, hand over hand. Killick was a deadweight now, limp and half-conscious from the strain, and when his body reached the ledge Blythe had to free an arm and wrap it around his shoulders to lift him the last six inches.

They huddled like that on the ledge for a long moment, clinging to each other, Killick's thin body shaken by spasms of remembered horror and Blythe tightening the arm around his shoulders to steady him.

But it was Killick who said, when the big man started hesitantly to speak: 'Not here, Blythe. Not on this darned awful spot. Let's climb higher before we talk.'

They climbed higher. It was almost dark now and they had to feel for the handholds blindly, but the same thought steadied both of them. Henry Killick and Albert Blythe, those two dead men, had never climbed beyond that ledge below.

Thirty feet above the ledge, they found a deep cleft in the face of the rock. They tumbled into it; lay for five endless sweet minutes out of the flaying wind.

After a while they talked. It was a long, quiet talk that lasted most of the night. Blythe started it by saying, in that slow, honest voice of his: 'So it was Albert Blythe who cut the rope.'

'Yes, Blythe. He must have overbalanced cutting it, or the end of the rope whipped back and knocked him off the ledge after Henry Killick had fallen.'

'So that was the way they died,' Blythe said. He looked at

his hands, frowning. 'So it was my grandfather who murdered yours.'

'Does it really matter,' Killick said, 'now? They were both guilty. It was jealousy which killed them, and they were both guilty of that. We know they were, Blythe, because they came back from the dead to take over our bodies, to work out their hatred for each other through us.'

Blythe grinned at Killick and shifted his big, solid body on the ledge. He said: 'That sounds fantastic now, doesn't it?'

'It happened,' Killick said simply.

They talked about it for a long while throughout that night, huddling close together on the ledge on the north face of the Henker. And by dawn the strange story seemed less real than ever.

What was real now was the mountain itself, the sheer endless drop of black rock below them, and the one thousand-odd feet above. And Killick was looking up at the summit, when the sun rose.

It was a clear, bright sun. It shone peacefully across the steep rock wall of the Henker north face, and the mist had cleared and the wind had dropped. There was no debris falling either.

And Killick said, turning a bright, tranquil face to Blythe: 'We've got to get down, Blythe, somehow. But getting down is going to be as tricky as getting up. And once we got to the top, it would be easy walking down the south side of the mountain. So...'

'So we go up,' Blythe said, standing suddenly, stamping his feet, grinning his eager grin. 'Heck, we go up! We'll be the first men to climb the north face of the Henker to the summit, and maybe that's the way to end this whole gruesome business. Maybe *that* will make those two dead men lie easy at last.'

They went up. The weather held good, and made climbing possible without pitons. And as old Paccard had said, even inexperienced climbers could conquer the Henker north face if they had weather and good luck on their side.

Killick and Blythe already had the weather. They had the good luck, too, or perhaps it was just that they had escaped from the looming shadows of the past and it was their joyous relief that sustained them during that freezing last night on the ice ledge and held them steady on the last tricky ascent five hundred feet below the summit.

At noon on their seventh day on the north face of the Henker, Killick paused one step from the narrow cone of ice that was the summit, and waited for Blythe to climb up beside him.

Blythe knew why he had waited. He heaved himself to Killick's side and grinned at him. He put his hand under Killick's shoulder blade.

'Up with you, Killick,' he said. 'One of us has got to set foot on the top first, and our names aren't Henry and Albert — so it doesn't matter who it is.'

So Killick took that last step to the summit of the Henker with Blythe's big hand helping him up, and he turned when he got there and helped the big man up beside him, and that was really the end of the high quest. They had conquered more than a mountain — they had conquered the past.


And to the question Paccard asked, the same question that he was asked by the press at the impromptu news conference in the hotel later, and by the television interviewer at London Airport when he flew back to England five days afterwards, by the landlady at his lodgings in Inkerman Road, Cambridge, even by his chief when he started work on a new research programme at the laboratories a month after he had gone out to Chamonix, Killick gave the same answer.

The question Paccard asked was: 'Did you find out what happened up there, *m'sieur*, that day in 1892, between Henry Killick and Albert Blythe?'

And Killick's answer, the quiet answer which put back the smile on Blythe's big, friendly face, was: 'No. We didn't find out. But it doesn't really matter, does it? After all, it happened a long time ago...'

# Spell of Magic

by

HARRY HARRISON

Merlo sat with one leg dangling over the ten-storey drop to where the ocean lashed the jagged rocks below. In his hand he held a thin thread, woven from one of the new miracle plastics. In another moment, Merlo's life would be hanging from it. The knot where he had tied the thread to the radiator inside his hotel room held firm when he put his weight against it. It would do.

Carefully, so that no sudden jerk would come on the strand, he eased himself out of the window until he was hanging from the sill by one tanned and muscled hand. Then, very carefully, he loosened his fingers so that his weight shifted to his other hand, and on to the strange gun-like device he held there. It had a stirrup-shaped handle that he held and a round case above, out of which came the gleaming strand of thread. He hung from the handle now, his feet swinging free over the blackness of that awful drop. Below, in the Bay of Naples, he could hear the pounding of the waves. Merlo ignored it, concentrating all his attention on the thin thread from which he hung. It had a breaking strength of three hundred pounds... and any sharp tugs might snap it. He gently pushed a button on the handle and the reel inside began to turn, letting out more thread. Slowly, he dropped down the smooth wall of the hotel.

He passed a lighted window on the floor below, soundlessly as a ghost. Inside it, a man stood before a mirror adjusting his tie. He never noticed the dark shape that slid past the

**170**

window and was gone. Then Merlo was on a level with the window on the floor below, and his feet touched soundlessly on the window-sill. The window was closed and dark.

Balanced easily on the four-inch wide ledge, Merlo stopped the unreeling thread, then cut it with a knife-edge built into the handle. For an instant there was a tiny flare of flame from his gas lighter. Flame leapt up the thread, which burned to ash in an instant. It blew away, leaving no trace.

Merlo pocketed the thread machine, and slid the window open. Silently as a shadow he slipped into the room.

It was the bedroom of a suite, and from the partly-open door of the sitting-room came a shaft of light and a murmur of voices. Still moving without a sound, Merlo went to the door and looked in. He smiled grimly. He had arrived just in time — the vultures were gathering.

There were four men in the room. Two of them looked like the professional gunmen that they were. Hired killers. The other two were a cut better, though not much. A fat man sat at the table across from a thin, grey rat of a man named Ravali. He was a gang leader, a member of the Mafia, the dreaded international crime syndicate, and the man whom Merlo had been watching for weeks ... waiting for this meeting.

'Here they are,' the fat man said, handing a small box across the table.

'Good!' Ravali whispered, licking his lips and twitching his moustache like a rat. 'They have been a long time coming.'

Both men spoke in Italian, which was one of the half-dozen languages that Merlo spoke as fluently as his native English. He smiled when he saw the box — his weeks of waiting had not been in vain. While he memorised the positions of the men, the table and the box, he slipped what looked like an ordinary fountain pen from the pocket of his dark suit. When he twisted the barrel of the pen, the end flipped open and the pocket clip stuck down like a trigger — which it was. For the 'pen' was a small but deadly single-shot pistol. Sighting along two grooves in the top of the pen, Merlo pulled the tiny trigger.

He had aimed at no human target, but at the tiny 'off' button of the light switch across the room. The gun cracked and the room instantly plunged into darkness. Merlo threw open the door and dived in. With a single jump he reached the table and grabbed the box. Ravali still had his hand around it, but his fingers sprang open when Merlo tapped his wrist with a sharp judo blow.

'Someone's here!' Ravali squealed. 'He's got the shipment!'

A gun blasted a tongue of flame through the darkness and strong hands grabbed at Merlo. He planted a fist into a solid body and the hands were gone. Other fingers brushed him, but they were too late. He was back through the door into the bedroom. Slamming it behind him, Merlo sprinted through the other door into the hall. The corridor was empty and, with the package safely in his pocket, he ran towards the turning that led to the lifts and the stairs.

Behind him a gun boomed and a slug whined over his head. One of the thugs had some brains, and instead of following into the bedroom had opened the other door into the hall. Another shot followed the first, thudding into the wall near Merlo's head. Then he was around the turning.

Without slowing his pace, he tore off his black jacket, turned it inside out, and put it back on. It had become yellow tweed. A beret and dark-rimmed glasses were in the pocket and he put them on. Skidding to a halt in front of the door to the stairs, Merlo ripped the black plastic coverings from his shoes to reveal them as hideous orange. Still kneeling, he stuffed the covers into his pocket, pushed the door open and fell backwards just as the first thug skidded around the corner, gun ready.

'Stop him!' Merlo gasped in Italian. 'A man... in a black suit... knocked me over, ran down the stairs!'

Without giving Merlo a second glance, the man pounded down the stairs. Merlo smiled, brushed himself off as he rose, and went down in the lift. No one noticed him nor recognised him as he crossed the lobby. A cab was waiting outside.

'Rondinella Club,' he said to the driver and sank back into the soft seat.

The cab stopped by a large sign that read: MERLO THE MAGICIAN — MASTER OF THE DARK ARTS! And in smaller letters, *Every Night!* It was decorated by a large photo of him, without the dark-rimmed glasses and wearing evening clothes. Under the sign stood a small figure who waved to Merlo as he stepped out of the cab. It was Tommy, Merlo's assistant, who had been training as a jockey before he met the magician. Tommy looked no older than twelve — but he was actually nineteen.

As Merlo walked into the club with Tommy, he reflected how valuable Tommy's youthful appearance was to him — not only in his magician's act, but in other ways. For, like Merlo, Tommy Archer had a double role in life.

'How did you make out?' Tommy asked, as they made their way to Merlo's dressing-room.

Merlo turned on the lights in the empty dressing-room and closed the door. 'Take a look at that,' he said, handing Tommy the mysterious package.

Tommy stripped off the brown paper covering to reveal a rough wooden box held shut by a thick rubber band. He took this off and turned the box out on to the glass top of the dressing-table. Sparkling stones poured out, reflecting the light with dazzling brilliance.

'Wow!' Tommy said in a hushed voice, holding one of the gems up and admiring the rainbow twinkle. 'Diamonds!'

'More than just plain diamonds,' Merlo said. '*They are cut* diamonds, worth a small fortune anywhere in the world. Do you remember those rough diamonds a native smuggler tried to sell us in South Africa?'

'Sure. They looked just like any pebble you could find on the beach. Dirty little rocks.'

'Right — and that gives us a mystery that we are going to have to solve.' The smile vanished from his tanned, hawk-like face and Merlo was suddenly serious. 'We've been lucky, Tommy. So far, no one has suspected that a magician and his assistant might be working for Interpol. We've managed to get into a lot of places the normal police never reach. We found who was buying the rough diamonds and smuggling them out of Africa, and we even found out the name of the man here in Italy who is smuggling them into Europe. But our information is not complete. The most important part is missing. Somewhere between Africa and Naples these rough diamonds were cut and polished.'

Tommy frowned down at the gems. 'I don't dig you! As long as we find who the smugglers are, what difference does the polishing make?'

'The *big* difference. Every diamond cutter in the world, and there aren't many, is licensed and well-known. None of them would cut stolen gems. Yet these diamonds were cut. How? Where? By whom? Until we find out the answers to those questions we don't know enough to move. Interpol can only pick up a few of the small-time smugglers who won't be able to tell us a thing...'

'... while the boss, and the real gang, and those invisible diamond cutters are laughing up their sleeves at us!' Tommy interrupted.

'Perfectly correct!' agreed Merlo. 'So now, we are going to find out how...'

'No, you're not!' a voice grated from the suddenly-open door.

One of the gunmen from the hotel room stood there, a large automatic in his fist. It was aimed at Merlo's back.

The gunman fired twice. And the shots were as loud as a cannon's in the small room.

But the gunman had made a single mistake — he had taken the time to talk, to say that he was going to kill Merlo. Even as his finger tightened on the trigger, the two men he meant to be his victims were going into action. They were used to working together on the stage, and in danger, and they moved at the same time.

Tommy threw his small weight against the partly-open door, jarring the gunman. Merlo hurled himself sideways from the chair, rolling as he hit the floor. The gun barked loudly and one lead slug ripped through the chair where Merlo had just been sitting, and the other whirred by his head and dug a hole in the wall. The gunman cursed and shifted his aim — but there was no third shot. Even though he was lying on his back on the floor, Merlo was far from helpless. He was well-practised in the French form of boxing known as *la savate*. In *savate* the feet are used as well as the fists.

Fast as a striking snake, his foot lashed out and the sharp toe of his shoe caught the gunman's wrist. The man grunted with pain and the automatic spun away through the air. As the would-be killer jumped after the gun, Merlo seized him.

'I'll kill you!' the gunman grated through his teeth, fighting to free himself. 'You can't buck the gang...'

'We'll see about that,' Merlo answered grimly. 'Get my cigarette case from my coat, Tommy. It's time for our friend here to take a nap.'

'I dig you!' Tommy gave the struggling man a wicked grin and slipped Merlo's slim cigarette case from his pocket. It was made of platinum and should have held nothing more than the lighter and cigarettes. Yet, when Tommy pressed a concealed button, a small, liquid-filled plastic globe fell into his hand.

'Know what this is?' he asked, holding it before the gunman's face.

Before the man could answer, Tommy squeezed — the thin skin broke and a cool liquid ran out, turning instantly to gas. Both Merlo and Tommy were holding their breath, but the unknowing prisoner took one lungful of the vapour, struggled for an instant and fell limp. Merlo laid him on the floor.

'You can breathe again, Tommy — after fifteen seconds in the air the sleeping gas loses its power. Now the problem is, what do we do with sleeping beauty here?'

'He knows we work for Interpol!'

'Exactly. Therefore, Interpol will have to take care of him.'

Tommy locked the door while Merlo took down from the shelf an ordinary-looking transistor radio. Merlo had rebuilt it completely and, in addition to receiving programmes, it cantained a compact transmitter. The plastic grille slipped off and revealed a hidden set of controls and a telegraph key. Merlo tapped out a brief signal, waited until it was answered, then sent a longer message in code.

'That takes care of our gunman,' he said, changing the radio back to its normal guise. 'The local Interpol operator will pick him up and deliver him to a special prison where he will be held until this case is over. He will be allowed to contact no one, so that he can't give us away to his smuggling friends. You wait here until he is picked up.'

'Where will you be?'

'Visiting the gang! The time has come for us to get much closer to them if we are to find anything out about the secret diamond-cutting operation. I'm going to try to join them!'

Merlo's rented car spun him quickly out of the city and

down the *autostrada* along the Bay of Naples. Within minutes, he turned off at the small town of Torre del Greco. Ravali, the sinister leader of the gang, lived in a high-walled house here that seemed to be the local headquarters for the smugglers. Merlo had followed him here and noted the barbed wire, armed guards and vicious dogs that guarded it. He chose the easiest and simplest way to get in — the front door. He rang the bell. A surly-looking servant finally answered and said that Ravali could not see him. Merlo ignored this, and passed an envelope through the barred window in the door.

'Give this to Signor Ravali. He'll see me.'

The envelope contained two of the smuggled diamonds and it worked like a charm. Within a minute the door was thrown open and two toughs — with their hands on suspicious bulges in their jacket pockets — ushered him inside. Ravali sat slumped in a chair, looking more like a grey rat than ever as he plucked at his moustache, in a room filled with smoke and his bodyguards. It looked as though Merlo was interrupting an emergency meeting of the gang.

'Who are you?' Ravali snapped.

'The name is Merlo,' he said, coolly taking a cigarette and tapping it lazily on his thumb nail. 'Even you should have heard of me.'

'I know him,' one of the men growled. 'He's a tin-pot magician — plays the night clubs.'

'Where did you get these?' Ravali asked, holding up the diamonds from the envelope.

'Out of this box with the others,' Merlo answered calmly, and threw the box on the table. The cover flew open, and a fortune in glittering gems spilled out. The silence in the room was so thick it could have been cut with a knife.

'Where did you get them?' Ravali breathed, gaping at the diamonds he had thought lost forever.

'From your room at the hotel. I have been following the messenger who brought them to you. I recognised him on the boat. I do a good bit of smuggling myself. As a magician I find it really very simple to conceal things — even from customs officers. When I'm not smuggling goods, I like to relieve other smugglers of their goods. They rarely complain to the police.'

'Why are you telling me this? Why did you bring the diamonds back?' Ravali rasped, his fingertips inside his coat, touching his gun.

'Because I'm not a fool. I'll buck lone wolves and small-time smugglers. But I'm not going to buck a large organisation like yours. I would rather join it. That way, there will be a larger profit for both of us. You can use me — and I can use your money!'

An angry mumble went around the room, and Ravali leaned back and scratched his jaw. 'Something might be possible,' he began. Then a voice interrupted him.

'Wait a minute, Ravali!' One of the gunmen from the hotel room lumbered forward. 'What happened to Gino? If this Merlo hijacked our shipment, he must be the one Gino followed. He just had time to tell me that he was following someone from the hotel — then he left. He ain't back yet. Where is he? Ask this guy!'

All eyes were on Merlo. The magician relaxed and blew a perfect smoke-ring. The mystery of the vanishing gunman would have to be faced some time, best to get it over with now.

'Was his name Gino? I never found out. He followed me to the club and tried to kill me. That has been tried before... always with the same results. Gino is dead.'

'He killed Gino!' one of the men gasped, then in instant anger: '*Kill him!*'

Their guns were out now, and shining knife-blades as well.

A ring of death was closing in on Merlo, yet he never flinched.

'Kill him!' they shouted.

Merlo sat calmly ignoring them! This bothered even these professional murderers and slowed them down for one vital moment.

'Don't make any mistakes!' Merlo said softly, yet the menace in his tone was unmistakable. 'I didn't come here to get knocked off. The first one that tries anything will die — I promise that!'

And while he talked. he stubbed out his cigarette and took a fresh one from his case.

One man ignored the warning. He pushed forward, carrying a long-bladed knife in his hand.

'You killed Gino,' he growled. 'He was my friend. For that *you* die!'

'It was a fair fight,' Merlo replied grimly. 'Gino tried to murder me — only I shot first. Be careful, or you'll be joining him in the river.'

The man snarled in answer and leaped forward. But what happened next shocked everyone in the room.

'*Then die!*' Merlo snapped, and pointed his finger at his attacker. The man jerked to a halt, clutched his throat in sudden pain and fell to the floor. The knife dropped from his limp fingers and he did not move again.

'Anyone else want that?' Merlo asked, and no one moved. 'Then clear out of here until I'm through. I have some things to talk to Ravali about.'

The rat-like leader nibbled his moustache for a moment, then nodded his head. His gangsters quickly left the room.

'He is not dead,' Merlo said, pointing to the body on the floor with his toe. 'He'll come to in a few hours.'

'But... but how did you do it?' Ravali asked, fear and amazement in his voice.

Merlo smiled. 'Trade secret; you should never ask a magician how he does anything.'

As he talked he·took a fresh cigarette from his case, at the same time slipping back into it the 'cigarette' he had just used. This was a white metal tube containing a tiny pressure tank of carbon-dioxide gas of the same sort that makes soda bottles fizz. In front of it was a plastic dart tipped with a strong drug. A squeeze on the tube projected the dart with a blast of gas. The dart had hit the would-be killer in the neck.

'I don't suppose you are too sorry about losing Gino?' Merlo asked.

'Gino! I can hire a hundred like him by lifting a finger. And a killer who can't kill is of no use to me,' Ravali replied.

'Just as I thought,' said Merlo, 'which is why I was sure you wouldn't have me killed if I came here. And you have the diamonds as proof of my good intentions. Now, can you use me? I can get diamonds into any country in the world for your organisation — and I'll never be caught.'

'Yes... yes, we could use a reliable messenger,' Ravali mumbled over the thought, darting little glances at Merlo. 'But I cannot decide myself. There are others, higher up. They will tell me. Stay in Naples and I will get in touch with you.'

Merlo left then, without any trouble, and found his assistant, Tommy Archer, waiting anxiously at the club.

The magician grinned at the sight of Tommy's anxious face.

'Relax, Tommy! I'm as good as a member of the gang. They'll try me out — and keep a close watch for any funny moves on my part. So we'll just finish this run at the club, then enjoy the beaches on Capri until they make up their minds. It's about time we had a holiday!'

But they never did. The same day their show closed, Merlo had a call from Ravali and went out for a luncheon confer-ence. He returned in high humour, hurling his hat across the room to score a perfect landing on the light bulb over the mirror.

'Time to pack,' he said. 'I'm going on a little sea voyage.'

'But what about *me*?' Tommy asked.

'You are going ahead by train with our props, and we'll meet in Cannes, the pearl of the French Riviera. I'm going alone by ship, the *King Hercules*, which docks here tomorrow. She is on a cruise to Canada, but I'm only going as far as Cannes, a short, two-day trip. And while I'm on board I'll have a chat with the second mate, who will slip me a small box worth a few hundred thousand pounds. All I have to do is land it safely ashore in France. They are Ravali's orders.'

'But ... it's not going to be easy ...'

'You can say that again, Tommy,' Merlo aswered. 'Interpol can't help me this time; I'll be watched too closely. I'll have to do a genuine job of smuggling that can't possibly be detected. And I have just the gadget to do it with.'

'Not that toy rocket ship you have been working on all week?' Tommy asked, pointing to the silvery tube that lay on the workbench.

The tube lay among a clutter of half-finished gadgets on the bench. For Merlo spent much of his time inventing, building and experimenting with contrivances that he used both for his act as a magician and his work as an Interpol agent. The gas 'blow-pipe' with which he had stopped the gangster's knife attack at Ravali's house had, in fact, been invented and built at this workbench.

'The very thing,' Merlo said, picking it up, 'though it's not a rocket ship. Here, hold it, and I'll show you something.'

The tube was about two feet long, pointed at both ends, and had a tiny propeller and fins at the back. Tommy took it and held it unhappily. Merlo turned on some of his radio and electronic machines, and when the valves had warmed he pressed a button. The tiny propeller began to spin and whir, while the fins flapped up and down. Tommy was so surprised that he almost dropped the machine.

'Hey — it works!' He looked at it more closely. 'I bet it's a boat of some kind, and that it can go by itself in the water!'

'Right both times. Now help me pack these things up. My ship sails at eight in the morning.'

They parted at the club the next morning, and a taxi took Merlo and his single suitcase to the dock where the big, brightly-coloured *King Hercules* was tied up. There was only a small crowd, and within a few minutes he was through Customs and boarding the ship. He did not notice the two men who stood well back in the shadows of the shed and watched him climb the gang-plank. One of them glared at Merlo's back, his fingers opening and closing on the knife in his pocket.

'Don't get into any trouble, Tonio,' the other man warned. 'This Merlo is pure poison.'

'He killed my friend,' Tonio snarled, 'and I'm fixing him for that.'

'He's tough — he'll be hard to get.'

'I know what I'm doing. It'll be two days before he can get to France in this tub. And I'm flying there at noon. When he tries to walk off that ship at Cannes, Signor Merlo is going to have a big surprise waiting for him ...'

The two-day trip from Naples to Cannes should have been a holiday — but Merlo could not shake off a nagging fear. Soon after the ship had cast off, the second mate slipped into Merlo's cabin, handed him a paper-backed German thriller — and vanished.

The pages of the book were glued together. Merlo cut them apart, and took a handful of glittering cut diamonds from the hollowed-out inside.

Then he threw the book out of the porthole. Merlo would have relaxed then, but for the feeling that things were going too easily ... that he was walking into the open jaws of a trap.

When the ship dropped anchor at Cannes, he was glad that he did not have to walk ashore with the smuggled diamonds.

In a matter of seconds, the mysterious torpedo-like device he had brought with him was unpacked and checked. The concealed motor spun the tiny propeller and the guiding vanes flipped up and down. Merlo opened its pointed nose and slipped the diamonds inside.

From the top of the machine sprang a length of insulated wire that vanished into a piece of bleached driftwood. A crooked piece of rusty wire stuck above the wood.

Merlo opened his porthole and looked out. There was no one at the rail above nor were there any boats in sight. Everyone would be at the other side of the ship watching the small boats come out from the shore for the passengers. It was only a moment's work to let the little machine down into the sea on its length of wire — then throw the wood after it.

Immediately, the torpedo-like device vanished, and only the innocent-looking piece of driftwood floated on the surface. It was weighted so that the rusty wire stuck straight into the air.

Merlo walked up to the deck. The shore boat was already loading with disembarking passengers. He stepped aboard, and a minute later was heading towards shore with the other passengers who were also landing at Cannes.

'Will you step in here, please?' an officer asked, waving to an office, as Merlo walked into the Customs shed.

Merlo's eyebrows rose. 'Why?' he asked. 'All the other passengers are going right through.'

'A routine matter,' the officer murmured, touching his arm.

They had been speaking English, so the officer was caught off-balance when Merlo snapped a question at him in his own tongue, Provençal-accented French. Merlo's voice was low.

'You have been tipped off about me?'

Looking at the man out of the corner of his eyes, Merlo saw him start as the barb sunk home. This, then, was the trap. The Customs had been tipped off that he might be smuggling.

The Customs men were experienced and complete, and the only reason they found no contraband was because Merlo was carrying none. They searched him and they searched his bag. They prised open the heels of his shoes, and even opened his transistor radio. Finally they offered polite apologies for the delay and called a cab to take him to the Hotel Majestic where he had reserved a room. Only when the cab had started and he was safely on his way did Merlo allow himself a small smile of victory. He had expected trouble and had found it. And he was sure he could look forward to more.

It arrived a moment after the pageboy had pocketed his tip and left the room. As Merlo locked the door, a man stepped from the bathroom and said: 'I'll take those diamonds now.'

Merlo did not answer or even look at the intruder until he had put his radio on the table and had walked across the room and opened the blinds.

'I have no idea what you are talking about,' he said, turning to face the man.

'The diamonds you just smuggled into this country. Give them to me.' The stranger raised a large automatic that was almost hidden in one great, meaty hand. He was fat and he was tall, and he bulged like a pear in the middle. Yet there was nothing of the funny fat man about him: the icy-blue eyes were as cold as death.

'Get out!' Merlo snapped.

'Only with the diamonds. You have ten seconds to hand them over. Then I shoot!'

'You do make it difficult, Merlo sighed. 'What would you

do if I told you there was someone standing behind you with a gun pointed at your spine?'

'I'd laugh. That trick is so old it has whiskers!'

'Really?' Merlo asked, raising his eyebrows. 'Then we had better have a demonstration.' He clapped his hands together twice, sharply.

'Just freeze, or you're dead,' a voice snapped behind the intruder. 'Now raise your hands over your head ... *slowly!*'

The fat man's eyes bulged and his mouth gaped open. As he raised his hands over his head, Merlo reached out and took the gun from his limp, trembling fingers.

'Tell him not to shoot!' the man begged, his skin damp with sudden sweat. 'I'm your contact man. Petritz is my name. The code word is *blue summer*. I was told to do this ... to try to frighten you. Orders from upstairs. They wanted to see how well you would take care of the shipment.'

'I thought as much,' Merlo laughed. 'You can relax. There's no one here.'

'B ... but the voice — I heard it behind me!' Petritz gasped, looking around at the empty room.

'Magic. Call it ventriloquism, if you like.'

Merlo had no intention of telling how the trick had been done. He had turned on the transistor radio when Petritz had first appeared ... then deliberately stood on the other side of the room so the man would have his back to it. The two sharp hand-claps had been his signal, picked up by a sensitive microphone in the radio. This had turned on a tiny tape-recorder, also hidden there, which had spoken the recorded speech. It was a useful gadget that had saved his life more than once.

'Can I have the diamonds now?' Petritz asked weakly, mopping at his damp face.

'Tomorrow. They are in a place where even the Customs guards could not find them when they searched me. Do you know anything about that? Someone must have told them.'

'No... but I'll look into it. It sounds like they were tipped off. And that could only have been done by someone inside the organisation. This is bad. Will you have the diamonds in the morning?'

'Join me here for breakfast and I'll turn them over to you,' Merlo replied.

Petritz, satisfied, hurried out. After unpacking, Merlo went down to the hotel restaurant and enjoyed a leisurely dinner. He was one step closer to his goal.

It was near midnight when he left the hotel, carrying his portable radio that contained so many secrets. After making sure that he was not being followed, he walked far out on La Croisette, the street that runs along the shore, until he came to one of the dark and deserted beaches. Standing at the water's edge, Merlo raised the whip antenna on the radio, turned on the power and waited. A powerful signal beamed out from the little transmitter, and out in the bay his miniature submarine stirred to life. The rusty wire on the driftwood was really an excellent aerial, and it picked up his broadcast signal. The electric motor started, the screw turned, steering rudders flipped and the machine headed towards the shore.

It landed almost at Merlo's feet and he had only to remove his sandals and wade out to get it. He wrapped it in paper he had brought for this purpose, so that it looked like a package bought in some tourist store.

'Now, I'll just take those diamonds!' a voice gloated from the darkness, and the hulking form of Tonio appeared. The blade of the knife in his hand glittered viciously.

Merlo turned to escape the knife... and too late realised that he had been tricked. An iron bar in Tonio's other hand crashed against Merlo's head, knocking him to the sand. The package was torn from his hands and the knife plunged into his side like a finger of fire. Merlo groaned with agony.

'You kill my friend!' Tonio cried. 'Now I kill you!'

Merlo fought to escape the haze of red pain that was flooding his senses, but he could not. The blow on the head hadn't knocked him out — but it had paralysed his body. When Tonio struck down with the knife he could only lie on the sand without moving, even when agony tore at his chest. In the darkness the blow had missed its mark, cutting his side and sliding from his ribs. But the next blow would not miss. The knife was raised and he could not force himself to roll out of its way.

A whistle shrilled suddenly, and running footsteps thudded on the hard-packed sand at the water's edge. Tonio cursed, jumped and ran in the opposite direction with the precious package under his arm. The policeman who patrolled beaches at night hurried over to Merlo.

'Monsieur is hurt...?' he asked.

'No...' Merlo almost gasped the words. 'Just knocked down... I'll be all right. But stop that man — he stole my money... winnings from the Casino!' Merlo did not dare mention the stolen diamonds.

The whistle shrilled again and the police officer pounded into the darkness after the vanished Tonio. From the street a second whistle sounded as another policeman heard and joined the chase.

Merlo sat up groggily, angry with himself that he had allowed Tonio to follow him, outwit him and get the diamonds. Only the fact that a policeman had happened to be close by had prevented Tonio from killing him, too. Merlo had been over confident. He had thought that the tip-off to the Customs was the only danger that he had to face. He had let his guard down for an instant — and had lost the diamonds and almost his life as well.

That was over now. He dragged himself to his feet, ignoring

the pain in his throbbing head, and touched the cut in his side. It was narrow and not too deep, and was not bleeding too much. He would just have to ignore it. In less than eight hours he would be meeting Petritz to give him the diamonds. If he did not have them by then he would be signing his own death warrant. If he told about Tonio's attack he would not be believed. He *had* to get the diamonds back.

At a stumbling run he made his way down the beach after the policemen. Bit by bit his head cleared and he could think more clearly. He was surprised to find that he still clutched his portable radio.

The road turned to go around the yacht basin, and it was silent and empty.

'Stop and think!' Merlo said to himself, sinking down on to the sea-wall. 'You can run all night and never catch Tonio. He has the entire city to hide in. Or has he?'

Merlo looked closely around at the empty street, the darkened yachts and boats tied in even rows, and at the black mouths of the side streets. Would Tonio, a stranger in this city, have run into these side streets, not knowing if they were dead ends or if other police were coming? The policemen seemed to think so; they were out of sight now. But Tonio could have hidden somewhere else.

On one of these boats or yachts?

The idea seemed a good one, and he had to put it to the test. Tonio would still be carrying the tiny, radio-controlled submarine until he had a chance to examine it and remove the diamonds. And the radio Merlo carried would control the tiny sub! The magician carefully set the controls on the transmitter and pressed the button that would start the sub's electric motor.

From somewhere among the yachts there came a tiny, whining sound. Tonio *was* there! Silently Merlo slipped along the dock and pressed the button again. The sound was closer.

He must be careful. He was still weak, and Tonio was armed and deadly. Merlo had only one thing that might even be called a weapon. The jewel on the heavy signet ring he wore flipped open when he turned it. Inside was a glass globe containing tear-gas. With this he might even the odds.

A last touch on the radio control brought an answering buzz from the bow of a nearby yacht. Carefully putting down the radio, he swung on to the yacht. The glass ball of tear-gas was ready in his hands as he moved towards the dark bow.

Suddenly, footsteps hammered along the deck behind him and an iron-hard arm closed about his neck. He had been tricked! Tonio had known what the buzzing of the sub meant and had put it in the bow whilst he hid in the stern. His baited trap had worked!

With the last of his strength, Merlo turned and grasped the arm that was tightening on his neck like a band of iron. He held on, and both men staggered off balance and plunged from the deck into the water. Merlo had time for a single breath before they went under.

As a slum child of Naples, Tonio had grown up near the water and was a good swimmer. He smiled into the darkness and tightened his arm about Merlo's throat. He would hold him under water until he was dead!

The idea should have worked — but long seconds passed and Merlo still struggled. Tonio, fighting for breath, pushed the other man away and made towards the surface. But they had drifted beneath the yacht, and instead of air his face met barnacle-covered wood. He fought to get out... fought and fought...

Merlo's head broke out of the water and he gasped in a wonderful breath of air. Around him the water was smooth and unbroken. Tonio had met the death he had meant for his victim, Merlo. Really it was quite an ironical situation.

Tonio had been a good swimmer — but he had forgotten that Merlo was a professional magician. And one of Merlo's most famous tricks had been an under-water escape from chains and locks. He had trained himself to hold his breath up to five minutes, if necessary. This training had saved his life yet again.

When some of his strength had returned, Merlo wearily dragged himself from the water and found the tiny sub. The diamonds were still there! He wrapped them in his hand-kerchief and sank the sub in the deep water at the other end of the basin. He would look strange enough in his battered and soaked condition, without carrying that around with him.

He rested while his clothes dried a bit, and did what he could to make himself look more normal. The police passed back by the yachts but did not see him in the shadows. When they were safely out of sight, he made his way by back streets to the Servants' Entrance of the Majestic Hotel.

Once in his room, Merlo had a hot bath, shaved, dressed the sore spot on his head and the slash in his side. Then he lay down for some rest. It was almost dawn and Petritz would soon be there for the diamonds.

A distant knocking pulled him from a deep sleep, and he went yawning to the door. It seemed a little early for the expected visit of the agent of the smuggling ring. He opened the door.

The man in the hall was a stranger, a grim-looking one.

'My name is DuPont,' he announced, holding out an opened wallet with his identification. 'I'm a detective. You had better let me in. I want to talk to you about smuggled diamonds.'

Merlo tried to blink away the fatigue and sleep as he stared at the man outside the door.

'I don't quite understand what you want...' Merlo began.

190

'You understand well enough,'the detective answered coldly. 'Let me in and we'll have a nice, private chat about smuggled diamonds. I think you could tell me a lot.' He pushed past Merlo and into the room, a lean, grey man with short-cropped hair and a web of wrinkles around his eyes.

'I can call the desk and have you thrown out,' Merlo said.

'Why do that?' DuPont asked, dropping into a chair. 'I'm not here to cause trouble. I want to do you a favour. You saw my identification, didn't you?'

'Yes. It said only that you were a private detective working for a firm in Paris.'

'That's all I am, believe me. I don't want to put you into jail or cause you any trouble. I just want some information.' He dug into his side pocket and produced a thick wad of bank notes that he threw on the table. 'That could be yours. Four thousand new francs. Just for giving me some information about diamond smuggling.'

'What could I possibly know about that?'

'Don't kid me,' DuPont snapped angrily. 'The Customs men gave you a shaking up yesterday on a tip from a thug named Tonio ... who has been mixed up in illegal diamonds himself. You *know* something. Tell me and I'll pay for it. I work for a syndicate of diamond buyers in Paris who want to stop illegal gems from flooding the market. They don't want to see you in trouble. They just want to stop the diamonds from coming into the country.'

Merlo found a cigarette and lit it before he answered.

'You have me interested ... but not here and not now.' He pushed the money back. 'Meet me at eleven o'clock tonight, DuPont, at the end of the ferry dock. It'll be empty then and we can have a private talk. I might well have something for you.'

'You're a smart man,' DuPont said, climbing to his feet

and stuffing the notes back into his pocket. 'At eleven then.'

When the detective had gone, Merlo yawned and slowly dressed. Yesterday had been a hard day — and this one was not going to be any easier.

As he strolled out on to the main terrace he saw that Petritz was there and had already ordered his breakfast. Merlo slid into the empty chair and casually dropped his newspaper on to the table.

'Well?' Petritz asked. 'Where are they? You do have the diamonds... don't you?'

'Relax, read the paper — plenty of time for business later.' He pushed the newspaper across the table, ignoring the pistol that suddenly appeared in Petritz's fat hand.

There was no mistaking the menace that crept into Petritz's voice. 'Don't play any games, Merlo. I want those diamonds...' Then his hand fell on the folded newspaper and he felt the bulge in it. He opened it as if he was going to read it, but instead took a long look at the plastic bag pinned inside.

Petritz breathed a sigh of relief. 'Very good,' he finally said, and slipped the gun back into his pocket. 'It looks like you are as good at this business as they said in Naples. There is something else we would like...'

'Don't tell me now,' Merlo broke in. 'It's too early in the morning, and besides, I have some things to take care of first. Can you be back here at ten tonight?'

'Ten it is.' Petritz heaved his fat bulk to his feet. 'I want to get rid of this shipment first, anyway.'

After breakfast, Merlo went back to his room and was not at all surprised to find his assistant, Tommy Archer, waiting there. The little ex-jockey jumped to his feet happily.

'You're all right! I can tell you now, Merlo — I was worried about this job.'

'So was I... with good reason,' Merlo admitted, and told

Tommy about the attack by Tonio and the earlier visit of the detective. 'I don't like it, not at all. Too many people seem to know my business and to be lying in wait for me. Breaking into this gang is going to be a lot harder than I thought. I have the feeling that someone is watching me and laying traps. When I get out of one there is another waiting.'

'Let's turn the whole thing over to Interpol and get out while our skins are still in one piece.'

'No... I'm too close to the inside now. The more I know, the more dangerous it gets. And the way things are happening to me, I begin to feel that the answer is very close. If I can find out how and where the illegal diamonds are being cut — and who is in charge of this international ring — I'll have a real case for Interpol. If they act now, all they'll pick up will be the small fry. I have a little plan that might crack this business open, and I'll need your help to carry it out.'

Tommy listened. Then he set off to obey the magician's instructions.

Merlo spent a quiet day preparing for what was sure to be a very busy evening. He met Petritz at ten and they strolled along the waterfront, looking out across the bay at the lights of the American fleet lying at anchor.

'I don't get you...' Petritz complained. 'What's this all about?'

'It's very simple,' Merlo grinned. 'I just want you to stand behind that building on the dock out of sight, but where you can hear a conversation.'

'Why?'

'You'll know why, once you hear it. Now, come on... we don't have too much time.'

The diamond smuggler was stationed behind the dark ferry office when DuPont walked out on the deserted dock. He went over to where Merlo stood at the very edge.

'Well?' the detective asked. 'You got the information for me about the diamond smugglers?'

'I have something for you right here,' Merlo said, reaching into his pocket. The detective gasped when he saw the wicked-looking knife that Merlo brought out.

'What are you doing?' he gasped.

'Taking care of a rat,' Merlo said coldly. 'You want to know about diamonds? I'll tell you this much. You should have asked someone else. I'm not a stool-pigeon.'

With those words, before the detective could protect himself, Merlo's hand lashed forward. DuPont staggered backwards and fell over the edge of the dock. There was a splash in the water below.

'What are you doing?' Petritz gasped, running up at a fast waddle. 'You killed him!' He looked down at the dark water below, but nothing was visible.

Merlo had a strange smile as he put the knife back into his pocket. 'You heard what he said to me. He wanted me to sell him information on the organisation. That means he knew about me... and he may have known about you and the others. A man like that is dangerous, my friend, even if you tell him nothing.'

'But... but to kill him like — like that!'

Merlo looked down at the water, now smooth and dark and holding its mystery.

'That is the way — the *only* way — to treat people like that. Don't you agree?'

Petritz took a long time to answer, and when he did there was a new tone in his voice.

'Yes. That is the only way to treat them. Now come with me. I have something very important to tell you.'

Petritz had been shocked by the cold-blooded killing and his immense form was dark and silent as they walked back along the dock. He was reflecting on how mercilessly Merlo had pushed the body into the ocean. It had been so frighteningly casual.

When Merlo spoke it was almost as if he had read the diamond smuggler's mind. The big man started, because the words were so close to what he had been thinking.

'Killing that man didn't bother me at all,' Merlo said quietly, 'so it shouldn't upset you. He was a spy, so I did us all a favour by killing him. Now, what was it you wanted to talk to me about?'

'You're going to have a chance to work for the organisation,' Petritz finally said. 'I'll pick you up at your hotel in the morning. Pack your bag, because we are going to be away for a few days.'

'All right,' Merlo answered, knowing better than to ask any questions. 'I'll be waiting for you.'

Merlo returned alone to his hotel, the Majestic, and the calmness of his face did not show any of the feelings that were churning inside him. Only when he was safely in his room did he relax.

He burst out laughing... and he was still laughing when his assistant, Tommy, came in a few moments later. And Tommy joined in the laughter.

'The look on Petritz's face must have been something to see,' Tommy finally said. 'Now can you tell me what this whole thing is about, now that your 'dead' man is safe under lock and key?'

'It's really very simple. As soon as DuPont, the detective I 'killed', talked to me, I suspected that he had been sent by the smugglers as a test — that is why I arranged to meet him later. A call to Interpol proved that he was a private detective, but he was certainly not working for any diamond organisation.'

Tommy's eyebrows rose. 'Then he was a spy for the gem

smugglers? A colleague of Petritz and the rest of the gang?'

'Exactly. That is when I set up the 'murder'. The smugglers wanted to see how I would react to a bribe. So I showed them. I stabbed their spy... except the knife was one of my stage props. The blade slides back into the handle without doing any harm. I changed it a bit by putting a hypodermic needle on the tip, filled with a sleeping drug. The needle hurt a bit, DuPont shouted and grabbed his stomach — then passed out. So I pushed him off the dock with my most evil laugh, knowing that you were there to take over.'

'On - the - spot - Tommy, that's me all right! I had one of those rubber raft things out of sight under the dock and was enjoying a bit of a swim. DuPont splashed in right under my nose, and I had him under the dock with his head on the raft long before anyone looked over. The Interpol car picked him up as soon as you and that elephant-sized smuggler were gone.'

'Well done, Tommy. So right now, DuPont is in a "maximum security" prison and will be allowed to contact no one. The smugglers will think he is dead.'

'Aren't they going to get angry at you for knocking off so many of their men?'

'Maybe — but that's a chance I must take. They are ruthless men, and now they believe I am the same sort, I hope they'll want to use me! I'm going somewhere with Petritz tomorrow. You stay here until I can contact you. Check the post office box twice a day.'

'All right,' Tommy said gloomily. 'But I wish I had some of the fun, too.'


It was a longer trip than Merlo had thought. With Petritz, he boarded a private plane at the airport a few miles down

196

the coast. As they climbed above the clouds, Merlo noted that their course was roughly south-east. A few hours later, there were mountains visible through a break in the clouds, then water again. They must have passed over Italy. Petritz slept most of the way and told him nothing of their destination. But when the plane finally swept down through the cloud cover and Merlo saw islands below, he knew they were somewhere between Turkey and Greece.

Seconds later, the little plane swept down towards a short, bumpy field. The aircraft was unsuited to such a landing strip. With a spine-jarring crash, it slewed round on to a wing as a tyre burst on touch-down. Desperately, the pilot fought with the controls as the machine careered across the ruts and hollows, the rubber tearing off in shreds from the burst tyre. With brakes jammed on, the plane came to a halt in a flurry of dust and flying rocks — a few yards from the ditch at the end of the field.

As they stepped from the plane, Merlo had never been happier to be on firm ground. But he had no time to think. Petritz hurried him over to a waiting car. Then they were careering down a dusty road and through a small town.

'Stop here!' Merlo told the driver, and the man obediently put on the brakes.

'What are you doing?' Petritz asked suspiciously.

'Buying some cigarettes in this hotel,' Merlo answered, already half out of the car. 'Come in with me if you are worried.'

Petritz did come, and looked on with suspicion as Merlo ordered and paid for the cigarettes. They had left the counter and had gone just a few steps when Merlo turned back.

'I forgot matches,' he said loudly enough for the clerk and Petritz to both hear. The clerk reached for the matches as Petritz was still turning. That was the moment when Merlo pressed his elbow against his side and, like magic, an envelope

*The plane came to rest a few yards from the end of the field.*

suddenly appeared in his hand. He dropped it on the counter along with some coins from his change that he had palmed a moment before.

'Mail that, will you please,' he said, just loud enough for the clerk to hear, then turned quickly with the matches so that his body blocked the letter from Petritz's sight.

'Thank you, sir,' the clerk said, looking at the extra coins.

Merlo walked away, face relaxed, but tense as a coiled spring inside. If the clerk mentioned the letter there would be trouble.

But the clerk said nothing as they walked out of the door, and climbing back into the car, some of the strain left Merlo. If the clerk was honest and mailed it, that letter should tell Tommy where he was. There was just a blank piece of paper inside — but the envelope would tell Tommy all he needed to know. The postage stamp would name the country and Merlo hoped for a clear postage mark that would name the town.

Merlo had prepared the letter in his hotel and clipped it into the 'hold-out' up his sleeve. This was a device that strapped on to his arm. When it was 'triggered', a combination of springs and folding metal arms shot the letter down his sleeve and into his hand. Crooked gamblers used such gadgets to produce aces at the right time, while magicians used them to make small objects appear from nowhere.

Now the car was climbing in low gear even higher into the mountains at the north end of the island. There were no buildings here, except for a large, walled building — almost a castle. They swept through a gate in the wall and Merlo saw guards locking it behind them.

'You'll be shown to your room,' Petritz said when they had stopped in the courtyard. 'You will wait there until The Duke is ready to talk to you.'

199

'The Duke? Who is that?' Merlo demanded quickly.

'The man in charge of the organisation. He is known by no other name. Now — take my advice, and don't ask too many questions. People who ask questions lead short lives.'

Merlo thought about this warning as he was shown into a well-furnished bedroom on the second floor. He locked the door and, after a quick look around the room, went to the window. There was a balcony there, and when he stepped out on it he could hear the drone of machinery and a murmur of voices from the next window, not five feet away. It had a balcony, too. There was no one in sight at the other windows in the wall, so, in instant decision, Merlo leaped over the gap and landed lightly on the other balcony.

Inside the room were a number of gem cutting and polishing machines being operated by small, dark men in turbans. This was where the illegal diamonds were cut.

'I warned you not to be too curious,' a chill voice said, and Merlo looked up.

Petritz stood on the balcony above, leaning over, pointing a large revolver at Merlo's head.

'You're not going to shoot me just because I was curious, are you?' Merlo asked, outwardly calm, looking up at the threatening black muzzle of the gun above him.

'Why shouldn't I?' Petritz growled, leaning out from the balcony, the big revolver aimed and unmoving. 'You have disobeyed me, snooped when I warned you not to...'

'Get this straight!' Merlo snapped in icy fury. 'Until The Duke tells me differently, I do just as I please. He is in charge of the organisation — not you! I'm interested in the set-up here and I mean to find out as much about it as I can. If The Duke wants me to trust him, he is going to have to trust *me*!'

'That is for The Duke to decide!' Petritz's fat cheeks were

red and shaking with anger. 'He sent me to get you — so make your excuses to him!'

'Happy to oblige,' Merlo said cheerfully, and, ignoring the man and his threatening gun, he swung smoothly back to his own balcony and into the room.

Petritz was waiting in the hall when Merlo came out, and without a word led him deeper into the large building. They stopped before a giant door of carved mahogany. Petritz knocked twice, then threw the door open without waiting for an answer. He waved Merlo ahead and followed him into the room.

They walked into solid blackness, black in every way. Dark tapestries hung in thick folds from the walls, their midnight fringes brushing the thick, black rug that soaked up their footsteps as they entered. The only light came from black candles set in smoked metal holders, and their light was so weak that it only accented the gloom of the dark chamber. Merlo did not laugh, even smile, at this tomb-like atmosphere: he was far too good a magician not to appreciate a fine set of props.

'You may leave now, Petritz — I will talk to this one alone.'

The voice came from behind a black curtain at the far end of the room and had a strange, muffled quality, as though the speaker were talking through many layers of cloth. Petritz nodded his head and almost bowed at the order. Then he shuffled quickly back through the door. As soon as it was closed, the voice continued:

'I am The Duke. You are the one called Merlo the Magician. It has been reported that you wish to work for me. But I know very little about you.'

'I'm sure you know all about me by now,' Merlo said. To show his calm, he leaned against the wall and folded his arms.

'My history is just what it appears to be. I'm a professional stage magician and have never been anything else — if you don't count the war years, that is. I have never been in jail or been arrested, if that is what is bothering you. Some years back I realised that I was not making enough money from my act, but it made a perfect cover for other activities.'

'What kind of activities?' The Duke's muffled voice asked.

'Smuggling for the most part. My sleight-of-hand skills and my constant travelling make that kind of work childishly easy. But I'm sure you know all this. What do you want me to do — and how much are you willing to pay?'

This time the answering voice had an edge of cold anger.

'It is I who give the orders here and ask the questions — not *you*! I could have you killed...'

'No threats, please,' Merlo said in a highly bored voice. 'If you wanted to kill, you could have done it far more simply and easily than by bringing me to this island hide-away of yours. You want help from me, so it would pay you to be frank. Now that I have seen the diamond cutters and know how you operate here...'

'You have been snooping!'

'I have. I like to know what I am getting into. When I saw those gem cutters wearing turbans I knew you were a man of imagination whom I would enjoy working with. While all the diamond cutters in Europe are licensed and carefully watched, the Orient is a different matter altogether. And the art of gem cutting was invented there. You could train them in the modern style of diamond cutting. They'll do your work for you, they won't ask any questions and won't be able to talk because they don't know any of the local languages.'

There was a long silence before The Duke spoke again.

'You have been very curious, Merlo. I do not know if I like it.'

'You had better learn to like it if we are to work together.

202

I don't go into *anything* blind. I particularly don't like to work with people I cannot see.'

'You will have to grow used to that. No one may see my face. It is forbidden.'

'Is it?' Merlo asked, a tiny smile pulling at the corners of his mouth. 'But if I were to pull the curtains aside...'

'It is forbidden! You will die...'

But even as the muffled voice of The Duke was raised in anger, Merlo was quickly stepping forward. He grasped the curtain in both hands and jerked it to one side.

'I thought it would be like this,' he said. 'It was the way your voice sounded, Duke.'

The Duke was silent. And he wasn't there. In fact he had *never* been there.

The end of the room that had been curtained off was empty and dusty. It contained a single table. On the table was a loudspeaker, a microphone and a small television camera. The camera had been placed behind a hole in the curtain and this was what Merlo had first noticed.

'Your curiosity has gone too far this time,' The Duke's muffled voice rasped from the speaker.

'Has it?' Merlo asked calmly, and paused to light a cigarette. 'I know nothing more than I did before — except for the fact that you are seeing me through that TV gadget and listening to me through the microphone. I still have no idea of your identity, and we can keep it that way if that is the way you must work.'

The Duke's answer was cut off by a sudden hammering on the door. Merlo drew back against the wall as the knocking broke off and the door was flung open. A man in dirty, travel-worn clothes stood there, panting with fatigue. Behind him were two of the guards, armed with rifles. The man stumbled into the room and, for the first time in his life, Merlo lost his self-control. He stared in amazement and his jaw dropped. It just couldn't be!

But it was. The man in the doorway was DuPont, the detective who had been hired by the smugglers to trap Merlo; the man Merlo had 'killed' and sent to a maximum-security Interpol prison. He could not be here — yet he was.

'Duke! Are you here?' DuPont shouted. 'I managed to escape, to warn you — Merlo is a *police spy!* He works for *Interpol...*'

At that moment he saw Merlo and his teeth clenched with anger.

'Still here! So I am not too late. You will suffer before you die!'

DuPont and the armed guards blocked the door — and there was no other way out. Merlo's stomach sank as he realised that he had taken one chance too many. This time there would be no escape.

Merlo dived to the attack, moving a single instant before the man in the doorway.

DuPont tried to turn to face the charge, but there was no time. Merlo hit him with all his weight, knocking the man across the room. This barely slowed his charge. He went on to crash into the door and slam it shut in the surprised faces of the guards before they could follow DuPont through the door.

But their rifles were raised, and if they had the sense to use them, the thick door would offer as little protection as a piece of paper.

The steel slugs would tear through it, and through Merlo's body. He could almost feel their impact as he shot home the heavy bolt and turned the key in the lock... He was diving to get clear of the door when a sharp pain shot through his shoulder.

His first thought was that one of the bullets had hit him so fierce was the agony. But the force of the blow had spu. him about. He had a quick glimpse of the wickedly grinnin DuPont swinging his fist and was just in time to dodge th blow. It whistled by his head, then he had to move back agaii as DuPont forced home the attack.

'Do not kill him, DuPont — I will do that myself after h has been questioned.' The Duke's muffled voice spoke fron the speaker on the table. 'Hurt him all you want, but keep him alive. I'm sending men now to break down the door.'

'You speak and I obey, Duke,' DuPont shouted toward the microphone, and closed in on Merlo.

Merlo dodged another blow and backed away again. Ther was little else he could do. DuPont moved and fought lik a professional boxer — and on each fist he had a savage knuckle-duster with spikes on the outer edge. The single blow that had struck Merlo had half-paralysed his arm. Weaponless as he was, Merlo had no defence against this terrible attack

He turned and ran.

'Come back, you coward!' DuPont shouted. 'We're locked in this room together and you can't get away. Stand and fight...'

DuPont's bragging words ended in a nowl of anger as he saw what Merlo was doing. He had not been running away — he had really been preparing to kill two birds with a single stone. He grabbed the edge of the table and lifted, and the TV and radio apparatus fell crashing to the floor.

'Stop him...' The Duke's voice shouted, then broke off as the loudspeaker smashed.

'That takes care of your mysterious boss,' Merlo said, gasping with pain as he took the weight of the table on his injured arm. He forced his fingers to cling on and to lift — to hold the table clear of the floor while he spun about.

'And that should take care of you,' he gasped as the plunging DuPont crashed into the table and fell.

The table had only knocked the smuggler down, but before he could rise to his feet, Merlo was on top of him. This was no time for fair fighting: there was nothing fair about *this* gang's dealings. Merlo chopped his open hand down. The outer edge caught DuPont on the side of his neck. The smuggler's eyes rolled back in his head and he collapsed.

Merlo wasted no more time on him. With a quick jerk he pulled the black hangings from the wall. It was solid, without openings of any kind. Behind him there was a thud as some heavy object struck the door, and it shuddered. Merlo jumped over the unconscious body on the floor and tried the other wall. The cloth fell away and he saw a window-frame. But the sudden spurt of hope died. The window was bricked and cemented, sealed for ever.

The door shook again to a heavy blow and this time there was a cracking sound as the lock broke. Pieces of metal flew across the room. The bolt still held — but for how long?

When the door went down, the chase would be over and Merlo would be as good as dead. He sprinted to the rear wall, but it was as solid as the others.

Yet it did contain one opening — a small hole no bigger than a man's thumb — that had been pierced through the plaster a foot above the floor. Through the hole ran the wires from the television and radio equipment that allowed The Duke to speak to anyone in the room.

'Good enough!' Merlo thought, and with controlled speed pulled his cigarette case from his pocket and thumbed a hidden release catch.

This thin platinum case was Merlo's constant companion, containing many of the small devices that he used with a magician's skill. It contained plastic pellets of sleeping gas, and it also held a small supply of micro-grenades. One of these tiny bombs fell into his waiting palm now.

Small, black and no bigger than a sixpence, it held almost as much explosive power as a full-sized hand-grenade. It had a three-second fuse in it. Merlo squeezed the fuse, pushed the micro-grenade into the hole in the wall and fell to the floor, to one side.

Behind him there was a crash and a howl of victory from the hallway as the door splintered and almost went down.

'Once more!' a voice shouted — then the words were drowned out in the boom of the explosion.

Dust and smoke billowed and Merlo could just make out a ragged hole that had been blasted through the plaster to an adjoining room.

Without looking behind him, Merlo dived for the hole, and forced himself through it, despite the ragged ends of wood and cement that tore at his clothes. Behind him, the shouts turned to cries of anger as they saw his escape.

The door was open and the room deserted, but against one wall stood a bank of television and radio equipment. This was where The Duke watched and talked to the other room — he could have left only moments before. For one instant, Merlo wondered at the identity of this mysterious leader of the diamond smugglers — then forced the thought from his mind. He could solve this puzzle only *if* he escaped.

There was another door leading from the room, and Merlo tried it, in the hope that he could confuse his trail a bit. It opened easily and revealed a rising stairway. Merlo slipped through, silently locked the door behind him and began noiselessly to climb the stairs.

Muffled shouts echoed from the room he had just left, and someone rattled the knob of the door, then went away. Quicker now, Merlo ran up the stairs, feeling his way in the darkness.

They seemed to go on for ever, and there were no doors at any of the landings. Merlo was gasping for breath when he saw a dim light above him. A few seconds later he had reached the door at the top of the stairs.

Sunlight came in through the keyhole and, when he pressed his eye to it, Merlo could see only blue sky. But waiting solved nothing. Merlo opened the door.

Before him stretched a few feet of sun-blistered tar roofing, and beyond this was a stone parapet. He stepped forward and looked down at an immense drop. The house was built on the very edge of the cliff, and it was a straight drop from the roof to the rocky ground below.

There was a low chuckle behind Merlo, and he spun round to face Petritz and two guards with levelled rifles, who stood facing him across the flat roof.

'Jump,' Petritz said, 'or surrender. It makes no difference. The end will be the same either way.'

Painful, tense seconds ticked by as Merlo stood at the edge of the roof, facing the levelled guns.

What Petritz said was true. A jump to the rocky ground far below would be suicide. Merlo caught a glint of water beyond the far wall of the house. There might be a way to dive into the sea on that side — but he would never reach the edge alive. He would be shot before he was half-way there.

'For once we agree, Petritz,' Merlo said, and forced his taut muscles to relax. He sat down slowly on the parapet. 'The next move, I'm sorry to say, is yours.'

The big smuggler stepped forward, his fat cheeks suddenly burning with anger. His meaty hand lashed out. It hit Merlo full in the face, almost knocking him backwards off the parapet. Then the other hand struck before Merlo could regain his balance. When Merlo straightened up, the smuggler had stepped back again behind the protection of the guns. Merlo was

208

'Jump,' said Petritz, 'or surrender!'

helpless, and knew he was completely at the mercy of Petritz.

'That is my next move,' Petritz said. 'A small sample of what is to come. The Duke wants certain information from you — and I am going to get it. By the time I am through, you will be wishing that you had made the other choice and jumped from this roof when you had the chance.' He waved the guards forward. 'Take him to the cellars.'

Merlo waited for his chance, but there was none. The guards knew what they were doing. One kept his gun pointed while the other handcuffed Merlo's wrists. Then they prodded him at gunpoint towards an open door farther down the roof. Stairs wound down and down, through the building and deep into the earth below. The plastered walls gave way to joined stone, crumbling and dusty with age. Petritz was waiting here, in the damp and musty cellar.

What followed was bad, worse than Merlo had ever imagined pain could be. There was very little Petritz did not know about the terrible art of torture. He worked hard, but he did not wring a single word from Merlo's sealed lips. He asked about Interpol, who their agents were, and how much they knew about this diamond smuggling gang. But he got no answers. Merlo knew that men in pain will say things without meaning to, so he resolved to say nothing. Only once did he break this promise to himself, half-way through the endless night.

'Who is The Duke?' Merlo asked. 'If he came here and asked the questions himself, I might give him some answers.'

'You are curious, aren't you? You know you are going to die, but you would like the answer to this little mystery before you go. You shall not have it. The Duke does not choose to reveal himself to you — or even to me. You will talk, and you will die with your curiosity unsatisfied.'

But Merlo did not talk. That night seemed to go on for ever, yet he did not speak again. Other endless days and nights followed, when Merlo still stubbornly refused to speak.

'Well — it's the third day,' one of the guards said, lighting a fresh cigarette. 'I think you can torture this one for ever and he will never speak. He is that kind.'

'I think you are right,' Petritz agreed, dropping into a chair. 'And I think The Duke knew that in advance. He ordered that if Merlo doesn't talk this time, we're to put him in the water cell.'

'Very good,' the guard nodded. 'A very unpleasant kind of death. But we must be careful. He is a magician and an escape artiste, remember.'

Petritz nodded. 'We will take his shoes, coat, belt — everything that might conceal trickery. We will empty his pockets. He will not escape.'

Handcuffed again, Merlo was dragged down another flight of stone steps, damp and slippery, smelling of the sea. The room below was hollowed out of the solid rock and Petritz pointed to a dark mark half-way up the wall.

'See that line? Down here, we are below the level of the sea — which will flow in through tunnels in the rock. At high tide, the water will reach to that mark. And you will be locked in the water cell which is lower than this floor. Can you imagine what will happen to you?'

Merlo did not bother to answer, nor did he resist when he was pushed across the stones to an opening in the floor. It was covered with a metal grille of thick bars, now held open by the other guard. Below was only blackness, unlit by the single bulb in the ceiling above. Merlo stopped at the edge of the opening, but Petritz laughed and gave him a shove.

'Goodbye, magician — goodbye for ever!'

Merlo struggled to keep his balance as he fell, to keep his legs beneath him and bend his knees for the shock. The water cell was at least 12 feet deep, but there was about 2 feet of water in it, which softened his landing. But he still fell hard, crashing into the water and stone below, struggling to his feet in spite of this new pain.

Above him, the metal grille crashed down and he heard the footsteps retreating across the room. He stood in the rising water, listening, hearing nothing from the chamber above. Only when he was sure he was absolutely alone did his lips separate. He laughed!

'I should thank you, Petritz — you and your boss,' he shouted up into the empty room. The echoes rolled. 'You're really being too kind — locking up an escape artiste in this simple way.' He laughed again, still weak with pain, but happy with the thought that there still might be a slim chance to escape alive.

The handcuffs were in the way and would have to go first. He carefully unbuttoned his shirt and reached up into his armpit. His groping fingers felt for the flesh-coloured piece of sticking plaster that had escaped the notice of his searchers. He worked his fingernail under its edge and carefully tore it loose. Concealed beneath it was a tiny, steel lock-pick! It was only a tiny bit of curled, pointed metal, but, used skilfully, it would open any lock in a matter of seconds.

Deftly inserting it into the lock of the handcuffs, he probed a bit, then pushed and turned. There was a click... and the lock opened. The other hand was freed with the same speed.

'I'll hold on to these,' he said to himself, stuffing the hand-cuffs into the top of his trousers. 'They may be of some use later. And now I'll just look around this water cell to see if there is anything else that might come in handy.'

He talked to himself to stay awake; to combat the tiredness that fogged his brain; to forget for a moment the bruises on his body, stung now by the salt water. The sea was rising swiftly, almost to his chest now. With his fingers, he made a search of the wall, feeling the floor with his feet at the same time. There was nothing. Just slippery rock and water. The metal grille that sealed the cell was far above. He could not reach it. After putting the lock-pick into his mouth so he would not lose it, he tried to climb the wall. There were tiny cracks between the blocks of stone — but they were not big enough. He managed to drag himself a few feet up the wall before his tired fingers could find no grip and he splashed back into the dark water below. It was up to his chin now.

'Just relax,' he told himself. 'Tread water and float and the rising sea will carry me up to the level of the grille.'

The water flowed in slowly through unseen channels and he floated higher and higher. The grille was almost at his fingertips, but he made himself relax a few minutes more until he could grasp it easily. His fingers closed on a bar and he pulled his face to examine the lock, to see how to open it.

A pang of horror shot through him.

'A combination lock!' he gasped. There was no keyhole! It might take hours to open this lock.

Merlo's fingers slipped from the rusty iron of the bar and he slid back into the dark water of the cell.

'I'm not finished yet!' he thought to himself, and his fingers probed the waistband of his trousers. He had a number of interesting devices concealed in his clothing, and the searchers had not found them all. With the lock-pick he tore open the stitches that sealed the waistband, and his probing fingers pulled out a two-foot length of stiff wire with a loop at either end. This was his last ace. If it didn't work, he would drown.

This was no ordinary piece of wire, but a surgical tool known as a Gigli saw. Tiny teeth had been cut into the hard metal, turning it into a saw blade that could cut in any direction. It would cut easily through bone and, given enough time, it could saw through iron or mild steel. But *was* there time? Merlo did not even dare to think about that.

Treading water, he looked up at the grille. The combination lock was concealed behind a metal plate and there was no way to get at it. He might be able to get the saw next to the bolt of the lock, but this was sure to be made of hardened steel and impossible to cut. The hinges! These were two simple rings set into the stone. If he could cut through them, the grille could be lifted free.

Reaching the grille was easier this time, for the rising water in which he swam was almost up to its level. It was easy enough to get the Gigli saw around the hinge pin — but he needed three hands!

'There has to be an answer! I need two hands to use the saw — and at least one more hand to hold on with...'

For a long moment the answer escaped him — until he remembered the handcuffs. Quickly snapping one of the cuffs around his wrist he locked the other one on to a bar of the grille. It hurt, but he could hang from it. And the water held up part of his weight. With slow, strong movements he began pulling back and forth on the blade and it sank slowly into the thick iron.

But had he enough time? He tried to ignore the rising water. Panic would only make death certain — and he had to keep his sawing even and firm.

Slowly, painfully slowly, he worked on. The handcuff chafed his wrist... and his strength was failing. How long could he hold out?

The water reached his chin and the first bar still held. He could no longer see what he was doing, since he had to keep his face pressed through the bars in order to breathe. His moving arms raised waves that washed salt water into his mouth and over his nose.

Then the saw was suddenly loose in his hands — he was

through! When he pushed upwards, the end of the grille lifted. But it was still held by the other hinge and the lock.

Racing against the rising tide, Merlo freed his arm from the handcuff and filled his lungs with air. Then he lowered himself below the water, braced hands and feet against the edge of the pit and pushed up against the bars with his back. Harder and harder, until fire tore at his muscles and his lungs ached...

The lock twisted out of its seat and the grille crashed open. Weakened but victorious, Merlo climbed out of the water-filled cell. Water washed over his ankles as he waded towards the stairs. A half-minute more in the cell and he would have been drowned. Silently, he climbed the stone steps and looked carefully into the room above.

'Empty — except for my clothes!' he breathed, in a delighted whisper.

Most of his gadgets had been taken when the guards had emptied the pockets, but some remained. There was a slight tell-tale bump in the thin shoulder-pad of his jacket, and he opened the seam and squeezed a tiny camera into his hand. It was no bigger than a matchbox, yet the fast film with which it was loaded would take a clear picture in any light — even that of a single candle. The case was waterproof and shock-proof, and the camera in perfect working order. He dressed quickly and bounced the tiny camera in his hand.

'Now to get a little evidence. If I get out of this den alive, I want to be able to come back with the police and clean it out.'

Silently as a ghost, he went up the stairs. Luck was on his side in the deserted hallways. He met no one as he climbed. Two floors above he recognised a doorway. He slipped through it into the room where he had first been left. It was empty, and once more he made the leap between the close balconies.

But this time there was no one to observe him as he stood outside the window and watched the busy, native diamond cutters at work on smuggled gems. The çamera blinked silently as he took careful pictures of the scene. With this film, Interpol would have a perfect case.

Now to find a way out of the building. The shortest way out was from the room where The Duke talked to his men through his TV and radio apparatus. The door was still half-way off its hinges. Through the opening, he could hear the familiar, muffled tones of The Duke.

Merlo risked a single quick look into the room. Four men faced the curtain, their backs to him, receiving instructions about a shipment of diamonds. While he memorised the orders, Merlo held the camera at the opening and took a quick picture. More evidence against The Duke and his gang.

Then the curiosity bug hit him. If The Duke was talking to his men, he must be in the control room. Merlo could see him — find out who he was! It was almost like suicide to go farther into the building, but The Duke's identity would be the final piece of evidence needed to close this case. Even though he was running a terrible risk, Merlo knew that he *had* to do it!

A minute's search found the door to the other wing of the building, and there, before him, was the door he had last seen standing open — the door to the control room. The Duke would be inside. He tried the knob gently, it was unlocked. He turned it...

'It's Merlo! Get him!'

An instant after the shout, a gun was fired and the bullet screamed down the hall. It did not find its mark. Merlo moved at the first sound and was already away from the door and on to the stairs. Someone was coming up from below, so he had to climb. He ran.

There were shouts from below, and the heavy thud of feet coming after him. Ignoring his fatigue and the pain of his aching body, he climbed. He forced his tired muscles to run at top speed. And he stayed ahead of his pursuers. The roof door was ahead.

A man stepped through it, his gun raised and pointing at Merlo's chest.

Merlo hit him, putting all the weight of his body behind a pile-driver punch to the jaw. He had no time to fight, just time for one blow. The man sagged and Merlo was jumping over the fallen body even before it had hit the stairs. The roof ahead was empty. Merlo's hope rose, but his nerves were tingling.

There was a desperate choice to be made. Merlo might find one of the other stairways and go back into the building. Yet he felt in his bones that this would be suicide. He was unarmed and one man against countless others. Was there another way off the roof? He remembered the brief sight of the sea he had had several days before. Could he reach it? He ran for the far edge of the roof.

Far, far below the ocean frothed white as it washed over the fanged rocks of the bay. Could anyone possibly survive such a drop and still have the strength to swim away? Could he dive and miss the rocks? Was the water deep enough to cushion his fall?

Voices roared behind him — dangerously close — he knew he had no choice.

As Merlo leaped from the roof the guns behind him cracked. Bullets screamed past him. None of them came too close, and Merlo scarely noticed them. He was thinking of the sea below, and the waves and rocks rushing towards him. The air tore at him as he struggled to dive straight. If he turned and hit the water sideways, the impact would kill him.

217

The white wall of the building rushed by him, then the cliff, and he was still falling. He would miss the rocks — but there was another danger below he had not counted on. A man in a rowing boat at just the spot where he would enter the water!

The sound of the shots had been heard by the boatman. He looked up. His mouth dropped open with shock when he saw Merlo's body falling straight towards him. He pulled madly at the oars. This was the last thing Merlo saw when he put his arms over his head, his fingers clasped tightly together. His chin was tight against his chest. He would have to hit the water as cleanly as an arrow if he were not to kill himself. *If he missed the boat...*

Then a spine-jarring crash shook his whole body.

Stunned by the blow, his first thought was that he had hit the boat. But the water rushing past told him he had missed. Pressure pushed on his chest and he bent his arms to curve his dive back to the surface. But the water was not deep enough. A deeper blackness crashed into him — the sandy bottom of the cove. The impact drove precious air from his lungs. Fighting against the numbness that wanted to drag him down, Merlo began the slow battle back to the surface.

Above him was the dark shadow of the rowing boat, and he could make out the outline of the boatman leaning over the side. In spite of the burning in his lungs, Merlo forced himself to swim to the other side of the boat, to raise his face silently from the water, and to breathe in the life-giving air without a sound.

'Can you see him?'

The voice floated down from the cliff above. Merlo could not see the speaker, he was covered by the side of the rowing boat. Neither could anyone see him.

'He hit right here!' the boatman shouted. 'I saw him go

down. Just like a rock. Probably broke his neck. The undertow around these rocks will carry his body out to sea.'

'Keep looking!' the voice called from above. 'We must be sure he's dead...'

'He's dead — take my word for it!'

While they talked, the pain slipped from Merlo's body and the ache died from his lungs. He breathed deeply, preparing for a long underwater swim. The entrance to the cove was two hundred yards away. He should be able to swim that without coming up for air. The cove was in shadow. If he swam deep he would not be seen from the house above. Once out of the cove he would be safe.

With a last deep breath of air he slipped beneath the surface again and began to swim.

No ripple disturbed the surface from Merlo's strong, steady movements. The dim shape of the rocks at the entrance of the cove came towards him and he rounded them, staying underwater as long as he could. When he finally surfaced he was safely out of sight behind the cliff.

From out at sea he heard the beat of a powerful engine. When he rose on a wave he caught sight of a big motor-launch. Both her colour and lines indicated she was a war-ship. On the next wave he made out a Greek naval ensign at her stern. Merlo swam towards the boat and wondered what chance had brought her here at this time. He had a feeling it was more than luck.

Merlo was right. When he was close enough to wave, there came an answering shout from the boat — in a familiar voice!

'Tommy Archer!' he laughed, as his assistant reached down to help him from the sea. 'Ugly as your face is, I can't think of a prettier sight at this moment! You made fast time getting here — and brought the navy, too.'

'That was their idea,' Tommy said, helping Merlo into the

boat and wrapping a blanket around him. 'As soon as I got your letter I flew to Athens and talked to the Interpol guy there. He got all excited about the diamond smugglers maybe having an HQ in his country, and everyone wanted to help me. There just happened to be a naval ship on manoeuvres near here.'

'So you found yourself with a naval escort instead of looking around quietly on your own!'

'You said it! They pin-pointed that big building on the cliff as the only spot where the smugglers might be, and we've been sort of keeping an eye on it.'

'Well, you found the right place. They are all in there now. I wonder if the Greek Marines would like to see some action?'

'Like?' Tommy snorted. 'They have been breathing fire! The Interpol man has been working full-time with the cruiser captain to stop them from landing and wiping the island clean!'

'Well, they are going to get their wish!'

Merlo found that Tommy had been right. Holding back the Marines was harder than getting their aid. Each one of the sixty Marines on the ship wanted to be the one to personally stamp out the international diamond smugglers who dared to use a Greek island as the centre for their world racket. They grumbled, but agreed to have the building surrounded by an hour after dark — and not to attack for a quarter of an hour more. This was to give Merlo, Tommy and five rugged Marines a chance to climb the steep part from the sea and to enter the house from the rear.

It was after dark when the rubber dinghy nosed into the dark cove. Merlo led the way, climbing the rough trail by touch alone. Someone coughed at the cliff edge above — a guard. Merlo leapt into silent, lethal action. A few seconds later the guard sighed gently, and one of the Marines helped Merlo ease the unconscious body to the ground.

'Single file in the house,' Merlo whispered. 'Stay close behind me.'

He led his raiders in through a window he opened with the tip of his flick-knife. They were in a dark room, and when Merlo checked the hall outside it was empty also.

Merlo hissed his orders.

'We'll move fast from here on — but try to avoid any extra noise. Keep the guns for last. We have four minutes left before the attack starts and we are going to try and capture The Duke, the leader of this gang; and hold him until the building is taken.'

'Let's go!' Tommy whispered. 'I'm itching for a good brawl.'

'Watch out you don't get stepped on,' one of the big Marines said, picking up the tiny ex-jockey and holding him out at arm's length.

'Three minutes... up the stairs... NOW!'

They went in a silent rush. One of the guards was coming down the stairs. But before he could raise his gun or even shout, a weighted cosh spun through the air and he fell. The attackers ran by a closed door and Merlo stopped them.

'Listen!' he said. Through the dark wood came the muffled tones of The Duke giving orders.

'Two of you stay here,' hissed Merlo. 'There will be some of the gang in this room. The Duke is talking to them through a radio set-up. He must be in the control room. The rest of you come with me.'

They reached the door of the control room exactly at zero hour. Merlo crashed the door open and they plunged in. The Duke's voice went on without change.

The room was *empty!* His voice was coming from the spinning reel of a tape-recorder, playing into a microphone to the other room.

'He knew we were coming!' Tommy shouted. 'He got away!'

In the distance a whistle and scattered shots signalled the beginning of the main attack.

'But the Duke *has* to be here!' Tommy raged. 'There's no possible way he could have known we were coming.'

Merlo looked at his assistant thoughtfully. 'You're right, Tommy,' he said. 'I think there is another reason altogether for this.' He pointed at the tape-recorder playing The Duke's orders into the microphone to the members of the gang in the other room. He could see them on the television screen, six of them, with two familiar figures in the front row.

'Look who we have caught in our trap,' Merlo said. 'Standing there next to Petritz...'

'It looks like that gang-leader from Naples — Ravali. His gang is being arrested right now. Interpol has carefully timed raids in every country to bring in every member of every gang in this ring...'

Shots sounded outside the building as the Marines closed in — then suddenly blasted louder inside the building. They saw the smugglers on the TV screen turn startled faces, then run from the room.

'After them!' Merlo shouted. 'Something has gone wrong.'

When they reached the other room, the smugglers were gone. The two Marines who had been left on guard outside the door were lying the floor. Both had been shot.

'They're still alive,' Merlo said, bending to them.

'Surprised...' one of the wounded Marines gasped. 'Two others... from down the hall... the ones in the room... got away...'

'Don't worry about them,' Merlo said. 'They can't get far. The house is surrounded and they don't know that we are inside with them.'

One Marine was left to bandage and guard the casualties

222

while the rest followed Merlo down the stairs. A crackle of gunfire from the front of the building told them where the smugglers were fighting back.

The building would have been hard to capture if Merlo and his Marines had not been inside. At the first alarm, steel shutters had dropped in front of all the windows, and the smugglers were firing back through gun-slits. They had heavy machine guns and boxes of ammunition. But they had no defence against attack from inside. The Marines cleared out one room after another until they reached the last. Merlo himself stood in the doorway, a captured gun in his hands, pointed and ready.

'Drop the guns and turn around!' he ordered.

'You!' Ravali gasped, mouth open and teeth showing, looking like a trapped rat. 'I should have killed you when I had the chance...'

'Yes,' Merlo agreed, 'you'll have plenty of years in jail to think about that.'

'I must say you had me fooled,' the other man said coolly. It was Petritz. 'But I can get some small pleasure from the fact that you have not captured The Duke — he left here this afternoon!'

'Really?' Merlo laughed. 'A good try — but not good enough. You see, I *have* captured The Duke. Because *you* are The Duke.'

'You're mad,' Petritz said calmly. 'We were together when The Duke talked to us...'

'Easy enough to rig. I know a thing or two about tricks with tape-recorders myself. You recorded the first speech, telling yourself to leave, and turned it on by a concealed switch when we came into the room. Then, while I was answering the prepared questions, you ducked round into the control room and took over from there.'

Petritz looked flabbergasted. 'You cannot prove that. I am only a member of this organisation.'

'You are The Duke. I'll wager that your fingerprints are all over the machines in the control room — and no one else's. As Petritz, you might get a light sentence. As The Duke you will face more than one charge of murder...'

'Lies...' Petritz mumbled in a thick voice, his face suddenly white. He stumbled and leaned against the wall. 'Just lies... my heart...'

'Watch out!' Merlo shouted, but it was too late.

One of the Marines had stepped forward to aid what he thought was a sick man. As he came close, Petritz straightened up with movements astonishingly fast for a man so big. Large hands clutched the Marine, lifted him clear of the floor and sent him crashing into the others. Before they could fight clear of the tangle, Petritz was out of the door and running for the stairs.

'Take him alive if you can!' Merlo shouted, and led the pursuit. Only Tommy and a single Marine followed him; the rest guarded the prisoners.

Petritz started to go down to the ground floor, but hurled himself about at the last instant. He turned and ran upwards instead.

'We have him trapped now,' Merlo shouted as they charged after the escaping man.

They did not gain an inch on him, and they were still a floor below when he banged out through the door on to the roof. Merlo ran out in time to see him dive behind a water tank.

'Surrender, Petritz!' he shouted. 'You don't stand a chance.'

'I do not die — and I do not surrender,' the voice came back. And a bullet thudded into the door near Merlo's head.

'Is there another door to this roof?' the Marine sergeant asked.

'Yes,' Merlo said. 'It comes out on that side, over there...'

'Draw his fire. I'll try and work behind him.' The Marine was gone before Merlo could stop him.

A full moon rode the sky, a tricky light to shoot by, but strong enough to see any detail. Petritz — The Duke — was trapped by their fire, but he must have expected them to try the other stairs. As soon as the other door opened, he jumped into the clear and raced across the roof, towards the side that faced the sea.

A single shot broke the darkness and the running man stumbled, clutching his side. Then he was up again and staggering on to the very edge of the roof.

'Take him!' Merlo shouted as they rushed forward.

'Never!' answered The Duke. Then he was gone. He toppled over the edge of the roof and fell towards the ocean far below, vanishing instantly in the darkness of the night. They looked down at the unseen water, listening to the rumblings of the waves.

'He's dead,' Tommy said. 'The bullet... then the fall...'

'*I* lived,' Merlo said quietly. 'I wonder if we will ever know what happened to him? Know for sure...'

# The Ship That Vanished

When 21-year-old engineering student Vic West and his younger brother, Tony, collected their mail at the British Consulate in Istanbul, Turkey, the first thing that stopped them dead in their tracks was the telegram.

It had been sent from their London home... three days ago! There were also several letters, but these bore old postmarks, and Vic automatically pocketed them.

'Well...' said Tony uneasily, 'I suppose you'd better open it!' At fifteen, Tony was a stocky, red-haired boy with a pleasant but determined face covered in freckles. Only now that face was masked with a worried expression.

Vic was taller, slimmer than his brother, and his legs were long and muscular. He wore khaki shorts and a shirt that had once been white and clean. Now he was frowning, but his numbed fingers made no effort to open the envelope. There was something ominous about the telegram!

Nearly a month ago, Vic and Tony had set out from Blackheath in South London, determined to drive across Europe in a battered, broken-down two-seater sports car.

'Istanbul or bust!' they had boasted to friends. Everyone had said it would be bust, since Vic had bought the car from a college friend for a fiver and a second-hand tennis racket.

But Vic's skill at 'tinkering' with motors had somehow seen them through. Despite a dozen agonising breakdowns in various countries en route, the two-seater had actually brought them within three miles of Istanbul before clanking to a final stop. They had walked the rest of the way.

But now, after having been on the road so long, the two brothers seemed strangely out of place standing inside the air-conditioned, plush-carpeted lobby of the Consulate building. A long, hard journey had given them a somewhat scruffy air, and a blazing sun had burned their skins almost as brown as beans.

Finally, Vic ripped open the envelope and ran his eyes over its contents.

Tony saw the blood drain from his brother's face. 'What is it?' he demanded.

'It's... it's Dad.' Vic's voice was a ghostly whisper.

Tony's eyes widened: 'What about him?'

'He's been lost... with his ship!'

'Lost?' Tony echoed. 'You mean... drowned? The *India Star's* gone down? Don't be silly...'

Vic thrust the telegram at him.

'Here — read it for yourself,' he said roughly.

Tony read it in shocked silence. It was true. The *India Star* had been lost in the Mediterranean on a run to South Africa. There had been no survivors.

It had happened four days ago! It seemed incredible that they had heard nothing about it until now. But the fact was, they'd been out of touch with the world for a month.

Vic was still stunned. 'We've got to get back home,' he stammered.

The Consul did all he could to help when he heard about their trouble.

'I'm sorry you've had such bad news,' he said. 'There's a plane leaving for London in the morning. I could get you on that. And I'll have your car and gear collected and stored here.'

After that there was nothing to do except wait. They were given a room at the Consulate for the night, and baths and food were laid on for them. They were glad to get clean, but they couldn't eat.

Later, the Consul brought them a stack of newspapers. Vic hastily began thumbing through them, hoping to uncover more details of the mystery.

'Let me have a look, too,' said Tony. He took one of the papers from the stack. 'H'mm... not much in this one. The front page is all about an unsolved robbery that happened last month. They got away with bullion worth almost a million pounds! Let's see page two... nope, not there, either!'

Vic thrust another newspaper at his brother. 'Here... this one tells about Dad's ship,' he said.

The affair was as mysterious as it was tragic. The headlines read: BAFFLING DISAPPEARANCE OF STAR LINE VESSEL. MYSTERY OF THE *INDIA STAR*. SHIP HAS VANISHED. NOTHING LIKE IT SINCE THE FAMOUS *MARIE CELESTE*.

The facts were few. The *India Star* had had her engines re-fitted, and had gone on a trial run, which took her through the Mediterranean and down the east coast of Africa as far as Durban. There were no passengers aboard. Just the crew and captain. She had left Malta on schedule, bound for Port Said, but had never arrived there. Somewhere in the Mediterranean she had simply disappeared.

The whole affair was completely baffling. She had radioed no message indicating any trouble, and she had certainly not been lost because of the weather.

'But — how *could* it have happened?' Tony said. 'A ship of over twenty thousand tons doesn't just dissolve into thin air!

'And what's more, Dad was the Star Line's best captain,' Tony went on. He shook his head miserably. 'It just doesn't make sense!'

'Of course it doesn't make sense!' Vic said irritably. It seemed to him that they had been talking about it for hours and getting nowhere at all. 'Of course it doesn't — but it happened just the same!'

Neither of them slept much that night. In the morning, they sat wearily in the car that took them out to Yesilkoy Airport to catch the plane.

Under ordinary circumstances they would have enjoyed the flight, but today they couldn't take any interest in it at all. It was late afternoon when the plane landed at London Airport, in pouring rain.

'Ugh!' Tony said, as they hurried across the tarmac. 'What a day! I could do with a bit of that heat we had out there!'

'Oh, shut up!' Vic exclaimed, turning on him fiercely. 'Why can't you be quiet for a change?'

'O.K,' Tony said. 'Keep your hair on, chum. It's just that if I don't talk, I keep thinking about Dad!'

Vic had kept a small emergency reserve of English money on him throughout their tour, so that they were able to take a taxi from the air terminal right out to their home in Blackheath.

By the time they got there, the rain had become a thick misty drizzle. They could hear ships' sirens as they groped up and down the Thames at Greenwich below them. Under the circumstances, it was an unwelcome sound.

They found their mother pale but composed.

She was overjoyed to see them, of course, and hurried to get them tea while they washed and changed out of their holiday clothes. And over tea she talked so sensibly about the tragedy that both Vic and Tony wondered how she could be so calm.

She wasn't really calm, though. There was something unnatural about her control. They would have been less worried, in a way, if she'd burst into tears. After a while, Vic realised that there was something very strange indeed about her attitude to their father's death. She kept saying: 'If *he's dead*'... and 'If *he doesn't come back*'... as though there was nothing certain about it. Was it just that she wouldn't accept the fact that he was dead? Or — was it something else?

In the end Vic had to speak up.

'Mother...' he said, 'is there something we don't know? Is there anything about — about Dad that you haven't told us?'

Mrs West suddenly became very still. Then she clasped her hands, almost as though she were praying. For the first time she seemed really agitated.

'Vic...' she said, almost in a whisper. 'Yes. Vic... there is... something.'

'Tell us, Mum,' Tony said quietly.

'I...' She was obviously very uncertain what to do. 'I don't know whether I ought to tell you. I... I promised not to tell anyone at all...'

'You can tell us,' Vic said gently.

'Yes,' Mrs West said. 'Yes. And I've got to, because if I don't talk to somebody about it, I shall go mad!' She drew a deep breath, as though what she was about to say would be an unspeakable relief. 'It's just that... well... I'm not really sure that he isn't still alive. And it's not simply because that's what I want to think. I've good reason for what I'm saying!'

Both Vic and Tony stared at her in blank astonishment.

'But...' Vic said. 'What on earth...?'

'You won't tell a soul?'

'Of course we won't,' Tony said. 'You ought to know that, Mum.'

'All right.' Mrs West smoothed back a wisp of dark hair from her forehead. 'Well... of course, I don't *know* whether he's alive or not. But one thing I *do* know — and that is not all the *India Star's* crew went down with her!'

'But she was reported lost with all hands.'

'I know,' Mrs West said. 'But, all the same, there was at least one survivor. One of the young able seamen.'

'How do you know that?' Tony asked.

'Because his mother had a letter from him only a day or two ago.'

Vic drew a sharp breath. 'After the ship disappeared?'

Mrs West nodded. 'Yes,' she said quietly.

Vic frowned. 'Do you know what the letter said?'

'Yes.' His mother paused. 'It was a very strange letter. The boy — his name is Albert Saunders — said he was alive and well, but in fear of his life. He said he'd only written because he knew his mother would be worried, but he begged her not to say anything about it. He said that if it got known that he was alive, "they" would kill him — whoever "they" are. He said he would get home as quickly as he could.' She lifted her hand helplessly. 'That's all.'

Tony leaned forward. 'Where did the letter come from?'

'We don't know. There wasn't any place or date.'

'Postmark?' Vic asked.

Mrs West shook her head. 'Mrs Saunders didn't bring the envelope. She said she'd thrown it away. She didn't think of the postmark. She's a simple soul, and doesn't really understand about things like that.'

'She brought the letter to show you?' Vic said.

'Yes.'

'Why?'

'Because I was the captain's wife. She had to talk to someone about it — just as I've had to tell you.'

Vic looked thoughtful.

'She came to see you,' he said. 'That means she lives somewhere near?' Vic seemed keyed-up, his voice full of urgency.

'Yes,' Mrs West said. 'Just down in Greenwich.'

Vic suddenly got the set look about his jaw that always meant he'd made a decision.

'I'm going to see her,' he said.

Mrs West looked apprehensive. 'Do you think you ought to?' she said. 'After all, I promised...'

Vic reached over and put his hand on hers. 'Now, Mother,' he said, 'don't be silly. We all know what this means. If that chap Saunders is still alive, then Dad may be, too! But he may be in some sort of danger himself. Do you think, knowing that, I'm just going to sit here doing nothing?'

'Or me!' Tony said quickly. He turned to Vic. 'Don't think I'm going to be left out of this! And to start with, if we're going to see Mrs Saunders, why don't we get cracking?'

They left the house shortly afterwards and took a bus down to Greenwich. Mrs Saunders lived at Number 10, Admiral's Walk.

Admiral's Walk turned out to be a narrow alley running parallel with the river and only a few yards from it. There was a timber wharf on the riverside and a row of small, drab cottages on the other. It was getting dark now, and in the rainy twilight the cottages looked depressingly humble and poverty stricken.

They found Number 10 and stopped outside. The curtains were drawn, but a narrow chink of light showed that someone was at home.

Vic had raised his hand to knock when a queer sound came from inside the cottage; a sort of bumping, accompanied by a hoarse gasping.

Vic looked at Tony sharply.

'What the...?' he said. 'What's going on in there?'

He raised his hand again and knocked loudly.

For a moment there was silence inside the cottage. Then there came a high, shrill scream, followed by a heavy thud. Vic wrenched at the handle of the door. It was locked.

'Break it down!' Tony exclaimed.

Vic charged the door. The lock was flimsy and gave at once. They rushed in.

The furniture in the little cottage parlour was in wild disorder. And lying senseless on the floor was an elderly, grey-haired woman.

Vic knelt down at her side. She moaned when he touched her, and tried to move away.

'It's all right,' he told her gently. 'You're safe now.' He pulled out his handkerchief. 'Soak it in cold water, Tony. I want to clean this cut on her forehead.'

'Whoever attacked her got away through the back door.' Tony said, when he returned. 'He left it wide open.'

Five minutes later, Mrs Saunders was sitting in an armchair, her head bandaged.

'Now,' said Vic, 'we can't just leave you here alone. Is there anyone who could come in?'

'There's Mrs Brown next door,' Mrs Saunders said reluctantly. Vic felt that she would have covered up the whole affair if she could.

'Do you know who it was?' Vic asked, as Tony went off to fetch Mrs Brown.

She shook her head. 'No.'

'What did he want?'

'I don't know.'

Vic left it at that. She was in no state to answer questions. Her condition was a mixture of fear and shock. Perhaps she was still a bit stunned. She didn't even seem curious as to who he and Tony were, or how they had happened to be there.

Tony came back with the young Mrs Brown and her husband, a tough, but kindly-looking character.

'We'll come back tomorrow,' Vic told the old lady as they left, relieved at being able to leave her in such good hands.

He and Tony walked up to the bus stop.

'Well — that didn't get us far,' Tony said.

'No,' Vic said grimly, 'except that it proves there's a lot more in the loss of Dad's ship than meets the eye.'

'You think the attack on her was something to do with that? But why go for an old woman?'

'Why?' Vic echoed. 'To stop her talking!'

'You mean he really meant to kill her?'

'That's the most effective way of stopping anyone from talking, isn't it?' Vic said.

When they got home, they didn't tell their mother about the incident at the cottage. There was no point in alarming her. They simply said that they hadn't been able to see Mrs Saunders.


That night Vic lay awake for hours. It was quite apparent now that there was some secret behind the loss of the *India Star*. A secret that someone was prepared to go to any lengths to hide!

He decided to go up and see someone at the London office of the company that owned the *India Star*. After all, he was the son of her captain. They might just possibly tell him something that hadn't been made public.

Vic telephoned soon after breakfast time and asked for an appointment with Mr Robinson, the general manager. Mr Robinson seemed a bit taken aback, but arranged to see Vic at half past three that afternoon.

Vic arrived promptly, and was received by a smart secretary.

234

'Good afternoon, Mr West,' she said politely. 'Sir John won't keep you a moment.'

'Sir John? Vic said. 'But I have an appointment to see Mr Robinson...'

'I know.' The young woman smiled apologetically. 'Unfortunately, Mr Robinson had a sudden call down to the docks, so Sir John thought you might like a word with him instead.' A buzzer sounded on her desk. 'There — he's free now.'

Sir John Pember was Chairman of the Star Line, and a very important figure in shipping circles. He was a tall, grey-haired man with a lean, hard look about him.

'Well?' he said abruptly. 'What can I do for you, young man?'

Vic leaned forward.

'I want to have a word with someone about my father, sir,' he said.

Sir John shook his head.

'A very bad business,' he said. Then his manner changed and he asked, almost sharply: 'But just what did you want a word with someone about?'

Vic drew a deep breath.

'I only wondered,' he said, 'if all the facts about the sinking had been made public.'

Sir John's bushy eyebrows rose.

'I don't understand you,' he said. 'The incident was very fully reported at the time. Why should you think there might be anything further?'

Vic stayed silent. He couldn't mention the letter Mrs Saunders had received from her son.

Sir John broke the uncomfortable pause. 'I'm sorry, my boy, but I'm afraid the facts are quite definite. The *India Star* was lost with all hands.'

On his way home in the train Vic sat frowning thoughtfully.

He knew now that there was something very fishy here — and so did the Star Line people! Otherwise, why had Mr Robinson been so disconcerted when he'd asked to see him? And why had Sir John Pember intervened?

He was quite sure that the general manager hadn't had to go down to the docks. It was simply that Sir John had wanted to see him personally — to find out what he was after.

Vic walked up from the station feeling that the whole thing was extremely odd. And he hadn't been home long, before it began to look odder still...

The Wests were having tea when the doorbell rang, and Tony went to answer it. On the doorstep was an elegant young man wearing a bowler and a dark overcoat.

'I'm so sorry to bother you,' he said. He smoothly produced a card. 'I wonder if I could see Mrs West for a moment?'

Tony glanced at the card. It read: *Vivian Loring, Charles Mansell & Co, Underwriters.*

He showed Mr Loring into the lounge and introduced him. The young man sat down gracefully and accepted a cup of tea.

Vic said sharply: 'You're an underwriter, Mr Loring — an insurance man?'

Loring nodded. 'Yes.' He hesitated. 'Forgive me for raising a painful subject, but I'm inquiring into the disappearance of the *India Star*.'

Vic was suddenly very much on his guard.

'I see,' he said. 'But just why have you come to us?'

'Oh, it's just a routine check, really,' Loring said. 'It's my job to find out if there was anything suspicious about her loss. Naturally it would affect any insurance claim, if there were.'

All at once, Vic felt that this conversation was a strange reversal of the one he had had with Sir John Pember. Then, he'd been the one who had been trying to find out something. Now this Mr Loring was trying to find out something from him.

'But the ship just disappeared with all hands, didn't she?' he said, repeating almost exactly what Sir John had said to him.

Mr Loring smiled, and turned to Mrs West. 'I was wondering if your husband perhaps said anything to you, Mrs West, which might suggest that his last voyage was in any way an unusual one?'

Mrs West shook her head.

'No,' she said. 'It all seemed quite normal.'

Mr Loring stayed for another cup of tea, then politely took his leave. A little later, Vic and Tony set out to call on Mrs Saunders.

Neither Tony nor Mrs West seemed to have thought the insurance man's visit in any way strange, but Vic did.

'That chap,' he said suddenly, as he and Tony walked to the bus. 'I don't think he was an underwriter at all!'

Tony stared at his brother.

'He turned up jolly quickly after my talk with Pember, didn't he?' Vic went on. 'I reckon the Star Line got on to him after I left. And they wouldn't do that if he were an insurance man. They wouldn't do anything to stop their claim getting paid.'

'But what do you think he was, then?' asked Tony.

'I don't know,' Vic said slowly. 'Scotland Yard? M.I.5? Something like that.'

Tony whistled.

'Secret Service stuff!' he exclaimed. 'Then this really could be something big!'

'Yes,' Vic agreed. 'And dangerous!'

When they reached the Admiral's Walk cottage, the door was opened to them by Mrs Brown, who was spending the evening with Mrs Saunders.

Vic wondered how he was going to talk to the old lady

privately, with Mrs Brown there. But the younger woman solved that problem herself.

'Seeing that you're here,' she told Vic, 'I think I'll pop home for a while.'

A minute or so later, Vic and Tony were alone with Mrs Saunders.

He introduced Tony and himself and explained why they were there. The old lady was worried at first, when she realised that they knew about her son's letter, but they quickly reassured her.

'We promise not to tell a soul,' Tony said.

'We might even be able to help,' Vic added. 'May I see the letter?'

Mrs Saunders hesitated, then got up and went across to her sideboard.

'Here it is,' she said, 'and the envelope, too. I hadn't thrown it away after all.'

Vic felt a sudden excitement as he took it.

'The stamp is — Greek!' he said. He took out the letter and handed the envelope to Tony. 'The postmark's very faint — see if you can make it out.'

The letter was an illiterate pencil scrawl on a sheet of cheap paper. It read:

'Dear Mum,

This is just to let you know I'm O.K. in case you're worried over the ship. I am O.K. but laying low in case they get me, as they will if they get to know where I am and all that. I will get home as soon as I can but Mum, please don't tell anybody about me being alive in case it got in the papers or something. Then if they read it they would get me. But don't worry Mum, I am O.K.

Your loving son,
Albert

Vic read the hasty, frightened words twice, then looked across at Tony.

'Any luck?'

'It's somewhere beginning with a P,' Tony said. 'I can't quite...'

'Let me look.' Vic took the envelope. 'Yes — it's a P. And it ends in S. It's... it's Piraeus!'

'That's in Greece, isn't it?' Tony said.

'You bet it is!' Vic exclaimed. 'It's the country's biggest seaport!'

They looked at each other. At last they were getting some clues to the mystery!

Vic put the letter back in the envelope and returned it to the old lady.

'Thank you,' he said. 'That's helped a lot. We'll have to think about it, then we'll let you know if there is anything we can do.' He was anxious to get away now. 'Tony — I think we've bothered Mrs Saunders long enough.'

They were at the door when she stopped them.

'That man who went for me last night,' she said. 'He was only a common workman.'

Vic turned quickly. 'How do you know?'

'Because he dropped his dirty old cap in my kitchen.'

'Have you still got it?'

She left the room and came back a few moments later with a greasy cap.

'I wonder if there's a name in it?' Tony said.

Vic looked in the cap, and started visibly.

'There's a label,' he said. 'The maker's name and a place. The place looks like — Piraeus!'

They left then, and walked up to the bus stop.

'All right,' Vic said grimly. 'We know where the letter came from. We know young Saunders is in hiding there. We know he's in danger — great danger.' He paused. 'And all this means that Dad could be still alive — but in the same sort of fix!'

Tony nodded. 'I've been thinking that myself.'

Vic stopped suddenly.

'O.K.,' he said. 'I've got plenty of time before term starts, so I'm going out there — to see what I can do. I'd never forgive myself if I didn't.'

Tony turned and faced his brother.

'And I'd never forgive you if you didn't let me go with you!' he said. 'Anyway, try and stop me!'

Caught in the rays of the afternoon sun, the giant Boeing airliner looked like a gleaming dart of silver as it droned through the blue, cloudless sky. Far below was the shimmering Mediterranean Sea. The airliner was scheduled to land in one hour at Athens Airport.

Vic and Tony leaned back uneasily in their seats. Since taking off, they had hardly exchanged a word, and now that they were about to land in Greece, gloomy doubts gripped them.

Tony finally broke the silence. Turning to his brother, he asked: 'What happens if we can't find Albert Saunders in Piraeus? What do we do then, Vic?'

'Don't worry,' Vic replied, trying to sound confident. 'We'll find him, and I'm sure he can lead us right to the *India Star* . . . and to Dad!'

Tony swallowed hard and said nothing.

'Besides, we've got Albert Saunders' letter,' Vic added. 'And someone must have wanted it pretty badly to try to kill Albert's mother to get it.'

'Well . . . you've got a point there,' said Tony. 'But I wonder what Albert meant when he wrote *they* were out to get him. Who are they?'

240

Vic's face took on a grim expression. 'I don't know. But whoever they are, I wouldn't be surprised if they were out to get us, too. We've got to be more than careful in Piraeus.'

Vic thought about the letter, which was now safely concealed in the lining of his suitcase. Albert's mother had parted with it reluctantly.

They had paid her a final visit just before flying to Greece. She had shown them a picture of Albert. Then Vic had asked: 'Does he have any identifying marks?'

'Yes, one ... a tattoo,' she said. 'It's on his hand, between his forefinger and thumb. He said he had it done at sea. It looks like a ... snake, and when he moves his fingers, this ... snake opens its mouth — as if it were about to strike!'

Vic's mind was still lingering on this strange tattoo when the voice of the hostess suddenly broke into his thoughts.

'Fasten your seat belts,' she called out. 'We are arriving at Athens Aiport shortly.'

Minutes later the plane was nosing its way earthwards.

From Athens Airport to Piraeus was only a short trip. And, by the time evening fell, the two were finally settled in at the Neptunian Hotel, a small paint-chipped boarding house situated near Piraeus harbour.

'Some place!' said Tony gloomily, as his eyes scanned the four cracked walls lit by a single 40-watt light. The one window, that overlooked the harbour, was thick with grime.

Vic nodded. 'I have the feeling that a cheap hotel like this is the best place to begin our search for Albert. He's laying low somewhere and certainly not in an expensive hotel.'

'But right now, we'd better get some rest,' Vic added. 'Tomorrow, we'll try to find the tugmaster Dad's friend told us about.'

Earlier, Vic had figured that they would need at least one dependable contact in Piraeus. So he and Tony had gone to an old friend of their father's, also a ship's captain, seeking help.

The captain had told them to see a Welshman named Stokey Griffiths, who was tugmaster of a small outfit operating somewhere in Piraeus harbour.

Vic was wondering how to go about locating Griffiths, when a sharp knock sounded at the door. It was their landlord.

'Telephone... someone wants to speak to Vic West,' announced the grubby, sallow-faced man.

Vic walked over to the shabby telephone, mystified. Who on earth knew that they were in Piraeus? He picked up the phone apprehensively. 'Vic West speaking. Who is this?'

The voice at the other end of the line was curt, menacing.

'If you want to know more about the disappearance of the *India Star*, come to the lobby of the Waldoria Hotel in exactly one hour. And bring your brother!'

Then there was a click. The buzzing tone indicated that the connection had been broken.

Vic and Tony decided to risk it. They couldn't come to much harm in the lobby of the Waldoria, which was a large tourist hotel. 'Besides,' as Vic had pointed out to Tony in the taxi which took them there, 'it could be someone genuinely trying to help us.'

They arrived at the Waldoria a little before 8 p.m. and walked into the plush lobby, their hearts pounding tensely. But no one paid any attention to them at all. It was 11 p.m. before they gave up. On the way back to their hotel Vic said bitterly: 'Someone sent us off on this wild goose chase for a reason. I'm sure of it.'

They paid off the cab, unlocked the front door of the

242

Neptunian, and gloomily walked up the dimly-lit staircase which led to their room. Then Tony cried out in surprise: 'Vic... look, our door! I'm sure I locked it.'

Cautioning Tony aside, Vic flung the door wide open. The room was empty! But their luggage was strewn about the floor, and the dresser-drawers were turned upside down. Vic knew at once what the intruder had been searching for.

Swiftly he walked over to his upturned suitcase. He probed the lining desperately. Then at last he turned with despair to his brother. 'They got what they were after,' he said. 'They got Albert's letter!'

Then his voice climbed in key. 'But who are *they*, Tony?'

Tony looked grimly across the room. 'I don't know, Vic. But when we find out, we could be half-way to solving the whole mystery.'

'Come on, Tony! We're going to have a few words with the manager of this hotel. It's not so big that anyone could slip in and take this room apart, unseen and unheard.'

They hurried down the rickety stairs to the manager's office.

The man looked at them in surprise — then broke into a gabble of broken English. He was sweating and plainly frightened. He had heard no evil. He had seen no evil. Even if he had, he certainly wasn't going to talk about it.

Angrily, Vic West gripped his brother's arm. 'We're doing no good here, Tony. Leave him.' And he led the way down the narrow hall, and out into the dark street.

'Where are we going?'

Vic's reply was abrupt. It was brief. 'To find this Stokey Griffiths, the tugmaster Dad's friend told us about. Maybe he can help us.'

'But where do we start looking for him?' Tony said. 'All we know is that he works his ship out of this port. We don't know where he lives when he's ashore. We don't even know the name of his tug.'

'But we've got to do *something*, Tony!' Vic's voice was an unaccustomed growl. The events of the evening had left him very angry. 'We came out here to find Albert Saunders as a first step to discovering what's really happened to Dad and the *India Star*, and that's just what we're going to do. After all, Albert was a seaman on Dad's ship...'

Tony looked at his brother quickly. 'You think Griffiths might know where Albert is?'

'There's chance, isn't there?' Vic was walking so fast that Tony had a job keeping up with him. 'Dad's friend told us that Griffiths has worked out of this port for years, so he's bound to have his ear pretty close to the ground hereabouts. He may have caught wind of some word of Albert.'

They were out on Piraeus's garishly-lit waterfront now. 'And where,' Tony murmured, 'do we start looking for Mr Griffiths?'

'At this end of the waterfront,' his brother told him. 'And, if we have to, we work right through to the other end.'

The other end was several rough and tough miles away.

Neon signs glared. Music from the waterfront cafés was a jangle which ripped at the night. The noise was continuous; fights frequent. This was a hard, vicious neightbourhood. But the brothers were determined.

'*Stokey Griffiths...? You know Stokey Griffiths? Where can we find Stokey Griffiths?*' Vic and Tony asked the same question over and over again. And they kept the question simple to defeat the language barrier. But, for a very long time, it seemed as if they might just as well not have bothered.

Hardly anyone they tried to buttonhole in the rowdy, unruly cafés and bars even troubled to answer. Still the two brothers persisted, working their way from one end of the

244

waterfront to the other. And then, at four o'clock in the morning, when they'd almost given up hope, their dogged persistence suddenly had its reward.

They stopped a squat, barrel-chested, grey-haired and bushy-browed man in the road.

'Stokey Griffiths...? You know Stokey Griffiths?' they asked, wearily. Dawn was breaking and the whole world was growing perceptibly lighter minute by minute. 'You know Stokey Griffiths? Where can we find him? Can you tell us?'

The squat, barrel-chested man stared.

'I'm Stokey Griffiths,' he said, and something akin to deep suspicion thickened the Welsh lilt in his voice. 'Who are you?'

Vic told him, and his expression softened instantly.

'So you're Captain West's boys, are you? I never met your Dad, but I've read about what happened to him and his ship. Terrible thing — disappearing like that, leaving no trace. So many good men... all lost. Terrible!'

Stokey Griffiths sighed and shook his grey head. 'Some mighty strange things happen at sea...'

He sighed again.

Then he said: 'And old Billy Forbes told you to look me up, eh? But why are you here, of all places? And what's the idea of hunting me all the way down the waterfront, eh? You must have spent most of the night at it.'

'We have,' Vic agreed. 'And this is why...'

He told Stokey Griffiths the whole story.

And, as he did so, the little Welshman's expression changed yet again.

It had been suspicious. It had been sympathetic. Now it was very uneasy...

Vic concluded: 'So you see why we just had to come here, and why we must find Albert Saunders. Can you help?'

The Welsh tugmaster cleared his throat nervously. 'I wish

I could, boys. I really do. But I haven't heard a whisper about this fellow Saunders being here in Piraeus.'

Griffiths went on quickly — too quickly — 'I get to know pretty well everything that goes on in this place, and if *I* haven't heard anything about Saunders, you can take it he isn't here. I'd go home if I were you. You're not doing any good here. You...'

Vic sensed the man was afraid. He cut in swiftly: 'Who are you scared of, Mr Griffiths?'

'Me? Scared?' The squat grey-haired little man tried to laugh. It was a mistake. It was horrible. Then the truth flared out. 'You'd do well to be afraid of him, too! He'd eat you for breakfast! Both of you!'

'Who would, Mr Griffiths?'

The tugmaster hesitated; swallowed. He said, unwillingly: 'This is a bad place, believe me. Piraeus is a very bad place... and has been for years... ever since he came here.'

'Who, Mr Griffiths?' Vic West persisted.

'Katz. That's who,' Stokey Griffiths snapped back at him. 'Funny name, isn't it — Katz?' His mouth was grim. 'But. believe me, this gentleman's nothing to laugh at. He's the boss of a hundred rackets. He's clever, and he's utterly ruthless. Anybody that's fool enough to tangle with him...' Griffiths snapped his fingers... 'he's had it!'

He stopped abruptly, and he was sweating. There was a tense silence. Then Vic said slowly: 'And you're afraid of him, Mr Griffiths. You think he's behind everything that's happened to Tony and me since we got here. But you won't help us.'

'...I don't know anything...' the Welshman mumbled. Then his voice climbed. 'But you'd better take my tip. Get out of here... if you stay, you'll only find trouble!'

'You should see our hotel room,' Tony said, dryly. 'We've

already found trouble, and I've a feeling there's more to come!'

'In any case, we're not running away,' Vic added. 'If Katz really is behind everything that's happened to us, he must know something about the strange disappearance of my father's ship. We're staying here until we've got at the truth. And, first, we're going to find Albert Saunders... without your help, Mr Griffiths, if you're really so scared.'

And the squat, middle-aged tugmaster flinched at the scorn in Vic's voice.

'I told you...' he mumbled, '...I don't know anything.' He licked his lips; looked away. Then he suddenly blurted: 'I don't know anything, but... but if you've really made up your minds to commit suicide, go to the island.'

'The island? What island?'

Stokey Griffiths jerked up a hand. 'That one. That one out there.' And he licked his lips, nervously, as though he already regretted having spoken.

All the way along the waterfront, the light was quite bright now, and the sea glittered. Winches were beginning to rattle, coffee was brewing on boats tied up to the quay, and the first Greek dockers had already started the new day's work.

Narrowing their eyes, Vic and Tony could just make out a hazily distant hummock of land out to sea.

Vic swung back to Stokey Griffiths. 'And what will we find there?' he demanded. But the tugmaster just shook his head apprehensively. He wouldn't answer.

'All right. Then how do we get there?'

'A boat... take a boat,' he muttered.

'What boat?'

'I'll show you, but...' Stokey Griffiths' eyes darted this way and that as though he were a frightened mouse.

Then he jerked his hand up again, to point unwillingly. 'There's a boat down there you can borrow. That rowing boat. Come on — quickly — before anyone sees you!'

They went along the quayside, Stokey Griffiths scuttling nervously ahead, and, as they did so, Tony saw a launch coming in over the shimmering sea.

It was a medium-sized launch, and a fast one. It cut through the water, spray flying high from its bows. It came landwards; slowed. It nudged the quay two hundred yards ahead, and a man jumped from the deck to land on the quayside, a line in his hand.

Stokey Griffiths gave a strangled yelp. 'That's one of Katz's men! That's Margolis!' The next moment, he was gone.

He left Tony and Vic staring at the man who had scared him so much.

Margolis...

He was a tough-looking thug type: a hard-bitten, villainous character. He bawled at some men on the quayside and they came hurrying and scurrying with drums of petrol and hastily started loading them on to the launch. Then, beside him, Vic suddenly felt Tony stiffen.

'His hand, Vic!' Tony hissed. 'For Pete's sake, Vic! See it? His hand!'

Margolis had a tattoo on the back of his hand between his forefinger and thumb. It was the same strange and sinister serpent which was tattooed on the hand of Albert Saunders, exactly as it had been described to them in every detail.

'It can't just be coincidence,' Tony whispered. 'It's got to mean *something!* But what?'

Vic wished he knew.

The next moment, Margolis was back on his launch again, half-a-dozen petrol drums loaded aboard. He was running the engine. He was off. The launch roared away, wheeled into a skidding curve, and gathered speed quickly. It headed out to the hazy shape of the distant island.

Vic looked at his brother. 'Come on!' he said urgently. 'We're going, too!'

They reached the boat Stokey had indicated. They scrambled aboard. Tony cast off and, in doing so, stumbled. He nearly fell. Saving himself, he knocked a small anchor over the side.

Vic said disgustedly: 'What are you playing at?'

Tony grabbed the anchor line to pull it in again. It wouldn't move.

His brother snorted. 'Here, give it to me!' He jerked at it. He pulled. Still nothing happened. Steadying himself, he said irritably: 'We'll never get out to the island at this rate! We'll never find Albert...'

But there, abruptly, he stopped.

The line had come up with a rush as he spoke. The anchor had broken surface. And not only the anchor.

Beside him, Vic heard his brother gasp, and he felt the blood drain from his face. He was staring.

Not only the anchor had broken surface, but a body had too! And they had found the man they had gone all the way out to Piraeus to find.

They had found Albert Saunders.

But he wasn't going to help them solve the mystery of the disappearance of their father's ship. He wasn't going to help anybody solve anything.

There he bobbed in the water, slack and inert.

They had found Albert Saunders all right — but Albert Saunders was dead.

His death had been no accident. The water ruffled the edges of a ripped shirt and showed where he had been stabbed.

Vic found his voice, and was not surprised to discover that he sounded hoarse with the shock of it all. He turned to his younger brother as he spoke.

*They had found Albert Saunders!*

'Help me get him ashore, Tony. Then we're going to call the police.'

Tony's face was drained of blood, as he turned to his brother. He looked as though he was in the grip of a nightmare.

'Albert Saunders was one of Dad's crew, and Albert's been murdered. Vic... what about Dad?'

Three quarters of an hour later, Vic and Tony faced a uniformed police officer across a battered desk in the old and decaying police headquarters building not far from Piraeus harbour. The policeman was smooth and sleek, rather oily-looking.

The boys had finished telling their story. This police officer understood English, that much was already established. And he spoke English, too — his own brand of the language — with a self-satisfied purr.

'It was a pity about Albert Saunders,' he was saying now. 'Such a very great pity. But, just the same...'

And his thick-fingered hands fluttered expressively as he gave a strangely delicate shrug.

'...sailors are sailors all the world over,' he said, showing gold teeth in a smooth, smug smile. 'Always getting into trouble, my dear young sirs. This incident will be looked into, of course, as will all the other things you have told me about. But...' and he shrugged again '...I hold out no hope of any early solutions...'

'But what about this character Katz?' Vic West exploded, his patience worn thin. 'And what about this island Stokey Griffiths told us about?'

'Yes, are you going to pull in Katz for questioning?' Tony broke in. 'And when you go out to that island, we want to come with you.'

Well...' suddenly the officer seemed far less sure of himself. He said, rather uncomfortably: 'You must understand, my dear young sirs, that arranging these things takes time...'

He did not finish, for Vic interrupted savagely. 'You mean you're going to do *nothing*,' he raged. Meanwhile, my father's life could be at stake! In fact, I'm darned sure that it is... if he and the rest of his crew haven't been murdered already!'

The fat policeman looked more uncomfortable than ever. 'But you've given me no *proof* of anything at all,' he protested. 'And I can't act without it.'

Abruptly, Vic West swung away. 'Come on, Tony! We'll get no help here!' So saying, he made for the door.

Behind him, the police officer scrambled to his feet. Now he was flustered. 'Be reasonable!' he cried. 'How can I act without proof? And where is the connection between Mister Katz and the island and the disappearance of the *India Star*? Your father's ship vanished hundreds of miles away from the port of Piraeus...'

Vic halted suddenly and wheeled around.

'So it's *Mister* Katz now, is it...? That's very interesting!' And his voice was grim. 'As for the connection you're talking about, it's staring you right in the face... if you really wanted to see it. Albert Saunders was killed here, wasn't he? And we were tipped off to look for him on Katz's island, weren't we? And he'd disappeared when the *India Star* disappeared, hadn't he? He was one of Dad's crew.'

Silence followed Vic's outburst. The boys and the policeman looked at each other.

'Come back here,' he said placatingly. 'Sit down, my dear young sirs. Perhaps something can be done, after all. Maybe...'

But Vic West was moving again, and Tony was with him. 'Too right, something can be done!' Vic flung back over his shoulder. 'And my brother and I are going to do it! If you won't investigate that island... we will!'

'Wait!' Suddenly sweat was beading the policeman's olive-skinned face. 'Wait a minute, my dear young sirs... please!'

But Vic West and his brother had gone.

The policeman was muttering to himself and sweating copiously, as he grabbed the phone on his desk, and dialled swiftly. He heard the receiver being lifted at the other end of the line.

'Popodulis here,' he blurted. He spoke in Greek, the words tumbling out on top of each other in near-frantic haste. 'They have just left me. You will be able to guess where they are going...'

Leaving the police station, Vic West quickly outlined a plan of action.

'We're going out to that island, Tony. But not until it's dark. We'll have a better chance of landing undetected that way. Meantime, we both need some sleep. When we land on the island we've got to be ready for anything.'

But, back at their dingy hotel, sleep was a long time in coming, despite the fact that they were both very tired. Anxious thoughts of their father were never far from their minds. Was he still alive? Would they ever find him?

When they did sleep, it was a light, troubled sleep full of violent dreams.

But when they awoke, it was night...

The boys slipped out of their hotel just before half past eleven.

A chill wind was blowing in off the sea and bringing rain with it. The streets leading down to the waterfront were dark and deserted. There was no moon.

'Couldn't be better!' Vic West muttered. 'Come on. Let's find a boat and get out to that island.'

Swiftly they made their way to the quay.

And they thought that they went unobserved. But they were wrong. Someone had been waiting for them in the dark streets outside their hotel, one hand thrust into a light raincoat pocket. In that hand was a gun.

And now this figure, just a shadow among the shadows, watched the boys' every move.

'We'll take this one!' Vic West gripped his brother's arm as they came abreast of a sleek, powerful looking motor-launch tied up to the quay. There was no one aboard. It was just the job!

Tony West jerked his head round, casting a swift glance behind them and to either side. Rain lashed across the quay and beat against the window of the brightly lit cafés and bars all the way down the deserted waterfront. But he saw no one in the open. Not a single person was in sight.

Tony looked at his brother again and at the launch. He said quickly: 'You know what this is?'

'Of course,' Vic West nodded tautly. 'It's the boat we saw one of Katz's men handling this morning... the thug with that tattoo on his hand. So what about that? Now, come on! You get aboard. I'll cast off. Let's move!'

Tony jumped for the deck of the launch and grabbed up a boat-hook. 'O.K, Vic.'

Vic started to follow him down.

But then, suddenly, so suddenly that neither brother knew for an instant just what was happening, a man lunged across the quay out of nowhere; a tall, lean man in a light raincoat. 'Not so fast!'

The words came out in English and, for Vic, twisting his head to catch a quick glimpse of the man's shadowed face, one shock came hard on the heels of another. For he knew this man. He had met him, even talked to him, back in England. *Vivian Loring*, that was what the man had called himself then.

Now, Vic saw, he was gripping a gun, and its long barrel jutted threateningly at Vic's chest.

254

Vic straightened up slowly. 'What's your game, Loring?' he asked.

'Game...?' Loring laughed, a hard, brittle sound. 'I'm not playing games. That's the whole point. Maybe we'll talk about it. But right now both of you come away from that boat! Come on, jump to it!'

Vic West jumped. But not in the direction Loring expected. He jumped for the deck of the launch.

And as he did so, Tony wheeled to hurl the boat-hook at Vivian Loring.

Vic hadn't re-fastened the mooring lines, and Loring was double-up on the quayside gasping over the boat-hook which had hit him squarely. There was nothing at all to hold the launch back. Caught by the cross-wind and borne by the tide, it swept seawards.

Vic clapped his brother hard on the shoulder. 'Good work!' And he started the engine. Loring hadn't stopped them doing what they'd set out to do, and no one could stop them now. The island, their immediate target, lay somewhere ahead. Vic saw distant lights and set course for them. And, as he did so, he asked himself more than once, what could Loring's game be?

What was the man doing out here in Piraeus? What was he really after? Who was he working for?

But these questions were soon thrust out of mind, for the launch had a fine turn of speed and the once-distant lights were fast looming nearer and nearer.

They were about half a mile from the island when Vic cut off all power.

The launch rushed on in silence, save for the whine of the wind. Gradually its speed slackened as the engine-thrust spent itself. Then the tide took over once more and the launch was carried into the shore.

In the teeth of opposition, alone and unaided, they had reached the mysterious island — Mister Katz's island — and they were safely ashore.

The tide had carried them around the island, away from the lights they had seen out at sea. They moved forward slowly through the windswept darkness, and carefully scaled a steep escarpment which lay directly ahead.

They reached the top, panting — then gasped. And they weren't only gasping for air.

Now they could see the same lights which they had seen earlier. They came from a small huddle of buildings on the crest of the escarpment. But it wasn't these which made Vic and Tony gasp with shock. It was something else away on the right, below them.

Away down there was a steep-sided inlet which very nearly carved the escarpment in two. It was a narrow-mouthed inlet, almost closed to the sea. And in it ...

'Vic ... that's Dad's ship! That's the *India Star!*' Tony blurted.

Vic and Tony had found their father's ship ... which the world had told them was lost for all time.

They had done the impossible. They had found the ship. Surely they must soon find their father?

Tony wanted to say this. But he couldn't get any words out. But someone else did ... suddenly and roughly from right behind them.

'Move just one muscle ...' a voice hissed, '... .and I'll blow you in two!'

Vic and Tony froze in sudden, heart-stopping alarm. The voice grating through the darkness behind them was loaded with menace.

'All right,' it growled. 'Now let's see who you are! Turn around. Slowly, now — slowly! Or I might be tempted to

*Hidden in the steep-sided inlet was the 'India Star'*

shoot — and I'm not bluffing — so do as you're told!'

Slowly Vic and Tony turned.

They saw a man behind them. A man with a gun. And they recognised him instantly.

This was the villainous, brutal-looking thug they had seen on the Piraeus waterfront the previous morning.

And this was the man with the same sinister tattoo of a snake that the murdered Albert Saunders had on his wrist.

He was one of Katz's men. They knew that. They even knew his name. It was Margolis. And the heavy revolver which jutted out of his hand at this moment made him, more than ever, a bad man to cross.

Recognition was mutual, and Margolis started to laugh deep down in his throat. It was a blood-chilling sound.

'Well...!' he said. 'Just look who it is! The West boys. The guys who just have to keep looking for trouble!'

Then he stopped laughing abruptly, and his voice grated at them. 'You've found it this time!'

He jeered: 'Too bad you had to come out here. Too bad — *for you!* All right, so you've discovered that the *India Star* isn't really at the bottom of the Mediterranean Sea. You've actually discovered it's here. Now isn't that marvellous? But what good do you think it's going to do you?'

His gun jerked forward.

'Go on!' he said. 'Get moving! Go on — along that path. The Boss'll be wanting to see you before you finally get what's coming to you.'

And he drove the two brothers ahead of him across the escarpment towards the brightly-lit huddle of buildings they had seen from the sea.

'The big building,' he said. 'Make for that one. And hurry it up! I haven't got all night!'

But, just the same, he never got there.

For, right at that moment, the two brothers went into action. Only one swift glance passed between them. Nothing more was needed.

And what came next was something they'd long rehearsed for such a situation. It was one of the oldest tricks in the world — but it worked.

Margolis was jostling them along. He was right behind them. Then Tony West dropped in his tracks as if he'd been pole-axed. Simultaneously, his brother wheeled.

Margolis tried to stop himself, but couldn't. He was too close. He fell over Tony. And Vic did things, one after the other. He did them so fast that his hands were a blur.

He chopped the big gun out of the thug's grasp, took it out of the air as it fell, reversed it, and used it as a club. He laid it across the back of the gunman's head with a sickening thud. Margolis was already falling. Vic helped him on his way.

Margolis hit the ground with a thud, and stayed there. Tony scrambled to his feet.

'We got him,' he said with some satisfaction.

'Save the crowing till later,' his brother advised. 'We're not out of the wood yet. Far from it. We've found Dad's ship — sure. But where's Dad himself? We don't even know if he's alive. Give me a hand to tie up this character.'

They went to work quickly.

They used the gunman's belt, his handkerchief and his shoe laces. They bound him hand and foot, gagged him and then rolled him well clear of the path and into a deep patch of thorny scrub.

They straightened up, both breathing hard.

'So now what?' said Tony. 'Down to the creek and the *India Star?*'

Vic thrust Margolis's heavy revolver into his waistband, and shook his head in the darkness.

259

'I don't think so. Not right away. Let's not charge madly at this thing. There's too much at stake. My guess is that the *India Star*'s probably crawling with Katz's men, and we don't even know if Dad's down there. We haven't the right to take chances like that.'

Tony started to argue, but Vic cut him short, grimly. 'Let's not allow a couple of small successes to go to our heads, and let's not forget that we're outnumbered here on this island. If we're caught again, chances are we'll be done for, without having helped Dad or anyone else.'

Tony sounded exasperated. He was on a knife-edge of impatience. He wanted to find his father, and find him fast. 'All right,' he growled. 'So what do we do?'

'Go carefully and run no unnecessary risks until we know what's happened to Dad,' Vic told him. 'Blow it, there's so much we don't know! So much we've just got to find out!'

'O.K.,' Tony sighed. 'How do we start?'

Vic jerked his head. 'Màrgolis told us where we can find his boss. In that big building. Presumably it's some sort of head-quarters, and we should find the answers we're looking for.'

They went swiftly but cautiously. Two dark, silent figures slipping stealthily through the night. And as they came close to the big building which Margolis had indicated, they moved more cautiously still.

Light blazed from many of the big building's windows. The boys flitted from shadow to shadow, working their way round. Skirting the light, they made for a dark wall which apparently had no windows.

Then, backs pressed flat to the wall, they held their breath, staring into the night all around them and listening. They heard the pounding of their own hearts and, distantly, a sudden clatter as a winch started up.

'That's down by the *India Star!*' Tony hissed.

'Quiet! There might be someone around,' Vic whispered.

Close at hand, generators were humming, but Vic could hear nothing more.

Slowly, he permitted himself to relax. In his whole field of vision, nothing moved. So far, so good. They had reached their primary target undetected.

Distantly, a second winch clattered into life, joining the first.

'All right,' Vic whispered urgently. 'After you, Tony. Get moving again. Along the wall.'

'But — but those winches...'

'We can do no good down there until we know what's going on! I thought we'd settled all that! Now, will you move!'

Tony moved and Vic followed. Then, suddenly, Tony stopped again, and swung round to grip his brother's arm. 'Vic, there's a window dead ahead, and it's open!'

He was right. And there was no light in the room behind it.

'Let me go first.' Vic slid forward cautiously, stopped beneath the window, then carefully raised his head. The room was empty.

It was some kind of workshop. Vic could see that. Sheet metal and timber was stacked on either side of benches mounted with machine-tools. Light slitted round a door in the opposite wall of the room.

Simultaneously, straining his ears, he heard a far-away mutter of voices from somewhere beyond the door, and he thought he made out the words... *India Star* ... That decided him. He whispered abruptly to Tony, 'I'm going in.'

'Not without me.'

'All right, then. Come on.'

Silently, Vic lifted the window off its stay and swung it wide open. He eased himself through. Tony followed. They crossed the dark workshop stealthily and reached the door.

Vic listened again. The voices were louder now, but still infuriatingly indistinct. All Vic could be certain of was that the *India Star* was being mentioned, and that the voices were speaking in English.

It was enough.

Silently motioning Tony to stand clear, he reached for the door handle and slowly, silently, turned it round. He opened the door an eighth of an inch and peered out through the crack. He saw two men.

They were thirty feet away from him, standing in a brightly-lit room which opened off the other side of a dark corridor. Vic could hear what they were saying quite clearly now, and what he heard made him catch his breath.

They were talking about the *India Star* all right!

One of the men was short, stocky and square, and definitely Asiatic in appearance. The other was big and blubbery, and as white and as bald as a billiard ball. And this man, Vic rapidly gathered, was the sinister Mr Katz.

He looked completely hairless. It seemed to Vic that he was even devoid of eyelashes and eyebrows, but it was the man's eyes which held him — and what he was saying. Mr Katz's eyes were a glaring green, and what he was saying was equally startling.

Now a lot of Vic's unspoken question were answered.

As the big, bald Mr Katz spoke, Vic learned exactly how the *India Star* had vanished without trace on her voyage through the Mediterranean Sea.

She had been hijacked.

And Vic not only learned how it had been done. More important still, he learned why.

British boffins had perfected an apparatus for the detection of atom-powered submarines over immense distances.

This was the first thing Vic West learned that night.

262

And straight away, he knew how deadly such an invention could be in the wrong hands. It could leave Britain defenceless. What it meant was that the British main defence system, soon to be based on the Polaris nuclear submarine, could be rendered useless.

Vic felt ice-cold fingers of apprehension clutch at his heart as, in the room across the dark passageway, the glaringly green-eyed Mr Katz continued to talk to his companion.

For it was immediately obvious that the British boffins' invention had fallen into the hands of potential enemies. Vic was looking at just two of them. The apparatus had been installed in the *India Star* for top-secret trials, and Mr Katz had hijacked the ship on the other man's orders.

One could almost hear some British civil servant stuttering into a phone: 'But — but — but how could they have known? I mean, the whole idea was that no one would ever suspect a small British merchantman of carrying such apparatus or of engaging in top-secret tests of this nature. That was why we chose a civilian ship like the *India Star*. There was a total security blackout on the whole thing into the bargain. So how could they have known?'

How indeed, Vic West wondered. But the fact remained that Katz and his men had hijacked the *India Star* and brought her here. But she wasn't staying here. Not indefinitely. Vic swiftly gathered that, too.

She had been hidden here while the mystery of her sudden and complete disappearance worked itself out, and while new international alarms blew up to replace all mention of the *India Star* on the front pages of the world's Press. That point in time had now been reached.

So soon, very soon, the *India Star* would be sailing again, under a new name and heavily disguised, to an unknown destination.

All this Vic and Tony heard — and more.

They heard enough to know that the stocky and square Asiatic-looking man was without doubt an agent of a foreign power, and that he and Katz were conversing in English simply because neither could speak the other's native tongue.

But then something happened that needed no words, in any language — and Vic and Tony saw it. The Asiatic man was handing money — a lot of money — to Katz. Having served his purpose to the man who had hired him, Katz was now being paid off.

Then something else happened in the brightly-lit room across the dark corridor. Something entirely unexpected by the two watching boys.

A door at the far end of the room opened, and Katz turned his head lazily. Genially, he waved a fat and very white hand — as if to a friend. And into the room walked someone Vic and Tony would have known anywhere, but never as a friend of a merciless crook like Katz.

The man Katz was welcoming now as a friend — and it came as a body blow to Vic and Tony — was no one else but their own father.

Unbelievingly, Vic and Tony saw their father as a traitor to his country. As a friend of the very man who had hijacked his ship and all its top-secret, strategically vital equipment, what else could he be?

Then Katz was speaking. His voice was a fat purr: 'You know how you can help us, Captain. We need to know how to operate the apparatus installed aboard the *India Star*, and you're the only man who can tell us.'

That was the very instant that Vic and Tony's nightmare dissolved.

For they heard their father say bleakly and very clearly: 'You'll get nothing from me!' And, abruptly, Katz dropped his show of friendliness like the mask it really was. His green eyes glittered dangerously. 'We'll see about that!' And the words leapt out in a snarl.

'I've been very gentle with you so far, Captain. I've treated you well. I've exercised considerable patience in the face of your continued refusals to help us. But I'm warning you, I've no more time to waste. I want to know how to operate that apparatus, and I want to know *now!* Tell me — or I'll have it dragged out of you! Don't fool yourself! One way or the other, you're going to talk!'

And on the other side of the dark corridor, the two boys hesitated no longer. They went into action.

Vic had the heavy revolver he'd taken from Margolis. And he would have used it on Katz there and then — if his own father hadn't been standing directly in the line of fire.

Instead, he wrenched the door of the workshop wide open, and he charged recklessly forward, gun in hand, all caution gone. And Tony was hard on his heels.

Both boys were deeply ashamed of their earlier suspicions. Now they had only one thought, to rescue their father. And they burst into the brightly-lit room on the other side of the passageway with the force of an exploding bomb.

Vic saw the amazement cross Katz's face. There was utter disbelief on the face of his own father. And he saw shock on the face of the other man whose Asiatic features he had glimpsed from around the door of the workshop.

Then it happened.

Too late, Vic realised that these three were not alone in the brightly-lit room. There were other men there — Katz's bodyguards, heavily armed. Men who had been leaning against the wall on either side of the door through which he and Tony had just charged; silent men, unmoving, unseen — until now.

Now they lunged forward — and struck.

Vic felt an agonising blow on the back of his head. Simultaneously, the heavy revolver was wrenched from his grasp. He couldn't defend himself. His legs started to buckle beneath him.

He began to go down, and was struck again as he fell. He had a momentary glimpse of horror repacing the expression of incredulity on the face of his father.

And he heard Katz's voice, hollow-sounding, as though reaching him across a vast distance. 'Well, well... your sons couldn't have come at a better time, could they, Captain?' There was malice and mockery in his tone. 'I'm afraid you're going to have to co-operate now — unless you want both your boys killed — slowly...'

The voice faded away.

After that, for Vic West, there was nothing at all — not even despair. He was completely unconscious.

A long time later, he stirred into painful life once again.

A hammer thudded and thumped inside his head. His tongue seemed to be swollen to three times its usual size. He heard himself groan. He tried to move his legs and arms, and he couldn't. He got his eyes open, and it hurt.

He was bound hand and foot. He was sprawled on his back on damp cement directly under an unshaded electric light bulb in some sort of underground room. The light knifed through his eyes and into his brain. He had to wrench his head round and away. Then he saw Tony — and somebody else.

Tony was an inert bundle on the cement floor, unconscious and breathing shallowly. And, not five feet away, the man called Margolis sat on a packing case, trimming his nails with a long, wicked-looking knife, a grin on his face.

It was a grin which made Vic's blood run cold.

'So we've woken up, have we?' Margolis said. 'Isn't that nice... I've been looking forward to having another quiet little chat with you...' He stood up and came closer. He paused, still grinning.

'Where — where's my father?' Vic got out.

'Where d'you think?' Margolis grinned. 'You've been dead to the world for some time. He's on the high seas, of course. Aboard the *India Star* — though she's not called that now. And Mister Katz and the other gentleman are with him. Your father's co-operating a treat.'

Vic's heart sank.

So this was what it had come to. This was all the use he and Tony had been. Their trek across half the world in search of their father had done no good at all. They had only made matters worse.

Margolis' grin grew wider yet as he sat down and resumed trimming his nails with his long, wicked knife.

He said: 'They'll be through the Dardanelles any time now, I should think. Then on across the Sea of Marmara and through the Bosphorus. And after that...'

Looking up and leering at Vic, he slowly drew the back of his knife across his throat.

'Just as soon as they're in the Black Sea,' he said, 'you and your brother will get what's coming to you. Isn't that a laugh? Your father's doing what he is doing to save you, but you're going to die, anyway. I'm going to kill you...'

At that second, Tony started to stir. Margolis, the thug who had been left to guard them, saw it, and grinned.

'He's coming round. He'll be conscious quite soon. Then we can have quite a party,' Margolis said unpleasantly.

'You would interfere, wouldn't you,' he taunted. 'And look where it has got you!'

Tony's eyelids fluttered. He groaned.

'Your interfering was the best thing that could have happened for us!' Margolis jeered. 'It made your father co-operate, and he thinks that will save you. What a laugh.'

The voice went on, now harsh with hate. 'Just as soon as I get word that the ship has reached its destination, I'm going to take care of you — just as Mr Katz will take care of your father when he's learned all he needs.'

Vic heard a horrified gasp, and turned his head quickly. Tony was conscious and staring at Margolis like a rabbit hypnotised by a snake.

The thug laughed shortly. It was an ugly sound, but it broke off abruptly.

For suddenly another voice was heard in the cold, damp underground room. 'Drop that gun and get your hands up high,' it said.

Vic's head jerked around. The mystery man he and his brother knew by the name of Vivian Loring had materialised out of nowhere. And in Loring's hand was a revolver which pointed unwaveringly at Margolis.

Then it happened.

Margolis wrenched round — and fired. And twin explosions blasted the damp, cold air of the room.

Margolis was punched backwards as if by an invisible fist. The wall over Loring's head was jaggedly scarred, but Loring himself was untouched.

Margolis was sprawled on the hard cement floor. He would never move again.

Loring jerked forward quickly to slash Vic's bands with a knife. 'We've got to get out of here!'

He swung round to free Tony. 'Come on! Those shots could bring plenty of trouble this way!'

'Who are you?' Vic West demanded, hurriedly stamping numbed feet and wincing with the sharp pain of returning circulation. 'What do you know about Katz and the *India Star*?'

'I'm an M.I.5 man,' he said. 'Satisfied?'

'M.I.5!' Tony's voice sounded incredulous. But Loring thrust them urgently forward.

'We can talk on the way. For Pete's sake get moving! We've got to get off this island and back to Piraeus — fast!'

Loring hustled them out the cold, underground room and up a flight of stone steps. He halted them at the top in front of a partially open door and left them a moment whilst he swiftly reconnoitred the way ahead.

He returned. 'It seems O.K. Come on!'

He hurried them down a dark corridor, through another door, and then halted them. Again he left them. But bare seconds later he was back. 'All clear. This way!'

Abruptly, they were out in the open air. A fresh breeze was blowing, and the night sky was pale in the east. Dawn was not far away.

Loring said: 'I came in a rowing boat. But we'll go back to Piraeus in the launch you borrowed. Every moment now is vital.'

They found the launch and, within minutes, were heading back to Piraeus at speed.

'What made you come and find us?' Tony shouted above the roar of the powerful engine.

'I knew where you were, didn't I?' Loring said. 'And I'd already guessed most of what I heard that thug telling you before I stepped in just now. That's why I tried to stop you going out to the island. I was afraid that Katz might get his hands on you, and use you to pile pressure on your father.'

Vic West looked at him sharply. 'Then you knew Katz had hijacked the *India Star*?'

'I said I'd guessed it.'

'And you knew Katz was holding Dad as a prisoner out on

the island? You knew the ship was there?' Vic demanded.

Vic's voice climbed. 'Then why didn't you do something about it?'

Loring ignored the bitterness in Vic's voice.

'I'd only finally added everything up half an hour before our last encounter,' he said. 'And I wasn't going out to the island alone. There were arrangements to make. I was taking a posse of Greek policemen with me. You think I could have stopped that boat alone?'

His voice hardened as he went on. 'I did everything I knew to keep you two out of trouble. I even got the Greek police to help — unofficially. That was the only way they *could* help at that stage. But, no, nothing would stop you. I couldn't even stop you myself!'

Vic said dully: 'By the time you'd got to the island with your policemen you'd have been too late, anyway.'

Now the shore line was coming up fast. The waterfront of Piraeus lay dead ahead. Loring said: 'Somehow we've got to stop the *India Star* before it's too late. We might have had a chance at the Dardanelles. But, by now, it will be through into the Sea of Marmara. We'll have another chance as it goes through the Bosphorus. But once it's into the Black Sea...'

He broke off. 'Let's not think about that. Let's hope it never happens.'

At the controls, Vic put the launch alongside the quay. Tony jumped with a rope. Loring leapt after him. 'Come on, both of you!'

He ran down the quay and he ran fast, heading for the harbour-master's office. Tony and Vic overtook him as he reached the door. 'The new name of the ship — the name they've given the *India Star* — did you get it?' he asked.

'No. All Margolis told us was that it had been given a new name and disguised. He...'

'Never mind,' Loring said. 'We'll just have to try to manage without it.' He thrust them ahead of him into the office.

'We'll just have to try to locate the *India Star* without knowing what it's called now.' And they did — commandeering the phone in the harbour-master's office.

They located the *India Star* by a process of elimination. But it took time — too long. When, finally, hours later, Loring swung away from the phone, his face was stricken.

'It's called the *S.S. Sophia* now,' he told Vic and Tony. 'And it's through the Bosphorus... it's into the Black Sea.

Vic and Tony were stunned. It seemed that nothing could save their father now.

But when Vic spoke there was a stubborn note in his voice. 'All right,' he said to Loring, 'so there's little chance of saving Dad now.' His jaw set. 'But we've got to try!'

Loring said worriedly: 'The Turks are our only hope. They are the only people who can reach her now.'

He grabbed up the telephone. 'I'll get on to the British Embassy in Ankara. Maybe they can get the Turks to send out a destroyer.'

Hope swiftly rose — only to fall like a stone. When Loring put down the phone, there was a desperate look on his face.

The Turks were not willing to send a destroyer racing out on an interception course across the Black Sea without proof that the *India Star* was now masquerading as *S.S. Sophia*.

Loring's mouth twisted sourly as he told Vic and Tony the news.

'The ship we're asking them to stop looks nothing like the *India Star*,' he said. 'Katz and his boys have worked overtime to make sure of that. And it's flying a different flag.'

Vic broke the awkward silence that followed. 'Then we've got to get the Turks the proof they want.' He looked up at Loring. 'Get on to Ankara again, and get the Turks to send a destroyer after Dad's ship anyway. They can shadow it, can't they? That's not asking much in the circumstances. And when we get them the proof they need, they can close in without any risk that they're making a mistake.'

Loring snorted with irritation. 'But how are we going to get this proof?'

'Get a helicopter,' Vic said. 'Put Tony and me down on that ship and we'll get all the proof anybody is ever likely to need!'

Loring stared.

Then he said: 'I believe you will, too!' He said it slowly, and with something like real admiration colouring his voice.

After that, he moved fast.

A few hours later, there was a puzzled, worried group of men on the bridge of the disguised *India Star*.

Astern, across the waters of the Black Sea, a Turkish destroyer was coming up fast. And overhead, a helicopter suddenly appeared out of the clouds to circle the ship.

Some of Katz's men started to panic. 'They're coming after us! They're going to stop us!'

Katz screamed abuse at them.

'We're the *S.S. Sophia* ... stop us?' he blustered. 'They wouldn't dare!'

But when he looked at the destroyer a split-second later, the sight was far from reassuring. For the warship's powerful guns were elevated ready to fire and all her men were at battle stations.

Katz started to sweat. His mind raced.

In its disguise, the ship didn't look a bit like the *India Star*. Far from it. He, himself, had seen to that. And all the crew of the *India Star* — except Captain West — had been replaced. They were his own men on board.

If they stood firm and bluffed it out, there were only two

things which could identify this ship as the *India Star*. There were only two things for any boarding party to find. There was the secret atom-submarine detection apparatus, but this could be dismantled swiftly and hidden in the bilges. No Turkish boarding officer would search thoroughly enough to find it.

The only other thing that could identify this ship as the *India Star* was the prisoner — Captain West.

Katz's green eyes narrowed coldly. Under threats against the lives of his two sons, Captain West had been very co-operative. He'd told all he knew about the operation of the secret equipment aboard the ship and it had been duly recorded. Katz had no further use for Captain West.

Abruptly, Katz swung round and barked out a string of orders. Then he swiftly went aft.

And there, in the stand-by wheel-house, directly over the stern and the churning twin screws and safely out of sight of the still circling helicopter, Captain West was dragged before him.

He was securely bound, hand and foot. He was gagged, and loaded with chains. Katz grinned. Once overboard, his prisoner would sink like a stone. His body would never surface to give them away.

Overhead, in the circling helicopter, Vic was fuming and saying impatiently: 'How much longer do we have to wait?'

'Not much longer,' Loring replied. 'Give the destroyer another two or three minutes. We want it really close when we put down on the deck of that ship.'

'But my father's down there!' Vic snapped. 'Every second could count!'

And it did.

Down on the disguised *India Star*, Captain West was bundled forward. Above the thick and choking gag in his mouth he had a brief breath of the salt air he had loved all his life.

He looked at the grinning, merciless faces around him. And he knew this was the end.

Then he heard: 'Goodbye, Captain West!' from the smug, smirking Katz, and the men holding him suddenly swung him up over the stern.

He plunged through space, plummeting down directly above the fast-spinning screws. Then he blacked out.

Up in the helicopter, Vic suddenly crouched forward, wide-eyed and staring. Ice-cold fear gripped his heart.

He had seen the gagged figure pushed into the water sixty feet below and he didn't need to be told who that man was.

He could guess all too well. With terrible certainty, Vic knew that the man plummeting down into the water, and now only split-seconds away from being hacked to pieces by the *India Star's* thundering screws, was his own father.

He had to do something, however desperate and however futile. Even while he knew in his heart that his father hadn't a ghost of a chance, he still had to attempt the impossible and try to save him.

Vic lurched to his feet and lunged for the cabin door. He wrenched it half-open. White as a sheet, Tony leaped up after him. 'No, Vic! You can't do any good! You'll just kill yourself!'

And behind Tony, Loring joined in: 'You can't jump! It would be suicide!'

But, the very next instant, beating away the hands that clutched at him, Vic leapt out into space.

Down he plunged, air screaming past him. Down, down, down, falling fast, like a stone.

This was not the first time he had ever dived into the sea. He was quite a good swimmer. But he'd never attempted a dive from this towering height before. He'd never had cause.

274

He hit the water with an impact that almost drove all the breath out of his body. It stunned him. Then he was below the surface of the sea — ten feet... twenty feet... thirty feet below it, and still plunging down.

He began to fight hard then, to break the momentum that was driving him deeper. He fought for control of his own movements. He fought to choose where he would go; in which direction. He fought hard — and won.

Then, with aching lungs that felt iron-hard and tight, he made for the spot where his father had been hurled overboard from the *India Star*.

Fifty seconds passed... sixty... seventy. And each one seemed like an hour. Lungs close to bursting point now. Vic swam along, frantically searching this way and that.

Whether or not his father had somehow survived the murderous twin screws of the *India Star*, he must be down there. The chains with which he'd been weighted made that quite certain.

But more seconds passed without result and Vic was in agony. He knew he had to surface soon.

And then, quite suddenly, on the sea-bed directly in front of him, he saw a dark, inert mass.

But although it seemed that his father had somehow escaped being mangled and torn by the *India Star's* screws, Vic felt only despair brief moments later as he gazed down upon him. For there was no movement in the still form.

'Dead!' Vic thought brokenly. 'He's dead!'

What happened immediately after that, Vic found hard to remember.

He was conscious only of the fact that he had to get his father to the surface. He would not surface without him.

He struggled with chains. He wrestled with ropes. He was only half-aware of what he was doing. The blood sang through his head, and he saw strange shapes and fierce, blazing colours. But then, suddenly, his father was free of the chains and rope.

And Vic took him upwards; broke surface with him. The light blinded Vic. Then he had a confused impression of a racketing noise overhead, and water flashing off oars nearby. He saw faces above him and the side of a small boat.

Then muscular arms reached down for him and for his father's body. Suddenly, there was a roaring explosion. After that, Vic knew no more.

What seemed like an eternity later, he awoke to find himself a patient in hospital. And the first people he saw on opening his eyes were his brother Tony and Vivian Loring, the M.I.5 man. Both of them stood at the righthand side of his bed.

And both of them were looking strangely cheerful. Vic couldn't understand it. What had they got to be cheerful about? It seemed to him now that his brilliant idea of chasing after the *India Star* in a helicopter had ended in disastrous failure. Hadn't his father been killed as a direct result of it?

Loring said brightly: 'You'll be very pleased to hear that Britain's anti-submarine secrets are safe.'

Vic only grunted.

Loring said doubtfully: 'Well you *should* be pleased...' He regained his confidence. 'And you should be very proud, too. You did a fine job. If you hadn't twisted my arm to go after the *India Star* like we did, Katz would have won the whole game hands down.'

Vic closed his eyes. There was a lump in his throat. A game, eh? That's all it was? Some game — with his father dead at the end of it!

Tony chipped in excitedly: 'And you should have seen that Turkish destroyer, Vic! You really should! As soon as her skipper realised what was happening, he put a shot across the bows of the *India Star* and forced it to heave to. Then he sent a boarding party aboard. The ship's back here in Istanbul now, and Katz and his gang have all been thrown into gaol...'

'...And we've cleaned up Piraeus,' said Loring. 'And one or two other ports as well. Katz was running an international crime syndicate among sailors and dockers all over the Levant and the Middle East. Gun-running, smuggling drugs... all that was under his control. He had quite a big organisation. That's what those tattoo marks you spotted were all about. They were an easy means of identification for members of his gang. They showed Katz's men who their friends were. Needless to say, we found those tattoo marks very handy as well. They've helped the authorities make a lot of arrests.'

Tony said: 'That seaman, Albert Saunders, must have been a member of the gang, specially put aboard the *India Star* to help in the hijacking. Though, of course, his mother never knew that...'

'And we'll never know why the gang turned against him,' Loring added.

The voices droned on. Tony was talking cheerfully, saying how pleased Vic should be the way everything had ended. '...and it's all thanks to you, Vic...'

Vic could hardly believe his ears. He barely trusted himself to speak.

'Yes, it's all thanks to me,' he said thickly. 'All thanks to me... that Dad's dead!'

There was a sudden taut silence.

Then, out of nowhere, a voice said very quietly: 'No, Son, you've got it wrong. It's all thanks to you that Dad *isn't* dead!'

And, jerking his head round, and opening blurred eyes unbelievingly, Vic saw at last that his bed was not the only one in the hospital room. Ten feet away to the left, in a far corner, there was another. And in that bed, lying back and regarding him steadily, was his father.

Vic choked out only one word. It was: 'Dad!'

Tony grinned and; suddenly, Vic was grinning too — almost insanely. His joy was so great.

Captain West said: 'I'll never know how I missed the ship's propellers, and I'll never know how the Turks managed to pump most of the Black Sea out of me in time. But here I am — alive and kicking. I've just sent your mother a cable to say we'll all be home in a couple of days, and to put the kettle on for us.'

# Adventure Incorporated

*by*
JAMES KENNER

Bob Hunter did not believe in ghosts! That was kid's stuff! And yet he could not rid himself of the cold, clammy shivers racing up and down his spine. It was after midnight now, and the prospect of having to spend an hour alone in a gloomy, deserted manor house was certainly not appealing.

They would soon be there! The shiny, hotted-up Model-A Ford thundered down Pacific Coast Highway, No 101 — its dual exhausts screaming like jet rockets, headlamps slashing through the darkness.

Bob was in the rumble-seat, practically hanging on for dear life. The wind howled past, tearing at his dark, wavy hair, coldly penetrating his blazer.

'What a holiday this is turning out to be,' he thought glumly. 'To come all the way from Devonshire — just to meet up with three American maniacs!'

One of these 'maniacs' was Bob's happy-go-lucky cousin, Stuart Dodd, who silently shared the rumble-seat with him.

It was Stu who had first written to invite Bob to spend a month in California. At first it seemed an impossible offer. Bob hadn't the money for a trip like that. But cousin Stu provided the solution. His father was an airline pilot on the trans-continental route. A free flight for Bob had taken a lot of arranging — but it had been done!

Yet now Bob was beginning to wonder if the trip hadn't been a mistake.

The Americans seemed so different from his friends back

home in Devon, if cousin Stu and his friends were typical examples.

Somehow, the three of them had managed to rope in Bob on this dare. Cousin Stu had said sympathetically: 'If you want to join our club, you'll have to pass the initiation test.'

Spending an hour inside a spooky house high on a cliff was to be the test. Bob hadn't exactly fancied the idea, but he was determined to see it through. Backing down would have implied cowardice.

A sudden swerve of the Ford threw these thoughts from Bob's mind. Its tyres screamed a tortured protest as it hurtled off the main highway into a dark, lonely side road.

Bob did not scare easily. But this particular place, so he had heard, had a frightening reputation. It was boarded-up; empty. No one had lived there for years. But there were tales of ghostly figures, flashing lights, screams. And not long ago, a body had been found nearby, apparently cast up from the ocean.

Now the car was straining up a winding road, climbing higher and higher. Looking out to his left and down, Bob could make out the dim outline of the swirling Pacific.

They stopped only inches from the edge of a steep incline. From below came the roar of breaking surf. It was a lonely spot, hidden from the highway by thick shrubbery.

Bob climbed out of the rumble seat and found himself being scrutinised by the other three.

Mick Kelly stood nearest him. Mick was the proud owner of the car. A gangling youth of Irish descent, he was temperamental, but big-hearted, too.

Alongside Mick was 'Fats' Connegan, and when it came to eating capacity, no one was Fats' equal.

The third member — and leader of this strange trio — was cousin Stu. An energetic, ambitious young man who was constantly getting in and out of scrapes, he seemed to live for excitement.

The three were members of the club known as *Adventure Incorporated*. This was the club that Bob was about to be initiated into.

According to the club charter the purpose of membership was: '... to devote all available spare time and energy seeking out adventure.'

Membership in such a club called for a certain amount of bold, rugged courage. And, naturally, each prospective member had to be tested.

Now it was Stu who spoke first. 'Are you ready?'

Bob nodded, and found himself wishing that he had never heard of *Adventure Incorporated*.

Stu continued: 'It's too risky to attempt breaking in from the front, so you must get in at the back. You'll have to scale this ravine. About half-way down you'll find a narrow footpath. That will lead you directly to the place.'

Mick broke in with a hurried whisper: 'It's quarter to one now. Don't forget... no matter what you see, or hear... or whatever happens... you've got to stay inside a full hour. According to the legend, the ghost walks from one to two.'

Fats added pleasantly: 'If you're still alive by two o'clock, that means you've made it. You'll be a member of the club.'

A minute later Bob was on the move. Gingerly, using a rope anchored to a tree, he lowered himself down the face of the ravine. A slip now would be dangerous. The sea below, broken by black, shadowy rocks, thundered ominously.

Suddenly, the gravel beneath his feet gave way. He dangled in mid air, with only the rope to support him. Sweating, he managed to get a foothold again.

It was a slow, painful descent. But at last he found himself standing on what appeared to be solid ground. Actually, it was a ridge of some sort and it was only a few feet wide.

The flashlight they had given him provided only a dim, wavering beam. He was terribly alone now, and, as the moon vanished behind the clouds, darkness folded in on him.

Bob shivered. At that moment all the evil stories and legends about this strange house seemed true. But he was not going to back out, no matter what happened. Mustering up his courage, he drew nearer the house. Then his blood froze in his veins. Coming from inside this uninhabited house was a strange, flitting light — its rays clearly visible through the dusty slats of window which had long ago been boarded up.

Someone... or *something* was inside. And Bob would have to face it!

Switching off his torch, he stood rooted in the darkness, staring up at the gloomy, forbidding house.

The ocean was just below him now, and he could hear the slap of water against rock. But it was the mysterious flashing light that held his attention.

He swallowed nervously. Stu had assured him the house would be empty.

The light continued blinking in a pattern that repeated itself. There was something odd about it, and a moment later Bob realised just what it was. The light was signalling in Morse code. The frantic message was the same: SOS... SOS... SOS...

But why? What could it possibly mean? There was only one way to find out. Carefully picking his way along the stony footpath, Bob approached the back of the house. He found a door and gently tried the lock. It was bolted.

He would have to enter through a window. Cautiously he tugged at one of the slats barricading the broken pane. With an agonising creak, it gave way.

282

Forcing an opening large enough to crawl through, he climbed into the house, his heart pounding fiercely.

The darkness inside made him shudder. A dank, musty odour filled his nostrils. He flicked on his torch and looked round the room.

Bulky, sinister objects loomed up in the shadows. He realised that it was furniture — long in disuse, and now covered over by protective sheets. A thick layer of dust had settled over everything.

Bob's mouth felt dry. He found himself wishing that he was safely back in Devonshire.

Getting involved in a crazy initiation stunt to join his cousin's gang was one thing — but *this* was different. A foreboding sense of danger swept over him: warned him to be on guard.

He frowned. He wasn't going to back down now. He had to get upstairs, had to find the answer to this mystery.

The beam of light picked out a door on the other side of the room. Scarcely daring to breathe, he inched his way over and slowly opened it.

From down the hallway he heard voices. A door, slightly ajar, showed light. Bob flicked off his torch.

He crept down the hallway and, crouching behind the door, held his breath, listening. He heard someone say gruffly: 'The boss will be here soon. Then we'll get rid of Harcourt, and that'll be the end of project R. And I, for one, won't be sorry. This house gives me the creeps!'

Another voice replied: 'Me too. But you couldn't find a better place for this job — and we're being highly paid, remember.'

Bob leaned forward to catch a glimpse of the speaker through the slightly opened door — and, as he shifted his weight, the floorboard creaked.

'What was that?' the gruff voice asked.

'I thought I heard something. Better take a look!'

Bob's heart thudded against his ribs as he pressed himself into an angle in the wall, desperately hoping he would be concealed in the shadows. The door was swung open and a swarthy fat man poked his head out into the hallway.

Bob held his breath. For one nerve-racking moment, it seemed as though the man's stare rested right on him. But then he turned away, walked down the hallway a bit, and finally returned.

'No one there,' he said. 'Probably the wind on a shutter.' Bob sighed in relief as the door slammed shut. But now it was impossible for him to overhear anything else.

Perhaps the answer to all this was the flashing light upstairs. He crept down the hallway, and tiptoed up a winding staircase at the other end, testing every tread before putting his foot down. Every step was an agony. He dared not use his torch. By the time he had reached the second floor he was soaked in sweat.

He paused and looked around. There were several doors. But which one led to the room with the flickering light?

The padlock gave him the clue. Why should a door be padlocked — unless there was something inside to hide? The key rested in the lock, and slowly he twisted it.

The lock clicked open. He took a deep breath, and edged the door open. What he saw shocked him!

A man was handcuffed by one arm to a bed which he had succeeded in dragging to the boarded-up window. His hair was unkempt. His clothing was dirty, dishevelled. He was thin and gaunt-faced, with a week-old beard.

He was too engrossed in what he was doing to notice Bob. With his one free hand he had managed to grip a lighted candle. He was using it to signal.

As Bob entered the room, the man whirled round in alarm.

His uneasy eyes swept over Bob. Then, at last, he spoke harshly. 'What do you want? Who are you?'

Bob approached. 'I — I saw your signal...' he began. The man cut him off. A gleam of hope traced its way across his face. He put a wary finger up to his lips. 'Shhh... they'll hear. Listen... you can help! This is urgent. Do you understand?' He spoke in a rasping whisper. It was obvious that he was desperate.

'One person isn't enough... There are too many of them... And they'll stop at nothing. You must bring help! Call the police! And hurry... or it'll be too late!'

It was no time for asking questions, but Bob couldn't stop himself from blurting out: 'Who are you, anyhow? And why are you being kept a prisoner here?'

The man was about to answer, when suddenly his eyes opened wide, registered a look of stark fear. Frantically he gestured towards the doorway, which was now half-open.

Then a voice boomed out: 'You're too nosey, kid. You've got yourself into trouble now... real trouble.'

Bob whirled round.

A gigantic figure was framed in the doorway. The man seemed at least eight feet tall, and his arms dangled down, almost as if they belonged to a gorilla.

Bob shivered. The voice said coldly: 'Yes, kid. I've got to kill you!'

Bob's blood froze. But it was the prisoner who was the first to act. His free hand still clutched the candle. Suddenly, he flung it to the floor, plunging the room into darkness.

'Run — run for your life,' he shouted desperately.

Bob threw himself towards the half-open door, then he was out on the landing and groping desperately towards the staircase, not daring to use his torch.

'Stop him!' the giant's angry voice boomed out just a few

yards away. And an answer came from the hallway below.

Bob was trapped. A torch flicked on, its glaring beam spotlighting him on the staircase.

There were two men waiting. Bob's chances of getting past them were slim. He reversed his direction, and lost the searching torch beam at a bend in the stairs.

The giant was now standing on the landing, closing in. But somehow Bob managed to slip past his groping arms in the darkness, and he began to race towards the third floor.

Footsteps pounded on the stairs behind him, and the searching beam of light again swept across his path. There was a sharp crack —the report of a revolver. A bullet buried itself in the plaster just above Bob's head.

He had to keep moving, to find a way out. These men were not playing games! At the third floor landing, Bob's heart was pounding like a sledge-hammer. The first door he tried was locked. He clenched his fist in dismay.

The footsteps grew louder behind him. The second door was open! Flinging himself into the room, he flicked on his torch. The door had a bolt, and he slid it forward.

It would give him a minute, anyhow, to gather his frantic thoughts. A second later fists pounded at the door. 'Open up,' someone shouted.

Bob was already surveying the boarded window. It was the only way out. Desperately, he ripped out the slats. The cold rush of air gave him new hope. He peered down. Below, the ocean swirled past, lashing the jagged rocks along the coastline.

He had only one choice. The thought made him close his eyes and shudder. He was a good swimmer — but . . .

A loud crash rang out, as the door was wrenched from its hinges. Someone called out viciously: 'Get him!' A pistol shot rang out.

But it was too late. Bob was plunging down, twisting wildly, towards the water below.

He struck the surface with shattering impact. Momentarily, he blacked out. A wave of pain swept over him. He felt himself being dragged down ... down ... down ... Then, slowly, the will to live surged up in him. He fought the terrible numbness, forced himself to think, to fight ...

His lungs began to ache. He made himself swim underwater, intent on putting distance between himself and the house.

Finally, with his lungs at bursting point, he broke surface. He gasped the cool, delicious air, and half-expected to feel a bullet crashing into his brain. But there was only silence — probably the gunmen had given him up for dead!

Wearily he swam to shore, where, at last, he rejoined his three companions. They eyed him incredulously. Stu was the first to rush over. A frown darkened his face. 'What were all those strange noises we heard? Sounded like gunshots ...'

Breathlessly, Bob told them.

'This is really serious! I think we'd better get the police,' Mick gasped.

Stu shook his head. 'Nothing doing! What do we call ourselves *Adventure Incorporated* for? This sound like *real* adventure to me. I think we ought to follow it through!'

The others agreed, then Stu continued: 'The first thing we will do is to get over to that house. Arm yourselves with hefty sticks, lads! And hurry it up!'

Bob showed them the way. Twenty minutes later they were standing in the room where the prisoner had once been kept. But now it was empty!

'I just don't understand it,' Bob said at last. 'Those bullet holes are still in the wall ... so I know that I wasn't dreaming. But what's happened to the prisoner?'

'Look — over there!' said Fats suddenly. He had been

standing near the bed, and he pointed towards the floor. There, freshly written in the dust, was the sprawling word SANTA...

'It's a clue of some kind,' said Mick. 'But what does it mean?'

Stu glanced up at Bob. 'Tell me... you say the first man who attacked you was big. Very big... almost like a giant.'

'That's right,' said Bob.

Stu paused, and then went on. 'Come on... we're going to tackle a giant — and I think I know where to find him!'

Torch in hand, Stu stepped over to the spot where the word was traced in the dust. Bob, Mick and Fats waited for him to explain.

Stu scowled, then finally spoke up: 'See how the last letter in the word is clipped short. Obviously, the prisoner meant to write more... but didn't have time. Someone dragged him out of here in a big hurry...'

Stu slid his torch beam along the floor. It came to rest on an enormous footprint outlined in the dust.

Fats sucked in his breath. 'Holy smoke... must be a size 20! Only a... *giant* could wear a shoe like that!'

Stu broke in: 'I'm pretty sure the prisoner meant to write a second word to follow Santa... and my guess is that the word was Monica! That's what the prisoner wanted to say: Santa Monica!'

'Of course... the fun fair at Santa Monica!' Mick exclaimed. 'The freak show there would make a perfect hideout for a giant. No one would even notice him!'

Stu glanced at his watch. 'We've got to hurry,' he said. 'It's nearly two in the morning now. The place closes down at three.'

'Hey,' said Fats. 'What about the prisoner? Maybe they've rid themselves of him by now... dumped him into the ocean!'

'I don't think so,' said Bob. 'They obviously want him alive.

If I could only remember his name... it was something like Hancard, or Hocart...'

He frowned and added: 'Anyhow, I think Stu's right! Let's track down that giant. Maybe he'll lead us to the poor prisoner.'

Stu turned towards Bob.

'Oh, yes... about your test,' he said, with a friendly grin. 'You've passed it! After what you went through, you deserve to be a member of *Adventure Incorporated*! Right, gang?'

'Right!' chorused the others.

Bob was pleased. But a grim thought continued to nag at the back of his mind as they hurried back to Mick's car. Those thugs who had chased him earlier were playing for keeps. They would show no mercy. The trail, wherever it led, would be fraught with danger!

Bob sat in front. His desperate plunge into the ocean had drenched him to the skin. Now, as they drove off, he began to shiver. Luckily, Stu's house was on the way. They stopped there just long enough for Bob to change his clothes.

It was 2.45 a.m. when they reached the Santa Monica fun fair. Mick had no parking trouble — many of the fun-makers had already gone home.

The four of them hurried down a cement promenade which faced the ocean. Bob glimpsed rows of wooden stands lying off in the shadows. Paint-chipped signs on top stated: 'Hamburgers', 'Hot Dogs', 'Win a Live Goldfish', 'Try Your Luck — Three Darts for 25 cents...'

Most of the stands along the promenade had now closed down for the night. Beyond, looming up into the sky, was an enormous circus tent. It, too, was closed. Occasionally one of the animals caged inside the tent would let loose a mournful roar.

The main part of the fun fair was situated on a wide pier,

jutting out over the ocean. Here, there were still remnants of life.

Coloured lights winked on and off, barkers shouted, bells clanged, people laughed and bustled about. A roller-coaster rocketed down a nearby track. The tense, excited screams of the passengers riding it tore through the night air.

Bob and the others hurried towards the tent that housed the freak show — only to meet with bitter disappointment.

'Sorry, boys,' said the tall, sallow-faced man guarding the entrance. 'Show's over. Come back tomorrow!'

'Darn!' said Mick, as they moved away. 'That's bad luck!'

'What now?' asked Fats.

'We'll take a general look around,' said Bob. 'Maybe we'll hear or spot something.'

Stu nodded. 'Good idea!'

Just then a swarthy, sinister face peered out from around the corner of the freak show tent. A pair of cold, scrutinising eyes slid over Bob. Then... the face vanished. Bob had failed to notice it.

The boys moved on. Fats suggested they start by investigating a hot dog stand. The others quickly reminded him they had more important things to do.

But a half-hour's relentless search failed to turn up anything.

Bob was weary now, discouraged. The hectic events of the night seemed to have caught up with him at last.

Now, even the stands and rides on the pier were closing down. One by one the twinkling lights gave way to darkness. The crowd, which had thinned out, headed homeward.

Suddenly Mick pointed. 'Look!' he said, 'that tent over there.'

Bob turned. His eyes took in a large tent. A shabbily-painted sign hanging above stated: MADAM TANYA — FORTUNE TELLER — Seances, Crystal Ball Readings,

Advice, Predictions. Reasonable prices. Everyone welcome.

'C'mon,' said Mick, earnestly, 'we're going in there.'

Stu scowled. 'Are you crazy? Fortune tellers are a lot of hooey!'

But Mick was insistent. The blood of his Irish ancestors pulsed through his veins. For centuries they had accepted superstition.

Fats nodded. 'Why not? It's the only place open now.'

Stu shrugged his shoulders. 'All right — but just wait and see. I'll bet she's a fake!'

The four of them walked over to the tent. The entrance was pitch-black.

Bob shuddered. He could not shake off the horrible feeling that something was wrong — that danger was near.

Mick called out cautiously: 'Is anyone here?' There was no reply.

The heavy silence was broken by Fats. 'I don't think I like this place,' he whispered. 'Let's get out while we can!'

'Shhhh,' said Mick. 'I can hear something.'

Bob looked up to see a tall, unsmiling woman in a flowing gown suddenly appear. Her eyes were dark, mysterious.

'I am Madam Tanya, foreseer of the future,' she said in deep, sombre tones. 'What do you want?'

Mick spoke confidently. 'Can you tell our fortunes?'

She frowned and shrugged her shoulders. 'I do not know. It is late. The spirits may be difficult to contact. But I will try.'

'Who is she kidding?' whispered Stu scoffingly.

Luckily she did not seem to hear and beckoned them to follow her past the curtain.

Outside, a sinister pair of eyes narrowed menacingly. They had been following the boys for the last half-hour. A grim-faced figure slipped stealthily from the shadows. And in his hand, glinting like silver, was a long, tapered dagger.

The boys filed after Madam Tanya into an even darker, gloomier room. In one corner, surrounded by chairs, was a round table. It was empty, except for a crystal ball on one side, and a lighted, brass candelabra.

'Sit down,' said Madam Tanya, nodding towards this table. 'I will do the best I can. It will cost you two dollars... payable in advance.'

When they were seated, Mick turned to his companions. 'All right, pay up,' he said. 'That's half a dollar each.'

There was a scrape of chairs and the clink of money being counted. Stu grumbled: 'If you ask me, it's a waste of good cash. Anyone can see that she's a fake.'

Madam Tanya knitted her eyebrows into a disapproving frown. 'So... there are disbelievers in our midst,' she said grimly. 'But you shall see... the spirits do not lie...' She broke off into a low, throaty chuckle.

Mick placed the money on the table. Her gnarled hands snatched it up. Then she motioned for silence. Leaning over her crystal ball, she peered into it intensely. An expression of deep concentration passed over her face.

The silence seemed to last for ever. The flickering candle-light cast an eerie glow over the table. Suddenly, Madam Tanya flung up her arms in despair. 'It's no use,' she sighed. 'The ball is clouded. I must hold a seance. It is the only way.'

Bob's heart pounded in his chest. He did not know what it was he feared. Yet he was certain that danger was imminent.

Madam Tanya's voice was serious: 'You must put your hands on the table. Fingers must touch all round, so that we have a magic circle. Then you must concentrate... understand?'

'What a lot of bosh,' said Stu softly under his breath.

'You're not kidding,' replied Fats.

'Shhh,' said Mick, nudging him sharply.

292

When they had formed a ring of touching fingertips, Madam Tanya nodded in approval. Then she closed her eyes. She began to chant softly at first, her words taking on a hypnotic effect: 'Spirits... we call upon you... we beseech you... come, rise up from your lonely graves... speak to us... let your presence be known. Speak... speak...'

Bob shuddered. Every nerve in his body was wary... alert for trouble. He tried to relax, to listen to Madam Tanya's droning voice. But the darkness closed in on him oppressively.

'Spirits,' she moaned, and her face had now taken on a strange, tortured look, 'spirits, can you hear me?'

A sudden gust of wind swept through the tent. The candles on the table flickered and went out, leaving the place in utter darkness.

Madam Tanya's voice had changed. It was deep, low... as though someone else were putting words into her mouth. 'I see a house...' she moaned. 'Inside there is darkness. No... now there is light. How strange... wherever I turn, I see myself! There are mirrors — thousands of them... but there is danger in this house... death lurks. I see... No! No!'

Bob gazed up. A look of sheer horror crossed his face. Something silvery seemed to be floating towards them. The object hovered in mid air, as if lazily suspended, and then it streaked towards them.

Just then Madam Tanya let loose an ear-piercing shriek, and slumped forward as if totally exhausted.

The silvery object struck the table with a thud, vibrating as it embedded itself in the wood.

Bob leapt up, clutched out in the darkness. But nothing — no one — was there. His arms clawed thin air.

'Quick,' said Stu. 'The candles... who's got a match?'

Fats fumbled in his pockets. An instant later, light flooded the room.

Madam Tanya rubbed her eyes, moaned, and looked around. 'What's happened?' she asked groggily. 'Have the spirits made contact?'

Bob reached over and, with a forceful jerk, withdrew the silvery object that was firmly embedded in the table.

'Holy smoke!' exclaimed Fats, his eyes widening in disbelief as he gazed at the dagger.

Bob handled it gingerly. Its blade was long and shiny. The handle was tapered.

'I don't know who threw this,' he said, 'but I know one thing. This was a warning. It'll be the last one we get.'

Madam Tanya wrung her hands nervously. Fear was written across her face. 'I don't understand,' she muttered. 'The spirits I contacted were friendly. But this one... it must have been a — a demon!'

Chairs scraped as the four boys tensely rose from the table. Mick seemed shocked.

Fats kept glancing apprehensively over his shoulder. Behind him were dark, gloomy shadows. 'M-maybe we ought to s-search the tent!' He was not anxious to do so alone.

Stu looked about and frowned. 'It's no use,' he said. 'Whoever threw that dagger isn't going to wait around for us to nab him.'

'I agree,' said Bob, who was now holding the weapon gingerly in his palm. 'Anyhow ...I don't believe in demons. Someone must have followed us inside.'

Madam Tanya's eyes darted furtively towards the dagger. They rested momentarily on the tapered handle. She gave a sudden gasp of recognition.

Bob wheeled about, caught the fortune teller's startled expression.'What is it?' he asked.

But already a set frown began to trace its way across her forehead. 'Nothing...' she replied, somewhat shaken. 'No...

it is nothing.' But Madam Tanya was obviously worried.

Bob gazed at her intently. 'She knows something,' he thought. 'Yet she won't talk. Why? What is she afraid of?'

There was a long, tense silence.

Suddenly Madam Tanya thrust her gnarled hand out towards Mick. 'Here... take your money,' she said excitedly. 'I don't want any part in this.'

'No!' said Mick with alarm. He waved her off. To take money back from a fortune teller could only bring them bad luck. 'Let her keep it,' he told the others emphatically.

Stu shrugged his shoulders. 'She's a fake, I say.' He began to lead the way out.

'Wait!' Madam Tanya's anxious voice cut through the darkness like a knife. They had just reached the exit. 'There is something I must tell you,' she called out. 'The dagger... it came from the house of strange people, beware... evil lurks there. And... I have seen into the future. I implore you... watch out... for *the wheel of death!*'

Her words trailed off.

'What is it? What are you trying to warn us about?' cried out Mick. But there was no reply. Madam Tanya had gone!

Outside, darkness swept over the pier. The twinkling lights had gone out. The amusement park was closed for the night.

Bob took a deep, steadying breath. The tang of the ocean filled his nostrils, reminding him that it was good to be alive.

Not even in his wildest dreams could he have foreseen an adventure like this. And yet, where had the trail led them? There was no trace of the mysterious prisoner. They had not found the giant. But someone knew that they were looking — which made the search doubly dangerous.

Slowly, the four of them walked back to Mick's car. Bob remained lost in his own thoughts. He tried to piece together the fortune teller's strange words — but they seemed as meaningless as random pieces in a jig-saw puzzle. He wondered what their next move would be.

Stu's voice suddenly broke in: 'What do you make of it all, Bob? Do you think that fortune teller has anything to do with those things?'

Bob glanced up, frowned. 'I don't really know. But we've got to be careful.' The dagger which he had slipped into his pocket was a deadly reminder. 'Anyhow — there's not much more we can do tonight.'

Stu nodded. 'Tomorrow, we'll rest up during the day. Then, at night, we'll take a look at the freak show. It'll be crowded then ... it won't be so easy to spot us.'

Mick had been unusually silent. Now he began muttering, as if in a trance: 'The house of strange people ... of course ... she means the freak show.'

'Relax,' said Stu. 'I think that fortune teller was taking us for a ride. You don't really believe in that bosh, do you, Mick?'

Mick's eyebrows narrowed. 'She knows what she's talking about,' he said. 'She saw something in our future ... something horrible.'

'Pack it in,' scoffed Stu. 'Don't be so superstitious!'

'Yeah!' agreed Fats.

Mick eyed them both coldly. 'All right ... just wait and see,' he said at last.

The conversation ended as they reached the car. Bob and Stu climbed into the rumble seat. A moment later they were on the move.

The first traces of dawn could be seen streaking their way across the sombre sky. The car thundered down Sepulveda Boulevard, practically deserted at this early hour. Finally, Mick turned off on the road leading towards Laurel Canyon. It would serve as a short cut.

296

Bob was the first to notice it. Anxiously, he tapped Stu on the shoulder. He raised his voice, so it could be heard above the roar of the motor. 'Quick ... take a look ... that car behind. It seems to be following us!'

A minute later they were certain of it! The steady glare of headlights bobbed up and down through the darkness, following them at each turn-off.

Stu half-leaned out of the rumble-seat, shouting frantically over the noise of the engine to get Mick's attention. Then at last, Mick returned a knowing nod. He could see the pursuing car in his rear-view mirror.

Mick scowled, realising that it was too late to change direction. They would have to keep on the Canyon Road.

It was a treacherously narrow road, one that snaked around itself and climbed higher and higher. There were no more turn-offs. And already the pursuing car was beginning to close the gap.

There was only one thing Mick could do.

Gritting his teeth, he slammed his foot hard on the accelerator. The motor whined. The speedometer needle wavered frantically: 50 m.p.h. — 60 m.p.h. — 70 m.p.h.

Grim-faced, he sent the car racing through dangerous hairpin curves.

They continued climbing — and the sheer drop on one side of the road increased.

Bob held on for dear life in the rumble. He caught his breath as he looked down, saw the car tyres screech scant inches from the road's edge. And beyond the edge — a sheer drop, perhaps fifty or sixty feet. If they went over they wouldn't stand a chance!

The headlights behind Bob seemed to grown in size. He swallowed nervously, aware that they made good targets.

He braced himself for trouble, not knowing exactly what

would happen next. He was certain about one thing. Their mysterious assailants had allowed them to escape from the fun fair.

But now they were on a desolate open road, miles away from Santa Monica.

The pursuing car recklessly began to increase its speed. And Bob was sure that the men in it, whoever they were, had murder in their hearts.

*Crack! Crack!* Pistol shots suddenly rang out through the night.

A hit on any tyre could send them over the edge to their deaths.

Bob squinted, tried to identify the men in the other car. But the glare of the headlights made it impossible.

Escape seemed hopeless! Up, up, they climbed. Each curve they took shielded them, momentarily, from a hail of lead. But keeping up this gruelling high speed for long was impossible.

In the driver's seat, Mick, his face drawn and grim, reached a sudden decision. Frantically, he explained to Fats, who in turn passed the message back to Bob and Stu: 'Watch the next curve! Hang on for all you've got!'

Bob wondered what Mick was up to. He found out an instant later.

As they reached the foot of the curve, Mick crossed his fingers for luck, and jammed hard on the brake pedal. Simultaneously, he spun the steering wheel.

Tyres screeched! The car swerved, began to skid towards the edge. Fats closed his eyes. Bob looked on in horror!

Mick clung frantically to the wheel, fighting for control.

For one horrible second it looked as if the momentum was going to hurtle the car over the edge. But, miraculously, this desperate stunt, which Mick had learned while racing hot-

298

rods, paid off, and his passengers breathed sighs of relief.

They completed their spin. The wheels threw up dirt at the road's edge. And an instant later, they soared away in the opposite direction.

Mick's face bore a triumphant expression as he shot past the pursuing car, practically side-swiping it.

A couple of pistol shots flashed out. But the pursuers had been caught flat-footed. They could not turn and follow, without delay.

With a sigh of relief, Mick kept up the break-neck speed until they were safe.

Half an hour later the car squealed to a halt in front of Stu's house, on a quiet, tree-lined residential street. It was dawn, and they climbed out exhausted.

'Hey, take a look at this,' said Fats, his voice filled with awe. He pointed to three neat little holes situated just above the top part of the rumble seat.

Mick grumbled angrily: 'Those dirty rats... they're going to pay for shooting up my car!'

They split up after agreeing to meet at seven that evening. It left them the entire afternoon to rest.


That night, when they met at the pre-arranged spot, all four seemed rested and ready to resume their strange adventure.

They piled in the car with grim, determined expressions on their faces. They reached the Santa Monica fun fair at eight.

Bob felt like a commando about to land at Normandy. Every nerve in his body tingled with excitement.

'Remember,' warned Stu, as they approached the glittering amusement pier, 'be on your guard. Mingle with the crowd as much as possible. Don't let anyone notice you! Anyhow... they won't dare try anything — not in public!'

Ten minutes later they were pushing their way through the crowded entrance of the freak show. The large tent was jammed with sightseers who had come to look on some of the world's strange marvels...

The boys split up in pairs, and kept as much in the background as possible.

Up in front was a large, curtained platform. A tall moustached man, in gold-braided uniform, his chest covered with medals, motioned for silence.

'Ladies and gentlemen,' he began, and waited until the coughing and clearing of throats had ended, 'I now want to present to you a unique sight — the man with one thousand tattoos!'

The curtain drew back, revealing a grinning man in bathing trunks. Tattoos were etched over every part of his skin, including his face which somehow resembled a map.

The spectators pressed in to see him better. The man in the braided uniform said with a flourish. 'Every single one of these tattoos required great patience...'

Mick and Fats had pushed their way through the crowd, and were now standing at the opposite end of the tent.

Fats looked on, wide-eyed, as the next performer appeared on stage. He was dressed in a leopard-skin costume. He had a dreamy look on his face, and in his hand he gripped a wooden flute. A large covered basket was at his feet.

'Ladies and gentlemen,' announced the moustached man, his medals glinting in the spotlight, 'meet the snake-man! He was found in the jungle by a missionary, when he was three. It is said that he was raised by a King Cobra.'

The basket opened and a vicious hooded head made its appearance, and slowly began to weave back and forth to the music of the flute. It was a cobra.

*'Ladies and gentlemen — the man with a thousand tattoos!'*

'Ugh,' said Mick. 'I wouldn't want to meet up with that on a dark night!'

Fats was enjoying this spectacle. He failed to notice the two men creeping towards him.

Hands shot out, locking Fats in a vice-like grip. He whirled in alarm, tried to yell. Too late! A pad, reeking of chloroform, was brutally thrust into his face.

Helplessly, he struggled. His muffled shouts went unheard, drowned out by the heavy applause. Mick was only a few feet away. But like the rest of the crowd, he, too, was engrossed in the act.

Fats felt his senses whirling, numbed by a sweet odour that seemed to pierce his brain. Then came merciful blackness.

Arturo, the sword-swallower, was completing his act when Bob's intense whisper to Stu hissed through the silence. 'C'mon ... get closer — I think I've seen something!'

They pushed through the crowd to the edge of the platform. 'I thought so,' said Bob grimly. 'See that set of daggers Arturo is using? They're the same as the one that was thrown at us in the fortune teller's tent!'

Stu was about to reply, when Mick suddenly broke through the crowd, a frantic look on his face.

Bob whirled about: 'What is it? What's wrong?'

'It's Fats,' came the anguished reply. 'When the snake-charmer was on stage he was standing by my side. Now he's disappeared! He's not in the crowd!'

'Good grief,' said Stu. 'That can only mean one thing. They've got him ... and there's no telling what they'll do ... no telling at all!'

Quickly, the boys swung into action. Arturo was the only

lead they had. And, as the lights went on and the sword-swallower stepped down off the stage, they rushed over and cornered him.

'Start talking,' said Stu harshly. 'Where's our friend? What have your gang done with him?'

Arturo backed away, licking his lips nervously. 'I don't know what you're talking about,' he stammered. 'Leave me alone!'

The commotion immediately attracted other members of the freak show.

'Anything wrong?' asked the snake-charmer, who came over with his basket in his hand. He eyed Stu and scowled. Mick moved aside, away from the deadly basket.

Another voice chimed in, a high-pitched one: 'Yeah, what's going on here?' It belonged to a tough-looking, barrel-chested midget. 'Is anyone making trouble, Arturo?' he piped up angrily.

The boys suddenly found themselves hemmed in by a hostile crowd. There was the tattooed man, the pictures on his face moulded into a frown; and the fat lady, waving a ham-like fist; and a tall, ugly man who worked as a fire-eater...

Bob was prepared to fight his way out. Stu went on undauntedly: 'A friend of ours is missing. We want to know where he is. I think Arturo, here, has the answer!'

The crowd hesitated, puzzled. Bob stepped forward, reached into his pocket and came out with the dagger. He waved it about for all to see.

Arturo's eyes narrowed.

'Recognise it?' asked Bob, sharply.

Arturo nodded. 'Of course. It is from a set I use during my throwing act.' He eyed Bob accusingly. 'How did you get it? It must have been stolen! Thief!'

The crowd gave an angry murmur and pressed forward.

It looked bad for the boys. But just then a sharp, commanding voice rang out: 'What's going on over there?' It was Professor Trilbini, the announcer. His moustache quivered, his medals clinked as he pushed through the angry crowd.

Shrewdly, he sized up the situation. 'All right... back to work!' he yelled. 'Let's see you earn your money.'

Trilbini, it turned out, was the manager of the freak show. He also ran several other side-shows and rides at the fun fair. Now, as the crowd dispersed, he patiently heard the boys out. Arturo, still standing off to one side, cried out anxiously: 'No... no, I swear... I did not throw a dagger at anyone.'

Trilbini dismissed him with an impatient wave: 'Arturo's not your man,' he told Stu. 'I'm sure of it! Anyone could have stolen one of his daggers. Forget him. Tell me about your friend. Why should someone want to kidnap him?'

Stu replied: 'There's no time to explain the whole story now. We must find Fats. I assure you he is in great danger.'

Trilbini scowled. 'Have you contacted the police?'

Mick shook his head. 'Not yet!'

Stu then asked Trilbini about the giant. 'Odd that you should mention it,' replied the Professor. 'We did have a giant. He left very suddenly just the other day. He didn't leave a forwarding address.'

Trilbini flashed the boys a sympathetic look. Reaching into his pocket he took out a pencil and paper and scribbled something out. 'Here,' he said, handing out one to each of them. 'These will serve as passes. They will get you any ride or amusement in the place, free of charge. Have a good look around. Perhaps you'll find your friend. If not... come back and see me. Meanwhile I'll warn my men to be on the alert.'

The boys thanked him and hurried off, determined to leave no stone uncovered until they had found Fats.

Meanwhile, not far off, Fats had revived with a groan. It

was dark. He did not know where he was. His head throbbed and waves of nausea racked his body. Feebly, he attempted to stand. Then he realised that his wrists were tightly shackled against a stone wall.

A sudden clatter caught his attention. It sounded like a passing train. The noise grew in volume as it approached... and finally roared past. On the heels of this came another sound, the high-pitched, macabre shriek of mechanical laughter.

Where on earth was he, he wondered? Still somewhat dazed he craned his neck about. His eyes scanned the shadowy walls. He seemed to be in a dungeon of some kind. Above was a small, barred window. A thin beam of light trickled in.

Suddenly he made another — terrifying — discovery. The dungeon was growing smaller with every passing moment. Impossible! His mind must be playing tricks on him! But no... that wall in front... it was definitely closing in...

His heart filled with despair.

Suddenly a voice penetrated the darkness. 'Are you ready to talk?' it questioned him coldly. Fats looked about. He could see no one.

'How much do you and your friends know? Talk! Unless you prefer to die!'

Fats clenched his teeth: 'I've nothing to say. Just wait!' he shouted. 'My friends will see that you rats get what you deserve!'

The voice chuckled. 'We've got something planned for them, too!'

A cold shiver raced down to the tip of Fats' spine. In the distance, the grim cackle of mechanical laughter welled up. And the dungeon walls continued to close in.

He shuddered, aware of what would happen to him if they

did not stop soon. Yet, come what may, a stubborn determination to remain silent was winning out.

'Talk,' said the voice threateningly. Fats gritted his teeth. The cell grew smaller... smaller, and then... abruptly, the walls stopped. Fats sighed in relief. It had been a trick, an attempt to frighten him. But it hadn't worked.

Meanwhile, Stu, Bob and Mick were walking away from the freak show, wondering at what point to begin their search. Outside, a thousand bright lights seemed to beckon aimlessly.

'If only we had something to go on,' said Stu, an anxious frown tracing its way across his face.

Mick put in uneasily. 'I've been thinking... maybe we ought to call in the police.'

Stu shook his head. 'No... they'd ask too many questions! It would be hours before they began searching the fun fair! We can't take the chance... not with Fats' life at stake!'

Bob said glumly: 'I thought we were on to something with that sword-swallower. But I guess not! Which leave us exactly...'

'... Nowhere,' Mick concluded, taking the words from Bob's mouth. 'Unless... hey, wait a minute... remember what the fortune teller said... about a house of mirrors?'

Stu did not bother to conceal his annoyance: 'Why don't you forget that superstitious rot?' he snapped. 'It's wasting time.'

Mick's face reddened. 'Don't be so sure,' he replied angrily. 'We've got to follow up every clue. I say we start at the fun house... 'cause that's obviously where we'll find the house of mirrors!'

Bob brightened. 'I say, Mick might have something. Anyhow, we've got to start somewhere... so why not there?'

Stu scowled. But it was two against one, and so they hurried down the crowded pier towards the fun house.

They were nearing the fun house entrance when Bob

stopped dead in his tracks and cried out: 'Look ... over there, by that side door!' Less than ten yards away was a sallow-faced man that Bob could not fail to recognise, even in the night shadows. It was the thug who had fired at him earlier.

Bob said sharply: 'He's going in! We've got to follow him. Hurry up! And don't let him see you!'

A moment later the three boys were hot in pursuit. The sign above the door through which the thug had just entered stated: 'Private!'

Ignoring it, they barged straight in!

What happened next took them completely unawares.

They found themselves standing, dizzily, in a room which tilted at a crazy angle. The light was dim.

'There he goes,' whispered Bob, frantically. Ahead, a figure darted into a shadowy corridor.

They gave chase. They seemed to be running downhill! But the exertion it required proved otherwise. It was up, all the way.

Bob took the lead, puffing hard. A grotesque, elongated figure flashed past. He realised that it was his own reflection in a trick mirror.

They reached the corridor. It was pitch black. Bob groped his way blindly, until he felt a door handle. He opened it. A shaft of light was visible. Crash! Some invisible force prevented Bob from walking through the doorway. It was a pane of glass.

At length Bob found the real door. He rushed through, caught sight of the figure again, turning down another corridor.

It led to a staircase. But even as Bob reached the first step, the solid weight beneath his feet suddenly gave way. The trick staircase had flattened into a slide.

An instant later Bob tumbled out into another room, Stu and Mick following on his heels.

Now, they were in the maze-like house of mirrors. Their reflections seemed to leer at them from a hundred different angles. But the man they were pursuing had vanished quite mysteriously, seemingly into thin air!

They spent ten minutes in a frantic search along the winding corridors. 'It's no use,' said Bob finally. His voice was heavy with discouragement. 'He's got away! Our last clue, at that!'

Grimly the three boys moved on. At length Mick discovered a 'mirror' door which opened into another part of the fun house, a part open to the public.

Crowds shuffled past, laughing, joking, enjoying themselves. The boys moved with the flow of traffic and finally emerged outside, each wondering what their next step would be.

The lights glittered, and overhead the giant Ferris wheel illuminated the entire area. Bob noticed it from the corner of his eye, and it gave him a sudden idea. 'Let's go up on it,' he said. 'When we're on top, maybe we'll see something we missed.'

'You two go ahead,' said Stu. 'I'll stay here and have a look around. We'll cover more ground that way.'

Bob knew it was just a slim, desperate chance. But they had to do something.

He and Mick queued up, showed their passes and a minute later boarded the Ferris wheel.

The attendant slammed the safety bar into place. They started with a jerk, rising slowly at first. As the ground moved away from them Mick suddenly turned to Bob. His eyes had widened as if a terrible realisation had just struck him. 'Bob...' he cried out, 'I've just remembered... the fortune teller... she said "Beware the wheel of death!"'

A sudden chill raced down Bob's spine. 'Don't worry,' he replied. 'Nothing can happen.'

The wheel was moving faster now. Bob glanced down. A thousand lights seemed to glare up at him.

As they reached the top, Bob instinctively leaned over the side to get a better view. Suddenly, he had a hollow feeling in his stomach. The compartment they sat in was beginning to swing back and forth.

'Bob!' shouted Mick, and there was sheer horror in his voice. 'Look — on top. That supporting rod. It... it's giving way!'

Mick's face contorted with horror. There was no time to think. The glittering Ferris wheel stopped just as the two boys reached the top. And, with a sickening lurch, their seat tipped over.

Bob's hands shot out, clawed frantically at air — and caught hold of a rusted metal spoke. He hung by his fingertips.

Mick's reflexes were a fraction slower. He pitched forward with a yell. Lunging out in desperation he managed to catch hold of Bob's dangling leg, saving himself from plummeting to a horrible death.

Bob's heart hammered wildly. Mick's weight was weakening his grip. The strain was agonising. The muscles in his arms seemed to cry out in protest. With pain-numbed fingers, he wondered grimly just how long he could hold out.

Below, he could see a crowd forming. They looked like ants scurrying about. The lights of the amusement fair made his head whirl with dizziness.

'Mick!' His cry was frantic. 'I can't hang on much longer! Swing over to one side. And hurry...'

Mick, his face beaded with sweat, kicked out his legs to gain momentum. Slowly, he began moving back and forth like a pendulum.

Bob gritted his teeth. Mick neared the side of the wheel, reached out... missed, tried again... missed...

Bob's strength had reached its limit. He groaned. His

fingers ached horribly. He could not hold on any longer... just couldn't!

But suddenly the oppressive weight was lifted. Mick had flung himself free, and was now holding on securely to a metal spoke.

The worst was over! Now it was just a matter of careful climbing.

Five minutes later the crowd heaved a sigh of relief as the boys safely reached the ground. Helping hands steadied them.

Bob and Mick edged their way to the nervous-looking attendant who had strapped them into the wheel.

'I can't understand,' said the attendant in a clipped tone of voice. 'Something must have gone wrong with the safety mechanism.'

Bob glared at the man. 'I'm not so sure that it was an accident!' he said angrily.

Meanwhile, in all the excitement, neither of the boys noticed the sallow-faced thug who suddenly tore himself away from the crowd and rushed down the pier to a waiting accomplice.

'It didn't work,' reported the thug nervously.

The other man scowled. 'All right,' he said, 'you know what to do. Come on — there's no time to lose!'

Meanwhile, Bob and Mick continued to argue with the attendant. A large crowd of onlookers had now ringed them in.

'I had nothing to do with it,' the attendant snarled. 'And you can't prove otherwise!'

Mick's face grew purple with anger. 'We'll see about that,' he shouted, lunging forward.

Bob pulled him back, desperately. 'Easy, Mick,' he coaxed. 'It won't do any good. We've attracted too much attention already. Let's get out of here and find Stu.'

Mick grimly controlled his rage. The baffled crowd made way for the two boys. The attendant muttered threateningly...

It took ten minutes for them to locate Stu. He had been searching around the circus Big Top, but with no results. 'Hey, where have you guys been?' he asked. But before they could explain he interjected suddenly: 'Never mind now... look what I've got! Someone handed it to me about a minute ago. He got away before I could stop him.'

Stu produced a torn, crumpled sheet of paper. Written across it, in large scrawling letters, was the message:

HELP! THE CHAMBER OF HORRORS!

'Is that Fats' handwriting?' asked Mick cautiously.

'Impossible to tell,' replied Stu. 'It's obviously been scribbled under difficult circumstances.'

Bob frowned. 'H'mmm... it could be a trap of some kind. But what choice do we have? This is the only clue we've got! I say we give it a try!'

The others agreed, and they hurried along the dark, crowded pier towards the entrance of the Chamber of Horrors.

They showed their free passes, and the attendant on duty waved them past the barrier. A miniature train clattered to a stop just in front of them. It resembled a roller-coaster. They boarded, and the train started with a jerk. Bob shivered apprehensively as they hurtled down the track, suddenly entering a pitch-black tunnel.

The darkness was heavy and oppressive. It took a few seconds for their eyes to grow accustomed to the grim sights.

A long, narrow box suddenly loomed up in view. Slowly, the lid opened. A ghoulish-looking vampire sat up. Its glassy eyes seemed to bear down on them. Mick shuddered. The train shot past and the lid closed.

A high-pitched cackle of laughter rang out menacingly.

Suddenly, their train gave a frantic whistle toot. It was unbelievable! Another train, on the same track, was hurtling head-on towards them! The boys flung up their arms protectively, expecting the worst to happen, but they were lucky. The two trains met — but there was no crash! They had been hurtling towards a mirror that had slid away at the last minute.

Now they were inside a dungeon — and gloomy, life-sized figures leered down at them from the walls.

As they clattered along a curve, Bob noticed a figure dressed in eighteenth-century French costume. The scene, terribly life-like, was of the French revolution. The costumed figure had its hands bound behind its back. Its head rested on the wooden block of a shiny guillotine poised ready to drop.

The train shot past. Bob had been staring intently at the figure. Now he rubbed his eyes in sheer disbelief! He cried out frantically: 'That's Fats! I'm sure of it!'

As the train slowed around another curve, the boys leapt off. They got up, unhurt, and groped through the darkness. Slowly, they made their way past a tangle of dangling skeletons and leering cardboard ghouls.

They reached the figure dressed in French costume. It was Fats, all right! He struggled desperately to free himself. He was gagged and his eyes were wild with terror.

Stu rushed over and removed the gag. 'Are you O.K.?'

Fats could not move. But he struggled vainly to crane his neck around. 'Y-you shouldn't have come here!' he cried out in anguish.

Stu scowled. 'What is it, Fats? What's wrong?'

'I think I can answer that...' a voice as cold as ice suddenly cut in. Stu froze! Bob and Mick whirled about.

Closing in on them, pistols levelled menacingly, were two men. And standing just behind them, an evil grin pasted on his face, was the man Bob had encountered once before — the giant who had threatened to kill him.

The boys had walked into a trap!

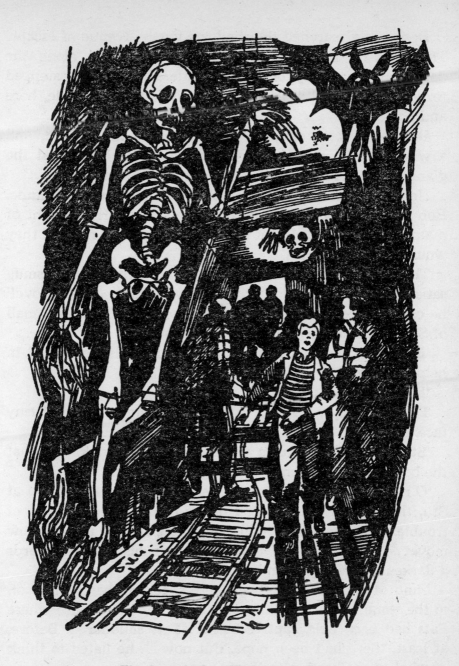

*The boys had walked into a trap!*

Bob wildly searched the shadows for an avenue of escape. There wasn't any. The boys were hemmed in along the darkened passageways of the ghost ride. The two thugs stepped forward. The giant snarled: 'Try anything and you die, here and now!'

Bob stood stock still, his feet rooted to the ground, and a wave of grim despair swept over him. He knew that the giant would not hesitate to carry out that threat!

Nearby, the clatter of an approaching train grew in volume. Bob momentarily sighted it rounding a bend. He thought of making a dash for it. But it was too far away. He realised they would shoot him down.

The fat, swarthy-faced thug eyed the captives with smug satisfaction. He walked over to Stu, who was nearest. 'Move!' he commanded, jamming the pistol forcefully into the small of Stu's back and giving him a violent shove.

'Keep your hands off me,' snapped Stu, fists clenched in helpless fury.

'Easy, mate,' warned Bob.

The thug's eyes seemed to bulge with anger in his fleshy face. He took careful aim.

'Stop!' the other thug's voice rang out. 'You know what the boss said. No violence — unless we have to!'

'O.K ... O.K,' muttered the heavy-set man. He glared at Stu, then at the others. 'You punks have caused us a lot of trouble. And in a while you'll get what's coming to you. Now move... and fast!' He motioned with his pistol towards a darkened, gloomy chamber.

Minutes later, all four boys were shackled, hand and foot, to the stone walls of a dungeon. It was the same place where Fats had been held captive earlier. Fats shuddered. Before, at least, there had been hope. But now... he hated to think of what might happen to them.

314

The two thugs left, satisfied that their prisoners could not escape. The giant approached the heavy steel door leading out of the dungeon. He paused, then glanced back at the struggling boys. His lips curled into a cruel sneer. 'You were too smart for your own good. Now you're going to pay for it!'

He strode out into the darkened corridor. The steel door swung behind him, locking with an ominous click.

Bob continued struggling with the shackles that painfully bit into his wrists and ankles.

'It's no use,' said Fats glumly. 'I've tried already. They won't come loose!'

'Blast it, anyway,' said Mick. 'We walked right into a trap.' He turned and looked at Fats. Despite all that had happened, Mick grinned weakly. 'Where did you get those duds?' He was referring to the eighteenth-century French costume that Fats was clumsily draped in.

'It's not funny,' scowled Fats. 'They forced me to wear it. If only you hadn't come... it's my fault that they caught you!'

The voice that cut through the dungeon next was sharp and unexpected. 'Are you ready to talk sensibly now?' it asked threateningly.

It seemed to be coming from the far corner of the dungeon, from the mouth of the leering skull which hung from the stone wall.

'There is no way out,' it went on coldly. 'Your fat friend knows that already. So it might be less painful for everyone if you tell us exactly what you're after.'

Bob stared hard at the bone-white skull. The voice must be coming from an amplifier hidden inside, he thought. 'You're not fooling us with a cheap trick like that,' he shouted angrily. 'I know that you're around somewhere, talking into a microphone.'

The voice broke into an amused chuckle. Then coldly:

'Very clever, my boy. And now that the preliminaries are over, we can start with you. Talk!'

Bob frowned. That voice. He had heard it before. But where? His mind probed desperately for an answer. Was it in the haunted house the other night? The night those men talked about Harcourt? Harcourt! The name he had forgotten. But now it burnt into his brain like a brand. It might be the way out of this mess...

'Talk,' repeated the voice sharply, 'or you'll be the first to die.'

Bob thought fast. He had to stall, play for time. 'Don't threaten me,' he said calmly. 'This afternoon I left a note with a friend. If I don't show up tonight he has instructions to turn it over to the police!'

'You're bluffing,' said the voice cynically. 'The police can't track down every kid that's missing. Why should they be interested in you?'

Bob hesitated. It was time to play his last ace. If it failed... but there was no time to think of that now. 'I'm sure the police would turn this place upside down. Not for us. But for Harcourt... your prisoner.'

There were several audible gasps of surprise in the dungeon. Bob's friends were stunned. Bob realised that though the name still meant nothing to him, its effect on the others was startling. If only he had told them about Harcourt sooner — but it was too late now.

The voice did not reply. The silence in the gloomy chamber was appalling. Stu said suddenly: 'Good grief! That explains a lot of things.'

Fats motioned for him to be silent. 'That microphone,' he reminded them, 'will pick up everything we say!'

Bob was desperately lost in his own thoughts. Would it work, he wondered? Or would they see through his bluff?

A moment later the steel door barring the entrance creaked open. The heavy-set thug entered and walked directly over to Bob. His pistol was gripped tightly in his hand, the muzzle pointed menacingly at Bob.

Bob half-shut his eyes... waited for the crashing explosion! But it never came. Instead, the thug said sharply: 'You're coming with me. The boss wants to talk to you... alone!'

The shackles were opened. Bob stood up, rubbing his aching wrists. The thug motioned with his pistol. 'Don't try anything funny!' he snapped. 'I've got an itchy trigger-finger!'

As Bob was being shepherded out of the dungeon Stu cried out: 'Don't talk... don't trust these rats. They'll find out what they want to know, and...'

'Shut up!' snarled the fat man. He lashed out viciously and gave Stu a cuff.

A moment later Bob stood outside in the darkened, gloomy corridor. The door clanged behind him. In the distance he could hear the clatter of a train. He had to make a break... it was their only chance. But the fat man hovered over him like a distrustful, watching hawk.

The train was approaching. 'Hold it,' said the thug. The shiny track was just ahead. A skull head dangled from the ceiling. Bob made a desperate calculation. Slowly his arm snaked up. The train was thundering towards them now. He lashed out, sent the skull flying. It glanced off the thug with a sharp crack, and knocked him off balance.

He yelled, and gripped the trigger. Two shots flared out in the darkness. They missed. The sound of the third shot was drowned by the clattering train. Bob leapt, somehow got a hold on the rear car, and desperately hung on.

The train shuttled around a curve. He was out of gun-range now. But he knew that he could not ride the train to the exit. They would be waiting for him there. Somehow... he had to outsmart them. Somehow he must escape, before the exit.

As the train flashed past another curve it slowed. He made up his mind. Without hesitation he leapt. The ground spun past ... but he had landed on his feet.

Desperately he raced down a darkened corridor. His lungs gasped for air.

Then he spotted it! A doorway! It stood there like a ray of hope. Frantically he clawed at the handle. He sighed in relief as it turned. He flung the door open, recklessly plunged inside.

Too late, he saw it! Only feet away a shadowy figure lunged for him.

'Trapped!' The horrible thought reared into Bob's mind.

Every muscle in Bob's body tensed as he anticipated the bone-crunching impact! But it never came!

The realisation of where he was hit him, and he let loose a tortured sigh of relief. The shadowy figure could not possibly harm him. *For it was nothing more than his own reflection in a full-length mirror!* In fact he was surrounded by reflections. He was inside the House of Mirrors.

Hurriedly, he slammed the door behind him, mechanically noting that six other Bobs were doing exactly the same thing.

He leaned on one of the mirrors. His heart hammered in his chest, his lungs gasped for breath. He was soaked in sweat.

He knew he could not remain there much longer. He had to move on. His pursuers might burst in at any moment. He shuddered, wishing that he had more time to devise a plan of action...

His bluff had paid off. Speaking the name Harcourt had been like touching off the fuse on a stick of dynamite. But why, Bob wondered grimly, was the prisoner called Harcourt so important?

He pushed the thought out of his mind. The important thing now was to get out — and quickly.

The police had to be informed. Trying to free his friends on his own would be foolhardy.

But which way out was the safest? He was certain that the gang would be watching every exit. Should he return to the Ghost Train, back-tracking his way? No — that was too risky. He had to think of something else.

He glanced about, ventured a step forward. Six other Bobs did likewise. He felt hopelessly confused.

He took a deep breath. Suddenly his mind picked up a fleeting memory. That thug they had chased and lost in the House of Mirrors! The man had simply vanished as if swallowed in thin air. Impossible! He must have gone somewhere.

He recalled what Madam Tanya had said. 'There are mirrors... thousands of them... but there is danger...'

What did she mean? Was it a warning of some kind?

Suddenly the answer clicked into place. Of course! There must be a secret panel, a door leading somewhere. That was how the thug vanished so mysteriously.

Bob let his eyes wander along the mirrored corridor. How on earth was he going to find such a panel?

Precious time was ticking away. He swallowed hard, forcing himself to remain calm.

He wandered along the twisting, maze-like corridors. One by one he touched the mirrors. He ran his hands along the sides, searched desperately for concealed switches, secret buttons...

Nothing!

Five minutes later his heart was filled with despair. But he did not give up. His eyes flicked along one corridor, past a row of mirrors. Suddenly they rested on a particular panel. It was shiny, clean... unlike all the other frames which were covered with grime and dust.

He stepped over, examined it carefully. His own reflection

stared back at him mockingly. It had to be the hidden door.

Slowly his fingers felt their way along the top of the mirror-frame. They stopped on a small knob-like protrusion. He pressed it down forcefully, and the miracle happened!

There was a soft whoosh, and a section of the wall just behind the mirror gave way. The mirror-door swung open, revealing a long, shadowy passageway.

Stepping inside, he located the second button and pressed it. The mirror closed behind him. Gaunt shadows leapt over the walls. A shimmering light seemed to be coming from the distant end of this passageway. Cautiously, and silently he crept towards it.

He froze suddenly, as voices drifted towards him. He recognised them. The giant was saying: 'We've got to get our hands on that kid before he talks.'

'He won't get away,' a second voice answered. Bob recognised it as that of the fat, swarthy-faced thug. 'Every exit is being guarded. He's probably lying low on the Ghost Train track!'

The giant said: 'Anyhow, we'll be getting Harcourt away from here in a couple of hours. Then we'll get rid of those snoopers. Even if the cops do come around, they won't find anything.'

Next instant, Bob heard the giant's heavy footfalls approaching. 'I've got to get back,' his voice boomed.

Bob felt a cold chill race along his spine. He shrank into the shadows, hugged the wall tightly. The giant entered the passageway. Bob held his breath. He forced down the panic which welled up in him. Concealed as he was in the darkness, his chances were good.

Sure enough, the giant strode past. The big man was in too much of a hurry to notice the darkened form huddled against the wall.

Bob thanked his lucky stars. He waited, tensely, until he saw the mirror-door open — and close.

Harcourt must be here, somewhere, he concluded. The fat thug was probably guarding him alone.

A grim determination swept over Bob. If he could somehow overcome the thug, he might find Harcourt — who was the key to this entire mystery.

Stealthily, Bob crept along the passageway. One gloomy thought continued to plague him. The giant had returned through the mirror-door, which probably meant it was the only way out.

Well, there was nothing Bob could do about it now. Steadily he edged forward. The passageway opened into a room that resembled an old warehouse of some kind. Bob cautiously peered around the corner. He spotted the thug, leaning idly against a large crate, reading a magazine, his back partly turned towards Bob. Just behind him was a door. Bob licked his lips. Perhaps Harcourt was on the other side of that door!

With bated breath, Bob tiptoed towards the unsuspecting thug. His muscles were tensed, ready for action.

He was half-way there, when a creaking floorboard gave him away. The thug whirled about, alarm written on his flabby face. His hand flashed down to draw his pistol.

Desperately, Bob flung himself at his human target. The heavy-set thug snarled, his eyes blinking in disbelief. Jerking his pistol upwards, he rattled off a wild, hurried shot.

The bullet screamed past Bob's head, and the thug had no chance for a second try.

Bob slammed into him with bone-jarring impact. The two crashed heavily into the wall. The pistol went clattering along the floor.

The fat man lashed out. But Bob's fist was already swinging and caught him on the jaw.

The thug tossed up his arms protectively, leaving Bob with an opening to smash home a sharp left to the midriff.

As the thug doubled over in pain, Bob unleashed a powerful uppercut. It connected, but still the man did not go down.

Instead, he got a grip on his attacker and the two toppled over, with the thug on top. His fingers clawed at Bob's throat like talons.

The man's weight gave him the advantage. Bob felt his strength ebbing as the grip around his throat tightened.

A wave of dizziness swept over Bob. The room began whirling about. Then—a grim determination took over. He had to break this grip if he was to save his friends.

With the remaining dregs of his strength, he got his knees into position against the thug's chest and kicked out desperately.

The fat man went sprawling head over heels. Bob was first on his feet. As the thug rose, Bob rushed in. A crunching left hook finished the fight. The thug reeled back, glassy-eyed, and slumped to the floor.

Panting for breath, Bob rolled the thug over and searched him thoroughly. He found nothing. He had to work fast now.

Tearing off the man's shirt, he used it to gag and bind him. Then, with a hurried stride, he stooped over, picked up the fallen pistol and stuffed it into his pocket. Now, at least, he would have a fighting chance.

His eyes darted over towards the door which the thug had been guarding. Would he find Harcourt in there?

He walked over, his heart thumping wildly as he drew the heavy iron bolt. The door opened with an eerie creak, and warily he peered inside.

The man known as Harcourt looked up furtively from a darkened corner of the small room. His haggard, unshaven face was that of a man who had given up all hope.

His hands were handcuffed behind his back to a rusty metal

pipe which jutted up from the floor. He was in an awkward sitting position.

There was fear and mistrust in his eyes. 'What have you come here for?' he said to Bob in a thin, cracked voice.

Bob hurried over to him. 'I've come to help,' he said.

Harcourt peered up at Bob intently. Suddenly a flicker of recognition crossed his face. 'Of course... the manor house... you must have got my message.'

Bob nodded. 'That's right. Finding you has been quite a job.'

A gleam of hope entered Harcourt's eyes. But it was clouded over by despair. 'You'll never get these cuffs off,' he said flatly.

Bob stepped over and inspected the handcuffs. He tugged at the pipe with all his might. It wouldn't budge.

Frowning, he said: 'The key.. who has it?'

Harcourt answered grimly: 'There is only one key. The man they call "The Boss" keeps it in his possession. He is responsible for kidnapping me.'

Bob put in bitterly: 'And for kidnapping my friends, too!' He eyed the handcuffs once more, then added: 'I'm afraid I'll have to leave you and come back with help. But first tell me... who are you? What is project R? Why are these men holding you prisoner?'

Harcourt sighed. 'I cannot explain it all,' he said. 'There isn't time. But I am a mathematician. I have spent three years working on R — that is, project Mars Rocket. I have made some vital discoveries — calculations which, if they are right, would enable our country to land the first manned rocket on Mars!'

Harcourt went on angrily: 'These men are... traitors. They are dealing with a foreign power... a country which would pay a great deal for the information I now possess. But please.. no more now.' He looked up frantically. 'Bring help and hurry! Time is running out.'

Bob nodded, suddenly recalling the conversation he had overheard between the giant and the fat thug. They were going to get rid of Harcourt... tonight!

He turned to leave. Then, remembering the pistol, he took it from his pocket and slipped it into Harcourt's cuffed hand. 'Here... your aim might be a bit off, but at close range it would prove useful. If they come for you before I'm back, you might need it.'

Harcourt palmed the pistol gratefully.

Bob left. He hurried past the thug, who was still out cold. Tracing his way back along the dark tunnel, he soon reached the secret panel which led into the House of Mirrors.

With bated breath he pressed the button. The mirror-door swung open. Cautiously he stepped into the House of Mirrors. He pressed the second button and the mirror-door closed behind him.

They would be still searching for him. He understood now what they were after! He had to escape, had to contact the police. This was important — not only to himself and his friends, but to the entire country.

He crept stealthily along the corridor of mirrors. He would have to break out through one of the exits, no matter how well guarded it might be.

Suddenly, he gave a start. A horrible image loomed up at him. The giant, with pistol levelled, could be seen coming from six different sides.

There was a sudden flash of gun-fire and the tinkling of crashing glass.

Bob swallowed hard. Which way should he turn?

The giant's voice roared out: 'There he is!'

From the other side of the corridor Bob saw the advancing

figure of the thin, furtive-eyed thug. He had to move, quickly.

Which way? He had to make a decision!

The thug raised his pistol. Bob shuddered as six pistols appeared to go off. There was a loud crash as another mirror shattered.

Bob had but one advantage. His pursuers did not have a single target — they had a choice of the real Bob and six reflections.

Wham! Glass splintered just behind him. That had been close!

He raced down the corridor, desperation written on his sweat-covered face.

The giant's reflection loomed up mockingly.

Bob gave the mirror at the end of the corridor a frantic shove. It slid open, and with a tremendous sigh of relief he bolted through.

The next moment he found himself jammed into a flowing, laughing crowd.

Desperately he elbowed his way through, spotted an exit and raced for it.

The night air gave him a sudden feeling of exultation. Outside, the lights were blinding, people were streaming past. He was free...

'Where do you think you're going?' A cruel, harsh voice suddenly demanded.

It was the Ferris wheel attendant, and he stepped menacingly towards Bob.

The giant and the thin thug would be on his heels any moment now. He had to work fast.

He tried to break away from the attendant. But the wiry man lurched out and caught him in a powerful, vice-like grip.

'You and your friend were lucky last time,' he said sarcastically as Bob struggled to break free.

A crowd began to form. It began to look as if Bob had bungled his escape attempt. The giant was now approaching.

Suddenly a sharp, clear voice rang out: 'Break it up!' It was Professor Trilbini.

The attendant glanced up, let go of Bob, and bolted away like a frightened rabbit. The giant and the thug stepped back and vanished into the crowd.

Apparently they feared attempting anything in public.

Bob said breathlessly: 'You came just in time!'

Trilbini stepped over, eyed Bob curiously. 'What is it?' he asked. 'Have you found your friends?'

Bob replied urgently: 'I'll explain later. Right now I must contact the police!'

Trilbini frowned. 'Trouble, huh? Very well... come to my office. You can use my telephone!'

A few moments later, as Trilbini closed the door behind them, Bob strode over towards the desk. 'There's no time to lose,' he said, reaching for the telephone. 'There's a band of dangerous men here — and they must be stopped.'

'I see,' replied Trilbini. 'But there seems to be one problem.'

Bob glanced up, questioningly. He froze as he found himself looking down at the menacing steel barrel of a pistol.

Trilbini motioned him to put down the telephone. 'You've forgotten The Boss,' he said coldly. 'And that was a big mistake!'

Bob stared helplessly at the shiny black revolver pointed at him.

'Put that telephone down!' commanded Trilbini coldly. Gone was the friendly smile. In its place was the sinister expression of a man who would let no one stand in his way.

Bitterly, Bob obeyed. With freedom within his very grasp, he had been tricked. '*So you're* The Boss! I should have known...' His voice trailed off in despair.

Trilbini's eyes narrowed in cold contempt. 'Did you think I would let a couple of kids ruin everything?' he said. 'We tried to warn you. But now... you know too much!'

A buzzer sounded, Keeping his eyes glued on Bob, Trilbini opened his top desk drawer and drew out a small microphone.

'Is everything O.K., boss? You got him?' came the giant's voice.

Trilbini replied calmly, 'There's no need to worry.'

'You know what to do now,' Trilbini went on. 'Those other kids must be taken care of. I'll be down in a while.'

Bob said grimly: 'I suppose you plan to take Harcourt out of the country.'

Trilbini's eyes widened in surprise. 'Exactly!' he confirmed at last. 'By submarine... in about two hours. You do know a lot, don't you? Actually, if you hadn't come snooping around that manor house the other day, Harcourt wouldn't be here now. You forced us to change our plans slightly.'

Bob licked his lips. He was stalling for time now. 'You expect Harcourt to give his secrets to a foreign power?'

Trilbini smiled. 'Our methods of persuasion rarely fail!'

Just then the office door banged open and Madam Tanya rushed inside, waving her arms hysterically. 'Enough!' she wailed. 'You're going too far! I will not take part in... murder!'

'Shut up,' snarled Trilbini. 'You're paid to follow orders. Now get out of here!'

Bob saw his chance. Trilbini's eyes were momentarily off him. He gripped the top of Trilbini's desk with both hands, and with a sudden, violent jerk heaved the desk over on its side. Trilbini cursed as it struck him. His revolver spat flame, but the falling desk spoilt his aim. Madam Tanya uttered an ear-piercing shriek.

Flinging himself across the desk, Bob slammed Trilbini's

arm downward, and the gun went flying. They were locked in furious combat, when strange hands suddenly began pulling them apart.

Bob was jerked roughly to his feet. His arms were pinned back behind him.

'What's this all about?' asked the tattooed man. Bob realised that the shooting must have attracted everyone. Looking around, he saw the sword-swallower, the fire-eater, the snake-charmer, the midget, and the fat lady.

Trilbini struggled in vain to free himself from the fire-eater's heavy grip. The Professor spluttered out desperately: 'He... he tried to rob the office. I caught him breaking in here...'

For a moment Bob found himself under the angry scrutiny of everyone.

But it was Madam Tanya who saved the day. 'That's not true,' she wailed hysterically.

At length Bob succeeded in blurting out his story. He concluded: 'So you see, we've got to get down there... fast. They're planning to kill my friends.'

'We'd better take a look for ourselves,' said the tattooed man, finally loosening his grip on Bob.

A few minutes later the group moved stealthily down the narrow, darkened corridors of the ghost train ride.

'Not a peep from you,' whispered the fire-eater menacingly to Trilbini who was in his grip. The Professor was livid with rage.

'Shhh —' warned Bob, as they rounded a bend. A set of skeletons dangled grimly from the ceiling. The dungeon was not far away. In the distance a train roared along the track.

With each cautious step, Bob's heart pounded frantically. The horrible question repeated itself in his mind. Would they be in time?

Then, suddenly, Bob stiffened, motioning the others to halt.

There, only a few yards away, stood the three men they sought. The Ferris wheel attendant was manipulating a long, rusty lever which jutted out from the ground. The giant and the tall, thin thug were at his side. 'Those walls will keep closing in now,' said the Ferris wheel attendant, with no show of emotion. 'The Boss will be glad to know we've taken care of those meddlers!'

An icy chill shot along Bob's spine. His friends were in the dungeon which Fats had spoken of earlier. They would be crushed to death!

Bob stopped thinking, and swung into frantic action. He flung himself towards the man manipulating the controls and crashed into him with the force of a pile-driver. The two slammed to the ground, a tangle of flaying arms and legs.

The giant and the other thug looked at the oncomers with heavy dismay. The thin man was the first to react. 'Stand back,' he shouted threateningly. He reached into his pocket. A knife glinted in his hand.

Arturo, the sword-swallower, reddened with anger. 'So it was you who stole a dagger from my set. Tried to implicate me, did you?'

The thug took a furtive step back, turned and desperately began to run. Arturo reached into his vest. Calmly, he took aim. The thug had not gone five paces when Arturo's dagger whistled through the air. It pinned the furious thug neatly by his jacket to the wall. Another dagger whizzed by, and another... each pinning the horror-stricken man more securely against the wall.

Meanwhile, bellowing with rage, the giant broke loose and ran.

It was the burly, thick-chested midget who threw himself at the giant's feet, bringing him down with a crash. The giant struggled in vain. The fat lady wobbled over and sat on him.

Bob exchanged furious, desperate blows with the Ferris wheel attendant. Then, suddenly, the attendant broke away. As he did so, the snake-charmer stepped forward, a cold smile on his face. He opened his basket — and a venomous head writhed out.

'No — no!' shrieked the attendant. Beads of sweat broke out on his brow, and he flung his hands into the air. A bite from the cobra would be fatal.

Professor Trilbini took advantage of the confusion and jerked free from the fire-eater's grip. He began to run.

Madam Tanya was the first to act. A solid, round object was gripped tightly in the fortune-teller's hand, her arm moved in an arc — and the crystal ball crashed against Trilbini's head.

Bob was running now, thinking only of the fate of his friends.

But relief flooded through him as he reached the dungeon. The walls were only about two feet apart — but Fats, Mick and Stu were unharmed.

'C'mon, Bob,' said Stu, as Bob freed their chains. 'Tell us what's been happening.'

'No time now,' replied Bob. 'First we've got to see if Harcourt's still O.K.'

While the circus people stood close guard over their battered captives, Bob led his friends into the Hall of Mirrors.

Harcourt could scarcely believe his eyes! Bob unshackled him. He rubbed his wrists and eyed the boys gratefully.

Bob explained all. At last, Harcourt put in sombrely: 'You've done a great service to the country.'

Stu pointed with pride towards Bob. 'It's my English cousin who really deserves the credit.'

Bob shrugged off the compliment modestly. 'Aw — cut it

out,' he said. 'Look, the police will be here soon. I think we'd better hurry.'

Bob turned to Stu: 'By the way — I suggest we put in a good word for Madam Tanya. Maybe she'll get a lighter jail sentence.'

Slowly the boys made their way along the secret passageway. They were happy! There was no doubting that. But a bit saddened too. Their great adventure was over! And, though no one said anything, each knew in his heart that Bob would soon be returning to England.

But Bob had a slightly different thought. Stu's father might be able to wangle three aeroplane tickets for Stu, Mick and Fats. After all, their next adventure could take place in England!

# The Speed Kings

by
ROBERT  BATEMAN

Ted King throttled down the weary old engine of *Lulubelle,* and the bows smacked down hard into the grey, choppy seas as she lost speed. Oily bilge-water sloshed around his bare ankles, leaving a dark tide-mark.

'Can you see the *X.1?*' he shouted to Charlie Fitch.

Charlie was balanced awkwardly, kneeling with his legs well apart on the short decked-in bow of *Lulubelle.* Spray was lashing against his oilskins and coating the lens-protectors of the binoculars which he was training on the grey outline of the headland.

'I can't see anything,' he yelled back. 'Come on, Ted, let's head for home. Your Dad's not such a fool as to bring out *X.1* in this weather — not for a first sea test.'

Ted stared at the vicious white caps of the seas rolling in towards the Essex coast. If anybody other than Dad were involved, he would have taken Charlie's word for it. This was no weather for testing speedboats still on the secret list. He grinned. That was the trouble about Dad. He simply did not know the meaning of weather.

'There she goes!'

Ted followed Charlie's pointing finger, and saw the lean shape of *X.1* nose out from the shelter of the headland at half speed, throwing up a small foaming bow wave, pitching heavily as she met the big waves thundering in from the North Sea. Enviously, he glanced down at *Lulubelle's* oily, clattering little outboard motor, and gunned the throttle to bring the

332

boat round on to a new course, heading straight for X.1. Charlie, caught off balance, gave him a look of fury, and slithered down into the cockpit, landing with a splash in three inches of water.

'Thanks!' he burst out bitterly, as he hoisted himself upright. Oily water streamed from his oilskins. 'What are you trying to do — tip me in, so I can swim for it?'

'Sorry.' Ted was thinking of nothing except bringing the two boats together at a point a mile from shore where X.1 would start her two-mile test run back to the shelter of the headland. *Lulubelle* rattled and groaned as he put on speed. New, ten years ago, she'd been the smartest and fastest boat of her class in the Coastal Championship Speedboat Race, but now she was a hammered old wreck. He touched his lifejacket for luck. One day he was going to need it.

He brought *Lulubelle* to within feet of X.1 then looked across at his father in his bright yellow oilskins and red woollen hat. 'How is she?' he bellowed.

'Good enough.'

Even at a moment like this, with a new secret boat that could wipe the noses of the Italians, French, and Germans in the big race, Dad never got excited. He took it all as calmly as if it didn't really matter.

Charlie was squatting in the cockpit, examining X.1 carefully. 'Crumbs, she's a beauty. Y'know, your Dad's not just an ordinary boat designer, Ted. He's a positive genius.'

He clutched the gunwale as a big sea lifted *Lulubelle* and slammed her down hard into a trough. 'Come on, what are we waiting for? Let's get started on the test.'

He was answered by a roar from the huge outboard motor on X.1's blunt stern. The grey and scarlet nose of the secret boat leaped into the air. Even after all the years he had spent with speedboats, Charlie Fitch whistled his amazement. It was a thrilling sight. As he and Ted watched, *X.1* swung round in an unbelievably tight circle which threw buckets of white foam into *Lulubelle's* cockpit. Ted looked proudly at the retreating stern. Well, if the Old Man didn't win with *this* one, he'd never win at all!

'Wake up, Ted! Aren't we going to chase her?' Charlie yelled.

Ted let out a bellow of laughter. 'What? In this? All right, if you want to knock the bottom out of her, I'm game.' He opened the throttle wide, ignoring the protesting clatter of the tired engine and the painful shuddering as *Lulubelle* tried gamely to recapture her old speed.

Far ahead, *X.1* was making a wide circle towards a red and white buoy which marked the safe channel round the headland. Ted could have shouted with pride as *X.1* presented her flank with white foam curling up from her bows and a thick white trail of wake behind her. Then *X.1* continued the turn, so that she raced towards him, half a mile away, cutting sharply round the buoy, canted over like a dinghy in a high wind.

Then, with a rending crash that sounded as if it were right alongside, she rose up by her bows, her engine screaming. He saw Dad catapulted into the air, arms and legs outstretched, his red hat blowing astern. Numb, unbelieving, he watched *X.1* fall back and disappear, leaving nothing showing above the water except the buoy.

He was racing *Lulubelle* at top speed now, not caring any longer if he tore the stern out of her. It was Charlie who shouted the warning, but a split second later, Ted himself saw the tell-tale patch of greenish water, calmer than the rest. He swung *Lulubelle* almost at right angles, his heart thumping as he waited for the dreaded tearing of the rocks against the thin plywood of the boat. Then he throttled down.

In horror he looked ahead at the buoy bobbing on the water. There was not a trace of *X.1*, and not a trace of his father!

'Look!' shouted Charlie, seconds later, 'there's your father's red hat. Go in closer.'

Ted tried to gauge the depth of pale green water over the razor-sharp rocks. He eased the helm round.

Then, as suddenly as if he were Neptune his father came up from below the surface, right out, with water up to only a little above his ankles.

'He's standing on the shoal, Ted!' yelled Charlie. 'It can't be more than 6 inches deep. That's what ripped *X.1*! The buoy that marked it must have drifted.'

Ted was not listening. He was easing *Lulubelle* nearer, with short bursts of the throttle, peering overboard as he did so for signs that he was near the edge of the shoal. Dad was about twenty feet away, plodding slowly nearer, testing his footing with each step he took. Suddenly he sank down with water up to his waist, and then struck out, swimming the final few feet to *Lulubelle's* gunwale. Ted and Charlie threw their weight to the far side, to steady the boat as he hauled himself aboard.

Ted looked at him anxiously.

'Don't panic,' growled his father. 'I'm not hurt — nothing's bust.'

'Only *X.1*,' Charlie corrected him.

'That's right. Only *X.1*.' The old man stared across the water, frowning. 'That's what comes of trying to keep a secret. If I'd tested her round on our own bit of coast, where I know every foot of water, this would never have happened.'

Suddenly, with a grimace of agony, he sat down hard in the bottom of the cockpit, clutching his back. 'I must have ricked something after all. It'd better be all right by morning — we've a rush job on our hands now. We must have *X.2* ready for testing within a week so there's not a moment to lose.'

Two hours later, as they walked out of Wildhaven Hospital, Charlie echoed Ralph King's words. 'Ricked something? Your Dad must be as tough as an ox! The doc says it's a wonder his spine isn't broken.'

'It's not his spine I'm worried about,'muttered Ted. 'It's his blood pressure. Why, there's hardly any time before the big race. Imagine the Coastal Championship Speedboat Race without a King boat in it!'

He tried, and couldn't. There'd been a King boat every year since the race started, and every year the new model had been a shade better than the one before it — a shade closer to the sleek continental boats at the finish.

'Hey!' he burst out, suddenly remembering. 'We'd better report that shifting buoy. Otherwise somebody else may go the same way as Dad did. Who do we see about it?'

'In Wildhaven? They won't have a harbour-master — we'd better try the Yacht Club.' Charlie kicked the engine of his scooter into life.

The road up to the Yacht Club would have been tough going on even the softest pillion — which Charlie's was not! Ted winced as Charlie steered a wavering course between boulders and potholes.

At the Yacht Club the only man in sight was busy with a roll of charts.

'We've come to report a drifting buoy,' Ted announced.

The man scowled at him. 'You've come to the wrong place, then. Must be one of the clubs farther down the coast. We've only got one buoy, and that can't drift.'

'This is a red and white one, marking the shoal just round the headland.'

The man stood up, abruptly. 'That's our buoy — but as I told you, it can't drift. It's not on an anchor — it's chained

336

to the rock. It's just impossible for it go get dislodged.'

Ted stared at him. 'Two hours ago my father wrecked a speedboat on that shoal — not twenty feet from the buoy.'

'Nonsense. Look, I'll prove it.' The man walked across the club-house to a telescope mounted on a stand. 'See the flagpole beside the moorings?'

Ted nodded.

'The buoy's dead in line with it through this telescope. See for yourself if you don't believe me.'

'You bet your life I will!' Angrily Ted adjusted the telescope, and hunted until he found the flagpole. The buoy, then, should be farther inshore — say a hundred and fifty yards from its normal position.

Then he gasped. It wasn't. Just as the man had said, it was dead in line with the flagpole! He beckoned to Charlie. 'Check this for me.' His heart was hammering. 'Well?'

Charlie let out a low whistle. 'It's dead in line, chum, just as the man said. And a chained buoy can't drift by itself.'

'No,' said Ted grimly. 'You know what that means?'

Charlie looked blank.

'Somebody shifted that buoy — to wreck X.1 — and put it back again afterwards. Somebody who came very, very close to being a murderer!'

His voice was almost drowned by a sudden roar, and then a shout from Charlie. Eyes staring, Charlie stood at the window of the club-house. 'Hey!' he bellowed angrily, 'somebody's pinched my scooter!'

Ted leapt over to the window — just in time to see Charlie's scooter disappearing down the road in a cloud of dust.

'Well,' he said, thoughtfully scratching his chin, 'that makes two mysteries today. First, the shifted buoy, and now the stolen scooter. There *must* be a connection between the two.'

For a couple of minutes there was a silence in the club-room.

Then Ted grabbed Charlie by the arm. 'Quick! Let's get out of here!'

'Ugh?' Charlie was still glaring gloomily after his stolen scooter.

'Hurry, man — we've got to get down the coast to Shale Haven.' Without waiting to explain, he dragged Charlie by the sleeve, ran out of the Yacht Club, and started down the hill at top speed. Behind him he heard Charlie panting to keep up.

At the foot of the hill he halted. 'Got any money?' he gasped.

'What — on the salary your father pays me?' Reluctantly Charlie opened his wallet. 'One-fifty — that's all I've got left.'

'It's enough. Where's the station?'

'There's no station. Ted. The only way out of here is by road. Look, there's the coast bus!'

They ran, and leapt on to the bus just as it was pulling away. Ted flopped into a seat at the front, and stared anxiously at the road ahead.

'Now perhaps you'll tell me what's up!' Charlie wheezed.

'Somebody wrecked *X.1*. There could be only one reason — to keep my Dad out of the race. Haven't you guessed why they pinched your scooter?'

Charlie looked blank. 'I'm no good at guessing.'

'Think, man, think! Because your scooter was the quickest way we could get down to Shale Haven to stop them wrecking *X.2*.'

He thought of old Harry Farmer, alone in the King workshop at Shale Haven, suddenly attacked by saboteurs who'd nearly killed his father in wrecking *X.1*. Harry would stand up to them, whatever happened. But, if they'd risked one murder, they'd be willing to risk another. He looked through the glass panel at the bus driver.

'Oh, come on, get a move on!' he muttered. 'Anybody'd think you'd got all day to reach Shale Haven.'

'He has,' said Charlie simply. 'He's not chasing saboteurs.' Then, without warning, his hands came up and Ted found his head was being forced down between his kness. Charlie held it there, tightly, for about twenty seconds while Ted struggled fiercely to break loose. 'What on earth d'you think you're doing?' he spluttered angrily, when finally Charlie released him. To his astonishment, Charlie was laughing. 'Cut it out, Charlie — this is no time for kid games.'

'For the first time in my life I'm thankful your Dad pays me so badly! Thank goodness I couldn't afford to buy a better scooter. D'you know where your saboteurs are? They're back there on the road, trying to fix the scooter!'

Ted turned his head. Far back along the road two men were squatting beside the battered two-wheeler. 'Did they see us?'

'Thanks to my amazing presence of mind, they didn't. So we'll get to Shale Haven first if we're lucky. They'll expect to face just one old man, but instead there'll be both of us as well.'

Ted jumped up from his seat. 'Next stop's the one we want. Just round the corner.' He scrambled after Charlie to the platform of the bus, and looked back for any sign of the scooter.

Charlie grinned. 'Don't worry — when that thing breaks down, it takes a long, long time to find out what's wrong.'

As soon as they were off the bus, they sprinted down a side lane towards the seashore and the rusty corrugated iron shed which was the headquarters of King Speedboats.

From inside came a steady hammering which meant that old Harry was hard at work. Ted burst in, and Harry Farmer looked up, startled. 'Why, I thought you were at Wildhaven with your Dad.'

Quickly, Ted explained. Harry's eyes grew round with astonishment and anger. 'Don't you think we ought to tell the police?'

'Yes,' echoed Charlie.

'There's only one policeman in Shale Haven,' retorted Ted. 'And we can't prove anything, except that somebody ran off with your scooter.' Suddenly he ducked down below the level of the window as he heard the roar of an engine at the end of the lane. Cautiously he raised his head again for a split second.

'Here they come! Charlie — get out of sight! Harry — start working again, just as if you didn't suspect anything.' He looked around him swiftly, then ducked under cover behind the bows of the almost-completed X.2. He was sweating. If they wrecked X.2, that would be the end. Every penny of his father's money had gone into X.1 and X. 2 — the secret boats planned to earn a fortune!

He clenched his fists as a shadow loomed in the open doorway.

Then, behind the shadow Ted was watching, appeared another. He groped on the floor for a weapon. He didn't care what it was, or what he did with it to the men who had already wrecked X.1, and nearly killed his father.

Charlie must have guessed that Ted was about to leap out from cover with a heavy spanner in each hand, for his hand came down on Ted's shoulder, restraining him. 'Wait!' Charlie whispered urgently.

'What about Harry? You don't know what they might do to old Harry!' Ted hissed protestingly.

But Charlie had already crept away, almost on all fours, behind the hull of X.2. Ted watched him move round the shed, keeping in the shadows, as the two men moved in from the open front door. The light was behind them; all he could tell about them was that they were heavily built. He heard a sudden cry of alarm from old Harry, then a crunch of some heavy implement biting deep into the thin hull of X.2.

It was then that he came out, fighting. Instinct made him drop the spanners and rely on his fists, already well proved in amateur boxing. He leapt across the floor, catching one of the men by surprise, and crashing a hard right into the pit of his stomach. The man doubled up with a grunt of pain. But his partner swung the heavy crowbar he carried round in a wild sweep that missed Ted by a hair's breadth.

Charlie ran across the shed to attack from the other side. The man with the crowbar jabbed the sharp end of it towards Charlie. Ted saw Charlie's eyes widen in horror as he swerved to avoid it. Charlie lost his footing, went down heavily, and cracked his head against a leg of the workbench.

Suddenly, the man changed his tactics. The crowbar swung round to threaten old Harry, then was aimed straight at Ted's stomach, and the two men backed to the door. Ted looked around him for anything heavy enough to throw to stop their retreat.

The door slammed, and then came the rattle as the outside bolt was thrust into place. Ted rushed to the window while old Harry pulled Charlie to his feet. Fifty yards away the two men were fiddling with the scooter. One was kicking fiercely at the starter, but the engine was refusing to fire.

Pale, his eyes dazed, Charlie joined Ted at the window. 'Quickly, let's force it open before they get her going!' But even as he spoke, the raiders abandoned the scooter and ran up the lane towards the main road. Ted thumped the window-frame with his fist in a frantic attempt to get it open, then halted, despairingly, as he saw a bus pass by the end of the lane.

'They'll get away on that.'

'We could catch them on the scooter, Ted!'

'It could be any one of four buses, all going on different routes. Anyway, the scooter won't start.'

Charlie gripped the window-frame with both hands. 'It'll start for me all right!' he grunted, and with a protesting groan, the window opened up. He clambered through, unlatched the front door, and sprinted up the lane towards the scooter. Ted left old Harry staring gloomily at a huge rent in the bows of X.2 and dashed after him. He ran past Charlie, and didn't stop until he was at the main road.

There wasn't a human being in sight.

He turned and went back. 'They've gone.'

Charlie had the scooter running again. He throttled the engine down to a gentle murmur. 'Why do they want to wreck our boats? That's what I don't understand.'

'Dad says there's something special about winning this year's Coastal Championship Speedboat Race. Something very secret. We can repair X.2 in time, if we're quick.'

'Repair her? Gosh, Ted, she isn't even completed! Only your Dad knows the final details.'

Ted thought again, fast. 'Then ride back up the coast to Wildhaven Hospital. Tell the doctor you must see Dad. Find out all we've got to do to have X.2 ready for a test next week. Hurry!'

He watched Charlie ride off, then went back to the workshop.

Old Harry had already begun shaping a new plank to replace the one ripped by the saboteur. Ted pulled off his jersey and joined in the work for an hour. At the end of that time the new timber was ready to be mounted in place.

The phone rang. Ted picked it up. 'Hello, who's that?'

'Ted, it's Charlie!'

'Where are you?'

'In a telephone box at Wildhaven. Your Dad's much

better. I've talked to him and he's told me what we have to do. You know the spare engine? We have to...'

'Yes?'

But there was no reply. Faintly, to his horror, Ted heard an unmistakable noise. The sound of a desperate struggle for life.

'Charlie!' he yelled down the phone. 'What's happening?'

But there was no reply. Ted put down the phone and looked across the workshop at old Harry. Then he picked up the phone again, and called the police.

It was hours later when he reached Wildhaven. The first thing he saw as the bus pulled into the town square was a narrow alleyway with an empty phone box at the end of it. Beside the phone box was Charlie's scooter, but no sign of Charlie.

Warily, he walked across and bent over to examine it. The petrol tap was still on, which meant Charlie had expected to return quickly. He switched it off, then walked up the hill to the hospital. There was nothing he could do about Charlie's kidnapping. He'd have to leave that to the police. Meanwhile, the urgent task was to get information from his father about how to complete X.2 in time for the big race.

He reached the hospital, and then halted just inside the gates. He stared unbelievingly towards the main doors. Edging his way out, looking guardedly from side to side as he came, was his father, in his blue fisherman's jersey and grubby dungaree working trousers. Puzzled, Ted backed into the shelter of a clump of bushes and waited.

'Dad!'

Ralph King spun round, then grinned. 'Ted! Whew! I'm glad it's you ...'

'Why, who were you expecting?' Ted asked quietly.

'Charlie told me everything, Ted — how the wreckers shifted the marker buoy to make *X.1* crash, and how they came to the workshop to wreck *X.2.*'

He screwed up his face in pain. 'That's why I've left the hospital, against doctor's orders. Where *is* Charlie, anyway?'

Hurriedly, Ted told him. 'The police are handling all that,' he added. 'And we can get down to the workshop at Shale Haven on the scooter. You know how to ride one, don't you Dad?'

'I know how, but I couldn't do it today. Not with this back of mine. Where's your boat?'

'*Lulubelle?* I'd forgotten about *Lulubelle.* She's down at the wharf. Come on, then — I've enough petrol aboard!'

Ten minutes later, they were afloat. Ted coaxed *Lulubelle's* weary old engine into life, and they were scudding out of Wildhaven Bay southwards towards Ragland Rocks and the open coast to Shale Haven. Ted looked at his father propped in the stern. His face was white and drawn because of the pain shooting through his injured back whenever *Lulubelle* leaped high in the choppy sea or dived down into the troughs between the waves.

'Dad, why should anybody want to wreck our secret boat? Why should they want to stop us going in for the Coastal Race?'

'Rivals!' growled Ralph King.

'Yes, but rivals don't try to commit murder — just over a race!'

His father shifted uncomfortably. 'Over *this* race they would! Why d'you think I've spent every penny we have on those two secret boats? This is the one race in which we could make our fortunes.'

'Make our fortunes?' Ted wondered if the pain in his back had made his father light-headed. 'How?'

'It's a long story, but Britain, America and the other countries in the West want a secret fleet of lightweight radio-controlled speedboats.'

'What for?'

'You've heard about the dam-busting planes in World War Two? The idea now is to have a force that can do the same thing by speedboat. A radio-controlled speedboat can skim over the top of harbour defence nets and carry a bomb right up to a bridge or lock gate. Whoever wins this Coastal Race will get the N. A. T. O. contract to build the boats.'

Ted gasped. 'You mean if *X.2* wins we'll get the job?' He swung the tiller to steer clear of Ragland Rocks which rose grim and black out of the sea a hundred yards away. Then, as he heard the engine splutter, he reached for a can of petrol. 'Keep her on course, Dad, while I fill her up! Then it's top speed for Shale Haven and *X.2!*'

He took the top off the petrol can, and held it over the tank of the outboard motor.

'Hurry up!' shouted his father. 'We're drifting in towards the rocks!'

A tight knot of fear bunched itself in Ted's stomach. He looked towards, the waves slamming against the Ragland Rocks and throwing up clouds of spray. Then he held up the petrol can, and shouted above the roar of the sea.

Frantically, he waved the can, then turned it upside down to drain over the side. He glanced again at the rocks, much nearer now. 'Somebody's tipped out the petrol!' he yelled. 'This is sea water!'

It was only minutes before *Lulubelle,* her old timbers groaning, had swung broadside on to the sea, and water was slopping into the cockpit with every wave that hit her. Ted glanced at the rocks, then at the water surging around his ankles.

It was an open question whether the boat would splinter to matchwood against the jagged teeth of the rocks, or be swamped and sunk by the vicious white-caps foaming in from the North Sea. At a pinch, he might be able to swim to safety, but Ralph King couldn't swim — not with that injured back.

'Ted!'

His father was pointing around the spur of cliff. And then they were both balanced precariously on their feet, waving and shouting as a powerful fishing boat wallowed through the waves towards them. In the bows a sailor braced himself against a winch, steadying himself to hurl a coil of rope. His arm swung back, then forward, sending the light line snaking out towards them.

As it fell neatly across the bows of *Lulubelle*, Ted leapt for it, catching it before the sea could drag it away. He secured it to the bows, then waved.

For a sickening moment he thought rescue had come too late. The rocks loomed up almost alongside. At any second he expected to hear the deadly crunch of an underwater spike of sharp granite piercing the planking of the hull.

Then, inch by inch, *Lulubelle* moved outwards to safety as the fishing craft went astern and the line drew taut. Clouds of spray hit Ted in the face, blotting out all but the vague outline of the rescue boat. Then he dropped on his knees into the water in the cockpit and began battling to clear it with the baling bucket.

On tow, *Lulubelle's* bows were too low in the water; as fast as he baled, more water surged inboard. His arms ached after the first few minutes. His father took over, but only for a short while, because his injury cut down his speed.

Then, almost unbelievably, they were in calmer water, and the line was being drawn in by the winch aboard the fishing

*Ted leapt for the tow line.*

craft. Presently, two of its crew grasped the line and moved towards the stern, bringing *Lulubelle* along on the lee side, away from the wind and sea.

Ted hurled the empty can into the fishing boat. It came back to him, full, and the crew of the fishing boat lined the rails while he filled *Lulubelle's* tank and started her outboard motor.

It was as they reached the smooth, sheltered cove at Shale Haven, and moved in towards the slipway of the Kings' Speedboat shed that Ted's father, still working slowly with the baling bucket, reached down into the foaming water in the cockpit and held up a penknife.

'Is this yours, Ted?'

Ted shook his head. 'Never seen it before.'

'Then maybe it belongs to the wreckers! You saw them, Ted, when they came here and tried to smash *X.2.* What nationality were they?'

Ted shrugged his shoulders. 'I couldn't tell.'

'It's important, Ted. As you know, there are German, Italian and French boats in the Coastal Championship race. They're all trying to beat us, and win the government contract for bomb-carrying speedboats. If we knew which of them was trying to put us out of the race...'

'Does it say anything on the penknife, Dad?'

Ralph King held up the knife, and opened the two blades. 'One blade's badly damaged. That must have been caused by cutting the seals on our emergency petrol cans.' He stared at the blade. 'Hey, wait a minute! This is a German knife! On the handle it says in German: "Presented by the Hans Bloch Speedboat Company of Hamburg".'

Ted felt his fists bunch up into tight knots. 'Then they're the wreckers! It's their men who nearly killed you in *X.1.*, then smashed a hole in *X.2*, and finally kidnapped Charlie Fitch on his way back from visiting you in hospital.'

A sick, helpless feeling surged through him. 'What can they have done to Charlie? I'm getting very worried about him.'

The answer came from the end of the slipway — a loud shout which brought Ted to his feet.

It was Charlie!

Puzzled, he stared at his friend. For Charlie was waving frantically with both arms — waving them to hurry!

'She's ready for a test!' Charlie shouted excitedly, as Ted brought *Lulubelle* in towards the slipway. '*X.2.*'s all ready. Harry Farmers's patched up the damaged bows, and we've mounted the engine just the way you told me, Mr King.'

Ted stared at him. 'Yes, but how did you get away? The last I heard of you was over the phone, when the wreckers kidnapped you in the phone box.'

Charlie looked anxiously at Ted's father. 'I didn't tell them anything, Mr King. Honest I didn't!' He brought up his right hand, revealing torn, skinned knuckles. Then he grinned. 'They put me in a car and started driving.'

'The same two who came here and damaged *X.2*?'

Charlie nodded. 'Yes. And they admitted they shifted that marker buoy so that you were nearly killed when *X.1.* ran on to the shoal. They knew I'd been to see you in hospital. Once they got me in the car they started asking questions while they drove. One of them sat in the back with me, twisting my arm.' He laughed. 'But the car broke down — right in the market square of *Wildhaven!*'

Ted blinked at him. 'What happened?'

'Well, they couldn't frog-march me away through the shopping crowds, could they?' He examined his knuckles. 'I socked one of them, and ran for it. But by the time I'd found a policeman, they'd started the car and gone. So I collected my scooter and came down here.'

Old Harry Farmer appeared in the open doorway of the

shed. 'Here she comes!' Inside the shed the winch clattered, and the sleek bows of X.2 began sliding down the slipway into the water.

Ted looked proudly at his father. 'If you can't win the Coastal Championship with that, then you never will.'

Tensely, Ralph King watched X.2 take to the water. 'If I don't, we shan't get the government contract. And that means the end of the *King Speedboat Company.*'He winced as the pain returned to his injured back. 'Ted, I can't go out in her. You'll have to test X.2 for me. You and Charlie.'

'Whew!' Ted stared at X.2, the boat which could go almost twice as fast as anything he'd ever driven. 'And what will you be doing, Dad?'

Ralph King held up the German penknife. 'I have a little unfinished business to attend to,' he said grimly. 'Go on — off you go.'

Ted stepped into the roomy cockpit of X.2. He started the powerful engine, keeping it throbbing in neutral until Charlie joined him as helmsman.

'Good luck!' shouted his father.

Ted waved. Then he gunned the engine and felt the fierce surge forward as X.2 began to move for the first time. Her bows lifted as she gained speed, and astern the water churned up into a white foam. Smoothly, with hardly any vibration, X.2 headed out of Shale Haven at half-speed towards the vast expanse of the North Sea.

But there was no pleasure for Ted in squatting beside the engine, checking the way the boat answered the helm; checking the response to each gradual opening of the throttle. Everything seemed O.K. — and so it should be — his father had used every secret of design he'd learned in twenty years of building speedboats.

Somehow, even if it meant paying for the best specialists

in the country, his father had to be fit in a week's time. *Had to be fit* to drive X.2 in the race against the French, Italians and Germans who were all competing for the defence contract. And the X.2 must win, despite the Germans' attempts to wreck her. Charlie's voice broke into his thoughts.

'Ready?' Charlie yelled. 'We're just coming up to the test course.'

Ted came out of his day-dream, and nodded. Cautiously, he gave the engine more throttle, and the bows lifted even higher. Ted watched for the starter buoy of the test course, then clicked his stop-watch as he set the throttle wide open.

X.2's engine gave an angry roar, like a waking giant. Spray whipped into the cockpit, lashing their faces. The coast seemed to move past them with the swiftness of scenery watched from a speeding train. Ted grinned at Charlie, who was steering for the marker buoy which indicated the end of the two-mile run.

Then, to Ted's astonishment, something smashed a neat round hole in the cockpit windscreen, only a few inches from his head. He turned, just in time to see Charlie leap to one side as another hole appeared in the edge of the gunwale.

Somebody — some skilful marksman with telescopic sights on his rifle — was shooting at them from the shore!

Ted swung X.2 off the test course and kept down as another bullet from the shore missed him by less than a foot. Behind him, Charlie was crouching in the cockpit, with binoculars ranging over the sand dunes to the north of Shale Haven.

'I can see him!' he shouted, then: 'Hey, your Dad's come up and ambushed him. There's a fight going on!'

Ted looked at the smooth quarter mile of water between the X.2 and shore. He was tempted to run the X.2 right up to the beach, but he knew there were hidden rocks whose jagged edges lay only a few inches below the surface of the water.

So Ted raced the powerful boat back to the slipway, jumped ashore, and left Harry Farmer to tie her up securely. He ran along the foreshore, with Charlie at his heels. His heart was hammering: what chance did his father, with an injured back, have against one of those huge German toughs?

'There they are!' panted Charlie.

As Ted looked across the sands, he saw his father go down, clubbed across the shoulders with the butt of the rifle. Then the Germans raced away across the dunes. Ted sprinted after them, but halted when he heard the roar of a car accelerating away on the coast road.

Ralph King stood up, clutching his back and staggering. 'Is the boat all right?' he shouted hoarsely.

'There's a bullet in the windscreen, that's all,' Ted reassured him. 'Let's get her back into the shed. Then we can keep watch over her for twenty-four hours a day until the race.'

It was a long, worrying week that followed. Ted took the night watches with Charlie, which left his father and Harry Farmer free for work during the day, putting the final touches to X.2. The boat stood white and gleaming in the centre of the workshop, guarded every moment.

The race began at Wildhaven, a few miles up the coast, and the course ran round the Norfolk beaches as far as Hunstanton. On the night before the dawn start, they cruised X.2 to Wildhaven, and moored her alongside half a dozen sailing craft close to the Yacht Club.

'They'll have a job trying to wreck her where she is now,' grinned Ted. 'Two of those yachts beside her have people living aboard.'

'We daren't take any chances, though,' said his father.

'Thank goodness my back has healed up. If there's trouble I can be of some use.'

Ted shook his head. 'You're not staying up to keep watch tonight, Dad.'

'Why not?' Ralph King looked indignant.

'Because tomorrow you have to pilot X.2 — and win!'

Ted settled down in a quiet corner overlooking Wildhaven Harbour, with the X.2 in full view. With him he had the binoculars, a flask of hot coffee, half a chicken, and a packet of sandwiches. It was dusk; gradually the lights came on aboard half a dozen of the yachts. Through the binoculars he watched a dinghy go out from shore and moor astern of an old cabin cruiser.

Then the harbour was silent.

It grew darker. Presently, to see anything at all he had to leave his hiding place and move down to the edge of the quay. He was racking his brains to think of anything new the Germans could still try, to prevent the King Company from taking part in the race. What *else* could they do, in the eight hours left before the race began?

And then Ted heard a faint splash alongside the old cabin cruiser. He trained the binoculars towards it, straining his eyes to see anything in the gloom.

The surface of the water rippled. On deck there was the shadowy outline of a man, crouched down by the rail, moving his arms steadily back and forth. Was he paying out a rope? If so, why?

Ted stiffened. He lowered the binoculars slightly, towards the surface of the water a few feet away from the side of the cabin cruiser. For a few moments he could see nothing, then there was a slight disturbance of the water which puzzled him. Keeping low, he moved along the quay until he was nearer, but in the shelter of a store shed. He raised the binoculars again and carefully surveyed the scene before him.

Then he let out a gasp. The Germans had not kept him guessing for long!

For their next attempt at sabotage they were using a diver!

He would almost certainly be carrying a small time bomb, set to go off just after the race began, so that when X.2 sank, the race judges would think she had struck a rock or a sand-bank. It would look like an accident.

For a moment, he thought of swimming out to X.2, starting the engine, and moving her to safety. Then a better idea came to him. *Let* them put a time bomb under the hull. Then, just before the race, he could go down and take it off again, using his frogman gear.

He grinned to himself. The Germans would get a nasty surprise when X.2 didn't blow up!

But his grin vanished as a large hand was pressed across his face. Something sharp dug into his side. 'Keep quiet!' whispered a harsh voice immediately behind him. 'Do not make a sound.'

A wild thought came to Ted — to bite hard on the hand, then jump clear of the knife as his attacker felt the pain. It *might* work.

On the other hand it might not, and the point of the knife felt extremely sharp in his side.

'Sit down! Here, on this box.'

Ted sat down. Fifty feet away across the harbour he saw the head and shoulders of the diver rise up from the water alongside X.2. But there was nothing he could do about it. The man behind him would not hesitate to use the knife, he felt certain of that.

The diver remained beside X.2 for several minutes, then slipped below the surface again. It was now so dark that not even a trail of bubbles was visible to show his course back to the cabin cruiser. Their next attempt at sabotage was completed.

The knife was moved a fraction of an inch, just enough to jerk Ted forward. 'Down the steps!' the man ordered. 'I'm taking my hand away, but don't try to call for help, because the knife will be at your back!'

Ted shuffled to the edge of the quay, and began to climb down towards a small dinghy at the foot of the steps. Again he wondered if he could leap away — jump into the water faster than the man could thrust home the knife. He stiffened, ready to jump.

But the man with the knife sensed that Ted was about to try something.

'I should not try it, boy. With this knife I am very fast.'

Then they were in the dinghy. Ted's heart sank. This was the end, then. He would be held prisoner aboard the cabin cruiser. The X.2, with his father driving, would sink. The Germans would win the race, and also the defence contract to build bomb-carrying speedboats. He realised with a sick feeling of hopelessness that afterwards the Germans would be unable to let him go. To keep him quiet, they would have to use the knife after all, and dump his body, heavily weighted, far out in the North Sea.

'Up the ladder, boy.'

Ted climbed aboard. In the darkness there was a muttered conversation between his captor and the man on deck. Then Ted's arms were pinioned and he was led below into a dimly-lit cabin. He recognised the men as the two who had come to the workshop and smashed a hole in the side of X.2. One of them pushed him across the cabin into a tiny store locker and slammed the door.

The luminous dial of Ted's watch showed that it was well past midnight. Silently he groped his way round the locker in search of a weapon, but there seemed to be nothing in it except a large square tin. He tried the door, just in case it was not properly locked. There were no voices from the cabin, so he put his shoulder to it and heaved. Nothing happened. After several more attempts to break open the door, he sat down, then looked at his watch. With horror, he realised that it was now barely three hours before the start of the race, at dawn. Another hour passed before he made a find which immediately had him grubbing at the deck with the sharp blade of his penknife. His discovery was that the deckboards were rotten, the timber soft and dry. With the point of the knife he scraped a hole, and gradually widened it until he could get his hand through. That done, he started to break off fragments of the wood, hearing them splash below as they fell into the bilges.

And then, suddenly, came the tremendous roar of twenty outboard motors. The race had begun!

With a new desperate frenzy, Ted tore at the rotten planking, pulling it away in handfuls. Crashing his foot on what remained, Ted burst his way down into the bilges of the old cabin cruiser that was his prison. Up to his ankles in water, he climbed aft, through a door into the engine room, and then cautiously out on deck.

The cabin cruised was deserted. He jumped over the side, and swam powerfully towards the quay. Long before he had reached it, he saw Charlie racing down the stone steps to meet him.

'What happened, Ted?'

'I'll explain as we go. Quickly, have you got your scooter? We've got to get to the R.A.F. helicopter station fast.'

Charlie drove his scooter as it had never been driven before. But it took thirty minutes of hard explaining before they took off in one of the powerful helicopters.

Ted wondered if they were too late. Had the explosion

already happened? Would they be able to stop the accident?

'There they are!' shouted Charlie, pointing to the north.

The pilot headed the helicopter down towards the twenty white streaks of foaming water.

Twenty! Ted's spirits began to rise. That meant X.2 had not blown up yet. A moment later, he spotten X.2 running neck-and-neck with another boat he recognised — the big red craft from the Hans Bloch Speedboat Company of Hamburg.

'Can you go down and lower me on a ladder?' he shouted to the pilot.

The R.A.F. man shook his head. 'It would be suicide!'

'It's my life or my father's,' said Ted shortly. 'Where's the ladder?'

A few moments later, he was climbing down, suspended above the X.2 and looking into the astonished face of his father. Lower and lower went the helicopter... then Ted jumped. His feet landed in the bottom of the boat, and he rolled to break the fall.

At that moment there was a terrific explosion. 'What's happened?' he shouted hoarsely.

Ralph King was already swinging X.2 in a tight circle. 'The German boat's blown up!'

Ted's jaw dropped. 'The *German* boat? But they're the wreckers!' Puzzled, he reached over the side and helped the dazed German driver into the cockpit. Then, remembering with horror the bomb on X.2, he scrambled into the water, hanging on to a light line while he swam underneath.

He found the bomb immediately. There had been no attempt to hide it, because the wreckers had not expected anyone to be searching for it. He didn't dare to stop to wonder if there was a booby trap attached to it. He wrenched at it until he broke the suction by which it was held to the bottom of the

*Lower and lower went the helicopter, then Ted jumped!*

boat. He dropped it, and was still hauling himself back aboard when there came the deep thud of an underwater explosion.

'Phew!' he gasped. 'That was a near thing!'

His father grinned at him, then opened the thottle of the powerful outboard, sending *X.2* streaking across the water to regain first place. Ahead, only a few miles away, Ted could see the houses and shoreline of Hunstanton. Soon, the marker buoys for the end of the race were in sight. With a final throaty roar *X.2* surged past them, to the cheers of the watching crowd.

Ted's father throttled the engine down to a gentle purr.

The triumph of a lifetime's work as a boat designer was in his face. Then it clouded over as he turned to the shivering German. 'I'm sorry about what happened. I would rather have beaten you in fair competition.'

The German's face was flushed and angry. 'Just let me get my hands on those swine!'

'But we thought they were *your* men!' spluttered Ted, and explained about the penknife the wreckers had dropped, and its inscription of the Hans Bloch Company.

'We *sacked* those men! They were spies for an Eastern power. That is why they blew up our boat and tried to blow up yours — they wanted to make the British Government lose faith in the plan for bomb-carrying speedboats.'

They were alongside the quay now. An official was coming down the steps with the championship silver cup. More important, a naval officer was beckoning to Ted's father. He gave a nod of congratulation, followed by a light tap on his pocket which probably contained the government contract.

'We're *made*,' Ted heard his father whisper. 'All those years of hard work weren't wasted after all.'

'What about the wreckers?' demanded Ted impatiently. 'Surely we ought to be getting after them?'

Ralph King pointed across the quay, and grinned. 'Your friend Charlie's been doing that for us.' Charlie, the two spies, and the diver, were climbing into a police car. 'Remind me to give Charlie a rise in pay.' Then, seeing Ted's face, Mr King laughed. 'You, too, of course!'